THE
WOMAN
BEYOND
THE SEA

OTHER TITLES BY SARIT YISHAI-LEVI

The Beauty Queen of Jerusalem

THE
WOMAN
BEYOND
THE SEA

SARIT
YISHAI-LEVI

TRANSLATED BY GILAH KAHN-HOFFMANN

 AMAZON **CROSSING**

Text copyright © 2019 by Sarit Yishai-Levi
Translation copyright © 2023 by Gilah Kahn-Hoffmann
All rights reserved.

Previously published as *Isha Me-ever La-Yam* (אישה מעבר לים) by Modan Publishing House Ltd. in Israel in 2019. Translated from Hebrew by Gilah Kahn-Hoffmann. First published in English by Amazon Crossing in 2023.

Published by Amazon Crossing, Seattle

www.apub.com

Amazon, the Amazon logo, and Amazon Crossing are trademarks of Amazon.com, Inc., or its affiliates.

ISBN-13: 9781542037556 (paperback)
ISBN-13: 9781542037563 (digital)

Cover design by Amanda Kain
Cover image: © fiberglass / Shutterstock; © Ildiko Neer / Arcangel

Printed in the United States of America

For my mother

If there were torments—they voyaged toward you
my white sail to your dark night
allow me to leave, release me, let me go
to kneel on the shore of forgiveness.

—From "Prayers of Atonement," by Lea Goldberg

Eliya

Enveloped in layers of sweaters, a sheepskin coat, and a scarf and hat, I hurried into the warm embrace of the corner café, Café la Rivière. It was nearly empty, with tiny candles flickering on the tables. Only those overwhelmed by loneliness had ventured into the fierce cold. It was hot in there, a pleasant warmth, just right. I sat at the table by the window, and rather than hang the pile of sweaters, scarf, hat, gloves, and long coat on the hooks by the entrance, as most people did, I piled them on the empty chair beside me.

Even though it was situated in the heart of the Latin Quarter, Café la Rivière wasn't the kind of place that attracted the casual tourist. It was a small neighborhood establishment serving unpretentious, traditional French food. I didn't need the menu. I knew exactly what I wanted to order—croque madame, a slice of ham and slice of cheese sandwiched between two pieces of toast and topped with a poached egg. I also ordered a glass of red wine, which the waiter delivered right away. While the croque madame was being assembled, I settled into my upholstered chair, stared out the window, and asked myself for the thousandth time, What the hell was I doing in Paris again? Why was I sitting in the café where my life had been ruined? Why had my legs carried me to the place where my heart had been broken into a thousand pieces? What was I looking for? I already had all the answers. Ari had supplied them fully. He had responded to every one of my questions, sinking the knife into me until it drew blood.

"Better this way," he'd said at the time. The whole truth on the table, nothing hidden, no lies, no excuses, and no apologies, a direct blow to the face, the heart, the soft underbelly. He didn't love me anymore, he said with icy simplicity. He'd fallen in love with another woman, a petite Parisian with green eyes and chestnut hair. He took care to provide a detailed description, as if I had never met the bitch myself.

She was the reason he'd moved to Paris. That was why he hadn't called me for weeks at a time, claiming he was staying at a cheap hotel that didn't have a phone. She was the reason I could count on one hand the number of times we had slept together during the previous months when he'd returned to Israel. The reason he'd weaned himself of his habit of dropping off to sleep with my nipple in his mouth, had turned his back to me in bed, claiming that he was tired, troubled, wrecked.

Exactly one year ago I'd sat here, facing him, in Café la Rivière, the realization trickling into me that the world as I knew it would never be the same. My body seemed to sag, as though the life force were draining from me, and I wondered if that was how it felt to die. I stared at Ari. I didn't really hear his voice, smell his familiar scent of aftershave and cigarettes, didn't even really see his short, lean body or his mane of brown hair or his dark narrow eyes. I only watched his mouth moving. Then he stood up abruptly, leaned over, brushed his lips against my cheeks, tossed some money on the table, and was gone.

I sat frozen in my chair, trying to reconstruct what had landed on my head like hammer blows. *He doesn't love me. He loves another woman.* A Parisian, fine boned and delicate, with big eyes and a small chest. I had come to Paris to surprise my husband, my love, but in the end, it was he who surprised me.

During the final year of our life together, he'd taken more and more trips to Paris. I'd asked to join him. I wanted to be with the man I loved in the most romantic city on earth. I dreamed of wandering with him where Ernest Hemingway and F. Scott Fitzgerald had roamed and written great books after the First World War. I wanted to see where they had lived, sit in the cafés where they'd sat, and I didn't stop asking until he finally relented, on condition that my father bought my ticket.

"Just don't get the wrong idea," he warned. "You're not going to come with me every time I go to Paris." And I agreed.

The alienation I felt in my husband's company began at the airport. He was distant and self-absorbed, and the moment the plane's wheels left the ground, he fell asleep, leaning his head back on the seat's headrest and not on my shoulder, as he used to do. I closed the space between us and rested my head on his shoulder, but he shook me off and moved away.

We took the train from the airport to the Latin Quarter. I was enchanted. Saint-Germain-des-Prés, the plaza, the luxury fashion stores, all so elegant and different from Dizengoff Street in Tel Aviv, which until then had seemed to me to be the center of the world. Ari started to walk very fast, carrying our suitcase, and I trailed along behind.

"Why are you running?" I asked, panting.

He ignored me and maintained his pace. We crossed Boulevard Saint-Germain in the direction of Les Deux Magots café, filled to bursting with American tourists, and turned down Rue Bonaparte toward Rue Jacob. We stopped by a corner café whose small, inconspicuous sign read CAFÉ LA RIVIÈRE.

"Wait for me here; I'll be back in a minute," he said as he disappeared into the entrance of number 40. It was the first time in my life that I'd been outside Israel, and I found myself on a strange street in a country where I didn't speak the language. I broke out in a cold sweat, suddenly paralyzed with fear. But I recovered quickly and raced after him before he could slam the outer door in my face.

"I asked you to wait for me at the café," he said impatiently.

"You are not leaving me alone," I replied. "Not even for a minute. I don't know anyone here. I'm afraid to be by myself."

"Are you a little child? Wait for me for five minutes; I'll be right back."

"Where are you going? What is this place?"

"This is where I live," he said. "I'm going up to put down the suitcase. Why can't you wait in the café?"

"I'm not waiting in any café. If the waiter asks me what I want to drink, I won't know how to answer him. I don't even know how to say *coffee* in French."

Ari grimaced, seeming to realize that his little wife, who generally indulged his every whim, wasn't going to back down this time. He began to climb the narrow spiral staircase, suitcase on his head, me following behind. When we reached the fifth floor, he fished out a key and unlocked the door. To my surprise, it wasn't a small room in a cheap hotel, as I had expected, but a tiny apartment. Most of the space in the living room was taken up by an olive-green sofa. Beside it were two gigantic futon pillows on the wood floor and a turntable flanked by a pile of LPs. A huge poster of *The Fat and the Thin* hung behind the sofa. A painted spiral covered the entire wall in shades of black, turquoise, and green. There were two doors leading to other rooms. Ari opened one to reveal a double bed that took up almost all the space. I immediately recognized Ari's Hermes Baby typewriter on the bedside table.

"It's a little cramped," I said.

"This is it," he answered curtly. "And anyway it's only for a few days, until you go home."

I almost choked. He wanted me to leave after only a few days? Who goes abroad for just a few days? Who spends a fortune on a flight to a distant country for just a few days?

I decided to ignore what he'd said. I'd been longing to snuggle up with Ari in bed, and here was my chance. The room might have been tiny, but it was situated on the same street Ernest Hemingway had lived on. Immediately my mood improved.

"I hope you'll take advantage of the few days you have in Paris and enjoy them." Ari's tone was suddenly softer. I didn't notice he'd said *you* and not *we*, simply snuggled into his arms, ignoring the fact that while my body was soft and clinging, his was stiff and unyielding.

My isolation continued into the night. He stayed in the living room for a long time, clacking away at his typewriter and smoking like a chimney. I sat beside him on the couch, rolling joints for him just the way he liked them, and although he occasionally offered me a drag, he didn't do what he usually did and blow the potent smoke into my mouth. It occurred to me that he hadn't kissed me once since we'd arrived. Eventually I couldn't keep my eyes open.

"Ari, come to bed," I said in a seductive voice. "I miss you." He ignored me and said, "You go; I'll come soon." But he didn't come. I lay in his strange bed, the monotonous sound of his typing driving me mad. When finally it stopped, I could hear him breathing, then coughing, and finally snoring. Rather than gathering me in his arms as I had fantasized, instead of making love to me all night long, he had fallen asleep on the couch.

I woke early the following morning and moved restlessly around the small apartment. I tried to open the door to the second room, but it was locked. I stared at the spiral painted on the wall until my eyes ached. I checked out the LP collection. I wanted to put on a record, but I was afraid to wake Ari.

I found some books on a shelf, but they were all in French. I wanted coffee; I wanted a croissant. But all I found in the tiny refrigerator were an open bottle of white wine and a wedge of cheese that smelled so bad it nearly knocked me off my feet. Why the hell was he keeping rotten cheese in the fridge? There was also a glass jar in there filled with what looked like creamy white cheese. I took a small taste and spat it right out. It was face cream. My mother always said that my snooping would get me killed one day.

I peeked out the window. Along the skyline I could see the pretty rooftops of Paris. The café downstairs was crowded with customers, who spilled out onto the sidewalk, their laughter spiraling upward, those sitting at the outdoor tables probably enjoying café au lait and croissants. Craning my neck, I saw people walking along the tiny street. I wanted to join them and come out onto that wide and beautiful boulevard, to see from up close the Les Deux Magots café that we'd raced past on the way to the apartment, but it was as though my legs were cemented to the floor. How dependent I was, how indecisive, how pathetic.

When Ari finally opened his eyes, he was, as usual, in a foul mood and said he was going down for coffee. He didn't ask me to join him, but I followed. After coffee we returned to the apartment, where Ari immediately started to type.

"Ari." I found the courage to speak. "This is my first time abroad; I'm dying to see Paris."

"So what's the problem?" he said. "Walk down the stairs, and you're in the very heart of Paris."

"Why can't you show me the city? I'll get lost if I go by myself."

He sighed and said we'd go to the Shakespeare and Company Café on the banks of the Seine.

Excited by the prospect of a visit to the famous bookstore, I dressed up like a Frenchwoman, hoping he would notice. I draped a scarf around my neck, colored my lips bright red, and pulled my hair into a ponytail. He never even glanced at me, didn't even notice my bloodred lips.

When we arrived, I was overwhelmed by the book-lined walls. People jostled each other in the narrow spaces of the small rooms as they leafed through the merchandise. Instead of feeling the delight I'd expected at the sight of the mountains of books, I felt lost. The crowded space closed in on me.

"Let's go," I said to Ari. "I'm suffocating in here."

"Go yourself," he told me. "And here, take this," he said, holding out a heavy key.

"What is this?"

"It's the key to the apartment. I'm not coming back tonight. I'll sleep here; don't wait for me."

"Here?"

"Here." He pointed to a wooden bench behind a curtain.

"What do you mean, here? How can you sleep in a store?"

"It's an arrangement they have," he said, without looking at me. "In exchange I'll dust the books tomorrow or work at the register."

"And me?"

"You do whatever you want."

My throat contracted. He was going to leave me alone in a strange city and this time not just for a few minutes.

Ari turned and walked away, and though I rushed after him, he disappeared among the people as though the store had swallowed him whole. I stood outside, staring at the church and feeling bereft. What was I supposed to do now, after my husband had shaken me off? I turned away from the bookstore and into the streets of the Latin Quarter. I remembered the name of the street thanks to Ernest Hemingway, and with the help of some impatient Parisians, I managed to make my way back to Rue Jacob and Ari's apartment.

I threw myself onto the sofa, my disappointment so deep I didn't know what to think. I found myself nosing around in Ari's things. Other than several lighters and a pile of pages covered in Ari's familiar scrawl, I found nothing interesting.

Under the sink, in the trash, I saw the heel of a baguette and bent swiftly to retrieve it. My grandmother's voice, her broken Hebrew peppered with Ladino, came rushing back to me. "You don't throw away bread," Grandma Sarina always said. "If, heaven forfend, bread should fall to the ground, you pick it up, kiss it, and put it on the windowsill for the birds, but heaven forbid you should throw it away!"

The wave of nostalgia swept me back to Saturday mornings as a little girl, when I would go hand in hand with my father to visit her and my grandfather in Neve Tzedek in Tel Aviv. As though it had breached an invisible barrier, my sorrow broke through, and I burst into bitter sobs. I wept for my grandmother and grandfather, whom I missed so much. For my father, Shaul, who'd paid for my trip to Paris, though he didn't want me to go. I even wept for Lily, my mother, who had never treated me like a mother is supposed to, but who would never have left me alone in a bookstore in a strange city. And I wept for myself, for Ari, for our miserable marriage, and for the heartache that had become my second nature. I wept and wept until I fell asleep.

Just as he'd said, Ari didn't come back that night—or the next morning either. I had two options: to keep on crying or to pull myself together and go out and find him at the bookstore. I tried to retrace the route we had taken the day before, but I made a wrong turn. I wandered aimlessly in the foreign streets, lost among picturesque alleyways. Soon my determination to find him faded, and loneliness crowded out everything else. Worn out and weary from my walk, I found myself back at the apartment. Only standing right outside did I realize I'd forgotten to take the key. In despair I banged my fists on the front door. To my surprise Ari pulled it open. Without a word I followed him inside. My mouth was totally dry. I wanted to say something, but the words wouldn't come. I thought the tension between us might kill me.

Finally I managed a deep, shaky breath and said, "Ari, what's going on?"

"Nothing's going on."

"Why aren't you talking to me?"

"I don't feel like talking. I'm thinking about my book."

"What am I supposed to do when you disappear on me?"

"Go back to Tel Aviv."

"Go back to Tel Aviv? I just got here."

"I told you there's nothing for you here."

At that moment a young woman with short hair emerged from the locked room.

"Pleased to meet you," she said, kissing me on both cheeks. "I'm Sophie, Ari's flatmate."

I was shocked. Ari never told me that he had a flatmate.

"Nice to meet you," I mumbled.

The young Frenchwoman wound a scarf around her neck, said goodbye, and left.

In that moment I made a decision. I was in Paris, and I would enjoy myself, with or without Ari. I wouldn't be tied to his whims like a marionette in a puppet theater. I could manage just fine without him. I wasn't dependent on him, damn it.

Over the next few days I wandered for hours among the narrow streets of the Latin Quarter, intoxicated by its beauty. I visited galleries, window-shopped at boutiques full of clothes far beyond anything I could afford. I watched enchanting Frenchwomen, how they did their hair, how they dressed, the delicate and sensuous sway of their walk. I thought I might learn something.

Every morning, long before Ari woke, I dressed like a Frenchwoman and went out. I had coffee at Les Deux Magots and wine at Café de Flore; ate croque monsieur at Brasserie Lipp and croque madame at La Coupole. The rich food and good wine made my head spin. I knew I was wasting money we didn't have, that Ari would be livid when he discovered the fortune I'd spent in cafés and restaurants that long ago had ceased to draw bohemian writers and intellectuals and were now just tourist traps. My small secrets gave me deep pleasure; I thrilled at doing things without his permission. I realized I'd rediscovered my independence. It was the first time in our marriage I'd done anything for myself and not just for Ari.

I spent so many hours in the Latin Quarter that I became familiar with its every nook. I found the house on Rue de Fleurus where Gertrude Stein had lived; I touched the stone walls and imagined the wild evenings at her famous literary salon, which drew the writers and painters who gathered in Paris after WWI.

In my imagination I set sail for that romantic period I'd learned about in the Department of English Literature at Tel Aviv University. I became one of the beautiful women of the time, wearing a short beaded dress and ready to dance the Charleston, a long cigarette holder in my hand, listening to jazz in the smoky basements of the Latin Quarter, and holding scintillating conversations with rough men who'd just returned from the Spanish Civil War. Unlike in real life, I always had a witty response, and my imaginary companions marveled at what I had to say.

I had always loved to escape reality, to dream that I was someone else, someone prettier, more successful, happier, and more important. As a child I'd escaped into books and lived in a world of my own creation. My rich imagination rescued me from the gloom of my parents' apartment, which always seemed run down and neglected, where mildew stains were a permanent decoration on the bathroom ceiling. I built a different life alongside the one I hated, a different house, a different mother. I think I was only happy in my dreams.

Every time I walked from our apartment at the end of Dizengoff Street to the pool at Gordon Beach, I passed Prime Minister David Ben-Gurion's house. Across from it was a luxurious mansion, and I peeked through the iron gate into the big yard with a staircase up to the front door and a fountain burbling away. That villa was the mainstay of my fantasies. I dreamed I lived there and that my father was an important man, a friend of Ben-Gurion's. Once they closed off the boulevard when a member of some European royal family arrived to meet with Ben-Gurion. I was so engrossed in my fantasy that I believed that at the conclusion of his visit with the prime minister, the royal guest would come stay in our mansion. I confided in a girl from our building, and she thought I'd lost my mind and told the whole neighborhood. I already had a reputation as a strange child, and this distanced me further from the other girls. I never had friends, but my imagination saved me from the misery of a sad and boring life.

During the time I lived with Ari, I imagined that I was his muse, the inspiration for the woman he was writing about in his new book. When he forbade me to peek at his manuscript, I thought it made sense; after all, the muse isn't supposed to read about herself. I dreamed of him winning an important literary prize, standing onstage, expressing his gratitude, and then handing his prize to me, the love of his life, the woman who inspired him and without whom the book would never have come into being. I was still lost in fantasy, dreaming dreams, deceiving myself. And that was how it was in Paris, too, where I imagined that I was someone else who lived in a different country, in a different world, and at a different time. And so in the City of Light, just as it had been in Tel Aviv, my imagination kept me from losing my way.

In time I came to love the French, their manners, their charming flirtatiousness. I loved how they rushed to light my cigarette before it was even between my lips, to take my coat from my shoulders, and to open doors for me.

I remembered reading that aesthetics were part of the French DNA and that manners were the aesthetics of behavior. I started to emulate the effortlessly chic women who waltzed through the streets. I began to prance daintily on high heels, a new expensive woolen shawl draped with casual elegance over my shoulders. I wore my hair up, a scarf round my neck, and the red lipstick I'd begun using my first day in Paris, and soon I didn't feel so foreign. A few weeks after arriving, I felt at home in Paris. More importantly, I felt like a woman in a way that I had never experienced before.

Once I discovered my independence, Ari stopped talking about my return to Tel Aviv. He even grudgingly introduced me to his friends. They were young intellectuals who had passionate political arguments and debated existential issues for hours in Café la Rivière, downing wine like water and eating oysters and horse salami. After they'd had their fill of laughing at my broken French, they welcomed me with open arms and a kiss on each cheek. Ari's friends flirted with me and paid me compliments, while Ari continued to treat me with cold politeness. He never asked me where I went or what I did. He seemed to be impervious to my existence. At night he turned his back, and we never made love.

Unlike Ari, Sophie made every effort to welcome me. The more he scowled, the more she smiled, and when I returned from a day of roving around Paris, I was always pleased to find her at home, where she would pour me a glass of red wine and we'd talk. Somehow, despite Ari's behavior, I felt good in Paris, like I had discovered a new side of myself. I learned to enjoy things without Ari, and I was almost happy. Almost.

The party was in an impressive Ottoman house on Rue de Rennes. A last celebration before everyone went off for the summer *vacances*. We danced, talked, and laughed, and for once I even smoked a joint and had a cognac, so I was pleasantly buzzed. That was why it took so long for me to notice what everyone else had already seen. Ari stood by the big window kissing Sophie, crushing her to him and devouring her lips. They kissed as though they were alone, as if his lawfully wedded wife weren't dancing so close that she could have reached out and touched them. I froze. I felt my blood run cold. This was the enchanting Sophie who'd taken me to tiny secret boutiques known only to locals, the woman who'd become like my new best friend. I, who'd never actually had a best friend, was completely under her spell. What kind of game was she playing? And how had I not realized that Ari and Sophie weren't flatmates but lovers? How had I not realized I was the odd one out?

Overcome, I rushed out of the apartment and ran breathlessly, tears falling, down Rue de Rennes. My legs carried me to the only home I had in Paris, Ari and Sophie's apartment.

I lay awake all night. At dawn I heard a key in the lock, and moments later Ari dropped heavily onto the bed next to me, fully dressed, stinking of cigarettes and alcohol. Feeling nauseated, I moved to the edge of the bed, but he turned and held me in a viselike grip.

I felt strangled; he'd never held me like that before. I tried to wriggle away, but his arm was heavy as lead. Then just like that he fell into a drunken slumber, snoring loudly. Ari always slept quietly and soundly, but the man beside me in the bed wasn't Ari. He was a coarse drunk who'd humiliated me in front of my new friends.

Curled into a fetal position, I tried to make sense of what had happened. And then, as if Ari were still asleep and unaware of its actions, his hand groped toward me and grabbed my breast. He pulled himself over me and took my nipple in his teeth. This wasn't anything like the familiar intimacy that had given me so much pleasure in the past. I tried to get away, but Ari bit me harder and pulled me roughly toward him.

"No, Ari," I whispered, "you're drunk."

He mumbled something unintelligible and pinned me down with his full weight. I felt like my ribs were cracking as he ripped me apart from the inside. I cried out in pain.

"So we're enjoying ourselves now, aren't we," he rasped into my face, the stench of his breath turning my stomach.

"Ari, enough! You're hurting me! Stop!" But he didn't stop. It seemed like an eternity, but finally he came and collapsed on top of me. I tried to push him off me, to get his foul breath off my face, but I wasn't strong enough, and my body sagged.

My God, I suddenly realized, my husband had just raped me.

The next morning, as I stood in the kitchen making coffee, he came up behind me, fresh and showered, and asked me to make him a cup too. My throat closed up. Silently, I made him his coffee. I chose to believe that he didn't remember anything, that I had had a bad dream. He hadn't been himself, and it hadn't been me beneath him begging him to stop.

We never spoke of what had happened, not about Sophie and not about the fact that he'd raped me.

Gradually that night became a foggy memory, as if it had happened not to me but to another woman. Some nights I would wake in a cold sweat, remembering strong arms pinning me to the bed, but I forgave Ari, because I was certain that without him I would die.

I didn't see Sophie again. After the party she never returned to the apartment. But life with Ari didn't return to anything normal. Mostly Ari closed himself away with his typewriter. Sometimes we slept together, but it was like brushing your teeth or taking a shower. Ari slept with me to meet his needs while my passion suffocated. At some point he announced that he was meeting his friends on the French Riviera. He never suggested I join him.

Finally I understood. No matter what I did for Ari, nothing would make any difference. He didn't want my quiet, secure love anymore. He wanted excitement and thrills. The safe haven I had been wasn't enough for him.

My self-esteem in pieces, I returned to the energy-sapping heat of a sweltering August in Tel Aviv. I missed Ari desperately. My body ached; my soul was in agony. I paced like a caged animal in our apartment. I opened the closet and inhaled the scent of his shirts. At night I imagined him lying beside me, Ari as he had once been. I buried my head in his pillow, held it as though I were holding him. I talked to him, and I heard him answering me.

As more nights passed, me lying in our bed, my fingers moving deep inside myself, hearing him whisper in his hoarse voice to go further, push deeper, I knew that I couldn't give up on him. Not for Sophie or for any other woman. Despite his betrayal of me, I knew I would wait for him until he returned. Even if he'd forgotten it, I knew he was my man and I was his woman. It was a covenant I couldn't break.

I didn't know how I could live without him. I had nothing of my own. My few friends were really his friends. And I couldn't talk to my parents. My mother had sighed and cursed the moment I'd met the *shmendrik* who not only didn't support her daughter and didn't give her grandchildren but had abandoned his wife and run away to Paris, spinning stories about how he was writing a great novel, when it was clear no one would ever read his book.

Every time my mother started on her list of Ari's faults, I would clamp my teeth together and leave. I was tired of arguing with her, of defending Ari and his needs as a writer and an intellectual. I was so tired of telling her that Ari wasn't an ordinary person, soldiering through life like she was, but a respected artist, and that one day she would regret the harsh things she'd said about him.

Once in a while I received a letter from him in his usual terse style, or we talked on the phone. It was always me who called, begging him to come back. When he finally said I could come back to Paris, it was on condition that I empty our joint bank account and bring him the cash.

I would've done anything he asked. I emptied our account, and though one of his stipulations was that I only stay a few days, I bought a one-way ticket. I planned to tell my parents in the evening after Yom Kippur. The following day I would be on the plane to Paris, far from my mother's piercing eyes and my father's unhappy face.

On the Day of Atonement, I savored the wonderful silence that enveloped the streets during the fast while I packed my suitcase. Suddenly the wails of sirens rising and falling pierced the stillness. Terrified, I rushed to the window and saw people running, some clutching prayer shawls, others with knapsacks on their backs. With no warning, the empty streets filled with speeding cars, doors slammed up and down the block, and shouts emerged from my neighbors' windows. The phone rang, and I heard my father's voice. "It's war!" he shouted. "Come home immediately!" I switched on the radio to learn that the reserves had been called up. Lines of young people had formed at the El Al counter in London, Rome, New York, and Paris, all waiting their turn to be flown home to fight.

How could I go to Paris if war had broken out? How could I leave my parents? Could I even fly? Maybe all the planes had been commandeered. I knew I had to call Ari. Surely he would want to rush home. I started to dial, my shaking fingers choosing the wrong numbers again and again. Finally Ari answered, groggy as though I had woken him, "Hello . . ."

"Ari," I said, my voice shaking, "Ari, come home! There's a war!"

"What are you talking about?" He pulled himself together. "What war?"

"War. Cars driving on Yom Kippur. Sirens that won't stop, people going to shelters, the army calling up the reserves."

"And you want me to come home?"

"But Ari . . . I can't come to you now."

"Are you out of your mind!" he screamed. "I'm not coming back and fighting in some war. That crazy country that lives from one war to the next. It can fight all its shitty wars without me."

And just like that he hung up.

I could hear a woman wailing, "Don't go; please don't go." From the door I watched my upstairs neighbor clinging to her husband. "Take care of the children," he said, fleeing her grasping hands and disappearing down the street. The sirens continued their swinging cadence. My entire body trembled. I didn't know what frightened me more—the sirens, the chaos that had shattered the tranquility of the holy day, or Ari's shameful reaction.

I grabbed my leather bag and ran to my parents' house. The streets were a sea of chaos, cars flying past, sandbags piled at the entrances to houses. When I pushed their door open, I almost fell into my parents. "Good Lord, Eliya," my father said. "It took you so long to get here; we were beside ourselves."

"Hurry, hurry," Lily cried. "I'm going deaf from that siren. Let's get to the shelter." We rushed to the small underground shelter, which stank of disuse. The neighbors and their children were already squashed in, almost on top of each other.

"No," said my mother, "I can't breathe in here. I don't care—war or no war, I'm going back up."

My father was appalled, but unusually, I agreed with her. I also couldn't stand to be in that crowded, foul-smelling space.

"I'm coming with you," I declared, and my father followed. The sirens never stopped, and through the window I watched army vehicles picking up reservists.

My father turned on the television. Prime Minister Golda Meir, smoking a cigarette and looking more exhausted and ancient than I remembered, filled the screen.

"The war has just begun, and already she looks hopeless," my mother said.

From outside came the voices telling people to turn off their lights.

My father switched off the light and the television, and we sat in the dark.

It turned into nineteen days of shock and pain.

In addition to the terrible sorrow, the grief over so many young lives lost, so many fresh graves dug every day, I carried my private sorrow over Ari. He phoned once the entire time. His parents called almost every day, but he didn't call them either.

I postponed my flight indefinitely. My father begged me to look for work, to go out and meet friends, to come back to life, but I remained isolated and withdrawn.

I had finally stopped daydreaming about him and almost accepted that I'd lost Ari for good, when a letter arrived. The words were sweeter than honey, the sentences rife with double meanings in this uncharacteristically ambiguous, meandering style. He said even if it didn't seem that way, he was thinking about me. He apologized for not writing, saying he knew I was fine because I was such a strong woman while he was such a weak man, and he had done me a favor by not coming back for the war. If he had returned and died in the war, it would be on my conscience, and he knew I couldn't live with that. *And besides, don't you miss me? When are you coming to Paris with the money you took out of the bank?*

And so it was exactly one year ago, in a cold and wet November, in this same café beneath Ari's apartment, when my previous life had come to its end. The memory of the night I'd separated forever from Ari made me shudder. I wanted to bury it in the nearby Seine. To cast it away and never recall it again. But I knew I had to look hard at the winding labyrinth of my life and what had become of me. I allowed the memories to wash over me. For a year I'd repressed that night so I wouldn't have to experience the pain. Now it seared me as though it were happening at that moment. But with painful clarity I knew I was sitting alone in Paris to finally leave behind what had happened.

It had been late in the evening when Ari had walked away from our table, leaving me stunned and broken. The waiter lit candles, and streetlights came on with a golden glow. The café windows steamed up, and my tears threatened to spill over like the rain washing the street outside, but not one drop slid down my cheek. I sat erect in my chair like a pillar of salt, only moving to light one cigarette after another and stare into my glass of untouched wine.

I don't know how much time passed. The waiter didn't disturb my solitude, even to remove Ari's empty wineglass. People came and went; other waiters floated through the space like performers in a modern dance, carrying trays laden with drinks. They cleared tables and reset them, and still I sat.

Then the door opened and Ari walked in, an arm around Sophie's shoulders, gazing at her with that crooked smile I had thought was mine alone. Their palpable intimacy tore through me, shaking me out of my paralysis. As if hypnotized, I watched as he gently lifted Sophie's coat from her delicate shoulders, peeled the scarf off her lithe neck, and softly kissed the end of her nose. He pulled out her chair, as always ensuring that others witnessed his chivalrous performance.

I couldn't drag my eyes away from my husband and his lover. I had buried the kiss at the party deep in the caverns of memory and covered it with endless layers of justifications. But now an undeniable spectacle was taking place, and my heart was being wrenched from my chest. Ari brushed a stray curl from her forehead, pulled the gloves off her fingers one at a time, brought her palm to his lips. He leaned forward to whisper into her ear, and she caressed the nape of his neck, rubbing her nose softly against his. Against the quiet hum of talk in the café, I could make out Ari's voice, clear and distinct, speaking to Sophie's shining eyes and smiling mouth. I didn't understand the words, but their meaning was plain: they were words of love.

Almost floating, I crossed the short distance from my table to where my unfaithful husband and his treacherous lover sat together. I took the glass of red wine that had been placed before him and threw its contents into his shocked face.

Just before the door closed behind me, I heard the shriek of the woman who was now my husband's woman followed by Ari calling my name: "Eliya!"

It was freezing outside and a hard rain poured down. I ran through the wet streets in a daze until I couldn't take another step. I hailed a taxi and asked the driver to take me to the airport.

It was the next morning before I managed to get on a flight to Tel Aviv. I bought the ticket with money I'd withdrawn from our joint account, according to Ari's instructions.

"You're emptying our account; there won't be anything left," I'd said.

"You'll never be penniless," he'd replied. "You can always ask Daddy for money; he never says no to you." And I never said no to Ari. I emptied our account. I exchanged the money for francs on Lilienblum Street, my heart pounding wildly. I knew I was breaking the law. I shook with fear that an undercover policeman might catch me. I was terrified they would search me at the airport and confiscate the money. I was afraid someone would rob me; I'd never carried so much cash before. What would I say to Ari if I arrived in Paris without the money? In retrospect I would realize I was more scared of Ari than I was about being caught breaking the law or being robbed. I was afraid he would call me an idiot, like the time I forgot to get our change from a taxi driver who drove us from Tel Aviv to Jerusalem. I was afraid he would ridicule me, call me a coward, a stupid little girl, and I would be proving again that I wasn't worthy of him. I didn't dare confide my fears to him, so I overcame them instead and broke the rules, because when Ari wanted something, you had to give it to him, right away.

Now I knew why he needed the money. He had expenses, had to entertain his French whore, had to buy her presents. He loved to give gifts. I knew that well—a silk scarf, a ring, a string of pearls, a book of poetry. He was the king of loving gestures, large and small. They were what had first drawn me into his snare, made me want to be his woman, want to take care of him, cater to his every whim. He'd lulled me with those gestures. He'd known how to whisper the sweetest words in my ear, even during our last year, when—I could no longer hide from the knowledge—he'd been living a double life.

Ari had two sides. He could compose sugarcoated sentences that melted all my defenses, but then the pretty words would turn hurtful, dripping with venom. Though Ari had never hit me, I knew that I had been abused. His words were worse than blows: they had cut me like knives.

Ari always said I was his arms and legs, that he trusted me absolutely. "My little miracle worker," he called me, and I would burrow into the space between his shoulder and his neck, thrilling with pleasure. That was all I wanted to be—his little miracle worker, his arms and legs, his muse and inspiration.

"One day," he promised me in his seductive voice, "you will be the heroine of my book." He spoke as though he'd guessed my secret dream, and I knew then I was putty in his hands.

Even before we were married, Ari had me taking care of all the things he hated. I crossed the city by bus to do his errands, took care of all the little day-to-day tasks so he could concentrate "on what was really important—on writing," he told me. I never dared ask aloud how even though he was free of every obligation, he still hadn't finished his novel, which he'd started before I'd met him.

He declared the novel would revolutionize Israeli literature. "Bureaucracy stresses me out," he told me. "Just thinking about having to run errands makes me crazy." Under no circumstances did I want my Ari to go crazy. And so, though I also hated errands, I dealt with all his mundane issues. Knowing how intimidated I was by bureaucracy, my father even managed my bank account, and I was ashamed to tell him my husband gave me a list of tasks I had to complete to the letter to keep him happy. Secretly I hoped if Ari was totally dependent on me, he would never leave me. When he sent me to deal with his taxes or social insurance, to collect money from the newspapers he wrote for or to beg for an advance, to pick up his plane ticket from the travel agent on Gordon Street, I believed he was bringing me into the beating heart of his life.

So instead of spending my time in the university halls, listening to lectures and taking notes, I found myself busy with Ari's errands. Instead of sitting on the grass outside the Gilman Building with a book of poetry by Yehuda Amichai or David Avidan, I spent hours in gloomy government offices or at the pharmacy, surrounded by elderly, irritable people. Instead of immersing myself in Agnon's unique language or losing myself in Hemingway's *Islands in the Stream*, I learned what it meant to be overdrawn, just as I learned to plead with bank clerks. Because even when money came in from his lectures or articles, it disappeared as quickly as it arrived. Where did it go? I never understood. We lived modestly in Ari's apartment on Graetz Street, which he'd inherited from a childless aunt. When I asked him, he would get angry, say that he could do whatever he wanted with his own money and he regretted adding me to the account. If it bothered me so much, maybe I should contribute something to the joint account, which had my name on it only so I could take care of the mundane trivialities and he could concentrate on his writing. I believed he didn't really mean what he said, because after all, he had talked me into leaving my job at the university library.

"You earn almost nothing anyway," he'd said after we were married, "and what you do for me is worth much more. I earn so much more for us than you do working or studying at the university."

Since I was already torn between my job, studying at the prestigious Department of English Literature, and running errands for Ari, I listened to him. But I left the university with a heavy heart. Despite the department's stringent demands, which included reading long scholarly articles in foreign languages, I was sorry to leave. And the department head was sorry, too, for he believed I showed promise. But for me the dream of being Ari's muse was greater than anything my studies could give me. My father gave me money and never asked what it was for, but my mother exploded, "How many times have I told you that a man who doesn't earn a living is not a man—he's the lowest of the low."

I bit my tongue, swallowed my pride, and took the money my father had slipped into my wallet. But inside I burned with anger, not at Ari but at Lily, who refused to understand that Ari was an artist and shouldn't be bothered with petty issues like money. When I told them that I'd left the university to support Ari, my mother's anger became a volcanic eruption of fury. "All our lives we scrimped and denied ourselves so that you could study. Your father works like a dog at the store so that you can go to university, and then you throw it all away for that *shmendrik!*" Then she threatened to cut me off completely. "As far as I'm concerned, you can live in the street with that good-for-nothing who thinks the sun shines from his backside."

"I don't understand. Can't you be a married woman and also attend university?" my father asked. I didn't have an answer for him. There were other married women in the literature department, and I didn't really understand why I couldn't be one of them. When I told all this to Ari, he exploded, "I don't want to hear another word about your psycho mother and her opinions! I suppose she thinks she has keen insight into the value of a university education. Does she even know how to read and write, that illiterate? You think you can come here and repeat words of wisdom from your genius parents? I don't have time for this. You want to listen to them? There's the door—you can go back to living with them and go back to university. But if you want to stay here, it's me or the university."

I gave in. Of course I did. In the same way I gave up on my childhood dream of hosting a radio show about literature, because Ari was right—I couldn't study and also work for him full-time.

I lay awake the entire night before Ari's first trip to Paris, while beside me he sprawled on his back, taking up most of the space in our double bed, pushing me to the edge. I lay on my side, trying to wrap myself in a corner of the blanket he'd wrapped around himself as if he were alone in the bed. A thousand thoughts whirled in my head. Where had I gone wrong? What had knocked us off course? I promised myself I would be a better wife to Ari, more sensitive, more considerate. I berated myself, thinking there was something he wanted that I wasn't giving him, something he needed I wasn't supplying. I would make more of an effort, try harder, give more of myself to Ari.

The next morning I packed his suitcase, and we drove the red VW Beetle to the airport. Ari was distant, absorbed in his thoughts. I leaned my head on his shoulder and rested my hand on his thigh. He liked it when I aroused him while he was driving, and I loved to feel him swelling under my hand, until he couldn't wait another moment and stopped the car at the side of the road. We would devour one another, satisfying our desire with wild abandon while the cars passed by on the highway. The sense of danger and the possibility that someone might see us heightened the thrill, and we vibrated with passion as we moaned and moved together, rocking the car. But this time my fingers stroked the fly of his pants in vain, and he continued to look straight ahead and drive with deadly seriousness, although he didn't push my hand away. I finally removed it myself and shifted closer to the window.

When we stopped at the airport, I climbed out and leaned against the side of the car. Without warning, Ari pulled me roughly toward him and kissed me. He was holding me so tight I feared he was cracking my ribs. And then I felt dampness on my face. Ari was crying. His tears were wetting my cheeks, and I was kissing his tears. My body sagged with relief. Everything was all right; Ari loved me. Ari was troubled, but not because of me. It was his work; we were still fine. Just before he pulled away and disappeared through the automatic doors, I realized that even though our bodies had been pressed together, my breasts crushed against his chest, my legs entangled with his, the part of his body that always sprang to life at my touch was unresponsive. But I buried the thought and instead reveled in the comfort I felt in his embrace.

Only later, when he abandoned me in a Paris café, did I understand. It wasn't a gesture of love or desire. It was a sorrowful embrace, at the most a desperate effort to comfort me over what had vanished or died. He knew he didn't love me anymore. And I, stupid girl, misunderstood everything.

My life hadn't turned out the way I'd dreamed it would, the way I'd hoped. Ultimately I understood I couldn't continue on the dizzying roller coaster of emotions that was life with Ari, and here I was at the bottom, and I'd been kicked out, pummeled left and right with no defenses, my body exposed to the bone, and my soul had died.

Back in Tel Aviv, I went from the airport straight to my parents' house, not even stopping at the apartment I'd shared with Ari. It took three days to gather the courage to return to the place that I had thought was my home.

I wasn't sure what I'd do when I got there, but in a spur-of-the-moment whirlwind I grabbed my clothes, cleared my books off the shelves, took my favorite records, and removed my toiletries from the bathroom. I took every item that belonged to me, leaving not a trace of myself behind. When everything was packed in every suitcase and bag I could find, I took one last look around. I saw Ari's notebook on his desk in the living room. I opened it and for the first time read what was inside. I felt as though the blade of a knife were being twisted in my chest. It wasn't me who was the heroine of Ari's novel. It wasn't me who was his muse but Sophie, his French lover. He described her in painful detail—her spiky hair, her infectious laugh, the way she rounded her vowels. His Sophie was divine, larger than life, sensuous, and delightful. A woman who filled any room she entered and every chamber of my husband's traitorous heart. Not one word referred to me.

The pain I'd felt when I'd seen Ari kissing Sophie at the party was a trifle compared to what surged through me now. It was the pain of humiliation and the tearing away of the illusions I had wrapped myself in, the pain of the scorching truth written in black on white in Ari's cramped handwriting. The final nail in the coffin of my demolished self-esteem.

Before I left, my eyes swept the apartment one last time. On top of the television, in a silver frame my father had made especially for us in his tiny jewelry store, stood a photograph of Ari and me. I took the picture in which we looked so happy and threw it down, smashing it on the floor. The glass splintered into tiny shards. Then I brought my heel down on it hard, grinding the fragments into dust. I left behind the other few photographs of us and some letters he'd sent me. I didn't have the energy to pick them up and set fire to them. I decided that he could do it himself.

I tossed the key into the garbage can in the yard. I didn't want any reminders of Ari. Over the next few weeks I worked methodically to erase him from my life. In an attempt to forget him completely, I wouldn't set foot on any street we had walked along together or sit in any of our favorite cafés. Anything that reminded me of him, any person or place, was cut out of my life.

Ari did try to reach me. He sent letters written in a legalistic, impersonal tone. He wanted to come to an arrangement about our possessions, the apartment, the car; he wanted a divorce. There was no need to meet if I didn't want to, he wrote. He could divorce me at the office of the rabbinical authority in Paris and send the divorce paperwork by messenger to the office in Tel Aviv. But I adamantly refused to respond, ignored his letters, wouldn't answer his calls, and when he came to Israel, I refused to see him.

At twenty-five, with no profession or real education, no husband, no possessions, and no desire to live, I went back to my childhood bedroom in my parents' house, where they watched me fade into a shadow of my former self.

Nothing helped. Not my father's despair as he begged me to go back to being my old self, or the torment my mother was clearly experiencing as, uncharacteristically, she refrained from announcing triumphantly, *I told you so!*

A year is a long time. The year that passed after Ari left me was a lost year for me. A year during which I lay on my bed in my old room in my parents' house and did nothing, except smoke myself to death. I didn't read, I almost never spoke, I hardly ate, and it drove my mother out of her mind. My father, who had never been a religious man, started to consult with rabbis and read psalms. In one year he aged ten, but all I could do was stare at the ceiling until he, exhausted and defeated, despairing of ever managing to repair what had gone wrong with his only daughter, finally left me alone. I knew he was praying that I would bounce back, that he awoke each day hoping things would improve. I knew, but I couldn't find my way.

Then one morning I rose from my narrow bed, walked to the window, and pulled up the blind. The sky was filled with gray clouds, the weak rays of a winter sun struggling to shine through.

I stood at the closed window as the winter sunlight penetrated the glass and warmed my frozen body. I stared into the sunlight until my eyes were completely dazzled. The realization swept through me that I was actually dead, though my body was going through the motions of living.

Suddenly I was disgusted with myself and hurried to the bathroom to wash away the feeling. The woman who gazed back from the mirror didn't look like me. But she was me. She was gaunt and emaciated, with breasts that looked smaller than ever. My bones jutted through my skin; my arms hung down like those of a little girl; my legs were as thin and brittle as two matchsticks. My haggard, lifeless face seemed tiny, framed by a wild, unkempt mane of red hair. My cheeks were sunken, their bones prominent. Examining my eyes, I saw that their green color had dulled, and they contained no spark of life.

I took a deep breath and closed my eyes, and as if welling up from deep in the earth, the tears that had been imprisoned for so long burst forth. I wept because of the insult, the pain, the bitter disappointment, and mostly the betrayal. For months I had dulled the pain in my heart, kept silent, and smoked, but now I gave myself permission to feel, and the pain was so intense that I curled into a fetal position on the bathroom floor.

I despised the person I'd become; I hated the figure in the mirror. Drops of water still glistened on my body as I pulled out the first dress I saw in my closet, a black one that Ari hated. I could still hear his voice in my head: *That's the work of a fashion designer who's so ugly that only a little black dress can compensate for her flaws.* He'd forbidden me to wear that dress. But Ari could no longer forbid me anything.

The moment I set foot outside, I backed up against the door. My ears were assaulted by the noise, and I was thrown off by the commotion of life outside, which I had forgotten existed. I walked down the street, hyperaware of the smell of the exhaust from the buses mixed with the aroma of food drifting from restaurants and the odors of the people walking by. They mingled together like the stench of rotting trash. I wanted to escape to my childhood bedroom, but I knew that once I was back inside, the walls would only close in on me, and I would feel suffocated and vulnerable there as well. On that cold day, with a chill wind blowing, in my flip-flops and a thin black dress, I took off running. I took off past Amiram's Bar on the corner, then along Dizengoff Street, passing by cafés, restaurants, boutiques, shoe stores, and other people, who stared in surprise at the young woman who ran as if pursued by demons. I didn't stop until I reached Nordau and crossed Ben Yehuda Street in the direction of HaYarkon, oblivious to the honking horns and curses of the drivers who had to slam on their brakes so they wouldn't hit me. Breathless, I slowed down, and at the end of the street, the sea awaited.

The beach was empty, the chairs folded and chained together, tethered to the lifeguard's tower. Simcha's kiosk was closed, its only window boarded up. Gordon Beach was my beach. The beach of my childhood, youth, and adolescence, the beach that was like home. Packed with people in the summer, it was desolate now, not a soul on the sand.

I stood at the waterline, the soft, gentle waves lapping at my feet. Stretching out my arms, I raised my head, inhaled deeply, and closed my eyes, praying to the sea to rescue me like it always had, to heal me as it had healed me in the past. Wearing my black dress, despite the bitter cold, I walked into the water.

In the distance I saw a young man balancing on a surfboard, navigating the waves with one oar like a practiced dancer. I longed for those waves to cover me like a snug blanket. I allowed myself to sink into the sea and the water to fill my nostrils, dragging me down with its ancient force. Just before I was swept into the depths, I heard a shout—"Hey, give me your hand!"—and strong arms were grabbing me, pulling me out, and lifting me onto a surfboard.

Freezing and bewildered, soaked to the bone, I sat on the board rubbing my arms, which were red where the surfer had gripped them, wondering how he'd covered the distance between us so swiftly and why he hadn't just left me alone.

In minutes the surfboard was nosing against the white sand, and the surfer was helping me onto the beach. A November chill was in the air, and he rushed up the steps to the lifeguard tower before flying back down with an army-issue blanket, which he silently wrapped around me. I held the ends of the blanket together with one hand, and with the other I tried to peel off the cold, soaking dress, which stuck to my skin. Meanwhile the surfer stared out at the sea, keeping his eyes politely averted. I was surprised to realize that I felt safe with him. And when I saw that he kept his face resolutely pointed away from me, I dropped the blanket and stripped off my dress. At that moment he turned back from the sea and looked at me. We held each other's gaze for a moment, and then again he looked away. Once more he climbed the steps to the tower, then descended this time with wide harem pants and a sweater, which he held out to me.

I tied the pants' strings around my waist so they wouldn't fall down and slipped into the warm sweater. I was suddenly suffused with a kind of serenity. Together, the benevolent sea, the anonymous lifeguard, and the dry clothes that were much too big for me combined so that for the first time in months I experienced a delicious feeling of security and vitality. And I breathed.

I sat on the soft sand. The surfer knelt and opened his backpack, lifting out a camping burner on which he made us strong Turkish coffee in a small blackened metal pot. Then he covered my trembling hand with his, as if trying to steady it. The instant he touched me, I stopped shaking and brought the cup to my lips so I could sip the dark, scalding liquid.

"Are you okay?" he asked.

I nodded, staring into my coffee, not daring to meet his eyes.

For a long time we sat in silence, sipping our coffee, until he spoke again. "So what were you doing in the ocean in the middle of November?"

"I wanted to purify myself."

"And I thought I was saving you. What an idiot!"

"Maybe you did save me; maybe if you hadn't pulled me from the sea, I would have been dragged to the bottom."

He looked confused. "So did you or didn't you try to drown yourself?"

"I didn't go into the water to drown myself. I come here when I feel bad; I go into the sea, and slowly the bad feeling is washed away and replaced with a good feeling, and then I feel better."

"I'm sorry," he said, and his tone made it clear he really was sorry. "I'm sorry I interrupted your ceremony."

"It's okay. Worse things have happened to me in the past year."

"Were they so terrible?"

I took a deep breath. If only I could tell him. Maybe, like the sea, the unknown surfer could heal me, but the words didn't come and I remained silent.

The surfer dumped the dregs of my cup onto the sand and poured me some more hot coffee from the pot warming on the flame.

"Listen," he said after a while, "I don't know what's going on with you, but if you have demons that won't leave you alone, I think you should ask for help. From my experience it helps to talk."

"You want to talk to me about my demons?"

"Not me," he laughed. "The most I can do is take you out on my surfboard, but I know someone who can help you, if you want. His name is Amir Kaminsky. Here." He took a newspaper cutting from his backpack. "This is an article about him."

I took the page from him. Amir Kaminsky was described as a groundbreaking psychiatrist who had discovered a new type of therapy for soldiers traumatized in battle and people suffering from anxiety and depression.

"Thanks." I returned the article. "But I'm not nuts, and I don't need a psychiatrist."

"Keep it," he replied, ignoring what I'd said. "Maybe you'll use it—you never know." Then he stood up. "I have to get going. I'll tie up the board and walk you up to the street. The beach is totally deserted. It's not good to walk around here alone."

It wasn't until I reached the street and he was driving away on his scooter that I realized I was still wearing his clothes.

Dr. Amir Kaminsky

I hesitated at the door. "Hello," said the doctor. I noticed he seemed to be looking through me and not into my eyes.

"Please sit down." He pointed to a chair facing his desk.

Dr. Amir Kaminsky was a bald, heavyset man, his half glasses attached to a string around his neck and perched precariously on the end of his nose. Every few minutes he would push them up to his glistening brow. An unfiltered Nelson cigarette was affixed to his lips. I counted four during our short session. The doctor wore a faded white shirt and black pants that hung below his large belly. His desk was imposing, and the topmost branches of the sycamore tree outside the window behind him cast their shade into the room. Light shone through the green glass shade of a brass lamp on his desk. It looked like something from the set of a play. Beside the lamp sat a white telephone flanked by an answering machine, its red light flashing incessantly with recorded messages, upsetting my equanimity.

"Before we begin," he said, "I would like you to answer a few questions for me. How did you get to me?"

"Through an article in *Haaretz.*"

"Ah. And an article in the paper, even a highly respected one, was sufficient for you to decide that I am the right doctor for you? You didn't ask for references; you didn't try to find out anything about me?"

"I learned about you from the article in the paper," I replied, and I didn't tell him about the recommendation of the surfer from Gordon Beach. And what would I have said: *Someone saved me from drowning in the sea and recommended that I seek you out?* I didn't know his name, and I couldn't remember what he looked like. And anyway, I couldn't even figure out myself how an anonymous surfer from Gordon Beach had managed to convince me to come to this man's clinic.

"Have you been in psychological or psychiatric treatment in the past?"

"No."

The doctor scribbled a few notes on the open pad on his desk and mumbled something, and I calculated that he was using up valuable minutes of my treatment hour. When he looked up, I noticed that once again he didn't look me in the eye but stared at a spot somewhere in the vicinity of my nose.

"And so you know that each session is fifty minutes."

"I know, and I can hear the meter ticking," I said, looking pointedly at the clock on his desk. I didn't like this fat doctor.

He chose to ignore my comment and continued, "We agreed to the price on the phone. I insist on receiving payment at each session. I don't believe in owing money, and I make no exceptions regarding payment."

I immediately withdrew the 250 lira that we had agreed to over the phone.

"There's no need to pay me at the start of the session. You can also pay at the end," he said, but he reached out for the money and shoved it into his desk drawer.

"Anything else?" I asked irritably.

"Anything else," he responded as though he wasn't in any particular hurry. "I suggest that you drop the cynicism in the waiting room. In this room it won't get you anywhere. And now, if you would be so kind, let's move over to the sofa."

With his hand, Dr. Kaminsky indicated the green couch and commanded me to lie down, while he sat in a leather armchair by my head.

The moment I stretched out, I panicked. Bad thoughts filled my head. Could I live with the demons he would awaken? Was it the right thing to surrender myself to treatment on this green couch and stir up what I wanted to leave dormant?

I sat up again quickly.

"Is something wrong?" asked the doctor tonelessly.

"I don't think I'm ready for psychoanalysis."

"Did you hear me say anything about psychoanalysis?"

"So why did you ask me to lie down on the couch?"

"Young lady, this is how I work. The patient lies down calmly and tells me what is bothering him, and I try to help. Psychoanalysis is a process we would have to choose together. Not everyone is suited to undergo such a process, and it isn't helpful to everyone. I don't know anything about you yet other than your name, your age, and the fact that you have no patience. I suggest you lie down on the couch now and close your eyes, and we will start. What difference does it make? You've already paid, so give it a try. If it's good—good. If it isn't—goodbye, I won't see you again; you'll be on your way and won't come back."

"What do I have to do?" I asked anxiously.

"Close your eyes, relax, and breathe through your nose."

Slowly I began to breathe more easily. I didn't know how long I had been lying there breathing slowly with my eyes closed when suddenly I heard the doctor's voice as if from a distance. "And so, Eliya, what brings you to me?"

I swallowed and, in a voice much weaker than usual, said, "A broken heart."

The doctor was silent for what seemed to me an eternity.

"Did you hear what I said?"

"I heard," he replied. "Who broke your heart?"

"My husband, if I can still call him that."

"How did he break your heart?"

"He left me, left me without a heart and without a life. For a year I covered my head with a blanket and wanted to die."

"So why didn't you die?"

"What?"

"You could have killed yourself easily, swallowed sleeping pills, slit your wrists, thrown yourself in front of a bus, or jumped off the roof. There are many ways to die. If you wanted to die, why didn't you do any of those things?"

"How do you know that I didn't?"

"I see that you're alive and kicking."

The ticking of the clock was driving me crazy. My anger swelled— I'd thrown away my father's money for nothing.

Again I sat up, a little dizzy from the swift transition, and I said, "Excuse me, Doctor, I didn't come to you so you could provide me with a thousand ways to kill myself; I can figure that out myself. I came to you so that you can explain to me why I allowed my dog of a husband to ruin my life, why I allowed him to take over my life and play with me as though I was a puppet on a string. And you. What are you trying to do? To persuade me that I should have killed myself? Maybe I'll take sleeping pills or jump off the roof or slit my wrists as you suggest? For this I paid you money that my father doesn't have? For this you made me lie down here on the couch?"

The doctor, it seemed, wasn't impressed by my speech. He continued to pull on his cigarette, to blow smoke rings, and to push up the glasses that threatened to slide off his nose, and only after some time, which felt like forever, did he ask, "So why did you really come to me?"

"I told you, to fix my broken heart."

"I don't repair broken hearts."

"So what do you do?" I asked, as I lit a cigarette of my own. "Crush the little that's left of them?"

"I'm not a welder or a builder. I don't even know how to change a light bulb. I use processes after which, I hope, the patient knows herself better and learns to live with who she is, to accept herself and avoid the mistakes of the past. In other words, the patient and I set out on a journey, sometimes a long one and sometimes a very long one. You need walking shoes to travel it; you can't do it in flip-flops." He cast a disdainful glance at my feet and my choice of footwear despite the wintry weather. "You can't do it if you're short of breath. If you think you are capable of this, I would be happy to accompany you on the journey. If you're looking for shortcuts, I suggest that we part as friends."

All the force I couldn't summon with Ari was at my disposal as I confronted the doctor. Who did he think he was to talk to me about journeys and effort? "Doctor," I said, enraged, "we are going to part, but not as friends. You wasted my time and mainly my money. Thank you very much."

I crushed my cigarette savagely into the ashtray and made for the door.

The doctor didn't get up. My hand on the doorknob, I stopped at the sound of his voice. "I actually think I can help you. If you decide you want to try after all, I'd be happy to give you a second chance."

"There won't be any second chance," I replied and slammed the door behind me.

His license should be revoked. I was enraged. How dare he send me off to commit suicide? As if I hadn't thought of it myself. Time after time I'd planned to climb up on the roof and smash my body on the sidewalk, but the thought of my rumpled dress and my splayed limbs on the main street of the city was enough to deter me. I didn't really want to die. I wanted to sleep. To sleep so that I could wake up and discover that it had all been nothing but a bad dream, that Ari was still mine and my life was restored as if it had never been taken away. But one thing I already knew for sure—Ari was not mine and nothing was the way it was, and I was so angry that I kicked the stone wall around

Dr. Amir Kaminsky's clinic and nearly broke the little toe that poked over the edge of my flip-flop.

When I got home, my parents were sitting on the brown couch in the living room watching the evening news. Lily was glued to the television from the moment they finished eating dinner until the channel stopped broadcasting at midnight after presenting a verse from the Bible. "She closes down the channel," my father liked to say. That was how it was every evening. She demanded absolute silence and stared at the talking box as though the words of the living God were emanating from it. My father was a passive participant in her viewing. When it came to her, he never expressed any will of his own, and even if he suggested they go to a movie or a play, he was still dependent on her whims. If my mother, his darling wife, felt like going to a movie, they went to a movie. If she gave in and agreed to see a play, they went to the theater, and if she didn't, they didn't. When I was young, I'd still asked myself why it was like that, but by now I knew that my father would never stand up to her. He would never go toe to toe with my mother, like he did with the customers at his tiny jewelry shop on King George Street. Many times I saw him insist on a price for a gold ring and refuse to budge, even at the risk of losing a customer. But with Lily it was different. He acquiesced to all her desires. He even remained silent as a clam evening after evening so that he wouldn't—heaven forfend—disturb her when she was watching her programs.

The minute they became aware of my presence, they dragged their eyes from the screen and stared at me, waiting for me to speak first. For an entire year they'd become accustomed to me lying in bed, sleeping or staring into space, barely responsive, and had begged me to get up. Now that I'd left my bed and their constant supervision, I saw they were even more frightened.

"It would have been better if you had stayed under the blankets!" My mother couldn't restrain herself. "At least then we knew where you were."

"For God's sake! What are you saying, Lily?" My father managed to say this to my mother in a soft, conciliatory voice. "Finally the girl gets out of bed—we should go to the synagogue and recite the Prayer of Gratitude."

"You can go to the synagogue and recite the Prayer of Gratitude," my mother spat as if I weren't in the room. "I promise we'll be dealing with many more calamities from her, never mind the Prayer of Gratitude and the synagogue, and stop biting your nails already. Ever since Eliya came back from Paris, you haven't had any fingernails. Pretty soon you won't have any fingers left either."

My father just sighed. He knew not to step on Lily's toes, not to antagonize her, not to argue with her. All the things I'd never been able to do. "Eliya, let her be," he had told me so many times. "That's the best thing for all of us."

"What good does it do you to let her be, never upset her, and never argue with her, if despite all that, things are never good for the three of us, not for you, not for her, and not for me?"

He never answered that question, just shook his head as if he were knocking around the troubles in there caused by the women in his life.

I took a cigarette out of my bag and lit it with a flourish, watching the curling smoke. It drove Lily crazy every time I lit up. She, who'd never smoked, loathed the smell of cigarettes that adhered to the furniture and, she claimed, to her as well. "I don't smoke, and people say that my hair stinks like an ashtray," she complained to me, but I had no desire to stop smoking. The more the smoke filled my room, the better I felt, while Lily would stride in determinedly, raise the shade, and open the window, and all at once blinding light would flood the gloomy space. "Close it!" I would demand and cover my eyes with my hands. "Get out of my room!" But she would ignore me, and I had to get up and close it myself. "If you want to suffocate, that's your problem," she would shout at me, "but your father and I don't want to, and because of you I am suffocating in my own home. And from now on"—she would switch tactics—"I'm not emptying your ashtrays. As far as I'm concerned, you can suffocate in your smoke and your stench. You can empty them yourself."

When she saw that her threats made no difference and the ashtray was overflowing, ashes spilling out onto the night table beside my bed, even onto the floor, she went back to emptying it. She fumed and emptied it, cursed and emptied it. Now I inhaled deeply and exhaled the smoke into the center of her holy living room, looking straight into her face, ready for the next assault. But she just looked at me and didn't say a word. My father's hands gripped the sides of his armchair. I imagined while I'd been out he'd been beside himself with worry. He looked at Lily, as though he anticipated that she would be the first to speak. He looked so lost and miserable, and it seemed that time and again he was trying to say something, but he kept swallowing the sentence. And all at once I understood: good Lord, my father wasn't just afraid of my mother; he was also afraid of me.

"What?" I barked at my father.

"Nothing," he replied in a weak voice. "We were worried about you; it's a little late."

"Why should you worry about me? I'm a married woman, remember?"

My mother glared at me in silence. My father looked away, and I thought I could see tears in his eyes.

I knew I was being cruel to them, especially given that it had been such a terrible year, ever since the Yom Kippur War. As if the heartache I caused them weren't enough, they were troubled by the state of the country after the war. My father, a soft and gentle man who was always walking a tightrope, was irritable in his own way. I'd never seen him like that before. He complained to me, never within earshot of Lily, that every fluctuation in my mood or Lily's caused an emotional tempest that rocked the boat of his life, every telephone call made him jump, and every time one of us was in a bad mood, he couldn't sleep. "I've had enough!" he told me once when he almost reached breaking point. "I've had enough of both your moods, and I've had enough of the mood in the country. As if it isn't enough that the war finished me, you are finishing me off, Eliya. Wake up already! How much more time do you plan to spend lying in bed?"

When they published the conclusions of the Agranat Commission, which had been set up to investigate failings on the military and political levels in the prelude to that accursed war, and they exonerated the main guilty parties—Defense Minister Moshe Dayan and Prime Minister Golda Meir—he lost it. My father, who never raised his voice, faced the television and shouted, "What nerve! The entire country knows that they should accept responsibility and resign!" And when the protests started after the war, my father—that most modest and retiring man, who wasn't interested in anything other than his small family and his shop—in a manner entirely out of character for him, went out to show his support for Motti Ashkenazi, who'd been the commander of the Fort Budapest fortification on the Suez Canal, who was on hunger strike outside the government buildings. When he returned home, he came into my room, sat on the edge of my bed, and began to speak emotionally and wave his arms around. "Never before in my life," he told me, though I showed no interest, "have I participated in any demonstration or marched in any protest. I've never even expressed my opinion against anything out loud; I've always kept things to myself, but not this time! This time I am supporting Motti Ashkenazi, and don't you dare tell your mother, so she won't make a scene."

And I thrust my head out from under the blanket and nodded, if only so he would get out of my room and leave me in peace, but he persisted. "Promise me," he repeated, and I promised him that I wouldn't breathe a word of any of it to Lily and would never reveal that her husband had been transformed from a *nebech*, as she called him, into a revolutionary.

But he continued to suffer the pain of that damned war, which cost the lives of so many boys, cursing—as he never did—Golda and Moshe Dayan and the situation in the country, as I lay in my bed and prayed he would shut up already, leave my room, and let me be. I couldn't have cared less about what was going on. I wasn't interested in anything taking place beyond my blanket. I didn't see, I didn't hear, and when my father stood in my room talking incessantly, I wanted to scream. And yet deep down I understood that my father wasn't talking to me, that he was talking to himself. He had to release his bitterness, or else—and I understood this even then—he would go crazy along with me.

For an entire year my parents cared for me as though I'd reverted to being their little girl. From the other side of the shared wall between our rooms, I could hear my father's tearful voice and my mother scolding him, "Enough, Shaul, stop behaving like a woman! That's all Eliya needs now, to hear you crying. Be a man. Show her that you're strong!"

I had no doubt she herself hadn't shed a single tear during that whole year. My mother was a tough woman who never showed her emotions.

"Eliya, where were you?" asked my father in his soft voice that was always so pleasing to me.

"I went to a psychologist. I wasted your money for nothing, on a screwed-up psychologist who isn't worth one lira."

"Why 'wasted'?" It was as if a burden had lifted from my father's shoulders. "It's good you went to a psychologist. It's excellent for you. He'll help you to recover."

"Recover from what?" Lily's voice rang out.

"What do you mean, from what? From Ari. She has to divorce him and start living again."

"She's not going to divorce him!" Lily's voice was imperious. "We will make him suffer just like he made her suffer. He'll pay for what he did to her, our little *yekke potz*. We'll teach him what's what!"

"Who's 'we'?" My voice was high and shrill even to my own ears, and my parents reacted as though someone had just planted an explosive device in the room. "I'm the one who'll decide if I'm divorcing him or not, not 'we.' Ari is my problem, not yours."

"He may be your problem, but you're our problem!"

For a moment the look on Lily's face made me pause. I knew that expression well. When my mother narrowed her eyes like that, it meant she was at boiling point.

But unlike before, I didn't flee to my room and lock the door behind me. I stood my ground and listened as Lily unleashed her fury. "He broke your heart, that piece of nothing, that freeloader. He took an entire year of your life. We had to take care of you like a baby, to force you to eat, to monitor you round the clock so you wouldn't kill yourself. So now when, thank God, you're finally recovering, we have to deal with the problem called Ari, and that problem is also ours, not only yours. And we will deal with that problem, not only you."

"Lily!" I screamed. "Because of you, only because of you I married Ari, to be free of you, to escape from this house. Because I couldn't live under the same roof with you anymore, because you were suffocating me. It's because of you that I was in such a hurry to get married. It's you who pushed me into Ari's arms."

"Do you hear yourself?" Lily stared at me in fury. "I begged you not to get married. I told you that you were rushing into it, that you were too young. I told you he was nothing but a narcissist; I told you that being an author is some kind of fantasy, not a profession! That a man is useless if he doesn't get up every morning and go to work and bring home money at the end of the month. But you went and planned a wedding behind our backs. You went to the singer's wife's little boutique, and without even consulting me, like every bride asks her mother for advice, you chose a dress hardly suitable for a day at the beach, let alone for a wedding. And you got married in the rabbi's office. At the rabbinate!"

I waited for Lily to stop, but apparently this speech had been building for years. "My daughter gets married in the rabbi's office. As if, heaven forbid, she has something to hide underneath her tiny dress. And the refreshments, God help me, the refreshments—I wanted to dig a hole and crawl inside. Some cheap pastries and lousy wine you might drink to make the blessing on the Shabbat. Two in the afternoon and everyone was drunk, including the groom. I was so ashamed, even in front of the two and a half people from our family who were there."

"Enough!" My father interrupted her tirade. I couldn't remember when my reticent father had ever raised his voice to her before. "Lily, I'm begging you—enough. What's the point in getting upset about things that can't be changed?"

Lily exploded. "I'm upset because your daughter ruined her life with her eyes wide open. I'm getting upset because she married that loser who was so drunk at his own weird wedding that he collapsed on the steps of the rabbinate in his lousy wedding suit. And your Eliya, your princess, instead of him lifting her in his arms, she had to *schlep* that *schlimazel* she chose to marry and drag him along King David Boulevard all the way to Rabin Square."

"How do you know that?" asked my father. "What nonsense!"

"I'm making things up? Ask the two and a half guests she allowed us to invite! I'm sick of you defending her all the time, as if she's just fine and there's something wrong with me!"

"Have I ever said anything like that to you?"

"You don't have to. I see it in that horse's ass expression of yours. When you don't say anything, it's worse than if you did. I remember your face at the wedding; you looked like a dead man."

"Maybe, like you, I felt Eliya was making a mistake by marrying Ari, but I certainly didn't feel like it was a disaster, and please don't put words in my mouth."

"And don't you try to shut me up. I will tell my daughter what I feel even if she doesn't want to hear it. And you"—she turned to me—"you should thank that Frenchwoman who took him from you. She did you a favor; you should send her flowers."

"I'll send her a cyanide bouquet," I said, and I turned my back on my mother, stormed into my room, and slammed the door.

I made straight for my bed and again covered my head with the blanket. The few moments of sanity that had brought me out into the street, that I had while drinking coffee on the beach with the anonymous surfer who rescued me, whose words led me to Dr. Kaminsky's clinic—they vanished as if they had never been. Again all I wanted to do was sleep. I prayed that if I hid my head under the blanket as I had done during my year of silence, the pain would disappear. I was so angry at Lily, who'd forced me to think about my time with Ari. I was incensed she'd reminded me about the life I no longer had with the man I still loved, though my love for him gnawed away at every good part of me. I was furious she'd transported me back to my wedding night.

I tried to banish thoughts about the "weird wedding," because for me it had been the consummation of a dream. From the first moment I'd laid eyes on Ari, I'd wanted to marry him, even if it was in the afternoon at the rabbi's office, even if the substandard refreshment choices featured sangria, pretzels, and sad little dried-out puff pastries filled with cheese, even if Ari wouldn't allow me to invite more than ten people.

I remembered every detail of September 25, 1972, my wedding day. Most of the guests were Ari's relatives and hippie friends, many of whom I didn't know. From my side there was a handful from my father's family, some uncles and aunts and cousins, as well as my Grandfather and Grandmother Zoref, who I hadn't seen in years and who'd stood off to the side, embarrassed and as lost as two strangers at their own granddaughter's wedding. Now I was overcome with regret as I recalled how I had dismissed them when they'd come to congratulate me, dressed in their best clothes. Remembering their kind faces, my grandfather gently taking my hand and my grandmother stroking my cheek with her wrinkled fingers, I was so ashamed I pinched myself hard beneath the blanket. God, how stressed I'd been at my wedding, unable to focus on anyone except Ari, my eyes glued to every move made by this one-of-a-kind man who'd agreed to marry me. My gaze followed him everywhere, my eyes widening with fear every time he approached a woman, flirting as though he weren't the groom on his wedding day, drinking too much, laughing loudly, with me following behind him like some idiot, my face distorted by a false smile. I was on alert, terrified he'd change his mind at the last minute and abandon me under the wedding canopy or, worse, get so drunk that the reason we'd been together that day at the rabbi's office would be erased from his memory along with why I was wearing a white dress my mother hated and a veil on my head.

And of course Lily scowled throughout the ceremony and left before the party was over, dragging my father away, as he tried to no avail to convince her that her behavior was inappropriate. "Inappropriate, my ass," I heard her answer him crudely, and I prayed I was the only one who had heard. "It's inappropriate that even before this big fat nothing who married your daughter smashed the glass, he was already swaying like a *lulab*, like a palm frond in the wind, beneath the wedding canopy, so don't talk to me about inappropriate. Are you coming or should I leave you here!"

I saw him from the corner of my eye, could read the thoughts on his face. The scandal his wife was likely to cause worried him more than the thought his daughter had made a mistake now enshrined in Jewish law when she'd married a writer they scarcely knew. In the end he gave in. "All right, Lily, we're going."

Lily was already on the steps leading to the street when my father came over, kissed my forehead, and said, "Your mother isn't feeling well, my child. We're going now; enjoy your wedding." I knew that he was lying about Lily, but I didn't know if he really meant to wish me a good time at my wedding or if this was his way of expressing his displeasure over the pathetic event that Ari had organized for us. I kissed him back and told him, "Daddy, don't be so surprised—this is how hippies get married," and for a moment I even believed it myself.

The wedding was over in under an hour. I was thrilled to be alone with Ari, but my new husband was so drunk he could barely stand. I tried to support his lurching form and dragged him outside the building. When he collapsed on the filthy front steps in his wedding suit, I tried to flag down a taxi. Turning back to look at him, I was horrified. Ari was now sprawled across the stairs. He had been gulping glass after glass of sangria prepared by one of his famous bohemian friends. It was said it could bring even Tel Aviv's tallest skyscraper, the Shalom Tower, to its knees.

When we finally arrived at Ari's apartment, now our apartment, it was packed with dozens of people, most of whom I didn't know. Jimi Hendrix was blaring from the turntable, scorching his guitar strings with the American national anthem. People danced, bumping into each other, in a thick haze of hashish, and someone yelled that they'd better close the windows before one of the neighbors called the police. Others were crowded together on the narrow sofa, and as I continued my circuit of our apartment, I discovered the same scenes in the kitchen and even the bathroom. With difficulty I managed to propel Ari into the bedroom, where even our bed was occupied, by a couple rolling over each other. Ari screamed a wild, high-pitched laugh, wriggled out of my grasp, and lunged at the bed, inserting himself between the unknown man and woman. I decided to leave him there and try to enjoy my wedding party among the strangers filling the rooms of the apartment.

I saw them opening my fridge and pulling out everything that was in there—cheeses and jam and vegetables and a fat sausage I had bought especially for Ari at an outrageous price. I watched as they plunged their grubby hands into my underwear drawer, searching for the rolling papers Ari told them he had placed among my bras and panties. I stood as if paralyzed, not knowing how to stop them from going through my personal things, frightened that anything I might say would aggravate Ari, who would explode if he thought I had offended his friends.

I never knew how to behave when he was drunk or stoned. I never got used to the smashed versions of Ari, so different from the sober Ari. Maybe, I thought, I was just naive; maybe what was happening was fine. Maybe it was okay to open the refrigerator in a stranger's home and eat everything inside. Maybe there was nothing wrong with rummaging through someone's bras and panties to find rolling papers and a hidden piece of hash. Maybe that was just how hippies acted. After all, what did I know about hippies when I'd never met any before Ari? I was a little Goody Two-shoes following him blindly through the streets of Tel Aviv.

Before Ari I'd never met anybody like Ari.

The party went on into the night, and not for one moment was I alone with my new husband. He circulated among the guests, laughing with some guy I didn't know, placing his hand on the hip of an attractive woman. I followed his progress with desperate longing and burning jealousy, watching as he fondled the ass of another woman, clung to her in a sensuous slow dance, pressed up against her and buried his face in her neck, only to disentangle himself a moment later to swiftly roll joints and prepare huge cones of hashish while everyone stood around admiringly watching his nimble fingers working the papers and their contents like a virtuoso.

Never mind, I consoled myself, my arms wrapped around my body. *Soon everyone will leave, and then we'll be alone.* But the time crawled, and it seemed to me that no one was planning on going anywhere and the party would continue until morning. I didn't feel like a bride. I was a wallflower at my own wedding. I couldn't find a single place to be in the apartment that was my home. In a frenzy I started to empty ashtrays, to collect filthy cups with cigarette butts floating in leftover wine. "Hey, honey, can you bring me a beer?" A well-known actor, his arms and legs stretched wide across my sofa, motioned to me.

Honey! I wanted to stand in the middle of the room and scream, *I'm not "honey"—I'm the bride, and this is my party!* I wanted to snatch the record off the turntable and force all the animals who'd taken over my home to stop their never-ending jabbering, shove my fist into the mouth of the gorilla who had called me "honey," but I didn't dare. Even if I'd downed a whole bottle of whiskey, I wouldn't dare; even if I'd smoked a whole kamikaze cone of hashish, I wouldn't dare. Even then I was afraid of Ari, afraid of embarrassing him. "If there's one thing," he once told me, "one thing that can drive me insane, it's when a woman makes me look stupid. I'm asking you, Eliya, never embarrass me in front of my friends."

He was so sweet when he said that to me, kissing the tip of my nose, running his fingers along my spine, and I swore I would never embarrass him.

True to my word, I didn't throw out the mob that had taken over my apartment. I didn't smash the Jimi Hendrix record to smithereens. I didn't slap the girl Ari was now crushing to his chest, his hands gripping her ass too. No, I didn't embarrass my high-as-a-kite husband; I just did my best to pass the time until the party wound down by itself, until everyone would get out and finally it would be just the two of us.

It was close to midnight when one of the neighbors pounded on the door and threatened to call the police if we didn't turn off the music. The word *police* worked its magic. Everyone was afraid of the Tel Aviv police intelligence unit, especially Detective Zeigel, who had the Tel Aviv hippies running scared. A short time before, the Lool Gang, which met to create art in a hut on the beach in Tel Aviv, had been arrested. The unit also watched the Third Eye association of filmmakers, among them the counterculture multimedia artist and anarchist Jacques Mory-Katmor and others of greater or lesser degrees of fame and notoriety.

While the guests at the party were almost shocked into sobriety, I breathed a sigh of relief. I wasn't afraid of the police unit or of the infamous Zeigel. I was afraid of losing control, and Ari didn't insist, content with having trained me to roll joints exactly the way he liked them and pass them to him one after the other. He didn't need me to join him when he smoked alone in our home, and if he did want to get high with other people, he had ample opportunity on the long evenings when he went out to places I was never invited to. And so I silently thanked the neighbor who threatened to call the police, for now they would all leave and I could be alone with Ari.

Except that then Ari planted himself in the center of the room and announced, "*Yalla*, we're going to the beach! You too, Eliya," he added as if it wasn't obvious that I was included, as if there was a doubt. I went. Of course I went. I squeezed into a car owned by a guy named Alex along with a girl named Sharona. I ended up sitting beside Sharona in the back seat. I looked out the window at the dark city, and my heart ached. I was gripped tight in a vise of disappointment. This was not how I had dreamed of spending my wedding night, not how I imagined a bride was meant to feel on her first night married to the man she loved. Bewildered and unhappy, I pressed my nose against the window, less and less able to discern how I was feeling. We drove to Gordon Beach, where some guests from the party were already waiting for us. We sat on the sand, and a singer who already had two hit singles pulled out his guitar and sang Beatles songs in an awful accent. They all sang with him, sharing a bottle of medicinal cognac and smoking joints. I rolled joints for Ari, who confirmed with an approving glance that my work met his exacting standards. And then Ari said, "I'm bored. We're going to the commune in Rosh Pina."

"All the way up north at this hour?"

It's a miracle we arrived in one piece. My heart sank as Ari sat next to Alex in the front, and once again I was squashed in the back next to Sharona. There were no passionate embraces where we lost ourselves in one another, forgetting about the outside world. He never even kissed me. We almost crashed at least a dozen times that night, because Alex, who was stoned and exhausted, kept nodding off and the car zigzagged across the highway. Lucky for us it was the middle of the night and there weren't any other cars on the road. Lucky for us God was watching over us.

Dawn broke as we drove into the town of Rosh Pina. Alex parked next to one of the stone houses in the old neighborhood, got out of the car, and without knocking pushed open the unlocked door, and we all filed in behind him. Mattresses were scattered across the living room floor, with another roomful of people I had never met asleep on top of them. If I'd had the tiniest glimmer of hope that at long last I would be alone with Ari and we would make love as a married couple for the first time, that flicker was now extinguished. Ari collapsed onto an empty mattress at his feet and was asleep before his body, finally immobilized by all the alcohol and drugs, connected with its dingy surface. I lay down beside him, but his limbs spread in every direction, and it seemed that my proximity as I tried to snuggle up irritated him, because in his sleep he shoved me off the mattress, and I rolled off onto the cold tile floor.

"Come over here," the beautiful Sharona whispered and showed me a vacant bed in another room. So I spent my wedding night in bed with another woman, an almost stranger, while my new husband lay wasted on a mattress in the room next door.

My weird wedding was now a distant memory, and even my childhood room, where I'd always found refuge from Lily's moods, provided cold comfort.

I was worn out by the argument with Lily. I wanted to escape, but my imagination, which had always saved me, refused to come to my rescue. I raised the blind and counted the stars in the black sky. After that I tried to remember the names of all the children who had been in my class at elementary school, junior high, and high school, then the names of all the people in our apartment building, our neighborhood, and my classes at university. I filled my mind with a thousand and one useless names, a thousand and one people, not one of whom was really of any interest to me. I didn't even wonder what had happened to any of them or what they were doing with their lives; I was just busy making lists of names, anything not to remember, not to have to deal with myself, and then a gentle knocking at my door pulled me out of my trance.

"It's me. Can I come in?"

I opened the door for him. I could never refuse the kind, beloved man who was my father.

"You okay, sweetheart?"

"So-so."

"Don't let your mother put you in a bad mood. Sometimes she doesn't know what she's saying. We're so happy that you're back. Sometimes we make mistakes, and your mother doesn't know how to cope with what happened to you. You have to understand her—your mother's no good at separations."

"But it's me who had a separation, not her."

"She's angry at Ari, sweetheart, not at you. It's just that you're the one next to her, so it spills out on you. Now tell me, why weren't you happy with the psychologist?"

"He's an idiot and a charlatan, and I don't want to go back to him."

"That's okay, sweetheart; we'll find someone else. I'll ask Dr. Galili if he can recommend someone."

"You don't care if Dr. Galili knows your daughter needs a psychologist?"

"Your mother cares, so we won't tell her." He fell silent, and after a long moment he continued, "Maybe it would be better if you didn't tell your mother anything for now. She's in that state she gets into, you know, when she loses her temper at the drop of a hat, when it's better to keep your distance from her."

I had never understood how my father had married Lily, the evil beast who was my mother, how a man so modest and quiet had tied himself to a woman so tempestuous and unrefined. This time I screwed up my courage and asked. "So why don't you keep your own distance from her? Daddy, tell me, why have you stayed with her all these years?"

"What are you saying, Eliya? She's my wife and your mother. All I'm saying is that she's in her sensitive state."

"She's always in her sensitive state, and the whole household has to stand at attention and keep its distance from her. So what else is new?"

"Eliya, for all that time when you were closed up in your room, she worried about you and took care of you like a baby. She didn't think about me or about herself or about anyone else, only you."

"Great," I answered irritably. "So maybe I should get back into bed and cover my head with a blanket so that Lily will pay attention to me."

"Okay, Eliya, I can't go on being in the middle, with you on one side and your mother on the other. Even a person with patience, lots of patience like I have, can explode sometimes," he said, and he left the room. I was familiar with the rituals that calmed my father, and in my mind's eye I watched him close my door behind him and make for his old coat, pull a pack of Ascot cigarettes from one of the pockets, walk out the front door, and climb the ten steps to the roof. A slight push to the broken wooden door to the outside, and it would give way. He would lean on the parapet and take a deep drag before releasing it in smoke rings. Below him Dizengoff Street would be bustling with traffic and people, and opposite he would see the lights on the edge of the tower at the Reading Power Station. He would try to slow his breathing and relax.

I couldn't save my father from my mother. If I couldn't save myself, how could I save him? I plunged my head under the blanket. In the darkness I felt lonelier than ever, as though I didn't belong anywhere, and I cried bitter tears. I tried to muffle my sobs so that my mother wouldn't hear me in the next room, so that my father wouldn't weep along with me. Why, I asked myself for the first time in a long time, why did Lily always manage to reduce me to tears?

As far back as I could remember, I'd always had to be considerate of my mother, and no matter how hard I tried to be a good girl for her, it was never enough. She would look at me with that eternally disappointed expression of hers. I wasn't the child she'd wished for. Her child was the boy in the picture on the sideboard in the living room, always there, though no one talked about it. Sometimes I'd catch Lily watching me, and then her eyes would move to the photograph, and she would sigh. My earliest memories were of the knowledge that I had to try hard to be good enough for my mother like the little boy in the picture had been.

"If he were alive," she said on one of the rare occasions when she spoke of him, "he would make me proud, not miserable like you do." I wasn't even five, and I already knew that I was in a no-win situation, because as far as my mother was concerned, the boy in the picture would always triumph. When I ran to my father in tears, he would tell me my mother didn't mean it, that she was sad and anxious, and that I had to be considerate of her feelings because she'd had a hard life and had suffered.

What about my suffering? I was the only child in the building, in the neighborhood, at kindergarten, or at school without a sibling. How I wished for one! At first Lily promised soon, when the time was right; then she would wave me away, saying that I was whining; and finally, though I was only six years old, she told me bluntly, "You're like ten children, Eliya. We don't need more children—you're more than enough for us!"

At night, before I closed my eyes, I prayed to God that He would make me into a good girl, so good that Lily would see that I wasn't like ten children, and then maybe I would have a little sister or a little brother after all, who I could whisper to about our mother, because Lily forbade any discussion with strangers about what went on in our house, and there was no point talking to my father. He always defended her.

Like me, Lily didn't have any brothers or sisters. And worse still, she didn't even have parents, so not only was I an only child, but I didn't have a grandmother or a grandfather on her side, or aunts or uncles or cousins, like all the other children I knew. At least my father wasn't an orphan; at least on his side I had grandparents. Even if I rarely saw them, because they irritated Lily too.

Daddy's parents, Grandma and Grandpa Zoref, lived on Shabazi Street in the Neve Tzedek neighborhood near the city of Jaffa by the sea, and my sole uncle, Shmulik, or Sam as he was now called, lived in America, where he'd gone right after he'd finished his army service. He'd married Ida, an American Jewish woman who Lily referred to as "Her Highness." I'd never met his children. This uncle would visit Israel once every two years, and every time he came, with or without Her Highness, Lily would get angry with my father and my grandparents for eagerly anticipating his arrival.

"I won't lift a finger for your Ameri-show-off brother," she would declare as Daddy did his best to prepare an extra-special festive meal, and she demonstratively refused to set the table. And when my grand-parents and my uncle arrived for dinner, she would sit there scowling, and the more she scowled, the more I smiled. I was happy that finally it wasn't just the three of us. For a moment we were like all the other families I knew, sitting around the table for supper, even if out of six people, five were adults and two of them really old. Despite everything we were cheerful, except for Lily, who narrowed her eyes at my father and was silent most of the time, hardly responding when someone spoke to her.

Those visits were special occasions for me and a break from the stifling routine that prevailed in my childhood home. Each time he came, he took the family out for dinner to Tziyon's Restaurant in the Kerem HaTeimanim neighborhood. Of course Lily would make her usual scene and say that he was flashing his dollars around as if he were some kind of American millionaire, when in fact he was nothing more than a garage owner from Brooklyn.

My poor father, torn between Lily and Sam, would make futile efforts to calm her down. "For goodness' sake, Lily, my brother only visits once every two years. Please don't force me to hurt his feelings for the two weeks he's here."

"I can't bear it when you make yourself into a doormat for him," she would say, losing her temper. "I can't bear it that your mother behaves as if he's her only son. As if he even bothers with her when he's in his precious America. It's you who runs all your parents' errands to the insurance institute and the health fund and the bank. He hasn't even introduced her to his children, and to her he's the king of the world . . ."

My heart contracted with envy when I saw other families hosting their relatives on the day of rest, Shabbat, and for holiday meals. And I hated the New Year holiday most of all. Through the open windows I heard the sounds of families chanting holiday blessings and prayers, laughter and commotion and the happy shrieks of children, while we were three silent people. The only way I could survive that pathetic meal was to lose myself in a fantasy world where I was surrounded by doting relatives. I squeezed my eyelids shut until Lily's voice roused me from my reveries. "Again you're dreaming. Finish what's on your plate and clear the table."

Until I was six, we spent holidays with Grandma and Grandpa Zoref. On the eve of the Passover Seder, Lily condescended to go to their house, and I would sit with the four adults, shy about declaiming the Four Questions traditionally recited by the youngest person present. I loved to visit them. I loved to go there because of the tight hug I always received from my grandmother, who seemed overjoyed to see me, and the touch of my grandfather's warm hand on the top of my head as he kissed my forehead and murmured a blessing. I especially loved being showered with presents. "Those toys aren't for a child her age," Lily would carp to my father, and "Those clothes are from the Carmel Market." I didn't care. I was so thrilled to receive gifts from people whose love for me was palpable, so excited to feel like a real family.

I longed for my father to take me to America to meet my cousins and to have someone my age who wasn't just a friend but a relative, a real member of my family, a cousin.

Once I asked, and my father laughed and said that as soon as he won the lottery, he'd take me to America to see my cousins, who lived in a building that almost reached the sky. All my father's dreams were channeled to the Mifal HaPais, the national lottery, and mine were swept up in the same current. Every time I asked for something he couldn't afford, he would promise that when he won the lottery, he would make my wish come true. We would travel to America when he won the lottery; he would buy me a bicycle when he won the lottery; he would sign me up for ballet lessons when he won the lottery. And every time I walked past the dilapidated little kiosk on Dizengoff Street opposite the David's Palace Movie Theater that sold lottery tickets, I couldn't understand how a place full of so much money could look so run down.

Now, I wished that when he finally won the lottery, my daddy would buy a machine that would turn me back into the person I had been before Ari. A promising young student in the Department of English Literature at Tel Aviv University who dreamed of having a Friday-morning radio show about authors and books.

Where were those dreams? What had happened to me? How could I have married a man who controlled me exactly the same way my mother did my father? Lord in heaven, I suddenly realized, I'd married my mother.

My thoughts assailed me, pouring relentlessly into my mind. I could hear them pounding in my head, straining my temples. Any moment now they would be putting me in a straitjacket, sending me to the nuthouse at Abarbanel. I couldn't endure the raging torrent of thoughts, couldn't abide myself—someone had to stop this dance of demonic images that was pushing me to the edge, had to rip up the horror movie playing in my head, disconnect me from it, release me!

My father told me my screams brought him and Lily racing to my room. "It was lucky," he said, "you didn't lock the door." They found me sitting on my bed, slicing at my wrists with a razor. Cutting and screaming, cutting and weeping. Lily, who in a crisis was always more quick witted than my father, knocked the razor from my hand as I struggled with her, crying and screaming.

While my father called an ambulance, my mother held my wrists with her thumbs and managed to stem the flow of blood. By the time they carried me to the ambulance on a stretcher, I had lost consciousness.

"My sweetheart," I heard my father say as if from a distance, "are you awake?" I opened my eyes and saw that I was lying in a hospital bed, hooked up to an IV. I couldn't sit up. My wrists were bandaged and painful, my mouth so dry that though I wanted to answer my father, it was hard to speak.

"What happened to me?" I whispered.

"Everything's fine now, darling," my father said. "Rest. The most important thing is for you to rest."

"What happened?" I whispered again.

"You tried to kill yourself—that's what happened," Lily said curtly, pulling no punches, as usual.

"Go outside, Lily." My father was unusually firm and decisive. "Go get some coffee; you've had a rough night. I'll stay here with Eliya."

"Sweetheart," my father said when Lily left the room, "let's wait for the doctor to come and talk to you. Then I'll tell you what happened."

"Whatever you say," I answered wearily, and I closed my eyes.

I was worn out, my heart beating so fast that I could feel it pulsing in my head. I kept my eyes closed. I couldn't even manage to kill myself. I had failed at even that. Tears poured from my eyes again, and I sobbed and sobbed until I plunged into another deep sleep.

Hours later, when I woke, my parents were standing by my bed.

"You have to eat," said Lily in a businesslike tone. "There's mashed potatoes and some soup. Eat—it will make you stronger."

I pressed my lips together like an obstinate child and refused to open my mouth.

I saw their exchange of glances. Lily seemed to be at her wits' end. She was trying not to show it, but she was on the verge of tears, and I'd never seen Lily with tears in her eyes.

I remembered hearing her voice from the other side of my locked door, reprimanding my father and telling him to stop behaving like a dish towel. "You have to behave normally around her, even though she hasn't left her bed for months. Only then, when she sees that despite the fact that she won't get out of bed, the household is still running normally, will she pull herself out of this state." How angry I had been when I'd heard what she'd said.

Now I detected a fault in the foundation of Lily, who I'd always believed to be made of stone, and I was mesmerized by this intimation that she had what I had never believed she possessed—sensitivity. And maybe she was capable of feeling fear. She looked frightened.

"I'm going to call the doctor," my father said, and he left the two of us alone.

Lily sat on the edge of the bed and took my hands in hers. "Look how thin they are, like chicken feet." I wasn't used to demonstrations of affection from her. She brought my hands to her lips and kissed my palms, her tears falling on them. That day in the hospital was the first time I saw her cry, and I think it was also the first time she kissed me. I'd never felt so confused and bewildered. I wasn't sure whether I wanted to grab back my hand or put my head on her breast and cry with her. But at that moment my father walked in with the doctor, and to my amazement the man at my father's side was none other than Dr. Kaminsky.

Dr. Kaminsky was overly jovial.

"So how are we feeling today?"

"She doesn't want to eat," Lily said.

"Aren't you hungry?" asked the doctor. "Maybe you don't like hospital food? Maybe your father should go downstairs and get you a steak in a pita?"

Just the thought of that made me sick to my stomach, and I grimaced. Dr. Kaminsky jumped at my reaction. "Ah, I see that you do have emotions, and when you want to, you can respond. Excuse me." He turned to my parents. "Leave me alone with Eliya for a few minutes."

When it was just the two of us, with no preamble, the doctor said, "I was in the Suez Canal during the Yom Kippur War. I saw young people dying like flies, people your age who were dying to live, and you want to volunteer to die?"

He paused, as if anticipating a response. When none came, he continued, "The medical treatment ends here. Your cuts will heal, but you'll always have a scar to remind you that you were ready to commit the gravest of sins—to take a life. You are not God, Eliya; you don't get to decide whether to live or die. Think about that, and while you're at it, think about your parents—you almost killed them along with yourself. I know that we got off on the wrong foot, and I'm sorry." He continued to talk while checking the medical chart attached to the foot of my bed, not pausing to take a breath or to see if his words were making an impression on me. "I'm truly sorry, but we can start over, and if you prefer that I don't treat you, I'll recommend another doctor for you. A broken heart is not a reason to die; it's possible to mend the cracks and go on."

"But you said that you don't repair broken hearts. You said you're not a welder."

"It's true I don't mend broken hearts, but that doesn't mean that you slit your wrists over one. There's a process. If you had listened, you would have heard that I propose you embark on that process and not remain stranded with your broken heart. You didn't listen to what I was really saying."

"And what were you really saying?"

"That I can help you if you want."

"What's happened to me?" I asked in a whisper. "Why did I cut my wrists?"

"That's something we'll have to learn through the treatment process I'm proposing."

"So what now?"

"You'll be released in twenty-four hours, if they decide it's safe to do so."

"What do you mean?"

"If you cooperate, start eating and getting stronger, if your psychological state stabilizes, you'll go home."

"And if not?"

"Why are you thinking about 'not'? Think about 'yes.'"

I was confused. I wanted to go home, but I was afraid to be back in the four walls of my room, my bloodstained bed. Afraid of the thoughts that tortured me, of the nothing that I'd become. All I could see before me was a futile black void.

And abruptly, just like in Paris when Ari had told me that he was leaving me, I couldn't hear the doctor anymore, could only discern that his lips were moving, but not a word of what he was saying reached my ears. My eyes closed of their own volition. I covered my head with the hospital blanket and blocked out Dr. Kaminsky, who continued to talk while I fell asleep.

I slept a deep and dreamless sleep, apparently the result of the tranquilizers they'd dosed me with. I awoke feeling uneasy, dim witted, and light headed. My anxious parents were once again sitting by my bed and seemed to have aged a decade overnight. Their faces were gray, and I saw fear in their eyes.

"I need to pee," I said weakly.

"Yes, of course." My father sprang to his feet to help me sit up and move off the bed. Lily approached and supported me from the other side, holding my waist.

"There's nothing physically wrong with me," I said. "I'm just crazy. I don't need you to hold me."

They immediately released me, and I wobbled and almost dropped to the floor. They rushed to support me again, and this time I didn't say anything.

"Come, I'll take you to the bathroom," Lily said as she helped me walk to the toilets at the end of the corridor. "Should I come with you?" she asked uncertainly.

"No need."

I held on to the door. The thought of my mother and me alone in the cubicle while I urinated scared me more than the possibility that I might fall and crack my skull.

When I came out, Lily supported me back to bed.

I noticed she was holding me with unexpected tenderness, as though I were something fragile, but when my steps faltered, she tightened her hold. How strange: her support filled me with a sense of security that I had last felt when I was really small, when I'd still called her Mommy and she'd called me Eliyush. When had I stopped calling her Mommy? When had she stopped using that nickname for me? When had I stopped feeling safe with my mother?

We reached the bed. I lowered myself onto it gratefully and closed my eyes.

"Open your eyes," ordered Dr. Kaminsky.

His command was so unequivocal that my eyelids flew open.

"Look around," said the doctor. "Is this what you want? To stay in the hospital? To worry your father and mother to death?"

My father rubbed his eyes with the back of his hand, struggling to hold back the tears. Lily stood next to him, clutching his arm so tightly I could see her knuckles whitening. I heard her heavy, frightened breathing. I saw how much effort she was investing in being strong for my father and maybe also for me. Again I had a strange thought that maybe I didn't really know my mother. The doctor said, "Please go outside and leave me alone with Eliya."

The moment I was alone with the doctor, I felt relieved, as though the difficult emotions lingering after my meeting with him had vanished. Maybe because, unlike my parents, Kaminsky didn't treat me like a lost child; he treated me as an equal and refused to cut me any slack.

The doctor sat by the bed. "Listen," he said. "I don't know what plans you have for yourself, but I am extending an offer of help, and I suggest you meet me halfway. As far as the hospital is concerned, you must seek treatment. I don't want us to meet again as the result of some other desperate action. Sometimes those go too far, and then we'll only meet in the next world. You understand what I'm saying?"

I was silent, and Dr. Kaminsky waited a long time, like someone used to taking his time, and then he said, "I would recommend that you start treatment at the hospital's outpatient clinic or come to my clinic as a private patient. Of course you can choose to see another doctor, but you must seek treatment; otherwise you'll be forcibly hospitalized."

"In a nuthouse?"

"Oh, I'm glad something else elicits a reaction from you. Yes, in a psychiatric hospital. A person who attempts to end her life is a danger to herself, and the law says that if she's not able to receive assistance of her own free will, then she must be compelled to receive help. So the choice is in your hands, to accept help either of your own accord or under duress."

"Do my parents know about this?"

"Your parents preferred that I tell you. They can't face you. Would you believe it? Two adults who have devoted their lives to raising their only daughter are scared to death of her."

I studied Dr. Amir Kaminsky. I had no doubt that the large doctor, whose untucked white shirt strained to close over his belly, knew how to talk. His words were precise, sharp as a knife, and reached the heart of my bleeding wounds. I knew he wouldn't tolerate any scenes from me, wouldn't swallow any lies. Behind his ridiculous John Lennon glasses, he had eyes that penetrated to the core of hidden truths.

"I want to be hospitalized," I said. "I want to go to the nuthouse."

"I don't know what fantasies you have about madness, but I don't think you would like the 'nuthouse,' as you call it. In any case, if that's what you want, it can be arranged," said Kaminsky in a quiet voice as he prepared to leave the room. When his hand rested on the door handle, I whispered, "I don't want to take a razor to my wrists again."

Kaminsky released the door handle and retraced his steps to my bed, and then, when he was very close, I continued, "I'm not sure my mother will get to me in time to save me next time."

Looking at me through narrowed eyes, he said, "I don't think you'll slit your wrists again. I believe it was a cry for help." Sitting down again, he said, "You aren't a suicidal person. You're going through a crisis. The separation from your husband is a big mess, but it isn't something that can't be treated through therapy or even with antidepressants. You don't have to be hospitalized in an institution for the mentally ill for that."

But I wanted to be hospitalized. I didn't want to die, but I also didn't want to start living again. I wasn't ready yet.

My attempt at self-purification to make a new start had failed, and if it weren't for the guy with the surfboard, I would have drowned. I had just almost died. I believed that the only way to save myself from myself was to be in a ward where they would take care of me, where strangers would watch over me day and night. Not my father, who'd almost collapsed because of me, and not my mother, who any minute now was going to lose it, but someone like this fat doctor, who didn't care about me, to whom I was just another case. No doubt once he moved on to his next patient, he wouldn't even remember my name.

"Dr. Kaminsky." I tried again, endeavoring to steady my trembling voice. "Even though you told me that you don't fix broken hearts, I'm asking you, help me. Give me back my life."

For his part, he regarded me with what seemed to be a half smile and said, "Oho, that's a big responsibility you're putting on my shoulders, young lady, a heavy load." But he didn't refuse.

"Your case, Eliya, is a classic case of reactive depression, a response to your separation from your husband, and so it should be possible to treat you with discussion and if necessary with medication," Dr. Kaminsky told me in our first conversation in his clinic after I was released from the hospital.

"And what would happen if I rejected treatment?" I inquired in an even tone, as if I were indifferent, as if we weren't talking about my life.

"If I were to diagnose you as suicidal, you would be forcibly hospitalized, you would be placed in a closed ward, and you wouldn't be allowed to leave. And if you were to continue to refuse food like you refused to eat at Ichilov Hospital, we would feed you with a feeding tube through your nose, and that is most unpleasant, young lady, really."

My father had emptied a savings account to finance the expensive treatment with Dr. Kaminsky, but he would have sold one of his kidneys to save me. And although penny-pinching Lily, who was far from philanthropic, didn't like the idea that the sessions with the doctor were so expensive, she preferred I go to his private clinic and not the offices of the health fund, where, heaven forfend, one of the neighbors might see me.

"My treatment method," the doctor explained to me, "is unusual. I am not just a psychiatrist who writes prescriptions, and I'm not just a psychologist who listens to his patient. My approach is based on a system I've developed in which I conduct a dialogue with the patient, and when the patient is ready, we start group therapy. But there's a long process before that, so no need for you to make faces. For now all that I ask is that you keep an open mind and help me to help you."

Then the doctor asked me to move to the couch. I complied with an obvious lack of enthusiasm and lay down in the fetal position.

"Lie on your back," he ordered. "Uncurl your fists so that the open palms of your hands face the ceiling." I did what he asked but kept my legs bent. "Straighten your legs, relax, and allow your legs to fall any way that is comfortable. Breathe through your nose like you did the first time you were here."

The miniskirt I was wearing made it uncomfortable for me to relax my legs, and I kept them pressed tightly together.

"Relax your legs!" barked Dr. Kaminsky. Slowly, I relaxed. I lay on the doctor's sofa with my limbs spread out, breathing through my nose as instructed, and to my surprise I felt a serenity I hadn't experienced in years.

"Let's start at the beginning." The doctor's now-sonorous voice broke through the waves of tranquility enveloping me. But I didn't know where the beginning was. Was the beginning the day I'd met Ari and become addicted to my irresistible attraction to him? Was it the day he'd left me in the café in Paris? Or maybe the day when I'd read the manuscript lying on his desk and discovered to my bitter disappointment that his muse wasn't me but Sophie, the French bitch?

Following the doctor's instructions, I tried to go one step at a time in pursuit of the most minute details of the events that had led me to slit my wrists. "Explain to me," said the doctor, "what it is about this man, why you refuse to let go of him."

I closed my eyes and found it difficult to come up with an answer. I'd never asked myself questions like these. Ari was Ari, and that was enough; it was always enough. After waiting patiently for some time, Dr. Kaminsky interrupted my thoughts and said, "Don't think too much; tell me the first thing that pops into your head."

I was silent. Eyes closed, I counted the minutes as they ticked past. Now Dr. Kaminsky raised his voice. "If you want to lie here on the couch without speaking, that's fine, but if you want us to make progress and not waste money your father doesn't have, as you took great pains to mention, I suggest that you start talking."

My voice when it finally emerged sounded small, almost childlike. "No one will ever talk to me like Ari does. We talk all the time, drive in the car and talk, walk through the streets and talk."

"You talk," the doctor interjected, "or Ari talks?"

"Sometimes he also talks about me," I reflected, "analyzes my personality and teaches me things about myself that I didn't know. Who will talk to me like that? Who knows me better than Ari?"

"What else does Ari have that no one else has?" The doctor pulled deeply on his cigarette, his fifth—I was counting. He wanted answers that I didn't have.

Maybe I had no intention of revealing this to Dr. Kaminsky, but I feared no one would make love to me like Ari. But did Ari really make love to me? I remembered all the things that I would have preferred to forget; how he'd made me satisfy him and then told me to pleasure myself while he watched. I remembered how he'd raped me on that terrible night in Paris.

Suddenly I was so tired. To get Kaminsky off my back, I finally said, "Who will love me like Ari loved me?"

"And who will leave you like Ari left you?" He had no mercy. "This man, into whose hands you placed your life, left you in a café in a foreign city. You told me yourself how you went to Paris specifically to meet your husband, and he took you to a café and informed you that he had fallen in love with another woman. I'm sorry, young lady, but I don't see anything in what you said that could be described as kind."

I shrank into myself on the couch, digging my fingers deep into the coarse fabric, but Kaminsky didn't spare me and continued, "I imagine you in a café in Paris, after Ari informs you that he's leaving you and walks out. This is a straightforward story, and after all that he did, Ari can still control you remotely. And that's what worries me. That you honestly and truly believe that no one will love you like he did."

This time he didn't wait for my response. I realized that from the scraps of facts I'd told him, he'd pieced together an entire story. I still had the urge to defend Ari, but I had to listen to the doctor. I didn't want to hear his words, but I knew that I had to listen. I noticed that Kaminsky's voice had softened a little. "To be clear, this man does not interest me. As far as I'm concerned, he's a corpse, and we will perform a postmortem on it in this room, but only after we understand what led you, what still leads you, to choose to be his prisoner, and when I use that word, I mean it literally. Even now you're this man's prisoner. After a year of not seeing him. After he wounded you, you are still his captive, and you refuse to extricate yourself and reclaim your freedom.

"So I want to know why. What makes you choose to be a prisoner? After all, you aren't weak or pathetic. I've seen that you have *chutzpah* and you have courage."

"I have courage?" I found my voice again, and I pushed myself up on both elbows, my hair falling over my eyes like a red curtain.

"And what courage! You were ready to be confined to a psychiatric hospital without giving it a second thought. That's courage!"

"That came from cowardice, from weakness, from my belief that I couldn't take care of myself, from wanting to be taken care of," I confessed to him, disappointed.

"To be hospitalized so that someone would take care of you? You could have gone to the convalescent home at Kibbutz Ma'ale HaHamisha, where they would've taken care of you under much more pleasant conditions."

At first I was silent, trying to process what Kaminsky had said, breathing through my nose as instructed, and then I said, "So where should we start?"

During our subsequent sessions, answers slowly started to materialize. More than anything I wanted to go back in time, to the person I'd been before I'd met Ari. I wanted to go back to being Eliya Zoref, student at the Department of English Literature at Tel Aviv University, with dreams of a career on the radio, a home, and children. I wanted to go back in time and be like everybody else.

"What's preventing you today from being like everybody else?" the doctor inquired.

"I feel like a rabid dog that everyone stays away from because it's mad. Like Balak from Agnon's *Only Yesterday*." I didn't wait to see if he'd read the book. "I can't fall asleep at night. I feel as though hatred consumes every good part of me. Instead of a heart, there is a devouring fire inside me; instead of blood, poison flows in my veins; instead of a soul, anger bubbles up inside me like lava. And I can't take it anymore. I don't want to hate anymore, to be jealous, to be angry. And until this anger is gone, until this jealousy has left me, I won't be able to make space for the good that is to come, for the love, the joy, and the innocence I had in such great abundance before Ari destroyed who I was."

"Scream," said the doctor. "Scream the pain, the anger, the jealousy, the hatred. Yell it out. That's how you'll cleanse yourself. Let it all out in private and in the open; let it out here at the clinic or in the shower. Scream in the ocean, scream, scream it all out until there is nothing left, until your broken heart, as you call it, and all its thousands of tiny shards turn to dust to be carried off by the wind and become nothing, nonbeing, something that doesn't exist and will not exist in your life."

So I screamed just as the doctor ordered. I screamed at his clinic and in the shower when my parents weren't home and at the beach. I screamed at the beach, until I lost my voice, until my heart almost flew out of my body and my soul blossomed.

For six weeks, twice a week, I met with Dr. Amir Kaminsky in his clinic. What began as hesitant conversations, almost forced, became the most important two hours of the week. I eagerly anticipated them, planning what I would say ahead of time. I never missed an appointment.

During our sessions I tried to understand what had caused me to lose myself in the abusive relationship with Ari. For the first time I admitted to myself that above all, I was attracted to him because he was a writer. I'd always admired writers and never thought that I could create anything. So from the moment we'd met, I'd eradicated myself to facilitate his writing. I wanted to be the tormented artist's wife, the one who took care of his every need, like the wives of writers I'd read about in the biographies of famous authors. I believed that like those women I was the muse for my writer husband, that I also was the source of sweet inspiration. That I would be written up in the chronicles of this writer who was about to be discovered by the world, and I would have a place of honor in his biography. The price I paid, that the wives of the famous authors paid, never occurred to me. Only later, when Dr. Kaminsky and I began to analyze my life with Ari and what had happened to my personality, did I return to those biographies and think about those miserable women forced to live alongside their egocentric husbands, who betrayed them left and right with lovers who became no less famous than the lawfully wedded wives.

So I came to understand something else about Ari and me, about how he had hurt me so deeply. I realized that the moment when I'd discovered I wasn't his muse was a watershed moment. A string had snapped inside me, and I'd shattered in splinters of pain.

"I think he's helping me," I said to my father once when I returned from the clinic, and my father said, "Thank God, sweetheart, finally the color is back in your cheeks."

My kind father turned to Lily, who stood by his side wearing her usual expression of mocking derision. "You see, this doctor, who we thought was a charlatan, is actually doing good work with Eliya. She's even started eating again."

"A person can't live without food," Lily decreed, as if I weren't in the room. "What did you think, that she would die of starvation? So she's eating. Now I want to see her smile. When her smile returns, you'll know the doctor has succeeded. Till then we have to pray she doesn't go crazy on us again and hide under the blanket. She's going to the doctor, and she feels good now, but who'll guarantee she won't revert because of that piece of nothing? When she goes back to university, when she has a new guy, when she starts to look for work, then I'll feel better. Until then I won't be able to relax," she said, and she left the room. Even I didn't have an answer for her.

Lily

When a child dies, his soul is transferred to a newborn baby. Lily believed this with all her heart. She had to believe it; if not, where would she find the strength to carry her pregnancy for nine months, especially through the oppressive heat of August, the hottest month in Tel Aviv? Where would she find the strength to trudge on swollen ankles along the dusty, exposed streets, where the blazing, burning sun dazzled her eyes and beat mercilessly on her head? Where would she find the strength to care for her baby girl? She hated the sun, she hated Tel Aviv in August, and she hated being pregnant. If she could have, she would have stayed home all day and sealed the blinds, hiding from the world and the rays of the sun. But she knew if she shut herself up at home, Shaul wouldn't be able to take it. He'd nearly gone out of his mind when, after the baby died, she didn't leave her bed for such a long time. Shaul would go to work in the morning at his jewelry store on King George Street, and she would stay alone in their house and pray that God would end her pain.

Now Lily refused to relive that terrible period and the neighbors' pitying glances. She made up her mind that she wouldn't go back to being a topic of conversation among the women at the public park, and she forced herself to run errands, to go to the grocery store, to wander aimlessly past display windows on Dizengoff Street, mainly so they would stop staring at her with eyes full of pity, stop asking with feigned interest how she was. She knew every woman who asked was secretly thanking her God that it was Lily who'd lost a child and not her. She knew when she walked past, the mothers hurriedly shooed their children inside, fearful of the evil eye. They were right: her envy burned like fire as the babies born the same time as her son grew and developed and were already learning how to walk and to babble their first words. They were alive, and her baby was dead. She envied the alley cats born around the same time as her son that lived after he died. She knew all of them; she remembered them as kittens, and now they were strong, hardy street cats, and her baby hadn't been strong and hadn't survived.

The *bishara* had told her that she had to hurry up and become pregnant again so that the soul of her child would enter the new baby who would be born, so that her son, her pride and joy, would live on in her new baby.

"The child is gone, dead, finished, Allah have mercy," the *bishara*, the Muslim witch from Jaffa, told her. "Now pray that he will be born again to a good mother like yourself and not to another mother, may Allah forbid it. And to make sure he will be born to you, you have to become pregnant! There's no time; twelve months is the longest the soul can wait. If not, another mother will smile, but you will cry, and I want you to be the one smiling. You and your husband. You can't cross the same river twice, my daughter; the person changes and so does the water, so go quickly to your home and do what is necessary so another baby will grow in your belly."

She didn't tell Shaul the *bishara* had ordered her to become pregnant. She'd never told him at all about her frequent meetings with the Arab fortune-teller who lived in Jaffa, near the clock tower. If he'd known, he would've thought she'd lost her mind for good.

They had barely spoken since their son had died. At the end of the weeklong shiva mourning period, the house had emptied of people, and now it was just the two of them and the silence that singed the walls. During the shiva his relatives had come to offer their condolences. His parents, Sarina and Albert; his younger brother, Shmulik, who arrived in his uniform with the sergeant major insignia; several neighbors; Shaul's childhood friends; even some loyal customers, for whom Shaul had made earrings and bracelets and chains of gold.

Those had been the longest seven days of her life, seven days during which her heart was nearly smashed to pieces and her head nearly exploded. People came and went, did their best to provide comfort, but she refused to be comforted, shrank into herself on the mattress on the living room floor, sealing her ears to the deluge of consoling words, crawling inside her disaster, declining to share it with strangers. Of all the visitors the hardest to bear were Shaul's mother and father, who, to her great displeasure, sat with them from dawn to dusk and sometimes even stayed the night on the mattresses in the living room, without asking her permission, without considering her wishes.

There was no one from her side. She didn't have a relative in the world that Shaul knew about. Lily was a lonely woman, and after their son died, her loneliness only deepened.

He tried to share the pain with her, but she rejected him time and again, rebuffing the comfort of his arms, ignoring the words he murmured to her, intended as consolation for himself as well. She barricaded herself in her grief, and there was no opening through which he could enter. At night, when the consolers left them to themselves, she turned away from him in bed, crying for hours into her pillow. Her weeping tore his heart, her wails like those of a kitten abandoned by its mother. And every attempt he made to touch her, to stroke her back or her head, was met with almost violent resistance.

Lily was a lone wolf. She'd always taken care of herself. If she hadn't, who would have? The nuns at the convent? All they'd done was give orders and scold her without an iota of gentleness or love. All except Sister Rose. From the day Lily was born, she learned not to cry so she wouldn't annoy the nuns, not to ask questions because she knew there would be no answers. She learned how to see without being seen, how to observe the smallest details, how to recognize impending danger, how to smell the nuns before they appeared. She found the hidden corners and learned how to blend in, how to be swallowed by the stone walls of the convent, and how not to fear the echoing sound of the nuns' footsteps or the jangling keys they wore on the belts that encircled their waists. From as far back as she could remember, Lily hadn't trusted anyone or become attached to anyone. As a child she barely spoke. She did what was asked of her without argument and taught herself to manage on her own.

Lily learned not to appeal to others for comfort, yet when she met the *bishara*, she sought her understanding and warmth. And against all odds, the *bishara* became the closest person to Lily, a substitute for the mother she'd never had. She was the only person in the world Lily could trust, for she knew that the *bishara* would keep all Lily's secrets to herself and never reveal them to a soul. If only she could, she would have burrowed into her wide body, among the folds of the djellaba she wore, rested her head on the large bosom, climbed into the enveloping arms, and rested.

Lily had been going to the *bishara* for many years, asking her to read coffee grounds, asking for advice, with one explicit request: "If you see something about my past, don't tell me. I don't want to know anything about the time before."

The *bishara* shook her head in sorrow. Early in her acquaintance with the light-haired Jewish girl, she honored the request. When she saw things in the coffee grounds that could have lifted the veil shrouding Lily's past, she kept them to herself. Until she couldn't any longer.

Lily was fourteen when Naima, an Iraqi girl from Baghdad at her boarding school, took her to the Arab witch. Naima had come on aliyah to Israel as part of a rescue program for Jewish youth in danger across the world, and her Arabic was better than her Hebrew. Naima was the only girl in the boarding school Lily spent time with. But though Lily didn't always understand what the *bishara* said, she refused to allow Naima to join her in the cramped niche.

"What do you care if I come with you?" Naima challenged, shaking her head at Lily in amazement. "What could you possibly have to hide? You don't know anything about yourself, where you were born or who your parents are, so what secrets could you have?" Lily was furious. How dare Naima talk about her parents when Lily had never mentioned them? She knew the children at the school talked.

Each of the girls at school had a story; no one went to boarding school because they came from a perfect home. In some cases, parents had stayed in the countries they were from while the children came to Israel on their own. Some had lost one or both parents. Some were children of new immigrants who struggled to adjust and couldn't raise their families because of their emotional or economic situations. Some were sent by parents who felt they would have a better upbringing at the boarding school, while others were plucked from their homes by social welfare services. But not Lily. She hadn't been taken from anyone's home. She'd been transferred to the institution when, at ten, she was discovered roaming the streets of Jerusalem, hungry and filthy and clothed in rags. A group of kindhearted women from the Memorial to Moses club found her on Jaffa Road searching for food in trash cans.

These good women would traverse the Jerusalem streets in the afternoons, looking for abandoned children. They would bring them to the beautiful stone building in the neighborhood of Mazkeret Moshe, where the children received a hot meal and a few hours of grace from the streets. Girls were taught embroidery and knitting while the boys played ball games. At six o'clock, when the club closed, the children returned to the streets and the women to their safe, warm, well-lit homes, to their husbands and their own children, considerably more fortunate than the street children of Jerusalem. In the 1930s the Jerusalem orphanages were full to capacity. The great epidemic had claimed thousands, leaving many homeless orphans to fend for themselves. Thanks to a collaborative effort with the local institutions, some of the children were sent to homes established specifically to deal with the problem.

Lily didn't know how much time she'd spent wandering the streets hungry and shivering after she'd run away from the convent. Her blue convent dress was scant protection against the chill of Jerusalem after dark. She was exhausted and bleary eyed from sleeping on benches in public parks or under the stands in the Mahane Yehuda Market. Jerusalem was foreign to her. She didn't know its streets, alleyways, and shops. She'd never left the convent since she'd arrived as a day-old infant.

As a little girl Lily had loved to walk slowly along the corridors of the convent, gazing at large paintings of Christian saints on the walls. Her meanderings took her to every corner, but her favorite place was the small chapel, more modest than the large church. She was happiest sitting on the wooden pews facing the altar, basking in the silence and the smell of incense. It was the only place she had any privacy, where the other girls never bothered her, and where she wasn't constantly on alert for the nuns' echoing footsteps. It was the one place she felt serene and at peace. Lily would sit in the first pew and gaze at the painting of Mary, mother of Jesus. She looked into the painted eyes of the Holy Mother, who seemed to her to be kind and protective, and spoke to her as though she were a creature of flesh and blood and not an image hanging above an altar. Sometimes she felt that the Holy Mother wasn't just listening but was also answering her, whispering words of comfort and advice, instilling her with strength and reassurance. The humble chapel was the only place in the large convent where Lily could be herself.

As she grew older, the high ceilings, stained glass windows, and pictures of saints on giant walls began to close in on her. She felt foreign in the one place she knew, as though the convent and the secrets it concealed were a sugarcoated prison. The strict daily routine that ensured there was never a moment of privacy; the stern countenance of the nuns became physically painful to her. She chafed at the enforced repetition of the same activities every day for years and began to feel trapped. Inside the shadowy halls of the convent, she yearned for the sun, which she encountered only briefly once a day when she was permitted to go out into the yard with the other girls. On her tenth birthday she began to fantasize about her escape. In her imagination she spun a detailed plan, plotting every step, and at the first opportunity that presented itself, she fled without a backward glance.

When the women from the Memorial to Moses club discovered her rummaging in piles of discarded produce at the Mahane Yehuda Market, they invited her to the clubhouse, tempting her with a hot meal. But Lily evaded them like a canny street cat. It was more than a week before the good women managed to convince her to accompany them, and from then on she was there every day. A quiet child, frighteningly serious, who rarely spoke or interacted with the other children, she sat and embroidered with great skill. Perhaps it was the strange girl's extraordinary beauty that attracted the attention of Mrs. Nachmias, one of the women who volunteered at the club, who determined to use her connections to find Lily a place to live. But Lily resisted, fiercely. Surprised by the fire in the eyes of the usually docile child, Mrs. Nachmias explained that she had no choice. "It's that or the streets," she told her. "I'll find a place where they'll take care of you and provide for your needs."

One day a young energetic woman arrived at the club and took Lily and two other children by bus to the city of Herzliya and the institution that became her new home.

Here as well, Lily didn't engage with the other children. She had no hair-raising stories about sea voyages that almost ended in disaster. She didn't pine for her mother's cooking and the aromas of the maternal kitchen, dream that her father would come one day to carry her home, or miss some old neighborhood and the games played outdoors. She'd never had a doll or a toy, and she had never been hugged or kissed. The nuns had been rigid and severe and forbade any indulgence, which was considered the mother of all sins. The one good thing she'd emerged from the convent with was excellent English, the dominant language at the British convent. She spoke as if she could've grown up in England. It wasn't until she started to attend classes with other Jewish girls there that she learned Hebrew, a language she found difficult to master.

Lily was eight years old when Sister Rose arrived at the convent. Unlike the older grim, taciturn nuns, young Sister Rose beamed and spoke softly. She was responsible for the sleeping chamber, where the girls' beds were crowded together against the walls. Sister Rose wended her way among them before the girls closed their eyes, making sure they said their prayers and made the sign of the cross before turning in for the night, and only then did she switch off the light. Unlike her predecessor, who was short tempered and easily angered, Sister Rose had endless patience. She would occasionally stroke the head of one of the girls or whisper a blessing in her soft voice. Even Lily couldn't resist her kind nature and waited impatiently every evening for the moment when Sister Rose would stand by her bed, pull the covers over her shoulders, and recite a prayer with her. Together they would cross themselves, and then she would rest her warm palm on Lily's forehead and wish her good night.

Sister Rose was the only one who managed to penetrate Lily's armor, and their relationship quickly deepened. Lily found herself longing for Rose, thinking about her, and seeking opportunities to be near her. The young nun felt a special connection to Lily and lingered longer at her bedside than by the other girls'.

One day, after Sister Rose had been at the convent more than a year, Lily was sitting in her usual spot in the first pew of the small chapel, communing with the image of the Holy Virgin, when the young sister slipped into the pew and sat beside her. Lily was surprised she hadn't heard her enter the chapel, then realized that unlike the heavy footsteps of the other nuns, Rose's were light and almost silent, as though she floated above the tiled floors. Lily was happy when Rose sat next to her. She felt the warmth of Rose's body and the pleasant smell that wafted from her. While the odor of the older nuns was sour and mixed with perspiration, Rose smelled as fresh and delightful as her personality. The two sat silently together for a long time.

"Do you see how beautiful she is, the Holy Mother?" Sister Rose whispered to Lily. "And how she looks at her son, our sacred Lord. How she loves him. There's no love in the world like the love of a mother."

"I don't know," Lily replied. "I've never had a mother."

"If only you had one," whispered Rose. "I feel so sorry that your mother . . ."

Lily jumped as if bitten by a snake and stood, facing Sister Rose. "My mother? What do you know about my mother?"

The young nun regarded Lily with dismay. Despite her age, the girl suddenly appeared dangerous.

"I don't know much," she stammered. "Only what I heard from the other sisters."

"What did you hear?" Sparks seemed to shoot from Lily's green eyes.

"They said you've been here longest, that you were practically born here."

"I wasn't born here?"

"No."

"So where was I born?"

"I don't know. Sister Katherine, you should ask her. May the Lord forgive me, I shouldn't have spoken. I'm sorry, my child," said Rose tearfully, turning to leave the chapel.

"No, don't go." Lily blocked her path. "I won't move until you tell me where I was born and who left me here."

"My dear," said Sister Rose in her gentle voice, as a flush colored her cheeks, "let me pass, please. You're making me behave inappropriately. I shouldn't have said anything."

"What did you say?" Sister Katherine of the bitter countenance strode into the chapel and saw the small girl blocking Sister Rose with her slight, determined body.

"I'm sorry," said Sister Rose. "It seems I said something I shouldn't have." She crossed herself and left the chapel.

Lily found herself standing before Sister Katherine.

"Well, Lily, what did Sister Rose say to you?"

"She said I should ask you about my mother."

"And why would I know anything about your mother?"

"Sister Rose said you know who left me at the convent. And Sister Rose never lies."

"True," said Sister Katherine. "Lying is a sin."

"So tell me the truth!" Lily demanded with newfound strength.

Although she'd known her all her short life, Sister Katherine contemplated Lily as though seeing her for the first time. The scrawny, wrinkled baby had grown into a beautiful, healthy child. It had been years since Sister Katherine paid any special attention to her. To her, the child was a fixture in the convent. She was one of thirty children who lived there, who needed to be fed, clothed, and educated in the ways of the Lord. Even if she occasionally remembered the baby Lily had once been, she'd hardened her heart and refused to allow sentiment to touch her, perhaps even treating her more harshly than the others. Now she faced the child, who looked more fiercely resolute than ever as she demanded to hear the truth she'd never been told.

The nun sighed deeply and said, "It's not a secret. We never wanted to hide anything from you; we just thought you were too young. We were waiting until you were older to tell you."

"How old am I?" It was the first time Lily had asked the question.

"Well, let's see. We found you at the convent gate on Christmas Eve nine years ago. You were a gift placed there for us."

"So I'm nine years old?"

"Next Christmas you'll be ten. You were born on an especially cold Christmas. The day we found you, snow fell in Jerusalem."

Sister Katherine remembered that freezing day well. Everyone else had already been in the church for Christmas Mass. Before joining them she'd gone to check the fire in the dining hall hadn't died down and that candles were lit. As she walked through the corridor by the great hall, she heard the bell at the gate ringing, insistently and repeatedly. As if someone was pulling on the bell rope for all they were worth.

"One moment," she shouted. "I'm coming." But the bell continued to ring. She rushed outside without a coat; they must be in great distress, she thought. When she opened the huge metal gate, she found a snow-dusted bundle wrapped in a woolen blanket, containing a newborn baby sleeping deeply and contentedly, seemingly unaware of the fierce cold of the storm.

"And who left me there?" Lily interrupted her reveries. "Who left me there to die?"

Sister Katherine hesitated. Should she tell the child what she knew or order her back to class immediately and scold her for asking too many questions? This was the opportunity to lay down the burden of the secret she'd kept for years. Although she knew it was unfair. She'd sealed off her heart to the girl and lived in fear of reliving the dangerous and confusing maternal feelings that infant Lily had awakened. But at that moment the memories were overwhelming, and she realized all her efforts had been in vain. The painful truth slipped through her defenses, and she realized all this time her conscience had been sore, and it now demanded she reveal what she knew.

"I don't believe," she told Lily in an unusually gentle tone, "that the person who left you there wanted you to die. She wanted you to survive. She dressed you in two outfits, swaddled you in a scarf, and wrapped you in a blanket."

"How do you know?" Lily had never addressed any of the nuns in such an outspoken and demanding manner, yet what shocked Sister

Katherine most was the expression in her eyes. Lily looked like a trapped animal that knew it had nothing left to lose.

"I was the one who found you," she told the girl. "I found you at the entrance to the convent."

"And who left me there?"

"When I opened the gate, there was only you."

"That's all? That's all there was?"

"There was something else." Sister Katherine spoke slowly, weighing each word. "But now is not the time. When you're older, we'll tell you."

"Tell me now!" Lily clutched at the nun's habit to stop her from leaving. "Now!"

Again Sister Katherine was astonished by the girl's fierceness. She lowered herself to the shiny surface of the hard wooden pew and said, "In the folds of the blanket there was a note, stitched to the wool wrapped around you. It was in English and said, 'Good Sisters, please rescue my baby as you rescued me. I cannot save her.' At the bottom was a sketch of a white lily, and the name Lily was written there, apparently the name chosen for you by your mother. We named you Elizabeth after Elisheva, mother of John the Baptist, but Lily was the name chosen by your mother, so we called you Lily."

"And after you found me, what did you do?"

"I scooped you up and rushed inside. Luckily you hadn't been harmed by the cold. Your mother's warmth protected you. It must've been her who rang the bell, so you'd only been there a moment before I opened the gate. And you've been with us ever since, a daughter of God as we are all His daughters."

Lily was astounded. She hadn't thought much about who had given birth to her. She'd believed that the fact she was an orphan was self-evident. Jesus and Mary and the nuns were her only family. But now her curiosity was aroused. "Who left me here?" she asked Sister Katherine again.

The nun remained silent for a time before responding, "We don't know. She left no trace."

"But what about the note?" Lily insisted.

"My dear child, many young girls have passed through here since the convent was established," Sister Katherine said, attempting to avoid the question. But the expression in Lily's eyes showed the girl wouldn't accept less than a direct answer.

"Your mother could have been any one of the many young women who lived with us for a while, and perhaps she never lived here—maybe she'd only heard of us, heard that we provide a home to girls who are homeless." She half hoped that Lily might settle for that.

"The woman asked you to save me like you saved her," Lily persisted. "That means that she lived here."

"All I know is her name," said Sister Katherine. "At the end of her note she signed her name in Hebrew letters, Rahel."

"Rahel?" Lily repeated, pausing between the two syllables. Her mother's name was Rahel. So much softness in the name of the woman who had left a newborn infant on a freezing snowy night at a convent. How was it possible that a woman with such a soft name could abandon her like that? "And you knew her?"

"No."

"But someone must have known her."

"There were some who said they remembered her, but I didn't."

"Who? Who remembered her?" Lily continued to question. "I want to know who she was."

Sister Katherine sighed a long, deep sigh, and after a moment that was an eternity for Lily, she said, "They'll tell you when you're older."

"But I'm old enough," Lily exclaimed. "You just said that I'm ten."

"Almost ten. You are more mature than other girls your age, though." Sister Katherine regarded Lily gravely. Had there ever been such a child who seemed to be a grown woman from birth?

"You were such a good baby," she told Lily. "You almost never cried. The Mother Superior gave me the job of caring for you the first week you were here, and then we all took turns looking after you."

"Is that all you know?"

Sister Katherine fixed her eyes on the stone floor of the chapel. Something in Lily's expression kept her rooted to the spot. She couldn't deny it any longer. For seven days she'd cared for the infant as if she were her mother, feeding and changing her, rocking her, whispering endearments. The baby slept in her bed, and she had been vigilant not to roll over and crush the tiny being. In no time she was bound to her with filaments of love. But when the Mother Superior noticed Sister Katherine's stirrings of maternal feelings, she immediately separated them. Other nuns were assigned to care for her, according to a schedule of shifts, while Sister Katherine was given different duties.

Ever since, she'd held herself in check and tried to erase the memories of finding Lily and loving her during the first week of her life. Much as she was tempted to tell the poor child what she knew about her birth mother, Sister Katherine couldn't disobey an explicit order from the Mother Superior. She was not to tell Lily about her past until she was grown. "That's all I know," she said.

"You're lying!" Lily protested, shocking herself that she dared to accuse one of the nuns of such a sin.

Under different circumstances, Sister Katherine would have punished her severely for her behavior. But again she found she couldn't bear to disappoint Lily.

"There was another drawing on the note," she said slowly. Lily froze, listening intently. "It was a drawing of a Star of David."

Lily's head spun. A Star of David, she knew from the Jewish girls at the convent, was an important symbol. Did that mean that her mother was Jewish? That she, Lily, was Jewish too? Lily had always believed she was Christian through and through. She thought about how the Jewish girls crossed their fingers surreptitiously to cancel out the Christian prayers. How, after they knelt and prayed to Jesus and the Holy Mother, they climbed into bed, pulled the covers over their faces, and whispered softly. Once, when one of the girls peeked out and saw Lily watching her, she was frightened and made Lily swear she would never tell the nuns. Lily agreed but wanted to know what she was whispering. "*Shema Yisrael.* Hear, O Israel." The girl's voice was so low Lily had trouble hearing her. "It's a Jewish prayer. I'm Jewish. Even though here they teach me to be a Christian, I will always be a Jew."

Lily rushed out of the chapel past the dismayed Sister Katherine, flew through the garden where some of the girls were pulling weeds, charged into the convent's main building, raced through the corridors, climbed the broad staircase to the second floor, and burst into the office of the stern-faced Mother Superior, who sat behind her large writing desk.

The Mother Superior looked up from her papers in amazement at the child who had barged into her inner sanctum without permission.

"Can I help you?" she inquired with feigned politeness.

"Am I a Jew or a Christian?" Lily demanded breathlessly.

"What kind of question is that?" replied the Mother Superior, directing her query to Sister Katherine, who had entered her office moments after Lily.

"I told her about the note, Mother, and about the Star of David," said the panting nun. "I'm sorry. I don't know how she managed to get it out of me."

"It's not a secret," the expressionless older woman responded, and turning to Lily, she said, "We never intended to hide anything from you."

"I want the note."

"You will have the note," she answered evenly, "when you are seventeen."

◆ ◆ ◆

But Lily couldn't wait; she was constantly restless. She no longer prayed with intent, only mouthing the words so as not to draw the nuns' ire. The foundations of her world were shaken; the convent seemed like a kind of prison shrouded in lies. She decided to venture into the outside world, where she might learn about her Jewishness and find the woman who'd abandoned her outside in a snowstorm on Christmas Eve.

Lily found it hard to adapt to life at the boarding school, and as was her nature, she kept her distance from everyone. The other children found her strange and different. Perhaps because of her fair coloring, they nicknamed her *"goya,"* meaning *gentile girl,* and the label, with all its negative connotations, stuck. Also, despite her best efforts, she couldn't divest herself of the Christian customs instilled in her from birth. Some nights she caught herself kneeling at the side of her bed before lights-out and hoped none of the other girls noticed. There were times when, seemingly of their own accord, her hands began to make the sign of the cross, and she would force them to her sides. But the other girls did notice, and they ridiculed her, imitating her gestures and her kneeling with exaggerated glee, deluging her in a flood of curses and scorn, which only served to heighten her sense of foreignness and loneliness.

Lily's Hebrew wasn't fluent. Besides what the nuns had taught her, the only Hebrew words she knew she'd picked up on the streets of Jerusalem, and she spoke the language like a new immigrant. For her, it was the language of survival, and she found neither comfort nor beauty in its guttural sounds.

In all her years at the boarding school, Lily was never invited to join the secret meetings of young people who later joined the youth brigades of the Haganah paramilitary organization that ultimately became the core of the Israel Defense Forces. By this time she'd perfected her own defenses and become expert at observing without being observed. But she'd also become a strange creature, quiet as a mouse. At least she no longer suffered from the mockery of her early days at the boarding school, as she'd shown she could give as good as she got. If anyone dared to invade her privacy, she exploded like lava from a volcano that threatened to burn anything in its path. Everyone learned it was better not to antagonize Lily, so they settled for laughing at her behind her back and otherwise left her alone. Everyone except for Naima, the new immigrant from Iraq, who arrived at the boarding school in a gray woolen skirt, a white blouse buttoned up to her chin, knee socks, and shiny black patent leather shoes. Her tight braids tied with pink ribbons encircled her head, and her round glasses seemed to float above her nose. From her first day she became the punching bag for the other girls. They pulled her braids and made fun of her clothes, though Golda, who ran the storeroom, provided her with the same clothes the others wore as quickly as possible: blue shorts with elastic around the legs and a white singlet. They mocked her broken Hebrew and her accent, laughed when she insisted on showering alone and wouldn't allow anyone to see her naked, snorted when she asked every day when her parents were coming to take her home to "the most beautiful house in Baghdad."

Every night before she went to sleep, Naima would pull out the suitcase from beneath her bed and remove a small wooden chest that held photographs and the letters her parents had written before they'd sent her to the Land of Israel. After bestowing a kiss on each picture, she would sit for a while holding a gold necklace with a heart pendant and pray her father would come soon. Then she would replace the necklace, the letter, and the photographs in the wooden jewelry box, put it in the suitcase, and slide it back under her bed. When Naima closed her eyes, she imagined the street where her family home stood in Baghdad, with the large living room windows that seemed to usher inside the beautiful gardens surrounding the house. She remembered the luxurious carpets, the large bookshelf from which her father would sometimes select one of his prized holy books to read her stories from the Bible. She envisioned the low stools on which the members of her family sat to enjoy her mother's fragrant tea and anise-flavored cookies, the big dining room table the family would gather around, and she could almost smell the aroma of the *tbit*, the chicken and rice slowly cooked over a low flame for the Shabbat meal. As she remembered, tears slid down her cheeks, and her strangled sobs disturbed the quiet of the sleeping hall.

One evening, the moment her head touched the pillow, a group of girls rushed over and surrounded her bed. One dragged out her suitcase and with a victory flourish extracted a white cotton nightgown edged in lace. She put it on over her pajamas and began to dance around the room, maliciously mimicking Naima's accent. Two other girls pounced on the jewelry box and examined Naima's prized photographs, then brought them to their lips, making loud smacking sounds. Naima stared open mouthed and horrified as the girls pawed her precious possessions and contaminated them with their scorn, and then all at once she leaped off her bed. Lily watched Naima trying to catch the girls with her wooden box and saw how easily they evaded her, laughing with spiteful glee. She tried to remain indifferent. Such cruelty wasn't unusual—the girls at the boarding school were always seeking a victim to torture—but when the box fell and its contents spilled, she sprang from her bed like an enraged tiger and fell upon the girl who had dropped it.

"Bitch!" screamed Lily. "Who do you think you are? You rotten *vooz-vooz*!" She used the slur she'd heard girls at the convent use to insult Yiddish-speaking European Jews as she pulled hard at her hair.

"And you're a rotten *goya*," screeched the girl as she tried to escape Lily's grip. In a frenzy of anger, Lily pummeled her, hurling a stream of insults, until the woman on night duty came rushing in and separated the two thrashing combatants.

"What's going on here?" she berated them and then commanded, "Into bed, all of you! You too!" she shouted at Naima, who was crouched on the cold floor gathering up the contents of her chest. "Give me that!" she ordered.

"No," Naima wailed, tightening her hold.

"Give it to me this instant!"

"No, please, don't take my box," she begged, clasping it to her chest. "Punish me; make me clean the toilets all day and all night—just don't take my box!"

The night matron wrenched the jewelry box from her grasp.

"Give it to her," Lily demanded as she snatched back the box. "It's not yours. It isn't anyone's other than Naima's. Her parents gave it to her, and it belongs to her. No one has the right to take it, including you!"

The matron was stunned. None of the girls had ever raised her voice to her or disobeyed her. The other girls stared at Lily in amazement, while Naima's eyes shone with gratitude.

Collecting herself, the stern matron instructed Naima and the others to get into their beds immediately.

"I'm keeping the box," she told Lily, "and tomorrow morning, when the director comes, we'll deal with you and the problems you caused. Now go to your bed."

"Not without Naima's jewelry box," Lily retorted.

"Don't you dare argue with me, or you will be severely punished."

"What will you do? Kick me out? You don't scare me. I've wanted to get out of here for a long time."

"Lily, I don't understand. You're always so obedient. Why are you behaving like this?" Her strict demeanor lapsed, so bewildered was she at the transformation of the normally silent, well-mannered girl.

"She's homesick, and for Naima that box is home, and the girls are always tormenting her. Before you walked in, they took it from her suitcase, and they threw everything in it onto the floor. Then you arrive, with no idea about what happened, and you're mad at her, mad at me, and you take away her box."

Lily felt as though she had nothing to lose and spoke calmly and quietly, which impressed the older woman, who softened further.

"Lily, dear, go tell Naima to come and see me." Nodding her head, Lily turned away, glowing with a sense of triumph.

"I knew you wouldn't let anything bad happen to my box," Naima told her the next morning, reaching for Lily's hand. "You're a real friend. I owe you."

"You don't owe me anything!" cried Lily, who couldn't bear it when someone was kind to her. "I just don't like to see people being mistreated. That's all."

She pulled her hand away, but her new friend was unmoved. She shook her head and said, "Still, thanks to you they gave me back my jewelry box, and the girls don't bother me anymore because they're afraid of you."

"They should be, and they'd better watch themselves."

From that day, Lily's carefully cultivated isolation was breached. Naima followed her everywhere, saved a place for her in the dining hall, made her bed for her, and willingly performed every task allotted to her by Lily. Even if she wasn't overjoyed about this girl trailing along behind her, even if she never really thought of her as a friend, she did enjoy the fruits of the other girl's loyalty. When Naima told her about the Arab fortune-teller from Jaffa, the *bishara* who could read coffee grounds, Lily asked her to take her there.

A year after she started going to consult the *bishara*, Naima's parents arrived and took her from the boarding school to their new home. Lily would never forget the pinpricks of envy that punctured her heart at the sight of the emotional reunion between Naima and her parents. She would never forget the sight of Naima falling into the arms of the glamorous-looking man and woman or how they kissed her over and over again, on her forehead and cheeks and the top of her head. She would never forget the happiness shining in the eyes of a girl who'd almost never smiled or laughed in all her time at the boarding school. The car receding into the distance along the sandstone drive with Naima safely inside it, going home with her parents, would be forever etched in her memory. She had no idea what became of Naima after she went home.

Home. What exactly that was, Lily could only imagine. She thought it was someplace warm, pleasant, and safe, with good smells coming from the kitchen, aromas that were nothing like the odors of the porridge bubbling in the gigantic pot in the boarding school kitchen or the murky vegetable soup. That was what Naima had and Lily had never had. She felt the envy twisting her insides and vowed never to think about Naima and her secure new life with her family. It hurt too much. Lily returned to her lone-wolf persona. The only remnant of Naima was the *bishara*. Lily had never asked Naima how a young immigrant from Baghdad had known how to find an Arab fortune-teller in Jaffa, how she'd figured out how to take two buses, walk a long way, and wind through the crowded houses of Manshiya that descended toward the sea and through Jebeliya, until she finally arrived, worn out, in the square by the clock tower, before continuing by way of twisting alleyways to the home of the *bishara*. She never asked Naima why she'd sought the *bishara* in the first place or what the *bishara* had told her, and when Naima tried to volunteer the information, Lily refused to listen. She didn't want to know. If she asked Naima about her conversations, then Naima might ask her, and Lily didn't want to be asked questions, certainly not ones for which she had no answers.

Lily continued to visit the Arab woman after Naima disappeared from her life. The *bishara* never asked about Naima, and neither did Lily. She went to see her every few months, and sometimes the line of people waiting for the *bishara* filled the neglected yard covered with small stones, bordered by a low stone wall covered with climbing plants. The woman's burly son made sure they went in one by one and each person waited their turn.

The *bishara* was a tiny woman, and Lily towered a head above her. She dressed in the traditional embroidered caftan worn by many Arab women of her age, with her head covered by a white kerchief with colorful fringes. The girl longed to attach herself to the *bishara*'s elongated earlobes, stretched out of shape by her enormous gold earrings, and hang there. The rich fragrance of boiling coffee welcomed Lily when she entered the room. The *bishara* greeted her with a nod of the head and, without wasting any time, poured out a small cup of bitter black liquid. When Lily finished drinking, the *bishara* would turn over the cup and say, "Ask," always careful to respect Lily's request not to reveal any information about her past.

Until the day when she had to break her promise. "Allah have mercy, my daughter," she said. "*Inshallah,* your life will be blessed with luck, but why, my daughter, should you pay for something that has no value?" Lily stared at her, wide eyed, not understanding. "What's done can't be undone," the woman continued. "What was, was, and you pay for something you didn't do, that neither you nor anyone else can change. It's impossible, my daughter, to turn back time, and you suffer greatly. It comes through the *finjan,* my daughter. See for yourself— every time you come to see me, again and again I see the same thing."

"What do you see?"

"My daughter, I see the sea, a great sea, and beyond the sea I see a woman whose heart is *aswad,* black. That's what I see. You always say to me, 'Don't tell me anything'; you don't want to know. And why shouldn't you know, my daughter? Your soul burns, and in the end all you'll have is the charred remains of a soul."

Lily was silent as the *bishara* continued to scrutinize the coffee grounds, turning the cup this way and that, mumbling, "A black heart, *aswad,* black as black, *Allah yostour.*"

"Is the black heart mine?"

"No, not yours. The black heart belongs to the woman on the other side of the sea, behind where the sun sets."

"And why is her heart black?"

"From sorrow, my daughter, from sorrow over the great sin she committed. What she did blackened her heart."

"What did she do?" Lily felt as though she would burst.

"That I do not see, may Allah be merciful. What she did I don't see through the *finjan*."

"But what does it have to do with me?"

"It comes from your *finjan*, so it's connected to you. Listen closely, my daughter. I don't know who the woman is or why her heart is black or why she went away beyond the sea, but I'll tell you one thing: it's connected to your life, it's connected to your past, and a person can't escape her past. Even if she runs to the ends of the earth, her past will go everywhere with her."

Lily fell silent, and the *bishara* didn't speak again until she said abruptly, "*Tayeb*, time's up," leaving Lily with the questions she dared not ask. "Hurry home and think about it. *Yalla*, off you go," she urged Lily, who remained seated on the stool, trying to process what the *bishara* had told her. "Go now. There are many people outside, and I'm an old woman whose eyes don't see so well anymore. Go home, and may Allah help you; may He watch over you."

Lily was assailed by thoughts about the great sea and the woman who lived beyond it, the woman whose heart was black because of her sin. She had no doubt that this was the woman who'd left her at the convent on Christmas Eve. She could feel it in her bones. But what was she doing on the other side of the sea? She had to know who the woman was. She had to find out why she was beyond the sea.

The girl who'd never wanted to know about her past, only her future, continued to visit the *bishara* and ask questions, ask about the woman, but the *bishara* never had answers. The image that formed time and again in the coffee grounds was of the great sea and the woman. After a while Lily stopped asking, but the woman with the black heart began to appear in her dreams.

The dream was always the same. There was a tremendous sea, smooth as glass, from which a woman emerged dressed in what seemed to be a bridal gown, her large breasts and erect nipples clearly visible through the filmy fabric, holding something in her hands. The woman moved toward her, but the closer she came, the more elusive her image was, and Lily never managed to see her face. As she moved closer, her hands seemed to approach Lily's closed eyes, hands holding a tiny newborn baby. When Lily's outstretched hand could almost caress the baby's face, when his eyes, which were her eyes, and his dimples, which were her dimples, were almost in focus, the woman hurled the baby into the sea and disappeared into the horizon. Lily asked the *bishara* to interpret her dream, and she only said, "May Allah help you, my daughter, what didn't you understand? It's the woman beyond the sea who comes in your dream, and the baby in her hands is the reason that her heart has turned black. She threw away the baby, my daughter. She threw you away; the baby is you!" Lily, who'd never told the *bishara* anything about her circumstances or what the nuns had told her, begged the *bishara* over and over again to tell her what her dream meant until the woman became annoyed, and Lily realized she had to stop asking about it. The thought that the *bishara* might refuse to see her was unbearable. Of all the women she'd encountered, the *bishara* was the only one to whom she'd opened her heart. Perhaps because the terms of their relationship were clear, with no hidden conditions, no covert messages. Lily paid, and the *bishara* read her coffee grounds. She told her about her problems and asked her for advice. Lily went to the *bishara* throughout all the years she lived at the boarding school, and even when she became a young woman in the world, she continued to visit her.

Before she met Shaul, the *bishara* told her she would meet a man who would kiss the ground she walked on. The *bishara* told her to marry Shaul, because she would never find another husband like him in the entire world. "He will be faithful to you as no man has ever been faithful to a woman. He'll fulfill your every wish. He'll support you. For you he will bring down the moon, and most important, he will put up with all your craziness, and he will not leave you."

Lily tried to protest. Was the first man she met really the man she was supposed to marry? She tried to explain to the face that was a mesh of deep creases and wrinkles, "But he's not the most attractive man in the world, and he only works in a small jewelry store that belongs to his father."

"You don't need a handsome man. You need a man who can support you. Jewelry is good. People always buy gold; a groom always needs a ring; a bride always needs her dowry. Being a jeweler is a job for life. It's money in your hand, a peaceful life. It's what you need, my daughter: a peaceful life, family."

Lily heeded her advice and married Shaul even though not once, not before the wedding, not on her wedding night, and not in the years that followed, did she ever thrill to his touch. What the *bishara* had foreseen came to pass. Shaul was a model husband who accepted all her eccentricities and antics. He made a good living at the jewelry store, which provided them with enough money to buy a small apartment on the well-situated Dizengoff Street near the port, and they lived a comfortable life. Neither of them was accustomed to luxury, so they spent little.

Only once did Lily disregard the *bishara's* advice. She'd been married only a few months, and she was trying unsuccessfully to become pregnant.

"No!" screeched the old woman, horrified. "Not now! Now is not a good time for a child. Wait one year from your wedding day. This is not the right time for you."

But Lily was pregnant before the year was out, and when she visited the *bishara* late in her pregnancy to learn about the child in her womb, she claimed she had a headache and asked her to come another time.

Why hadn't she heeded the *bishara's* advice? Why had she gone only when the baby had already been growing inside her? In retrospect she understood, but at the time she hadn't attached any significance to the *bishara's* unusual behavior, so overjoyed she'd been about her pregnancy. She was to become a mother. For the first time in her life, she wouldn't be alone. She would have a family, and she would have more children, and her baby would have brothers and sisters, unlike her, who had no one in the world. Her child wouldn't grow up in an institution but in a real home, with a father and a mother who loved him. She was smitten by the child still in her womb. She spoke to him lovingly as she caressed her belly, promising him the sun and the stars. Before he slipped from her body, bellowing at the top of his lungs, she was already madly in love with him. He lit up her entire world. She brimmed with pride as passersby stopped their baby carriage to exclaim over his beauty. "Honey," she said again and again to Shaul. "This child is pure honey."

Shaul was euphoric as well. She'd never seen him so happy. He even stood taller. "Your joy fills me with happiness," he told her, and she knew she'd given him the best gift in the world. Although Shaul had never caused her heart to race, although his touch had never awakened her passion, she believed now that theirs was a match made in heaven after all, for the baby born of their union was a shining, glowing child.

During the early weeks of his life, Lily and Shaul marked their firstborn's every milestone with obsessive wonder, watching in awe as the tiny infant bundle developed into a sweet, beautiful baby. His features became more pronounced. His tiny nose was perfect, as was the dimple in his chin. His eyes took on the chestnut brown of his father's. His fingers and hands were exquisitely formed, as were his tiny feet and toes, onto which Lily tugged the little socks she had knitted to keep him warm. Even the sound of his crying delighted her. And she knew that Ron, the name she'd chosen despite fierce battles with Shaul's mother, Sarina, who wanted to name him after her dead brother, was the right name. Sometimes she woke him up just to play with him, and above all she loved it when he nursed at her breast. Despite the clear warnings she received from the nurse at the Mother and Baby Clinic that the child was gaining too much weight, she encouraged him to nurse and fed him more than was necessary.

For the first time in her life, Lily opened herself to people. She talked to women at the park, trading recipes, finally feeling that she was like everyone else, not strange, not different, not someone everyone kept their distance from. She even allowed herself to feel sorrow that she didn't have parents, that her son didn't have grandparents. She dismissed the grandmother and grandfather from his father's side, even though they came once a week to visit their grandson. When Sarina held the baby, Lily almost stopped breathing, afraid that he would slip from her arms. Shaul's father never lifted him from his cradle, just made nonsensical sounds at him, which annoyed her to no end. Shaul's parents spoke to each other in Ladino, a language she had no desire to understand. Shaul told her they'd come from Europe, but the only people she knew from Europe were girls at the convent or boarding school who'd arrived by ship without their parents. They'd spoken Yiddish and been mocked with a name that mimicked the sounds of their language as "smelly *vooz-vooziot*." She'd enjoyed insulting those girls with the slur and watching them cringe. But neither did she like the girls descended from the Sephardic families of Spain and Portugal. She didn't know which group she belonged to. How could she know? After all, no one knew what her origins were. She was a stray, and that was one of the names they had called her behind her back at the convent.

When they first met, she never asked Shaul about where he came from and never expressed interest in his family. If she asked about his past, he would have to reciprocate, and she had no answers.

The only thing she was sure of was her Jewishness. From the moment she'd decided to run away from the convent, she'd alienated herself from everything in her previous life, especially from the Holy Mother. She found it easy to turn her back on the compassionate image. Although there were times when the Ave Maria rose to her lips unbidden, she quickly dismissed the prayer. Instead of *Jesus Christ*, she trained herself to say *God help us*. Yet when her baby's life was in danger, she beseeched both the God of the Jews and the God of the Christians. Then she prayed to anyone who could help her, including the Christian Jesus and Mary, his holy mother.

◆ ◆ ◆

With her firstborn, Lily dared to ask herself the questions she'd repressed her entire life. She would grasp him tightly to her breast, cover him with tiny kisses, speak to him with words of love, words that never before had crossed her lips. Only after her baby arrived did she understand what her birth mother had deprived her of. A feeling of belonging, the deep connection between mother and child. When he nursed at her breast, she wondered whether she'd even had a chance to suckle before being abandoned. Who was that woman with a black heart? And who was her father? She gazed at the face of the beloved baby and recognized Shaul's round eyes and dimples and her own little snub nose and heart-shaped lips. Who had she resembled when she was born?

Shaul had once dared to ask about her past, and she'd told him to stop asking her, saying bluntly that she had no past. She, Lily, had been reborn the moment she'd arrived at the boarding school, where they'd given her the family name Yisrael. She was Lily Yisrael. And from the moment she'd married Shaul, her name was Lily Zoref.

And now she had a son. And her son had a father and a mother. Lily couldn't decide whether to screw up her courage and travel to the convent in Jerusalem to ask about the woman beyond the sea, the woman who had given birth to her. Maybe the day had come to take the note left by the woman she'd never called Mother. For her child's sake, not hers, so the child would know where he came from and what his roots were on his mother's side.

But maybe it was better to bury the past. As the days passed, though, her conviction grew that she had to know the identity of her mother for his sake.

After the rain stopped, she decided, she would take the train to the convent and demand the nuns give her the note and force them to tell her more about the woman who'd given birth to her. And in the meantime she would go to the *bishara* in Jaffa so she could give him her blessing and tell her about his character and what life held in store for him.

When she arrived at the *bishara*'s house, with her son dressed in his finest clothes, pushing him in the carriage Shaul's parents had bought, from which he looked at the world with interest and curiosity, again the woman refused to see her. She sent her son to say, "This is a day when God has closed her eyes and her heart and given her a headache."

But Lily insisted, vehemently. She waited for hours outside the house with her son in her arms, nursing him under the scorching sun in the bare yard, and refused to budge. Finally the *bishara* conceded to go out to her, dragging herself on her ancient legs.

"My son told you I can't see anything today, my daughter. Is it not a shame for you and your baby to wait for nothing in the sun? Go back home."

"You have to look," Lily said, cradling her baby in her arms. "I'm not leaving until you read my coffee grounds."

"My daughter, there's no coffee today, nothing to see, nothing to hear, nothing to smell. It's a closed day, my daughter. Go home, light candles, and pray to God to grant you only good things. Go where the Jews go to the wall in al-Quds; put a note to God in the cracks there asking Him to take good care of your child and your home and your life. *Yalla*, may God help you. Go in peace and may God bless you, and remember, you can't cross the same river twice, because the person changes and the water flows." Before Lily could say a word, she turned, moved surprisingly quickly toward the door, and slammed it shut. Only after Lily left the yard, navigating the carriage carefully along dips and rises in the unpaved road, did she realize the *bishara* had not once looked at her child.

She reached home, and according to the Arab fortune-teller's instructions, she lit candles and prayed to her God to watch over her child, her, and her life, but she never made it to Jerusalem to wedge a note in the cracks of the Western Wall.

By now he was crawling, and she had to lift everything off floor level, because whatever he found, he thrust into his mouth. Her heart melted at the sight of his smile, and she forgot that the *bishara* had refused to turn her head for even a moment to look at him. He grew and his laughter filled the house, and she was reluctant to let him out of her arms, singing to him the lullabies she knew, chortling at him, playing with him with his stuffed animals, and rolling a soft ball along the floor for him to grasp.

The baby slept in their bed, and she wouldn't have relations with her husband next to her child. When Shaul suggested she put him in his own bed—after all, there was a special bed for him, with tulle netting stretched above it to protect him from mosquitoes and flies—she said, "In your dreams! This child will leave my bed only to go to his wife's," and Shaul laughed, although he suspected his wife was deadly serious. "I'm like a bird," she told him. "I like my chick to be safely under my wing." Shaul kept quiet and hoped that when the child got a bit older, Lily would relax her grip on him and grant Shaul something of herself.

It was a perfectly ordinary morning when Lily noticed that something was different. Her baby didn't respond to her, to her coos and loving sounds, didn't hold out his arms so she could gather him up, didn't laugh, and didn't cry. He stared at her as if he didn't know her, his small face pale, his expression glazed. Terrified, Lily wrapped him in a blanket and rushed to the clinic. Dr. Shpitzer diagnosed a seasonal flu. But Lily protested, "This is no flu, Doctor. My child doesn't recognize me. It's something much worse. I want you to send us to the hospital."

"We'll wait twenty-four hours and see," the doctor replied firmly and turned back to her prescriptions.

"You wait twenty-four hours with your children," Lily told her, running outside, the baby's head lolling. She stopped a taxi and commanded the driver straight to Hadassah Hospital on Balfour Street.

At the hospital they took him from her and instructed her to wait outside. She protested, wanted to stay with him. The nurse requested firmly that she wait outside and not disturb the doctors. It was the first time the child had been away from her, but she had no choice. She wrung her hands, paced the length of the long white hospital corridor, praying to the God of the Jews and the God of the Christians, praying to Saint Mary for the first time since she'd abandoned the Christian faith, to save her child. She addressed her with a prayer she'd thought she had forgotten, repeating the words over and over, desperate for her compassion: "Have mercy upon me, my mother; have mercy upon my child." She clutched her stomach, which felt as if it were on fire, and made repeated trips to the bathroom, which did nothing to relieve her pain or terror.

She realized she hadn't told Shaul and called the phone at the pharmacy next to his shop. She struggled to insert the phone token, her fingers trembling, and then she punched the wrong numbers several times, and by the time the pharmacist went to get Shaul and she finally spoke to him, she had died a thousand deaths. "The child is at Hadassah Hospital. Come quick!" she told him, only just managing to control her sobs.

"What happened?" he cried in fright.

"Just close the store and come right away."

He ran all the way from the store on King George Street to the hospital on Balfour Street and arrived breathless. "Where's the child?"

"Inside, with the doctors. They're treating him."

"What do they say?"

"They aren't saying anything, just that I shouldn't disturb them."

He went to the nurses' station and introduced himself, and the nurse told him to be patient.

It was a long time still before the doctors emerged, and the baby wasn't with them.

"Where's my child?" she asked in terror.

Shaul asked, "How is he?"

"We think it may be meningitis," replied one of the doctors in a thick German accent.

"Meningitis?"

The doctor shifted his gaze to another, younger doctor, who explained, "It's an inflammation of the protective membranes that cover the brain," and motioned for Shaul and Lily to follow him to his office.

"Please, sit down," he said, and Lily felt that at any moment she might faint.

"Your baby is very sick," he said. "We'll do our best to treat him."

"But how?" Lily asked. "How can he be very sick? Just yesterday he was fine, smiling, full of energy. How could this happen?"

"It's an infection resulting from a bacterium, fungus, or virus. If it's from a virus, it'll clear up by itself. If it's from a bacterium, we'll administer penicillin and hope for the best."

"Can it kill him?" Lily asked, scarcely believing she'd spoken the question.

"I'm not God," said the young doctor. "We'll do our job the best we can, and meanwhile you pray as hard as you can."

For ten days the baby was suspended between life and death. Neither prayers to God nor prayers to Mother Mary made any difference. Nor did the fact that Shaul and Lily went to the Great Synagogue to add *Chaim*, meaning *life*, to Ron's name. Despite the rising tension between the Jews and the Arabs, despite the shots fired by snipers from the direction of the Hassan Bek Mosque in Jaffa, Lily risked her life and went to see the *bishara*, but again she refused to receive her and would only send out amulets with her son, who met her with a furious expression and said, "My mother says not to come here again, and I am telling you the same."

The War of Independence was about to break out, and one could easily be killed in an ambush on the ascent to the Castel on the road to Jerusalem or by Arab shooters in Jerusalem's Old City. Lily insisted that Shaul travel to the holy city to place a note drenched in her tears in one of the spaces between the ancient stones in the Western Wall. She wrote her request to God with her tears, begging as she had never before in her life, beseeching Him to let her child live.

God did not respond to her prayers. Ten days after she brought him to the hospital, the baby died. Lily wanted to die with him. Her grief was so intense that Shaul thought he would lose her, too, and he refused to leave her side. They returned to their house, and she closed herself off in their room and spurned all consolation.

The funeral was sparsely attended. Shaul's parents, who stood close together; his brother, who'd received special permission from his commanders in the Haganah; his aunt and uncle and their children; and neighbors from their building, mostly men. Young mothers with children or babies the same age as Ron-Chaim didn't come, for fear of the evil eye. Lily wouldn't allow the man from the Burial Society to perform the customary act of tearing part of her shirt, refused to cooperate with the messengers of the God who'd cruelly wrenched away her only child. And when Shaul recited the mourner's Kaddish at Ron-Chaim's grave in the children's section of the new cemetery in Kiryat Shaul, so far from their home on Dizengoff Street, she fainted and had to be revived with a splash of water.

Lily detested the seven-day shiva mourning period. She didn't want strangers in her home and didn't understand why she was expected to share her grief with them. She loathed having to sit on the mattress on the floor and hated the prayers for the elevation of the soul. She wouldn't clasp the hands of those who came to pay respects because she knew the moment they left, they would forget all about her and return to their own lives, as was the way of the world. The few neighbors who came to offer condolences stopped coming after Lily asked in a cold, accusatory voice, "Why, why did the sun shine on you but turn away from me?" They looked down, absorbed her anger in silence, and one by one escaped back to their own lives, thanking the Lord for not taking their children. She couldn't even abide the kittens in the yard. Those young cats, born among the trash cans and abandoned to their fates by their mother the moment they'd stopped sucking her teats, had lived, while her baby, for whom she would have given her life, who she'd fed at her breast and embraced and kissed and washed and cared for and almost never let out of her arms, had died.

For a month she didn't leave the house. She forbade Shaul to take away the baby's things. She caressed his soft, tiny outfits, buried her face in them to inhale his scent, and sobbed. The sight of his first pair of shoes tore her heart to pieces. He'd begun to pull himself up and try to stand and take his first steps when she'd bought the tiny blue shoes, and he had hardly managed to wear them. She felt her life force slipping away as she brought them to her mouth and kissed them.

The howl that issued from her chest threatened to bring down the walls of the house. She fell to the floor, crying to the heavens, "Why? God, why? After You finally brought light to my miserable life, why take it from me? What are You punishing me for? What sin am I paying for? What was my child's sin, who never even had a chance to live, that made You take him? Why did I have to endure seventeen hours of labor if it was always Your intention to take him? If You hear me, God, answer me, why?"

God didn't answer, and the sky had never been so empty.

Spurned by the God of the Jews, Lily sought an answer from the Christian God. Ignoring the risks of those dangerous times, the bullets and the enmity, she brazenly walked, almost ran, to Saint Peter's Church in the heart of Jaffa. It was different from the church of her childhood. She knew that Jesus and his mother had been born as Jews and died as Jews and that only after his death had Christianity been separated from Judaism. She wondered, not for the first time, how the world would look if the two were one religion.

She'd walked past the church many times on her way to the *bishara* but never set foot inside. Determined despite her exhaustion, she climbed the steps to the beautiful building on the hill facing the sea, with its impressive bell tower visible from far away. The open entrance welcomed all who passed by. Lily paused before the large carved wooden door fashioned by a craftsman, took a deep breath, and entered the hall of prayer. The scent of lavender that pervaded the interior transported her back to forgotten times. The icons on the walls, the high ceiling, and the statues of the saints were not so different from those of her childhood. She made straight for the altar and automatically knelt, reverting to the child she had been at the convent, with thick braids hanging down her back, begging Holy Mother Mary to have mercy on her, to ease her pain. "For you are also my mother," she whispered. "You were also born a Jewess. Please, won't you tell me, why did my God take my child? What sin have I committed?" But Mary didn't respond, either, and she found no solace in the church.

Rising from her kneeling position on the stone floor, massaging her stiff limbs, and rebelling again against the training of her youth, she turned her back on the Holy Mother and left the church.

The cold wind blowing from the sea revived Lily, and despite the *bishara*'s refusal to receive her the time before and her son's threatening, Lily followed the alleyways leading to her home.

Once again the fortune-teller's son tried to ward her off with threats and warnings, but this time his mother said she would see her. When she was finally sitting face-to-face with the *bishara*, Lily felt the last vestiges of her strength slip away. She slumped over wordlessly, and this time it was the *bishara* who broke the silence. "My daughter, oh, my daughter, may Allah help you. God has given you a hard lesson. But now *khalas*, enough, it's over. Now we begin afresh," she told her. Lily didn't ask how the Arab witch knew her beloved child was dead.

"But why? Look in the coffee and tell me—why did the Lord of the universe take my child from me?"

"Oh, my daughter, there's no need to look in the coffee. I saw it when you came to me and said you wanted to have a child; I saw in your coffee grounds that it wouldn't end well with your firstborn. I warned you, and you didn't heed my words."

"When I left you, was I already pregnant with him?"

"No, you weren't. There was sun in the sky when you came to me, and the child entered you under the moon. If only you had listened . . . but you wanted a child so badly you didn't hear anything, didn't see anything, didn't feel anything apart from your desire. But *khalas*, we won't cry now over what was. May Allah have mercy on the child."

"Couldn't you have done something to save him?" Lily cried. "You, who have powers, couldn't you have saved my child?"

"The time and the place are determined, my daughter. Uzair came to take the soul of someone in Jaffa, and they told him, 'Uzair is looking for you.' So the man took a horse and fled to Damascus, went to the souk there, where he sees Uzair. '*Ahlan wa sahlan*,' Uzair greets him. 'Finally we meet. I knew I was meant to find you in Damascus. I didn't understand why they told me you were in Jaffa.' That's how it is, my daughter; it is written. A person, it doesn't matter what she does, cannot escape her destiny. No matter how many blessings I would have given him, how many amulets and charms I would have given you to protect him from the evil eye, if Uzair made his decision, *hada ho*, so be it; nothing can help. Be comforted and know that when you cry, another mother laughs, because the soul of your child enters the soul of her child who will be born."

"I don't want the soul of my child to enter the soul of someone else's child. I want the soul of my child in a child of mine."

"Then go straight home, and prepare your house for the master of the house, who this very night will place a baby in your belly, and not one day later! *Inshallah*, if the soul of your child has not yet entered another baby, it will enter your child. *Yalla, ruhi*, hurry and prepare yourself for your husband. *Yalla*, my daughter, may Allah be with you."

She did as the *bishara* instructed and hurried back home.

When Lily stepped into her house, she saw it clearly for the first time in a long time. Ever since the baby had sickened, she'd neglected its upkeep, and her home appeared tired and dingy. She threw open the windows, and the sea breeze somewhat soothed her burning limbs as she scrubbed the floors and dusted the furniture and the few paintings on the walls. When she had finished cleaning, she went to the flower shop, bought a bunch of bright-yellow buttercups, hurried back, and arranged the flowers in a ceramic vase that she and Shaul had received as a wedding gift and never used, because neither of them ever thought to buy flowers. She placed the vase on the low wooden table in the lounge. Then she directed her attention to herself. She scrubbed her body thoroughly, as Sister Rose had taught her, and washed her blonde hair. When she was a young girl, her hair had shone like burnished gold, and the hot Mediterranean sun had bleached it further. As the water washed over her body, she thought of Sister Rose, who'd combed her locks gently and woven them into two thick braids.

The first thing she did after she ran away from the convent was to shake out her braids and let her hair fall loose and free over her shoulders. At the boarding school Hedva, who helped supervise the girls, forced her to tie it back, but when a plague of lice descended on them, like all the others she was forced to have her hair cut. No screaming, kicking, or attempts to shield her head with her arms made any difference. Her head was shaved, and she vowed that when it grew back, she would never allow anyone to touch it again. But the lice kept returning, and all the girls had ugly cropped hair. Standing under the stream of hot water, she remembered how on haircut days she used to run away and hide on the roof, next to the dovecote, but Hedva had always found her there. Even when she devised new hiding places she was sure would never be discovered, in the end she was compelled to submit to the scissors of the barber brought specially to hack off all the girls' tresses. She would twist her head from side to side and fidget the whole time, ignoring his requests to sit still, and finally, after almost injuring her with his scissors when she tried to push away his hand, he announced that he would never touch this girl's head again. The housemother was summoned, and she ordered Lily to go to her room and not come out until she was called. Moments of privacy were rare, and Lily was delighted to find herself alone. Without removing her shoes, she jumped into bed and covered her head with her blanket, a habit she'd developed at the convent.

Lily felt safe underneath the blanket. No one could invade her privacy. There, in the soft darkness, she dreamed her dreams, made her plans, pondered the questions to which she never received answers. It was under that thin fabric where she allowed herself to think about the woman she had never known, the woman beyond the sea, whose heart was black. There, in secret, she read Lea Goldberg's poetry, which she'd discovered in a book at the boarding school library. She had no intention of letting anyone catch her reading "Prayers of Atonement" and discovering that beneath her mantle of toughness hid a gentle soul who read love poems. No one knew that Lily would wait for the other girls to fall asleep and then switch on her flashlight under the covers and strain her eyes in the dark:

> If there were torments—they voyaged toward you
> my white sail to your dark night
> allow me to leave, release me, let me go
> to kneel on the shore of forgiveness.

Lily closed her eyes and yearned to fall asleep, but her efforts were rudely interrupted. The graceless hand of the housemother wrenched off the blanket, and Lily hastened to sit up.

"You weren't sent to your room to have a rest," she scolded her. "Go straight to the kitchen! Bronya will know what to do with you."

Bronya the cook was a large, fleshy woman who spoke Yiddish mixed with broken Hebrew and couldn't understand why the Jews in

Israel didn't all speak Yiddish, which she had always assumed was the language of the Jews, and not this strange and difficult Hebrew so similar to the language of the Arabs.

The girls didn't like the fat cook, who was irritable most of the time and tyrannized them during their mandatory shifts in the kitchen. Lily didn't care about her one way or the other. When she had kitchen duty, she did what was asked of her uncomplainingly. Bronya had noticed the quiet, efficient girl who never irked her as the other girls did, was never rude, and even performed her tasks well, but she'd trained herself long ago not to become attached to anyone, and so despite the fact that she harbored a fondness for the girl with the green eyes, she didn't cut her any slack.

In the kitchen Bronya motioned her over to a gigantic sack of potatoes and instructed her to peel them and cut them into quarters. Lily stood by the cutting board and got to work.

"Why are you standing? Sit," the cook told her. "Otherwise you'll end up with swollen veins in your legs, like me."

Lily obediently pulled over a chair and sat down, then continued to peel the potatoes and cut them with precision. Bronya came closer to watch and saw that the girl cut the vegetables as though she were wielding a scalpel. They worked in silence, just the girl and the cook, and the only noises in the kitchen were the jangling of pots and pans and the sound of Bronya's heavy breathing.

Lily knew that pretty soon the silence would be broken. The girls on kitchen duty would jostle in, and the room would be full of chatter and laughter, so for the moment she enjoyed the short grace period of near solitude, peeling the potatoes and patting herself on the back once again for having emerged victorious in her skirmish with the barber's scissors and for being tough enough to stand up for herself.

Bronya hummed a tune Lily didn't recognize but found pleasant, the soft morning light streamed through the open windows from the yard outside, and the sack gradually emptied.

"Okay, enough," Bronya said abruptly. "The girls can do the rest when they get here. You come over here and help me stir the soup."

Lily stationed herself by the big pot where Bronya's lentil soup was simmering, and the aroma rising from it made her wince.

"What's the matter? You don't like Bronya's soup?"

She didn't reply.

"You don't talk? Someone zipped up your mouth?"

Lily remained silent, stirring the soup, whose smell was making her feel queasy. At the convent they'd eaten lentils morning, noon, and night until she could barely stomach them, but she composed herself and thought about the scent of the citrus orchards that surrounded the boarding school, imagining their sweet perfume in her nose.

Bronya's voice invaded her thoughts. "Why did you get punished? Were you rude to Hedva?"

She considered whether to answer Bronya or keep silent and decided it would be better to be cooperative.

"I didn't want them to cut my hair."

"Oh, who are you? Samson, who wouldn't cut his hair so he would be strong?"

And Lily felt that she really was like Samson the hero and that if they cut off her hair, she would lose her strength. Her thick hair was the only thing that she liked about herself, the only thing she felt attached to. A small smile played about her lips as she imagined herself as a version of the muscular Samson.

Pleased with herself, Bronya clapped her hands. "*Nu*, I see that you have a pretty smile. Why do you never show it?" and Lily grinned broadly until the other girls arrived and her smile froze and vanished.

From then on there was a secret pact between Lily and Bronya, who would sometimes bend the rules and sneak the girl a piece of cake or a crisp apple.

Her hair was cut off in the end. The plague of lice outweighed the obstinacy of even the most stubborn and insubordinate young girl.

Until the age of fifteen Lily, like the rest of the girls, had a short, ugly haircut. The length was determined by the severity of the latest bout of lice. When the lice plague abated, the girls were permitted to grow their hair, but if even one louse was discovered on one hair of one head, everyone's hair was summarily chopped off.

When Lily graduated to the older group, the lice problem had disappeared, and the girls were allowed to grow their hair as long as they liked. Then she gathered her golden tresses in a ponytail. And even when the fashion was extremely short hairstyles like those sported by models or Hollywood stars, Lily kept hers long.

Now she stood under the shower in her home, washing her long hair, relishing the sensation of water massaging her scalp until the reason for washing and shampooing at this time of day was almost forgotten.

It wasn't until the hot water ran out and the cold water began to flow over her body that she stepped out of the shower.

Soon Shaul would come home from the store, and she wanted to be ready for him. He would place a new child in her womb, and more than anything Lily prayed that the soul of her son would enter her new baby boy. Only in that way would her wounded heart be healed and could she begin to breathe again.

Shaul returned after a frustrating day at work when hardly anyone had come into the store, knowing he would find no solace at home either. He was prepared to return to the dark, gloomy apartment, as it had been every day since they'd buried their son, but to his amazement the blinds were open and a strong, dazzling light flowed in. A soft breeze blew from the sea visible from the windows, the floor and the furniture shone, and there was a clean, fresh smell in the air. He noticed the vase filled with brilliant yellow flowers atop the table in the lounge. For the first time in many weeks, Shaul breathed easy. Then he looked up to the sky and gave silent thanks to God. Only after he finished his conversation with God did he turn to Lily, who was in the kitchen.

"What are you making?" he asked as if she stood in the kitchen cooking dinner every day.

"Nothing special, pea soup with sausage."

"I love pea soup."

"I know. That's why I'm making it."

Could it be that God had heeded his prayers and Lily was herself again? Shaul decided not to ask too many questions, not to wonder why once again, standing before him, was the vivacious woman who'd captured his heart from the first time he'd met her. He undressed and went to shower, undeterred by the lukewarm water, an old song rising within him so that he had to bite his tongue not to sing out loud. No need to overdo it, he thought to himself.

When he came into the kitchen, Lily was still standing there, dicing vegetables into tiny pieces for a fresh salad, then slicing dark-brown bread. The table was set for two like in happier days. Lily spooned the steaming soup into deep bowls, and they ate in silence, slowly sipping the thick, hot liquid.

"Delicious," he said to Lily. "Really delicious."

"Thank you," she replied. "It's all there was at Kelman's. There's hardly anything to buy at the grocery store—I almost couldn't find dried peas. He didn't even have rice. He said there's none left, and there's nowhere to get it and no one to bring it."

Shaul looked at her and almost jumped up to cover her in kisses, so great was his happiness, but he knew he had to behave as though she went to the grocery store every day, as though she cooked him supper every evening. As though everything were routine.

"The situation is very bad," he replied, trying to sound ordinary. "Today at the store someone told me that the British detained her for half an hour and interrogated her as if she was some kind of underground leader like Yair Stern, and she was late for work."

"Damn them all," said Lily. "But who knows what will happen when the British leave? Who knows—the Arabs will probably slaughter us all."

"It's already dangerous to go anywhere near Jaffa. You might be able to get in, but who knows if you could get out," he said, and Lily swallowed hard. She hadn't said she'd just come back from Jaffa, ignoring the danger lurking at every corner.

Shaul didn't notice the way Lily's face changed when he mentioned Jaffa. He felt as though the three months since the death of their baby had never happened, as though Lily hadn't locked herself in the bedroom and refused to speak for all that time, as though things were set right again. And then, when Lily stood to clear the table, he felt a stab of pain in his chest, as though someone had torn through his flesh and plunged a knife into his heart.

The pain was so strong he grabbed onto the edges of the table and his eyes welled with tears. He tried and failed to subdue it. A sob burst from him, and Lily, who'd just come back into the room, gazed at him wide eyed. She hurried to him and sat on his lap, opening her heart to him, kissed his head with soft lips, and wept. For the first time they cried together about their dead child and their lives torn asunder. His tears fell on her soft robe, his sobs broke her heart, and they sat like that for a long time, holding one another, before Lily stood and led Shaul to the bedroom.

Twilight fell on Tel Aviv. The sea beyond the window was painted in pink and gold, and the soft breath of evening nudged away the heat of the day. Lily shrugged off her robe and lay naked while Shaul stood transfixed by her beautiful body, as the evening light washed it in gentle rays. He shook his head in wonder that this woman, this beautiful woman, was his wife.

"What are you waiting for?" she asked in a soft voice as he lay down beside her.

When he hesitated, Lily touched him with her fingertips, taking long moments to caress his chest over his heart as if trying to penetrate the skin. They lay face-to-face, and he held his breath, lifting his hand to stroke her lovely face, and his lips kissed hers with infinite gentleness and then with burning passion. She was exquisite in the evening light. Shaul dived into her, lost himself between her thighs, thrust himself into her roughly, then softly, as if trying to merge his body with hers so they could become one, inhaling her scent with a yearning for her good, familiar, addictive smell to banish the bad odor that seemed to have sprung up between them. He groaned and moaned, and Lily moved underneath him, matching his rhythm, scratching his back and sighing. He played with her nipples, squeezed her belly, discovered a new side of himself. They couldn't get enough of each other, and all the poison and fears were released in one great cry as their bodies exploded in unison.

Spent, limbs sprawled across each other, they lay on the rumpled sheets. Lily couldn't believe what had just happened in their bed. She'd simply followed the *bishara*'s instructions to go home and have relations with her husband so he would plant a baby in her womb, and they'd made love like never before. She'd never imagined her jeweler harbored such passion and desire. The last time had been when she'd become pregnant with their beloved child. And that session had been devoid of frenzy. Shaul had fumbled clumsily on top of her, and she'd forced herself to suffer his weight, hoping he would get it over with quickly and stop rooting around inside her so she could wash herself and get some sleep. And now he'd ignited in her what she hadn't known was there, proved that she harbored some vitality and that the flame of desire burned not only between his legs but between hers as well, and this revelation brought her back to life.

Shaul Zoref lay happy in his bed, the head of his beautiful wife resting on his chest. He was still amazed she'd agreed to marry him, a quiet man, a jeweler, son of a jeweler, another link in his family's inglorious jeweler dynasty, a well-behaved mama's boy. He couldn't fathom the source of the storm that had just buffeted him, the origin of the winds that had filled his sails and carried the two of them to such heights of passion. Had no idea where the wings had come from that had suddenly sprouted to carry them beyond the summit of pleasure and desire.

He longed for the moment to last forever so that he and Lily would never have to land back on the hard ground of their lives.

Lily lifted her head and stared in awe at her man, as though really seeing him for the first time, and he gazed back at her and knew that he would love her for all time, come what may. He would remain with this woman even if he had to forsake his own mother, even if Lily yelled and cursed, even if once again she took to her bed and wouldn't leave it, even if the demon hadn't truly left her—he would stay with her. He loved her like he'd never loved before, in a way that he could never love any other woman. For one moment, and for the first time in his life, he felt happy.

Lily became pregnant that evening. Her morning sickness soon appeared, her nipples swelled, and the tiredness she felt at the end of the day told her as much. She didn't even go to the lab on Gordon Street for a pregnancy test, not needing anyone to check her secretions to know that there was a baby growing inside her. She prayed that the baby would look like Ron-Chaim, that his soul had been transferred to the new child. She'd already decided to call the new baby by his dead brother's name, as though he had never truly died and was simply being reborn.

She adamantly refused to exchange the old crib for a new one or to give away the dead baby's clothes, making up her mind that her new son would wear them.

"You're inviting the bad luck to return," Sarina told her son when she realized Lily intended the baby's first pair of shoes, worn only once, to be handed down to the new child. "You're tempting fate," she warned him. "You have to repaint the baby's room, buy a new bed and a new stroller, new sheets and blankets. Everything should be brand new, and heaven forfend she should put the living child in the shoes of the dead one. That would be the worst thing. You have to get everything out of the house, give it to charity, to children who don't have anything, do a *mitzvah*, a good deed! I'll send my neighbor, Allegra; she'll purify your home with incense and sage and chase away the evil eye, and then you can start over."

When Shaul repeated his mother's advice to Lily, she yelled loudly enough for the entire neighborhood to hear. "Your mother can't tell me what to do in my own house! That barbarian wants to bring witches to perform exorcisms, let her come and do it—she's a witch herself," she fumed, forgetting that she'd become pregnant according to the instructions of an Arab witch from Jaffa.

"Please, calm down, Lily. This isn't good for the baby. We'll do whatever you want. You want to keep his toys and clothes, fine. You want the new baby to wear his shoes, so when the time comes, we'll give him Ron's shoes, may his memory be blessed. Just calm down so you don't lose the baby."

Shaul felt deep love for his woman, deep compassion. Sometimes she seemed like a rare, injured bird, and he wanted to enfold her poor bedraggled wings in his hands, to smooth them and soothe her. And now a child was developing within her, a new child who might replace the dead one, and still she suffered, was angry.

When Eliya was born, Shaul named her after Eliyahu, his mother's younger brother, who had died in the Holocaust. From the moment she left her mother's womb, wrinkled like an old woman, she carried a heavy load. She didn't know she was supposed to return her mother's dead child to her, had no inkling that the name she bore carried the tragic story of her father's family, nearly all of whose members had been murdered at the Treblinka extermination camp.

When the baby was placed in her arms, Lily searched for traces of her firstborn, but Eliya didn't resemble her dead brother in any way. He'd been born as beautiful as an angel, his face smooth, his features defined, while this baby was wrinkled and ugly. He'd had a tuft of fair hair, which Lily had known would grow to be as blond as hers, but this baby didn't have a strand of hair on her head, and Lily feared it would be as dark as Shaul's.

"What a beauty you brought us." Shaul was as excited as someone holding a baby for the first time. "What a little doll she is." Lily didn't think she was beautiful, and certainly no doll. She looked down at the unsightly creature and knew the infant needed to feel the warmth of her body, that she should cradle her and whisper words of love as she had to Ron-Chaim, her dead brother. But the words didn't come. She felt nothing for the baby, neither love nor hate. Her heart was empty, and all she wanted was for someone to take the baby away so she could sleep. She hoped if she slept, she would awaken with renewed strength and start to behave like a mother. Being a mother was the thing she did best of all; she knew from experience. She'd been a wonderful mother to her dead child. Intuitively she'd known how to swaddle him, feed him, calm him, change his diapers. She hadn't needed help from the nurse at the Mother and Baby Clinic. This ability couldn't have been taken from her, as her baby Ron-Chaim had been taken; she just needed some sleep, and she would wake again as a mother.

When Lily left the hospital, it was Shaul who bundled the baby into Ron-Chaim's powder-blue blanket. Secretly, Lily was terrified that the infant would slip from her grasp, fall on her head, and die like her brother. Wordlessly, they agreed that Shaul would take care of the new baby. From the start it was clear Lily couldn't nurse her. The fountain of milk that had gushed from her breasts with the birth of her first baby was dry. Despite being empty, Lily's breasts were sensitive and painful. When Shaul begged her to try to feed the tiny baby and she brought her nipple to the baby's mouth, Eliya wailed and her face turned red with fury. The baby screamed and screamed, and Lily thought she would lose her mind. She was sure it was a punishment from on high, for not taking good enough care of her first baby. No wonder she couldn't feel anything; no wonder her breasts were dry.

Lily refused to change the baby, feed her, or even hold her. Shaul had to leave his elderly father alone at the store. His father had aged, his eyesight was poor, and he couldn't manipulate the metals as he had in the past, yet Shaul had no choice. He was afraid if he left the baby alone with Lily, she might hurt the child or herself. He bottle-fed her and changed her diapers, and when she cried, he lifted her from the crib and held her, whispering endearments and calling her "my Eliyush."

After two weeks he had to return to work. Once Lily was alone with the baby, she froze, petrified to become attached to the tiny being who was totally dependent on her kindness, afraid to love her in case, if she loved her as she'd loved Ron-Chaim, she would also die.

How she yearned for the sweet mornings with her firstborn; how she longed for the smell of him, which had filled her heart with a love larger than life. No, the new baby could never replace her dead son. The *bishara* had been wrong when she'd told her that the soul of her first baby would enter the new baby. If only she knew which baby his soul had chosen, she would steal it from its bed and replace it with this new baby. They'd been joined by an umbilical cord, but this baby girl was like a stranger to her.

Summoning all her strength, Lily approached the crib and observed the two-week-old infant. Her closed eyes, her bright, round face, her smooth head, her button nose, and her tiny perfect ears. She lay in the dead baby's crib, wearing his clothes, sleeping under his blanket, but there was nothing of him in her. Other than the dimples in her cheeks, Lily saw no resemblance. A musical mobile hung above the crib, and when she turned the key, a wistful lullaby poured into the room, along with her tears. She ached for her dead child, who would fall asleep to that melody, and knew the baby girl lying in his crib could never help her forget him, would never replace him or be a substitute for him. Feeling weak, she lay down at the foot of the crib and let the stone floor cool the fire raging within her. That was how Shaul found his wife and his daughter when he returned home hours later. The helpless baby was howling, her face bright red with anguish and streaked with tears, her diaper sopping and her hands balled into tiny fists, while her mother lay on the floor, eyes wide and expressionless, ignoring the baby and her screams.

Shaul sprang to the crib and gently lifted the baby, who continued to cry hysterically, with no space in his heart for the woman lying life-lessly on the floor. Holding his daughter in one arm, he took a bottle of fresh-delivered milk from the icebox, diluted a small amount in water, and brought it to boil three times before pouring it into a bottle, which he cooled in the cold stream from the kitchen faucet. Then he fed Eliya.

"You aren't normal!" he shouted at Lily, who hadn't moved. "Do you want to kill her? One dead child isn't enough for you—you want this one to die as well?"

Lily covered her ears with her hands. *Why doesn't he shut up? Please let him shut up,* she thought in despair. *Why don't they both shut up, him and his baby? Let them shut up, or else I'll be silent forever.*

"I don't buy your theatrics," Shaul said with a toughness he was sur-prised to feel. "If you don't get up, I'm going to take the baby and leave, and you won't be able to find us! No one will, not the British police, the local police, not even Interpol. You'll never find us, and you'll be alone like you were when I met you, alone in the world without anyone, do you hear me? With no one!"

Shaul wiped beads of perspiration from his forehead. The baby gulped hungrily from the bottle. When she finished, he held her on his shoulder and patted her back until he heard the coveted burp. "Bravo, sweetheart," he said to the baby. "What a lovely belch, good girl. Now I'm going to change your diaper, and then we'll go for a walk and leave your mother on the floor to think about whether she wants to stay there or start behaving like a normal person instead of a nutcase who belongs in an institution."

Lily had barely allowed him to do anything for the baby boy, who'd belonged wholly to her, and here he was, taking care of Eliya, and not only did Lily not intervene, but she continued to lie motionless on the floor. He had to admit, though he kept it to himself, that he actually enjoyed feeding the baby, changing her diapers, and taking her for walks on bustling Dizengoff Street. He left without a backward glance. Let her stew in her own juices, he thought. Let her realize she was behaving like a lunatic. He was tired of her craziness. How much longer could he live with this woman when he had no idea what she was thinking, what she felt? Worst of all, he had no idea who she really was.

But how could he leave her? Who was he kidding? He loved her with all his being, was enraptured by her, was attuned to her every whim and mood. He couldn't conceive of life without her. How could he get up in the morning if she wasn't by his side? Come home after another overlong day at work and not find her there? He had threatened to leave, but they both knew he couldn't survive without her. After the death of May His Memory Be Blessed, he'd supported and comforted her as much as she'd allowed, neglecting his own grief, because he couldn't contain both his own pain and hers. At the end of the traditional week of mourning, he pushed away his parents, who only wanted to comfort him, as well as his brother, his beloved cousins, and his few friends. She didn't want anyone in their house, and he obeyed, apologizing as he closed the door in their faces. He didn't permit himself to shed a tear in her presence, as though she alone had lost the child and not both of them.

In the dark days after the baby died, he knew if he allowed himself to feel the pain, he would lose her as well. He sensed that if he didn't sustain her, she, too, would die. He feared leaving her on her own lest she harm herself, but what choice did he have? Someone had to make a living.

So when Lily closed the blinds tightly so that the daylight couldn't penetrate the rooms, he didn't open them. When she didn't get up, he brought her coffee in bed. When he came home from work, he cooked supper for them both and set it upon the small table in the kitchen and ate with her in silence, cleared the table, washed and dried the dishes, and put them away. When she went back to bed, he said nothing about the layer of dust that coated everything or the filthy floor or the pile of dirty laundry in the wicker basket. He dusted, washed the floor, laundered the clothes, and hung them out to dry, then folded them and placed them in the closet. He had two full-time jobs now, one as a jeweler and one as a homemaker.

Sometimes he wondered if he had turned into a trained and obedient servant. When had he become a doormat? "What's happened to you?" his mother lamented on one of his rare visits to his parents. "You've become a *schmatte*, a rag to clean the floor. What happened to the man I raised? What about the commandment to honor your mother and your father? We never see you; you almost never visit us, and when you do, it's for fifteen minutes, and then you're gone, without touching the *arroz con gansos o patos* I make for you. I spend hours cooking the beans in tomato sauce and preparing the rice to perfection, and His Highness doesn't even have time to taste the *sofrito* that used to make him lick his fingers and beg for more. You come and go like a ghost."

His mother was right. Because he was so frightened of Lily, visits to his parents dwindled, and when they wanted to visit him, he fobbed them off with flimsy excuses. Shaul had no idea how to respond to Lily's harsh criticism of his parents and family. He'd always been so close to them, enfolded in their comforting embrace, but Lily distanced him from everyone else he knew and loved. She became his whole world but never made him feel that he mattered to her. After the baby's life was cut short, their home became a bastion of silences where no one else was welcome. He tried to talk to her, to touch her, to hold her, but she would turn away, her back shaking with sobs, not allowing him to comfort her. He didn't understand why his wife wouldn't talk to him. For months after the baby died, she remained lost in her all-encompassing grief and never shared her feelings.

In fact, it had always been that way. She never said a word about her feelings. Sometimes it seemed to him that Lily was dragged along by life, passively allowing events to push her forward, and other times it was just the opposite, and she resisted and opposed everything. She'd confused him from the first moment, and he still felt he didn't know the woman by his side in bed every night whom he loved so deeply. He couldn't explain the essence of his love. Was it her intoxicating beauty? Her lovely face? Her thick blonde hair and her enormous green eyes? Was it her beautiful body with her small, perfect breasts? Or maybe the very fact that she was so distant, mysterious, and unattainable was what tethered him to her. What the hell did Lily have that drew him to her like a moth to the proverbial flame and scorched him time and time again?

It was easier to think about what he didn't like about her. He didn't like her aloofness, the way she closed herself off, or her disturbing silences, just as he disliked her outbursts that exploded like molten lava. And at those times the most terrible words would issue from her mouth, like she was a dockworker at the Jaffa Port. More than once her big mouth had gotten her into trouble, and it was completely at odds with her refined appearance. He was frightened by the intensity of her grief, her silence, and the long period during which she refused to leave the house. But he held his tongue and allowed her to mourn, moving to the far edge of the bed so that their bodies wouldn't accidentally touch and upset her. He rose silently after a sleepless night lest he disturb her, dressed in the darkness, then washed, neglecting to shave since the death of his son as a mark of his extended mourning, made coffee for them both and placed her cup on her nightstand, closed the door soundlessly, and left the house.

Everything changed after the appearance of Eliya. Shaul's soul was bound up with hers from the moment she was born. She was as surely her father's child as the dead boy had belonged to his mother. The boy, may his memory be blessed, had always been attached to her breast or in her arms, always close to her heart, while their infant daughter—his heart ached at the very thought—was mostly in her bed or in the stroller. Lily only picked her up when she screamed so loudly it seemed her lungs would burst.

"You spoil her," she scolded him. "And then when you're at work, I'm the one who has to deal with her wanting to be held all the time."

How quickly she'd forgotten that she'd never allowed May His Memory Be Blessed to cry for even one minute, that he'd never been out of her arms. Shaul gritted his teeth and ignored her.

"Let her cry," she berated him. "It develops the lungs."

"I don't want her to be an opera singer." He couldn't keep quiet a moment longer. "I want her to be happy, to know that we also love her when she cries."

"Really, Shaul, what garbage you spout." She mocked him with ugly words. "Love her, shmuv her. You'd think you're the only one who loves her. Keep on spoiling her, and in the end we'll have a little princess, and you'll regret the day when you ruined her."

"She's already a princess," he replied, planting a soft kiss on Eliya's forehead.

"Fine, keep it up then, but don't come crying to me when she turns into a rude, spoiled brat like your beloved cousin Esther's children."

He bit his lips. He was sick of her contempt for his family. She was merciless in her criticism of them.

He didn't understand. Before introducing her to his parents, he had formed a completely different picture in his mind. Lily, the orphaned child with no known relatives in the world, who had never lived in the bosom of a family, would certainly be thrilled to adopt his mother and father as her parents, to make his brother her brother, to transform his warm extended family into the one she'd never had. But none of that happened.

True, his mother complained behind Lily's back, but Shaul alone absorbed Sarina's nasty words and her anger at Lily. Still Lily seemed to sense the criticism, and she demanded he keep his distance from his parents.

He could never divine her mood, never knew what would anger or please her. That one time they'd made love with passion, nine months before Eliya was born, was forgotten as though it had never happened. His joy was quickly replaced with frustration when Lily returned to her angry, distant self the next day, as if they hadn't been transported together to such heights that his heart had nearly exploded, so full was it of love for the strange woman he had married.

"*Strange* isn't the word," his mother had said after meeting her. "The strangest of creatures," she said, placing her hand on her hip. "Of all the girls in the country, you manage to find the one who looks like doom and gloom? Is she one of us at least?" Sarina asked.

"I don't know," he replied. "I didn't ask her."

"So ask." She bristled like a porcupine. "What do you mean, 'I didn't ask'? Don't you want to know who you're running around with?"

"What difference does it make, Mother?"

"It makes a difference. I want to know, Is she one of us? Is she Sephardic? Ashkenazic? Where is she from?"

"She was born here just like I was."

"Fine, fine, suddenly everyone was born here, even those who weren't. Now it's the fashion to say you are native born. Ask where her parents come from, her family."

"My mother asked me where your parents are from," he said to Lily one evening, feeling awkward, when they went to get ice cream at Whitman's Ice Cream Parlor.

She looked down at her shoes. It was the very question she had feared. She'd known he would ask eventually and she would have to find an answer. She'd tried to create a life story for herself, her favorite being that her parents came from a distant kibbutz. She'd even chosen one, Kibbutz Hanita in the north of the country, in the Western Galilee. But then she'd realized Kibbutz Hanita had been founded a decade after she was born. For nights she'd racked her brains to come up with a story that wouldn't be too complicated and wouldn't raise too many questions so that she wouldn't become entangled in too many lies.

She'd chosen Kibbutz Degania at the southern end of the Sea of Galilee, which was old enough, and hoped that neither Shaul nor his curious mother knew anyone there. She was poised to tell the lie when something stopped her. Hadn't the *bishara* seen in her coffee that Shaul was the man she would marry and raise a family with? If she told him her parents were from Degania, she would eventually have to introduce him to them, and where would she find a set of parents from Degania? Maybe, she thought desperately, she could say her parents had stayed in Europe and she'd come to Israel with the Jewish Youth Aliyah organization along with thousands of Jewish children they'd rescued from the Nazis, like so many of the girls from her boarding school. But she had already told him that she was born in the Land of Israel.

Her brain worked feverishly. She hadn't touched her ice cream, which had melted into a sticky pool, and Shaul watched her with concern, waiting for her response.

"My parents died!" she blurted. "Satisfied?"

"I'm sorry. I didn't mean to upset you."

He took her in his arms, deeply and sincerely upset he'd hurt her feelings, but she pushed him away roughly and said angrily, "Don't touch me in public. It disgusts me when couples embrace in the street as if they don't have homes to go to."

He backed off immediately, she threw her strawberry ice cream soup into the nearest trash can, and they walked in silence along King George Street until they arrived at the women's residence where she lived.

She said good night and hurried away from him, her simple blue dress billowing around her like a bell.

"Tomorrow at the same time?" he called after her, hesitatingly. She nodded and disappeared behind the gate.

Shaul was confused. His heart went out to the beautiful girl with whom he was already head over heels in love, but she held herself aloof, and he, who was a naturally shy person, found it difficult to penetrate the shell she'd constructed around herself. He took a deep breath and walked back all the way to Allenby Street and down to the promenade. It was packed with people. British soldiers sat at cafés with young, heavily made-up women, and lovers walked arm in arm alongside the railing that separated the promenade from the sea. At Café Pilz a band played dance music, and couples pressed up against each other on the improvised dance floor. He would have given anything to be dancing there with Lily. How he envied the couples walking by with their arms entwined. He longed to take Lily for a romantic walk on the beach, where the whispers of the waves would fill their ears, competing with the beating of his heart.

Patience, he told himself. It had to mean something that Lily always agreed to another date. It wouldn't be long before she opened up, and meanwhile he would continue to see her every evening at six and buy her falafel pita at the Bezalel Market and ice cream at Whitman's, as he had every day since they'd met. Patience. Who knew, maybe next week she would agree to accompany him to the cinema.

"What do you mean, her parents died? They died? How did they die?" his mother wouldn't stop asking.

"She didn't say. She just said that they died."

"That's it? You didn't ask how or when? Did you swallow your tongue? Oh my God, you meet some girl and you're struck dumb?"

"She's not 'some girl.'"

"If she's not just some girl, why didn't you ask? And if she is just some girl, don't bring her home. I don't have time for girls like that."

"I told you, Mother, she's not just any girl." Shaul raised his voice and was shocked to hear himself. He had never shouted at his mother, never treated her with disrespect.

"Are you yelling at me? Are you being rude to me because of her? You know what, I won't ask any more questions about her, and don't bring her here. Better I shouldn't know that she exists."

"What do you want from the boy?" Shaul's father interrupted. "He's young; he's allowed to go out with whoever he likes until he gets married."

"Young? At his age you were already a father of two. God help us if this is the bride he brings home . . ."

"This is the bride!" Shaul pounded on the table with his fist, unable to listen for another minute to his mother's scornful, mocking tone as she criticized Lily.

"Over my dead body!" his mother declared. "You'll find a girl from our community or from the other one, but she had better be a girl from a good home with a family. Who knows where this one was born, where she grew up. She doesn't have parents, God help us!"

"It's not her fault that her parents died."

"So it's our fault? You'll marry a girl who has a living father and a living mother who we will meet and get to know, and we'll be like family, and not some stray cat you found who knows where."

"I haven't yet proposed to her, *madre querida*." Shaul raised his voice again, and for a moment he appeared taller than he was. "But you know what, today I will. I was going to wait for a while, to take things slowly, but thanks to you, I think I will ask her to marry me. This very day I'll get down on one knee!"

"Don't you dare!" Sarina slapped him soundly. "You should be ashamed of yourself! You could marry anyone you want. Well, you won't see my face or anyone from your family at your wedding. If the bride has no parents and no family, neither does the groom, and that's that!"

But Shaul wasn't listening anymore. He had rushed out of the house, slamming the door behind him. He ran all the way to HaYarkon Street, slowing down only when he had reached the Kaete Dan Hotel. He walked to the beach, took off his shoes, and let his feet sink into the soft sand. Shaul took a deep breath, stunned that he had argued so horribly with his mother. The commandment to honor thy father and mother was one of the most important of all, and neither he nor his brother had ever violated it. The respect he had for his mother was genuine; he truly loved and valued her, and here he was arguing with her, slamming the door, and fleeing the house in fury, and for what? He scarcely knew Lily, hadn't really spent much time with her. He hadn't even kissed her, not even on the cheek, hadn't stroked her beautiful gold hair. And the one time he had dared to touch her, to comfort her, she'd rebuffed him, and here his mother was already marrying him to her and forbidding their wedding in the same breath.

Shaul Zoref's world had been turned upside down. He'd been a quiet, mild-mannered young man who hid among the tools of his trade as an apprentice to his jeweler father. His entire social life centered on his relatives. The Zoref family was tight knit and warm, the last remnant of a glorious dynasty from Bitola in North Macedonia. The family had been almost entirely wiped out during the Holocaust, and his relatives zealously protected their traditions, spent most of their time together, and honored their dead.

He'd always thought of himself as an ordinary person with no special dreams, different from his confident younger brother, Shmulik, who was a member of the youth brigade of the Haganah paramilitary organization and always surrounded by a group of friends. Shaul had never had any interest in the Haganah or in any other underground movement that resisted the British. He'd never had any desire to change the world.

The difference between the two boys was plain to see. Shmulik disdained his father's wishes and sneaked off to participate in the youth movement. But Shaul, the meek mama's boy, never dared to defy his parents, and every day after school he came to the jewelry store, which had a good reputation among the women of Tel Aviv. He sat across the worktable from his father in the back of the tiny shop and did his best to copy his movements. Albert taught him to work with gold and silver, to set gems, to melt noble metals and separate them from the slag. But the more Shaul tried, the more it was obvious he was no artist like his father, who had golden hands that fashioned jewelry into works of art. Shaul was all thumbs. The torch's flame frightened him, and his clumsy fingers couldn't manipulate the metal or the gems. After countless frustrating afternoons, his father told him, "You deal with the clients; I'll deal with the gold." With a heavy heart, he said to Sarina that the eminent family tradition would not be perpetuated through their sons. "Who knows," he sighed. "Maybe we'll be blessed with grandchildren who will follow in my footsteps."

But Sarina was adamant. "You sit with him and show him as many times as it takes until the knowledge penetrates his head and his hands. Don't give up on him. Let him work at it and learn. And you"—she turned to Shaul—"if you don't learn what your father is trying to teach you, you won't go to the high school, do you hear me? You are part of a glorious line of jewelers, and you will not break the chain."

"*Madre querida*," he replied politely, "I don't want to be a jeweler."

"So what do you want to be, a parasite like your brother?"

"Excuse me?" he answered with the good manners she had taught him. "Heaven forfend. Shmulik's not a parasite. He gives of himself for the sake of the Land of Israel. But I dream of being a teacher. I want to study at the Lewinsky Teachers Seminary and then educate the children here. That's my aspiration. So I'll work at the store during the day, and in the evening I'll learn to be a teacher."

"You think you have it all planned out, don't you? You blockhead!" His mother was angrier than he'd ever seen her. "Without even consulting us! You won't be a teacher or anything else! You'll learn to be a jeweler. That's the profession of your father, your grandfather, and your great-grandfather, and it will be your profession too!"

"But why me? Why don't you make Shmulik do it?"

"Because you are the elder brother, and the elder brother carries on the tradition."

◆ ◆ ◆

"Why don't you stand up for yourself?" his brother asked him later. "Why don't you insist? If it's your dream to be a teacher, why shouldn't you make it come true?"

"If only I were like you," Shaul replied, "if only I could stand up to Mother, but you know there's nothing I can do. She'll never let me realize my dream. At least you can go after yours." If he'd known when he was a teenager that Shmulik would end up working as a mechanic in Brooklyn, maybe he wouldn't have been so envious.

With patience and persistence, he managed to learn the skills of the trade, and in the end he was a competent jeweler, but he would never reach the heights scaled by his father.

So who would have believed that he of all people, the timid and fearful young man who had surrendered his dream to please his family, would upset his mother to the extent that she slapped him across the face? He scarcely believed it himself, but he knew that he couldn't have behaved any other way.

He'd never forget the day his life had changed. The sun had almost sunk into the sea when he finished his day's work and closed the store on King George Street, and instead of turning in the direction of Shabazi Street, toward home, he decided to go to Yehiye's falafel stand at the Bezalel Market. He knew his parents were waiting for him at home to eat supper, but he simply couldn't resist the temptation of fresh, hot falafel in pita. All day he'd dreamed of the crispy, green, melt-in-your-mouth balls of falafel still hot from the boiling oil, stuffed into the soft pita pocket with a salad of finely chopped tomatoes and cucumbers, a generous dab of hot sauce, fenugreek, and a dollop of tahini. He followed the hands of the clock inching frustratingly slowly across its face, and when it was finally closing time, he put away the tools, took the jewelry from the glass display case, and secured it in the safe hidden behind the tool cupboard. As he did so, he could hear his father warning him: *A breach invites a thief, and we don't want to invite thieves into our store. Check, recheck, and check again before you close the store, and make sure all the gold is in the safe.* As far as his father was concerned, all the jewelry, even if it was made of silver, was gold. After checking twice that the lock was clicked in place, he ran across the street to Bezalel Market.

Yehiye's falafel stand was always the most crowded. Nobody prepared falafel like that old Yemenite man. Shaul waited impatiently in the long line, and then he saw her. The first thing he noticed was her golden hair, which hung down her back in a long, heavy braid, and then he took in the flowered dress that accentuated her slim waist and tanned arms. His eyes traveled down to her legs, and his heart skipped a beat at the sight of the sculpted ankles and perfect feet clad in red sandals with delicate straps.

What if, he wondered, *she turns around and she's scary looking?* The thought amused him and a goofy smile lit up his face, and that was Lily's first sight of him—a man grinning like an idiot standing in line behind her, waiting for a falafel. He stood dumbstruck by her beauty, and she barely registered his presence. That might have been the end of it, but when she stepped up to the counter to claim her falafel, she didn't have enough to pay for it. She searched for the missing coin in her purse, but Yehiye, never the most tolerant soul, began to lose patience. "*Yalla*, girl, I don't have all day. Either pay or move aside! Falafel, hot falafel!" he cried. "Who wants a half? It's ready!"

"I do," Shaul exclaimed, "and another one as well."

He paid for the half portions and presented Lily with hers.

"Thank you very much," she said to him. "But I don't need charity. If you walk with me to my dormitory, I can pay you back."

Shaul didn't want her money, but there was no way he was going to pass up the chance to spend another few minutes with this girl. They walked in silence eating their falafel, she with unabashed relish, while he felt embarrassed.

When they arrived, she said, "Wait here. I'll be right back with the money."

He didn't know where he found the wits to say, "You know what, instead of paying me back, why don't you invite me for a falafel tomorrow?"

"Okay," she said. "But not another falafel. I'll buy you an ice cream at Whitman's; that's even better."

"Sounds fine," he replied, unable to believe his luck. "So see you tomorrow?"

"Tomorrow. Wait for me at Meir Park by the first bench near the entrance at three."

◆ ◆ ◆

And so his fate was sealed. The beautiful Lily entered his heart and his life. After that they met every day at three in the afternoon at Meir Park, at the first bench near the entrance.

They didn't talk much. Both were shy and spoke softly, making small talk about the news or the weather, but the regular meetings continued. One day he would treat her to a falafel, and the next time she would buy him an ice cream. After they'd been meeting for a week, he told her, "I can't allow you to keep treating me. I was brought up to be a gentleman. From now on I'm going to take you out for falafel and for ice cream."

She nodded, relieved. She barely had two coins to rub together. Ever since she had left the boarding school and moved to Tel Aviv, she'd been looking for a steady job. At first she worked as a salesgirl at a clothing store on Allenby Street, but she was soon fired for not urging the customers to buy. With no alternative she answered an ad she found on the bulletin board for a cleaning position at the Carmel School near the market, but that didn't last long either. This time she quit. She hadn't found another job yet and wasn't sure how much longer she could afford the room she shared with three other young women.

She was so tired of sharing a room with strangers, always with strangers. For her entire childhood she'd shared living quarters with girls she had no interest in befriending, who annoyed her, interfered in her affairs, asked questions to which she lacked answers, and invaded her privacy.

Shaul was different from anyone she'd ever met. Unlike her roommates, he didn't ask any questions. It was pleasant to meet him each afternoon, and she even agreed to walk with him along the promenade. He eased her loneliness, and in his company she didn't have to make an effort or pretend. She felt comfortable in her own skin when she was with him.

Another week passed, and she said he could pick her up at the entrance to her residence, instead of meeting in the park. She ignored her roommates' questions and venomous remarks. Let them die of jealousy, she thought. Let them explode with it. She had a man and they didn't. She'd been in Tel Aviv only a few weeks and had already snared a man, and they, some of whom had been living in the city for more than a year, were still single.

Let them make fun of the way she got dressed for a rendezvous with Shaul and the way she sashayed on her heels, swinging her hips. They snickered and went to sleep alone, and soon she would be laughing at them. The *bishara* had promised her she'd find a young man who'd kiss the ground she walked on, and she had found someone. Even if he hadn't yet kissed the ground under her feet, or even her for that matter. She wouldn't have let him kiss her anyway, although he hadn't tried to.

Twilight was descending on the promenade, and a summer breeze blew in from the sea, providing a slight respite from the oppressive July heat. The beach was packed with bathers, and despite the impending darkness they preferred to remain by the water rather than go back to their blazing-hot homes.

Lily inhaled the salty scent. How she loved the sea, the sense of lightness and freedom, the cafés jammed with customers, the mixture of young and old, families with children, groups of teenagers, and couples. British soldiers and officers in their spotless uniforms wandered the promenade alongside Arabs from Jaffa wearing djellabas and kaffiyehs with agals securing them on their heads, while their wives and children trailed along behind. She enjoyed the babble of Hebrew, Arabic, English, Yiddish, and Ladino and the loud voice of the man selling ice pops that rang out from the beach: "Get your ices, chocolate banana!" These competed with the man shouting, "Hot corn, hot corn!" standing beside a steaming vat where ears of sweet, juicy corn bobbed in the water.

They walked along the promenade, keeping close to the iron railing. A big red sun was sinking into the blue ocean, scattering its rays, and Lily reached out a tentative hand and took Shaul's arm. His breath caught in his throat. He was thrilled she was walking next to him, her arm entwined with his, like the couples in the films he saw at the cinema. His heart was expanding with joy, but he continued walking as though it were the most ordinary thing in the world that a ravishing woman was walking by his side, holding on to his arm.

An orchestra was playing at the Snow of Lebanon Café, and Shaul asked Lily if she'd like to sit outside on the terrace, where he ordered them each an espresso and ice cream with whipped cream. She licked seductively at the ice cream, which was served in a tall glass, and a delicate white mustache perched above her upper lip. Although there was nothing he longed to do more at that moment, Shaul didn't dare to wipe it away. He gestured at his own mouth, and her tongue darted out to lick it off. He had never before felt this way about any person in the world.

He wanted to tell her how beautiful she was and how happy he was that she was having ice cream with him at the Snow of Lebanon Café, but he couldn't speak.

"It's so nice to be here, Lily." She spoke for him as if reading his mind and smiled.

"I know," he stammered.

Lily burst out laughing. For the rest of his life he would long to hear Lily laugh again, as she had that time at the Snow of Lebanon Café. It was a healthy, relaxed chuckle, free and uninhibited. He would yearn with all his heart to hear Lily laugh again as she had when she'd teased him about how they were sitting in silence like two strangers.

They continued to meet every afternoon, and finally he found the courage to bring her home to meet his parents. Lily sat in their lounge, dressed in her simple blue dress, taut as a bowstring, without satisfactory answers to Sarina's prying questions. Less than fifteen minutes after they'd arrived, she whispered to Shaul that she had to get back to her room.

As they left, he noticed his mother's questioning gaze, and she called down the stairs after him, "Come back quickly—we're waiting for you to have supper." Which was when he realized she hadn't invited Lily to stay and eat with them. They were silent all the way back. A few days later he asked her to join him for a movie at Esther Cinema in Dizengoff Square. Afterward, if someone had asked him about the film they had just seen, he couldn't have described a single frame. He sat through the entire movie rigid and tense. More than anything he wanted to put his arm around Lily's shoulder and lean his head against hers like the other couples around them. He didn't even dream of giving her a kiss, afraid that if he so much as touched her shoulder or took her hand, she would rush out and he would never see her again.

To his surprise Lily slipped her hand into his of her own accord, and he was so nervous he broke out in a sweat. Now he was afraid his sweaty hand would repulse her, but Lily didn't pull her hand away even when the movie was over. They strolled around Dizengoff Square, lingering at the pretty fountain, and walked up the street, passing the densely packed houses of the Nordia neighborhood, continuing in the direction of King George Street, and crossing Bograshov. He wished that the sweet moment would last forever, that they would never reach their destination. Because not for an instant did Lily let go of his hand. Instead of parting from him at the entrance to her residence, as she always did, Lily led him toward Meir Park, and instead of remaining near the first bench at the entrance to the park at their old meeting place, she pulled him deep into the dark grassy expanse until they were out of sight of the busy street. And there, beneath the sycamore trees, under cover of darkness, Lily bent her head toward his and kissed him. The kiss lasted only a moment, and her lips were soft, and in spite of the darkness her blonde hair glowed like a halo, but Lily pulled away abruptly and moved to the end of the bench.

"Lily," he whispered, bewildered.

"Do you want to marry me," she asked urgently.

He thought he'd misheard her. He already dreamed of proposing to her but had been certain he would have to wait at least a year before he dared to ask her to marry him, and here she was, proposing to him. He was overcome with emotion, but she misinterpreted his silence and pounced.

"Because if you don't want to marry me, just say so! I'm not inter-ested in going around with someone just to pass the time. I'm looking for a man to marry, so say yes or no; decide!"

"Lily." He closed the distance between them and for the first time took her in his arms, feeling her body freeze at his touch.

"Lily, my love, my darling, of course I want to marry you, but I thought it was too soon to ask. We hardly know each other. I thought you would come home with me a few more times, get to know my parents better."

"What's the point in waiting?" she replied, trying to control her anger. "We can get to know each other after we're married. We have our whole lives to get to know each other. And if you want me to get to know your parents better, then come on—let's go to your house right now!"

"Now?" He was startled. He needed time to soften up his mother and change her mind; he had to convince her not to oppose the match. Her harsh words still echoed in his ears. Her emphatic declaration that not she, nor his father, nor his brother would come to his wedding had hurt him, and that wound was still raw. Shaul knew his mother; she was hotheaded and quick to anger, but Sarina loved her children more than life. She would come around, she would take back what she had said, and like him, she would learn to love Lily. But that would take time. If he brought Lily home without advance warning, his mother would view it as defiance and disrespect and be even angrier.

"What do you say? Shall we go now?" she pressed him.

"Now it's late. My parents aren't young anymore; they go to bed early," he lied.

"Fine," Lily agreed as she moved away from him. "We'll see them tomorrow, but we have agreed that we're getting married, right?"

"Right," he laughed. "We're getting married, but first we have to get engaged."

"Why do we need to get engaged? Engagements are for parents, and I don't have any."

"But I do," he said, "and they are very traditional. I want to marry you, Lily, but we have to do this my way."

"What does that mean? To wait until kingdom come?"

"Heaven forfend, but we don't have to rush things as though someone is chasing us. One step at a time, everything in its season."

Lily wasn't pleased, but she understood she had no choice. She had to do things slowly, as he wanted to. And another thing she understood was that if she didn't want to lose her future husband, she had to show some affection. She moved along the bench so she was beside him again and burrowed under his arm. He stroked her golden head, and when he leaned down to kiss her, she didn't turn away. Even when his tongue pushed into her mouth and her teeth clamped shut, Shaul, overwhelmed at the unexpected turn of events, didn't notice that Lily was stiff and unresponsive, so lost was he in the idea of the joyful new phase of their relationship. He was already thinking about how to lay the groundwork for Lily's next visit to his parents, devising ways to soften his mother's heart when he told her that, against all accepted rules, he was planning a marriage without the slightest involvement of his parents.

Lily felt as though she'd been holding her breath until she passed through the gates that led to the women's residence. She'd followed the *bishara*'s instructions to the letter and gone on several dates with Shaul but never allowed him to touch her. Not that he'd tried to, for he was a polite, gentle, shy young man. When she'd told the *bishara* Shaul wasn't making the first move, the witch had told her she should take the initiative. "You Jews don't wait until you're married. If you don't do something, you'll lose this groom, and wouldn't that be a shame? Do exactly as I tell you: Take your hand, and put it like this, in his hand." She demonstrated for Lily. "Not too close, so you're touching but not quite, and then see what happens, my daughter. See how things go."

"And if nothing happens?"

"Then you make them happen."

"How? What should I do?"

"*Ya rabi!*" the *bishara* lamented. "Do I have to tell you everything? You make things happen."

"Should I kiss him?"

"*Hada ho,* a kiss."

"And what if he doesn't propose?"

"Then you propose. If you've already gone that far, go all the way. May Allah be with you."

And that was precisely what she did. She took his arm as they walked along the promenade, and when he didn't take the hint, she did as the *bishara* had instructed and kissed him on the bench in the park. Even after that he behaved like a schlemiel and said nothing. Only then did she suggest they get married.

"You've got to catch him," the *bishara* had told her, "so he won't slip through your hands. These days for every man there are ten girls who want to catch him, and they have a father and a mother and a dowry, and what do you have, my daughter?"

"Not a penny to my name, that's what I have," Lily replied.

"*Hada ho*, you said it, not me. So listen and do exactly what I say, one to *wahda*. First, hold his hand, then give him a *bosah* that makes his legs go weak, and after the *bosah*, when he's still seeing stars, catch him unprepared and tell him: *Either you marry me or you can go to hell, a thousand times over!*"

"And if he says no?"

"He won't refuse you. Come here and look at the coffee. You see the shape of two people?"

"I see."

"You see the heart shape between the bodies of the two people?"

"I see."

"It means they will go together and the heart will connect them *Hada ho*, the coffee doesn't lie!"

"But I feel nothing in my heart. Does his heart feel something?"

"I think it does."

The *bishara* leaned back in her chair and stretched.

"That's enough. If he has the feeling, he will never leave you, even if you drive him crazy, and may God help him, but you will drive him crazy. Even if he wants to kill you, he would kill himself first, but he will never leave you. Poor man, he doesn't know what fate has in store for him. But what can we do—that's destiny, and it can't be changed. Even if you run away to America, destiny will follow you and him. So *yalla*, go home now and do what I told you. *Yalla, ruhi*, hurry up. I've used all my energy on you today, and you've left me with nothing for other people."

Eliya

The sound of the alarm made me jump.

"Our time is up," said Dr. Kaminsky, and I pulled myself into a sitting position, straightening my rumpled clothes. It seemed to me many hours had passed since I'd lain on the doctor's sofa and started talking. I couldn't remember what I'd said. Kaminsky took me through my own private time tunnel, which wended its way between Paris and Tel Aviv, and I wasn't sure I was enjoying the journey. One thing for sure, it exhausted me.

"Now what?" I asked Kaminsky, as I shook out my hair and tied it back again in a ponytail.

"Now homework," he replied. "You have to talk to your mother."

"About what?"

"About her, about you, about your relationship."

"No chance! My mother doesn't talk. She just gives orders."

"Soften her up. Find a way."

"I don't know how to talk to her. My mother and I have never spoken more than a few sentences consecutively, and always in anger. How can I get her to talk to me?"

"Eliya, my dear, our time is up; the next patient is waiting. Your homework is to talk to your mother. I'm sure you'll find a way. Go in peace."

Kaminsky emerged from behind his desk and approached me, almost pushing me out the door. The fat dog, I thought angrily. He wouldn't give up one cent to give me a minute more. As I left the clinic, I couldn't decide if I hated or loved Dr. Kaminsky. When he got me talking about things I'd never spoken about before, I felt as though I were sweeping myself clean from the inside. But then he gave me homework there was no chance I could do. How could I go to my mother after all these years and say, *Hi, Mom, feel like talking?* Lily would give me that look of hers and say, *From the day you were born, you've been a pain in my ass.* She'd said that very thing often during my childhood.

There was nothing negative she didn't accuse me of. Even the day I'd been born was somehow something I'd contrived to upset her. As if I'd deliberately chosen to be born on the day when the temporary government, for the first time, had decided to hold a census. On November 8, 1948, there was a curfew from five in the evening until midnight. The census takers had already been to our house, taken my parents' details, and provided them with identity numbers so that they could vote the following January. When the contractions started, she screamed in vain. The streets were deserted, and no one in the building owned a telephone. The only phone was at the pharmacy on Hashlah Street, which was also closed because of the curfew. Despite the curfew, my father went to Dizengoff Street to see if he could find someone with a vehicle to take my mother to Hadassah Hospital. Luckily a jeep with members of the Civil Guard passed, and my father convinced them to take Lily to the hospital.

More than once my mother said, "Good thing it was a Jewish curfew. If it'd been a British curfew, I would never have made it to the hospital. The moment your father set foot in the street, the British would have arrested him and thrown him in the clink."

Lily said to me, "You were born when you felt like it. Curfew or no curfew—it made no difference to you. You wanted to come out, and out you came. From the day you were born, you never cared about how I felt. And that's the way you still are today. You never have any consideration, just come home with your garbage, drop it here, and off you go, and we're left with the stink."

And Kaminsky wanted us to talk!

I'd always been Daddy's girl. My father took me to the Kindergarten for Working Women and picked me up in the afternoon. I don't know how he managed to sign me up, since my mother never worked a day in her life. My father went to the parent-teacher meetings and dressed me in my Queen Esther Purim costumes, and when I came home miserable because of some kind of bullying, he comforted me. Where was my mother all those times? Holed up in her room or walking the streets, God knows where. If Lily hadn't told me over and over she'd suffered through fifteen hours of contractions and excruciating pain until I, the little princess, deigned to be born, I would've doubted I was even hers.

"Sorry."

I'd nearly collided with a young man running into the yard outside Dr. Kaminsky's clinic.

"Watch where you're going," I yelled. "You almost knocked me down."

"Sorry," he repeated and turned back. I saw blue eyes, a tanned face, and hair down to his shoulders bleached gold by the sun and the water. It was the surfer from Gordon Beach. A long time had passed, and I'd scarcely thought about him since, but here he was standing in front of me, in a hurry, apparently ready to disappear from my life again.

"Hey," I called to him, "aren't you the guy with the surfboard from Gordon Beach?"

He stopped, gave me a glance, and said, "I didn't recognize you with your clothes on."

I ignored his joke and said, "You're the one who sent me to Kaminsky."

"Guilty. I'm glad you took my advice."

"Do you go to him?"

"I'm late for him now," he answered in a rush. "Have a good day." He disappeared through the building's glass door. I was surprised to realize I was disappointed. There was something about him I liked. Something welcoming. Maybe it was his large bright eyes or the fact that he hadn't made a big deal out of seeing me again, and of all places at the entrance to Dr. Kaminsky's clinic.

To my total amazement, the brief encounter with the good-looking surfer from Gordon Beach excited me. I hadn't given a thought to any man since Ari, but I found myself feeling curious. What was the surfer doing at Kaminsky's? Was he also trying to mend a broken heart? Had he also taken to his bed for an entire year? Had he, like me, tried to take his own life?

I leaned against the wall and lit a cigarette. I wasn't in a hurry to get home, especially since I didn't want to break the cease-fire between me and Lily. For years we'd lived parallel lives while I'd done everything I could to avoid making her angry, and only when she'd pushed me to the limit, when I had no choice, would I explode at her and she would explode right back. My poor father, I thought as I slouched against the stone wall enjoying the last rays of the sun hitting my face. How he must suffer with both of us, always maneuvering between us, trying to appease and never succeeding. And I couldn't understand why he never put Lily in her place, why he didn't stand up to her. Ari wouldn't have allowed me to speak to him the way Lily spoke to Shaul. Ari would've thrown me out. But I'd never spoken to him like that, and Ari had thrown me out anyway, I thought suddenly, and my face colored in anger. He'd abandoned me even though I'd never spoken to him in a vulgar way, even though I'd been his devoted servant and had done whatever he'd asked. To hell with Ari and his Frenchwoman. Why was I thinking of Ari all of a sudden? I took one last deep drag and ground the butt under my flat-soled sandal. I had to talk to my mother because Kaminsky had given me homework. The doctor said the treatment would only work if I cooperated. So that was what I would do: I would go home now and try to talk to Lily. *Let's see what the fat doctor will have to say when he realizes that talking to my mother is like talking to a wall. Let's see what kind of homework he gives me then.*

◆　◆　◆

"Hi, Daddy," I sang as I walked into the house.

"Hi, welcome, sweetheart." My father was in his armchair, a glass of tea in front of him with a floating slice of lemon, totally absorbed in the evening paper.

"Why are you reading in the dark?" I asked as I switched on the lamp.

"It isn't dark yet," he replied. "No need to waste electricity. You know how much electricity costs?"

"Do you know how much reading glasses cost?"

"Fine," he laughed. "Your mother isn't home; we can switch on the light. But heaven forbid she should come back and catch us using electricity if it's still light outside."

"Where is she anyway?"

"She's out."

"Have you ever wondered, Daddy, where she goes when she isn't home?"

"Maybe she's window-shopping on Dizengoff Street or sitting at Café Stern."

"Who does she sit with at Café Stern? She doesn't have any friends."

"Your mother is special," he answered without taking his eyes off the newspaper. "Your mother doesn't need company. She knows how to be alone, and when she wants to go to a café, she goes. She doesn't need anyone. She even likes to go to the cinema alone; that's how it is."

"'That's how it is' is your standard answer, Daddy. Everything about Mother is 'that's how it is.'"

My father was starting to lose his famous patience. "You're disturbing me, Eliya. I'm trying to read the paper."

"Can I make you coffee?" I asked, accepting yet again that when it came to my mother, I would never hear any explanation from him, and certainly not a negative word.

"With pleasure."

"Two sugars and hot milk?"

"Good, thanks for remembering." He always said that. I remembered how proud I'd been when I was a little girl to make his coffee and serve it to him and how he would drink it and compliment me.

I put his drink on the table and next to it a ceramic dish with a piece of the coffee cake that my father bought regularly at the Ugati cake shop next to his store on King George Street.

"You eat the cake," he told me. "I'll wait for supper, when your mother gets back."

"I'm not hungry."

"Why don't you eat, sweetheart? Look at how skinny you are. It's not nice for a woman to be so thin. A little meat on your bones wouldn't hurt you."

"I don't care right now whether it's nice or not nice to be thin."

"Eliya, be patient just a little longer, and soon you'll forget all about that terrible man, and with God's help you'll meet a new man. You'll find the right person for you, a man who will truly appreciate you and love you, will put you on a pedestal and treat you like a queen."

"The way you treat Mother?"

"Exactly, to me your mother is a queen."

"Sure, a queen. Queen Esther."

"What's wrong with Queen Esther? She saved the people of Israel."

"Mother is busy saving only herself."

For a moment my father seemed to be thinking deeply. His previous amused expression had vanished, and he replied in a serious tone, "Your mother had to save herself. There was no one else to save her."

"What did she have to save herself from?"

"Ach," he sighed and looked at me with his kind eyes. "There are parts of your mother's life that even I don't know anything about. You can't get a thing out of her; she keeps it all inside and never talks. Maybe the life she lived before we met made her that way."

"What kind of life did she have that other people don't have?" I was losing my patience.

"Did you never ask yourself why she doesn't have anyone in the whole world, other than us? Why you don't have grandparents on your mother's side, no uncles, aunts, or cousins? How your mother has no family?"

"When I was little, she told me they died."

"And you never wondered how they died, when they died?"

"A little girl doesn't ask questions when she knows she isn't going to get answers. Anyway, there were lots of children in the neighborhood whose grandparents died in the Holocaust. It wasn't so strange."

"Your mother's parents didn't die in the Holocaust," he said after a long silence.

"So how did they die?"

"I don't know if they died. Lily herself doesn't know. She doesn't know anything about them; she never knew her parents. Your mother was born an orphan."

I didn't understand what he meant.

"She never knew her parents."

"So who raised her?" For the first time I was curious about my mother's past, which had been sealed away under lock and key.

"Nuns in a convent. Years ago she told me she grew up in a convent but made me swear never to tell anyone. If she finds out I told you, she'll be very angry. Eliya, promise me if she doesn't tell you herself, you'll never tell her you know."

"Daddy, what does it matter now whether she tells me or I tell her? Which convent? Where? How did she get to a convent?" I brought my chair right up to my father's armchair so he couldn't get away and looked straight into his eyes, demanding answers.

"The English convent in Jerusalem. Someone left her there as a day-old baby, wrapped in a blanket, outside the convent gate. She was raised by the nuns, and when she was ten, she ran away and lived on the streets, eating from trash cans, until some good women found her and took her to a place for abandoned children in Jerusalem, and from there they sent her to a boarding school in Herzliya. She lived at the boarding school until she was old enough to leave, and then she went to Tel Aviv and lived in a women's residence. That's when I met her, just a few weeks after she left the boarding school."

"Why didn't you ever tell me?" I asked, shocked and confused.

"It's not my secret, it's her secret, and your mother made me swear not to tell. She barely told me."

"So many times I was angry at Mother, so many times I didn't understand her strange behavior, and you always told me I had to be patient, but you never explained why."

"She said you didn't need to know there were things like that in the world."

"But it's not 'things like that.' It's what happened to her, and what happened to her also affected my life. That must be why she never shows me affection. That's why for her I'm nothing but wallpaper."

"Eliya, how can you say such things! Your mother loves you deeply. She almost died of worry when you went through your difficult period."

"Right, and she still makes sure to remind me every single day that I'm to blame for what happened to me, because despite her opposition I still married Ari."

"From the start she realized that Ari wasn't for you. She told me she would've given up her life if it would stop you from marrying that *shmendrik*, as she called him. It pained her that you didn't listen, and it hurt her that she was right. She loves you, your mother, loves you more than she loves herself, but she has trouble showing it. She doesn't show me, either, but I still know that she loves me."

"And what if one day she doesn't come back from wherever she goes out there, and what if one day she leaves us?"

"She'll never leave. You and me, we're the family she never had. We are her life."

"Some life." My father looked at me with pain in his face, and I immediately regretted my bitter outburst. I hadn't meant to hurt him. "You know, Daddy," I said to him, softening my words, "if only I'd been able to understand her like you do. She spends as little time as possible with us, especially with me."

"Eliya, your mother has a good heart. Patience, all that I ask of you is patience."

"Like she's patient with me?"

"More. All the sorrow and pain that you went through because of that terrible man you married is not even close to the sorrow and pain your mother has experienced, and she's a strong woman, like steel! Otherwise how could she survive what she went through? And you, you're your mother's daughter. You came out of your difficult situation thanks to your strength, that steel you inherited from your mother."

"Me? Steel? I'm a rag, a dishrag."

"Heaven forbid, sweetheart, don't say such things. Look at how you're coping! How you're taking care of yourself. And by the way, how was it today at the doctor?"

"He gave me homework."

"What, has he opened a school now?" My father smiled.

"To talk to Mother."

"About what?"

"About her, about me, about us."

It was as though a heavy cloud descended upon him. He withdrew into himself, and I felt like he was disappearing and leaving me far behind, as if trying to take on a burden that was too heavy to carry.

"What happened, Daddy? Where did you go?"

He took a deep breath. "I'm not sure that's a good idea. It's not good to awaken slumbering demons," he said in his quiet voice, speaking not like a father to his daughter but like one equal to another, needing the other person's help. "Your relationship isn't exactly warm now, but it isn't cold either. Ever since your crisis, your mother has softened. She isn't angry all the time anymore. She has a gentleness that I haven't seen in her since May His Memory Be Blessed died, so why ruin it? Why get into discussions that will bring up things that are best left hidden under the floor tiles? No," he concluded, "I don't think that's a very good idea."

"You think I want to talk to her? But Kaminsky says that until Mother and I have a conversation, he and I can't make progress with the treatment."

"What do you have to talk to her about?"

"For example, the baby that died." My father turned pale, but I kept talking. "You've never told me about what happened to him. If it wasn't for that picture, I wouldn't even have known that he existed."

"He died when he was still a baby," he whispered. "But your mother never forgets him, and he remains in her heart like an open, bleeding wound."

"You never talk about him. What did you think, that I would turn out normal when I grew up in a house with such a big secret?"

"It was never a secret. You saw his picture, didn't you? And we certainly told you that you had a brother who was born before you, who died when he was still a baby."

"But you didn't tell me that he was like a wound in her heart. You didn't tell me that the wound never healed and continues to bleed. And what, you think it didn't make me into the person I am today?"

"It's not black and white, Eliya. We did everything so that the death of May His Memory Be Blessed wouldn't affect you. Because of that, we don't talk about him to each other or with the family or with the neighbors."

I was seething with emotion. We had never spoken so openly about the brother I'd never known. The pain of many years washed over me and through me. "Well, I couldn't not see the picture; it's always there on the sideboard. Even if I really wanted to, I couldn't ignore it. Wherever I was in the room, that baby looked at me like he was the *Mona Lisa.*"

I could picture every detail of that baby's infant face without looking. I hated the picture of my dead brother. There was something so alive in the toothless smile that I couldn't bear it. Sometimes, when Lily hadn't been home, I'd turned it around so that it faced the wall and I didn't have to see his innocent gaze and the smile that revealed his two dimples, which were identical to Lily's and mine. I was embarrassed to have a dead brother, and when anyone asked, I said he was my cousin from America. That worked until I was caught in the lie.

Lily didn't like strangers in the house, especially not strange children. But once in a while I took advantage of Lily's absences to invite kids from the neighborhood over. Once we were sitting on the floor in the lounge playing truth or dare. When the bottle stopped spinning, it pointed at me. "Truth or dare?" a girl who'd never come over before asked, and since I didn't feel like taking off my shirt or kissing Idith on the mouth, I answered, "Truth."

"Who's the baby in the picture?" she demanded.

Without blinking an eye, I stuck to my usual story. "That's my cousin from America."

Unfortunately, the new girl had more questions. "Where does he live in America?"

"In Hollywood, where all the movie stars live."

"Liar!" Idith, who was the undisputed queen of the class, jumped up and went over to the picture. She held it in her hand and said, "This isn't your cousin. This is your brother who died."

I was stunned Idith was breaking the rules of the game, but I made a swift recovery and retorted, "You're the liar! That's my cousin from America, and soon he's coming for a visit, so you'll see."

"Don't try to trick us!" Idith wouldn't let it go. "My mother told me your parents had a baby that died."

"Your mother is making up stories!"

"You're the one making things up!" Idith shouted. "Let's go—we aren't going to hang around with this liar. We're leaving."

One by one the girls got up, carefully adjusting the elastic around the legs of their identical short shorts without looking at me. They walked out of my house in single file, the last slamming the door behind them. It was only later that I realized I'd been set up. Idith had suggested we play truth or dare, and she'd instructed the new girl to ask about the picture. She'd had it all planned so she could turn them all against me and officially ostracize me so I'd go from being one of the popular girls to being a social outcast. At the time I didn't know all that; I just felt angry and miserable. I was sick of the dead baby I wasn't allowed to mention, sick of lying and of getting caught in my lies because of him. I grabbed the picture and hid it under the mattress in my room, where, still fully dressed, I climbed into bed and, as was my habit, covered my head with the blanket and pretended that I wasn't there.

The boycott Idith declared on me at school was cruel. In one fell swoop I was totally cut off from the circle of popular kids I had previously belonged to and transformed into persona non grata. During recess, not only did they not play with me, but they demonstratively avoided me and taunted me with the pitiless rhyme they had devised: "Eliya *eahira*, garbage from Jebeliya." Everyone knew the huge Jebeliya garbage dump outside Tel Aviv, and even kids knew that "*eahira*" was Arabic for *whore*. Every time I heard the terrible rhyme, I shrank into myself and wished I were dead.

I was still lost in those bitter memories when the door opened and Lily slipped inside.

As always, she left her wallet on the table by the entrance, shrugged off her coat and hung it on the coatrack, removed her shoes, and walked barefoot into the house.

"What's with the two of you? You both look so glum," she said, and I noticed how my father's face lit up with joy at the sight of her.

"You're right on time. Eliya just made me coffee; come join us. Eliya, make coffee for your mother too."

"Turkish," Lily said, "two sugars and a drop of milk." As if I didn't know.

I went into the kitchen. Even something so mundane she turned into an order. How was I ever going to get her to talk to me? And Daddy said it wasn't a good time, as if there would ever be a good time.

I moved my face into the steam rising from the boiling kettle. It was a pleasant sensation, as though the steam were caressing my face. I longed for everything to be simple, that I could make coffee for my mother more often. But nothing was simple with my mother. Now we were both being careful not to upset each other, but I knew one wrong word could ignite the raging fire. When I was a little girl and my mother would have one of her moods, I would hide under the bed or in the closet. She would hurl to the floor anything that crossed her path—dishes, glasses, books—and my father would never do anything to stop her, just whispered in a tiny, weak voice that could barely be heard, "Enough, Lily, that's enough, Lily. The neighbors will hear," as he picked up after her.

I filled the glass three-quarters with boiling water, stirred the sugar and the milk into the coffee, and turned toward the living room. For a moment I stood in the doorway and watched my parents. Shaul dipped the cake in his coffee, and Lily sat beside him. They were both very quiet. He held out the moistened cake, and she brought her mouth to his hand to take a bite. Then he took a napkin and wiped the crumbs off her lips. I was fascinated by their coordinated movements. How had I never noticed before that my parents, despite all the difficulty, despite their differences, were so compatible? Despite and in spite of it all, how close they were.

Shaul

The doubts continued. True, Eliya was seeing Dr. Kaminsky regularly, but he feared the slightest incident might cause her to regress. And who knew, if Eliya improved, Lily might go back to criticizing her every move, as she'd done before the girl had collapsed. The fear nearly paralyzed him. "Lord of the universe, why did you give me these two to carry?" he inquired for the umpteenth time of the God whose existence he'd recently begun to doubt.

How he missed the comfort of his childhood home, the orderly world where the father was responsible for earning a living, the mother took care of the children, and the children, for their part, honored their parents and would never defy them. How he longed for the world where a father's word was law and a mother's word was sacred, where a woman would never dare treat her husband as excess baggage, like Lily treated him.

He'd turned his world upside down for her. Sometimes he felt like walking out the door and not coming back, finding himself the life that he had dreamed of as a young man, before he'd met Lily. Before he fell madly in love with his strange wife, before he became a pawn in her hands, before the disasters that had befallen them. What wouldn't he give to go back to being the person he was before he met Lily.

He would never forget the day after they'd met. She'd said to meet at three, without asking whether that was a convenient time for him. He didn't dare say that he always rested after lunch and then went back to the store with his father. He stayed up the whole night desperately trying to come up with an excuse that would allow him to leave the house before his father did and return to the store after him. In the end he lied and said he had to go to see Dr. Freeman.

"Oh no, what's the matter!" His mother jumped up. "Is something wrong, heaven forfend?"

"I don't feel so well," he replied, almost unable to believe he was lying shamelessly to his parents. "I think I may be coming down with a throat infection."

They believed him. Why shouldn't they? He'd never told them a lie before. And he hurried off to meet Lily, and his father went to the store without him. To his mixed relief, after sharing an ice cream Lily said she had to get back, and he was able to get to work on time. The following day he told his parents the doctor had said he should come back at the same time for more tests. And just as on the previous day they had no suspicions, for why should they doubt their obedient, goody-two-shoes, well-behaved son? But he knew he couldn't go on lying, and he decided to tell her the truth, that he worked as a jeweler at his father's store and it would be more convenient if they could meet when he finished work, at six. To his surprise she agreed, and from then on they met every day between six and seven, after which he rushed home for supper with his parents. His father and mother didn't know what he did during the hour between closing time and the family meal. Until the day he brought her home, they had no idea.

And then the trouble started with his mother and Lily, troubles that never ended. Lily didn't talk to his mother, and his mother didn't talk to her, and his father was torn between the two.

Lily had even managed to distance Eliya from them, had forbidden him from bringing their daughter to visit his parents. He almost never saw them, even now that they were old and needed him more than ever. He hadn't told them about what had happened with Eliya, about how the bastard had left her, about how she'd almost lost her mind, and he along with her. That was how it was: to have a peaceful life at home, he'd sacrificed his parents—and himself.

Lily

When Lily came home and the picture of the baby wasn't on the sideboard, she started to scream like a madwoman and accused Shaul of taking it away.

She turned the house upside down searching, and the stunned Shaul helped her. They moved the heavy sideboard, lifted the carpets, and looked under the couch, in the kitchen, in the bathroom, and in the bedroom. They looked everywhere except Eliya's room. "I've got to talk to the *bishara*," Lily mumbled. "I've got to understand why the child came down from heaven and took away his picture."

"Who's the *bishara*?" asked Shaul in amazement. "What are you talking about? How could the child come down from heaven? Lily, you're losing your mind!"

"I'm going crazy? So you explain how the picture disappeared. Who took it? The devil? I have to go to the *bishara* right now and ask her." Lily stood in the middle of the apartment, her eyes moving wildly in their sockets. Shaul stared in fright at the strange fire ignited in those eyes.

"Lily, you aren't going anywhere at this hour," he said, trying to stop her, but she shoved him out of the way, and without taking a coat despite the wintry weather, she dashed down the stairs. He rushed after her, forgetting that they were leaving Eliya alone at home. Like a woman possessed, Lily ran up Dizengoff Street until she reached a stop for the bus to Jaffa, Shaul following behind.

"Lily," he shouted, "Lily, wait!" but she started to run again. If there was no bus, she would run all the way to Jaffa. She was terrified, convinced that the missing picture was a sign from on high. She didn't understand what sin she had committed to make her child descend from heaven and take the picture. Maybe he was jealous that she had a new child? But why would he choose this moment to become jealous? Eliya was already ten years old; why would he suddenly react now?

As if lost in a fog, she was unaware of Shaul's pursuit. Lily crossed Nordau Street to HaYarkon and continued to race along as if she were running for her life. Shaul was barely keeping up, but when she reached the Muslim cemetery, he managed to grab hold of her shoulder and pleaded, "Lily, stop. What demon has possessed you?"

She pulled away from him and kept on running. "Stop for a minute," he begged, panting, and she shouted over her shoulder, "Go home, Shaul. Stop running after me."

"But why are you running?"

"I'm running to save our lives. Something terrible is about to happen to us; I feel it. Our child is angry at us, and I have to find out why."

Shaul tried to follow his wife's convoluted train of thought. He knew her grief over the death of their son hadn't lessened with time, but he couldn't have imagined the picture going missing would provoke such a reaction. He tried again, "Lily, I'm begging you—how will you find out why he's angry? Who will tell you why?"

"The Arab witch from Jaffa will tell me. She will know why."

"Lily, what are you talking about? Please wait. I'm out of breath. It's late at night, and it's dangerous along the promenade, dangerous now in Jaffa, full of pimps and whores and God knows what else. Wait, Lily!"

"Nothing is more dangerous than the missing picture. No whore or pimp can hurt us like it can."

"Stop!" he commanded her. "Stop or I'll slap you!"

Shaul, her gentle man. Shaul, who couldn't hurt a fly. Lily was so surprised she stopped in her tracks, breathing heavily. Shaul faced her, also panting, stooped forward, his face red. With the last of his strength, he took hold of her shoulders and said, "If you don't explain where you're going and who this Arab witch is, I'll hold on to you, and you won't be able to move, do you understand?"

She gave in. Her body went limp, and a cry rose from her throat. "Shaul, I'm afraid," she told him. "I fear for our lives. Trust me—I know what I'm doing. Let me go to the *bishara*. She will straighten out everything. Go home to Eliya; she must be scared to death. Let me go. I promise I'll be back in a few hours."

Until that moment he'd forgotten that Eliya was home alone. He thought for a moment. "Eliya will be fine. It's not the first time we've left her alone. I'm not going home without you. I'll go with you to the *bishara*, bishmara, or whatever she's called."

"No," she cried, "I have to go alone."

"Either I go with you or you don't go at all!" Shaul was the fiercest he'd ever been.

"Fine," she agreed. "But when we get there, you must wait outside, and I'll go in alone."

"I'm not promising anything. We'll cross that bridge when we come to it. Now let's get a taxi. If we have to walk to Jaffa, we won't get there till tomorrow."

They walked back to Ben Yehuda Street, and Shaul flagged down a taxi. Lily asked the driver to drop them near the clock tower, and the couple traveled in silence. Lily led him confidently through the narrow, twisted streets to a large open area of the city known for its dangerous activities.

"Good Lord, Lily!" Shaul was really shocked. He'd read about the menaces in the area in the newspaper, and here was Lily, about to stride in like she belonged there. "You put your life in danger here. This place is crawling with criminals."

"Don't be afraid," she told him. "Just walk as if you belong here, as if you always walk around here."

"I am not setting foot in this place," he retorted, "and neither are you!"

"Fine," she sighed, and instead she took him the long way on Yefet Street, which led to the Ajami neighborhood, until they finally arrived at a house that stood near the sea.

"You wait for me here," she said.

"I'm going in with you."

"Under no circumstances. You wait here."

He realized that he couldn't argue with her about this. "All right," he agreed, "I'll wait here."

She walked to the green-painted door and knocked.

A young man opened the door. Shaul couldn't hear what they were saying, but he saw that Lily was terribly upset again. And then the man looked over at him.

The door closed, and with defeated steps Lily walked toward Shaul, her eyes shining with tears. "Now I'll never know where the picture went. Now all we can do is wait for the catastrophe to come."

"What catastrophe? What are you talking about? What did that man say?"

"He said his mother died! May Allah have mercy, she died in her sleep ten days ago like a righteous woman, and I didn't even know. I was here a month ago, and she seemed as strong as an ox."

"What do you mean, you were here a month ago? Who is she to you? Is she a relative?"

"What are you talking about, Shaul? How could she be related to me? I have no Arab relatives."

"Don't be angry, Lily. You yourself don't know who left you at the convent."

"Shaul! My mother was Jewish."

"Who told you that, Lily?"

"Sister Katherine at the convent told me. Just before I ran away, she told me that in the note attached to my blanket there was a drawing of a Star of David."

"You never told me they found a note."

"I never told you a lot of things. They found a note, and in the note was a request to save me like they had saved her."

"That's what it said, to save you like they saved her? So there's a clue there. That means that she was also at the convent."

"So it seems. That's also where I got my name. The note said that my name was Lily. She gave me my name and drew a Star of David. The nuns kept it a secret all those years, and I didn't know anything until Sister Katherine told me. And then I found out that my mother was a Jew and that I'm a Jew."

"So if this Arab woman who died wasn't a relative of yours, who was she to you? And why have I never heard of her before?"

"She wasn't family, not a blood relative, but she was everything to me. Mother, grandmother, friend. She told me everything, do you understand? Once she told me that she saw a great ocean in my coffee and beyond the sea a woman with a black heart. She said that was the woman who gave birth to me and that her heart was black because of a sin she had committed. Probably because she dumped me with the nuns. She told me everything, even that I should marry you."

"That you should marry me?"

"I went to her for the first time when I was a young girl at the boarding school, and from then on every time I needed advice, I went to her. She would read my coffee grounds, Shaul. If only I'd listened, maybe the baby Chaim would never have been born, and if he hadn't been born, he wouldn't have died and left a hole in my heart. But I wanted to have a child so badly I didn't hear what she told me. She knew more about me than I knew about myself. For years I wouldn't let her tell me anything about my past, certainly not about the woman who gave birth to me and left me like a stray dog on the steps of the convent."

"You didn't want to know? You didn't want to know who your mother was?" Shaul regarded his wife, unable to believe that they were having this conversation at all, let alone in some dark alley in the heart of Jaffa. But Lily talked and he listened.

"I wanted to erase my past, I wanted a new life, but that new life was taken away from me when my baby died. I went to her and asked her why it all happened. All she told me was to go home to you and be with you so that a new baby would grow inside me, so that the soul of the dead baby could enter the new baby. I did what she asked, but I lost the baby's soul. It didn't go to Eliya; it seems it went into another baby born to another mother." Her shoulders shook and she wept uncontrollably, and at that moment she seemed to Shaul like a small, lost child. Lily kept talking, her words punctuated by her sobs. "I went to the *bishara*, and I asked her why there is nothing of the baby in Eliya, why did God punish me twice, and she said that you can't give new life if you don't know anything about your old life. She said that until I knew about my past, nothing in my life would work out. I told her that my life had been the life of a dog, because otherwise I wouldn't have been abandoned at the convent, and she said, 'My daughter, until you find out who left you there and why, you will always be like an abandoned dog.' I asked her to tell me everything she could about my past. When I finished my coffee, she took the cup and turned it over, waited what felt like an eternity, and looked at the dark grounds against the white of the cup. 'I see a very young woman, almost a child, poor thing. She has no one; she's alone in the world. No husband, no father, no mother. I see a baby in her arms, and she gives it away to save it and also to save herself.'

"I asked her what she had to save herself from, and the *bishara* sighed a deep sigh and said, 'My daughter, what woman has a child alone? What woman has a child with no father?'

"I asked her, 'Oh, *bishara*, where is that woman now?' And she showed me in the coffee grounds an immense sea with another country on the other side and said, 'The woman crossed the great sea and went to another land.' And other than what Sister Katherine told me at the convent, that's all that I know about the woman who gave birth to me."

Shaul was astounded. His knees buckled, and he collapsed onto the cold, filthy stone ground of the alley. He'd lived with Lily for so long and never heard of the *bishara*. Did Lily only marry him because the *bishara* told her to? How did the *bishara* even know about him? And that night that led to the birth of Eliya? The flowers, the shining house on that passionate night of lovemaking that had never been repeated— had all of that been according to the *bishara*'s orders? Had the woman who'd writhed beneath him simply been following instructions? He was confused and shocked, but Lily had collapsed in his arms, and hers was the greater need. He opened his heart to her, kissed the top of her head, and slowly felt her body relax.

"She wanted to give you a better life than she had." He kissed her again.

"Thank you," she whispered. "Thank you for being in my life. I don't have anyone in the world but you."

Shaul tightened his embrace and whispered in her ear, "Thank you, thank you for being my wife, and thank you for being Eliya's mother. I love you more than my life. We are a family, you, me, and Eliya, and I will keep us safe. I swear to you that I will always keep us safe!"

It was very late when they returned home. All the lights were on, and Lily didn't even say anything about the colossal waste of electricity. The front door wasn't locked. They walked into the living room. On the sideboard, in its usual place, was the picture of the baby Chaim. Lily sprinted to the photograph, hugged it to her chest, and then covered it in kisses. "Thank you, God. Thank you, my child, for not taking away your picture."

"Lily," Shaul said, trying to be as gentle as he could, "neither God nor the baby Chaim took away or put back that picture."

"So who took it, and who put it back?"

"I took it!" Eliya, bathed and wearing clean pajamas, stood at the entrance to the lounge and stared defiantly at her mother.

"You?" Lily couldn't believe it.

"Me. I took it and I hid it. And I also put it back."

"Why?" Lily asked. "Why would you do such a thing?"

"Because they called me a liar. The girls asked who the baby was, and I was embarrassed."

"But sweetheart," Shaul said softly, trying to appease the child as he'd soothed her mother, "lots of children have pictures in their house of people who have died."

"Yes." Now Eliya was really crying. "But no one else has a picture of a dead baby, so I told them it was my cousin from America, but then Idith said I was a liar and that her mother told her it was your baby who died before I was born. All the other girls heard, and tomorrow at school they're all going to call me a liar."

"They can all go to hell." Lily thrust out her chin. "Since when do we care what other people say. They only know how to talk, blah-blah-blah all day long, poking their noses into other people's business. All they do is gossip in this building. You hear me, Eliya? I don't want any children coming into this house."

"Of course not." Eliya raised her voice, which wasn't shaking anymore. "You can sit all day and stare at the picture of your dead baby, but I'm alive, and you never look at me. Because of you they're calling me a liar. And I can't invite anyone over because you hate guests. I hate you! I hate you! You're a bad mother!"

And suddenly her little hands balled into fists, and she rushed at her mother.

Lily recoiled.

"Enough!" At Shaul's shout they both froze. "Enough!" He took Eliya by the hand. "Go to your room right now."

"I won't go to my room!" she cried. "I won't go anywhere until you take away the picture of your dead baby! If you don't, I'll break the glass and rip it into tiny pieces!"

All the color drained from Lily's face. Both she and Shaul were shocked by Eliya's outburst. She was only ten years old, and they couldn't believe the things she was saying. Without another word Lily took the photograph into the bedroom. From then on it stood on the night table at her side of the bed, and calm was restored.

Lily took three buses to get to the cemetery in Kiryat Shaul. The last bus let her off near the Tzahala neighborhood, and from there she traversed an unpaved path to the cemetery. Her legs hurt, she was thirsty, and the August sun beat mercilessly on her head. She sat down to rest for a moment beside the path. The houses seemed to be much farther away now. Fear gripped her. The neighborhood was surrounded by citrus orchards, and who knew what demon might emerge from among the orange trees and attack her. Although she hadn't caught her breath yet, she rose hurriedly and continued toward the cemetery. Since his death two years ago, she hadn't set foot here even once, unable to bear the pain that gripped her stomach and crushed her heart. It was her child buried there under the ground, beneath the stone that closed him in forever.

The large cemetery gate was wide open. How would she ever find the children's section, and how would she find her child? When her son had died, there was no space at the Trumpeldor Cemetery, so they had to bury him at the newly opened Kiryat Shaul. Its location, in the middle of nowhere, intimidated her, but not Shaul. It was better that way, he thought. They'd buried the child, and now they must go on. The farther away the grave, the better it would be for Lily, he believed.

If they had buried him at Trumpeldor Cemetery, she would probably have spent more time there than at home. He didn't know that every day Lily sat for hours at the window, gazing eastward, in the general direction of the Kiryat Shaul, tormenting herself because she didn't go to visit her child. So tiny and so alone. He didn't know that each time that she was about to catch the bus to go to him, she was overcome with fear and paralyzing physical pain. Until she screwed up her courage and resolved to go through with it.

She walked past the new monument at the entrance dedicated to the victims of the Holocaust who'd never received a burial, then continued along what she hoped was the main path, under young cypress trees that had been recently planted. How would she find her way among the different paths and the trees?

A funeral was underway a short distance from where she was walking. A representative of the Burial Society led the way, followed by four men carrying a stretcher covered with a shroud. An old woman followed slowly, supported on either side by two young-looking men, and behind them walked several women wearing headscarves, and at the end of the procession was a mixed group of women and men. That was the right way, she thought. That was the right way to escort the dead. She decided the dead person must have been an elderly man who'd died peacefully in his later years. How she would have preferred to walk through cemeteries where only elderly people who had died of old age were buried, not babies who'd died before their lives had even begun.

The procession seemed to be coming her way, and she walked quickly to avoid it. How different this unhurried, silent funeral was from the funeral for baby Ron-Chaim. She didn't remember much of it because for the entire bleak walk her eyes had been filled with tears. Her son's tiny body was placed on a stretcher so much bigger than he was. Like a little bird he lay in the center of the stretcher, covered in a shroud, so diminutive she feared he would be jostled off by the four men carrying the stretcher. Who those men had been she couldn't remember, but

Shaul was not among them. He had kept his arms around her so she wouldn't collapse. When she'd heard the man from the Burial Society mumbling the name of God, a scream had escaped her. That she did remember, that she had cried out, "There is no God! If God took my child from me, a little child who never harmed anyone, who didn't have the chance to sin, then there is no God." No one had contradicted her, not even the members of the Burial Society.

But where the hell was the child's grave? So many names, so much life buried in the ground. Her paralyzing fear returned. And what if she wandered in the cemetery until nightfall and they closed the gate and she was locked in there, alone?

She continued along the central path. How would she ever find the child's grave among so many others? They didn't bury children in large graves; she had to look for a section of tiny graves. That was where her child would be. But no matter how much she searched, she couldn't find it, and the sun was moving westward. She should turn back. But she had come this far; how could she not kiss her child's resting place? She had to show him that his mother hadn't forgotten him. She wandered along the paths. *My child,* she said to him silently, *I've come all this way to see you. Won't you show me the way? Won't you show me where you are? Give me a sign that you hear me, my beloved child. Send me a sign.*

At that moment she saw a beautiful butterfly, bright lemon yellow. Again she spoke soundlessly to her beloved child and said, *I knew it; I knew you could hear me, my beautiful boy. It's you. It's you, my darling, whose life was the span of a butterfly's eternity.* Her heart was full, for her child had come to calm her fear; he'd come to show her the way. Peace and serenity enveloped her. The butterfly flitted here and there, disappeared and reappeared, as though guiding her. She found herself on a path that led to the adjacent military cemetery. She still hadn't found the children's section, but the fear that had nearly immobilized her had vanished. Lily moved sure-footedly, certain now that she wouldn't be lost among the paths and the gravestones, secure in the knowledge that the butterfly would lead her to her son's grave.

The trail seemed to go on forever. Then she spied two workers, sitting under a tree at the side of the path and eating pita sandwiches. *Some place to have a picnic,* she thought, but she was glad to see them.

"Pardon me, perhaps you know where the children's section is?" she asked.

"Just down there," they said, pointing. "Walk straight along the path, and on the right, under the cypress trees, that's where the children are," one of them told her.

She nodded her thanks.

"May the Lord preserve us," murmured one of the workers as Lily disappeared down the path. "May the Lord preserve us."

And as he'd said, off to the right she saw the children's section. Three rows of tiny graves in the heart of a cypress grove. Some tombstones had the names of the child and parents and their birth and death years in the Hebrew calendar. In other places only a small wooden sign affixed to a stake pushed into the ground indicated that a child was buried there. With no name, no date, no mention of parents, as though those children didn't belong to anyone.

She recognized her son's grave at once. Upon the grave sat a simple stone inscribed with the one year of his life and the words:

HERE LIES
OUR BELOVED BABY
RON-CHAIM
SON OF SHAUL AND LILY ZOREF
1946–1947
ONE YEAR OLD WHEN HE DIED

Ron. From the time he'd died, she had called him only Chaim, the second name attached to his first by the rabbi at the Great Synagogue, when he'd been in the hospital and they'd prayed God would spare their child. She'd gratefully added the name Chaim, hoping it had the power to give life, according to its meaning. But the name hadn't helped, and her baby's first name, the beautiful Hebrew name she'd chosen, had been almost forgotten. She remembered Shaul's mother had wanted to name the baby for her brother, who'd perished in the Holocaust. She'd gotten her way with Eliya, because Lily had been too weak to resist; in fact, she hadn't cared what name they gave to the baby.

Ron, whose name she'd fought for, had survived barely a year. Kneeling before the gravestone, caressing the inscription with her fingertips, wiping away the dust of the past two years, she whispered, "Ron, Roni, how could I have left you alone under the ground for so long? How could I not have come to visit you? But I didn't forget; you know I didn't forget you. In bed before I close my eyes, I look at you and I kiss you, and when I open my eyes, I look at you and I kiss you. Like the devout kiss the mezuzah on the doorpost. You're always with me, everywhere, at every moment, my child, but I couldn't bring myself to come here. I couldn't bear it that your sweet smile is crushed underneath a stone. Forgive me, my child; forgive me for not being able to come. Just the thought that you are here breaks my heart, but I promise you, my Roni, even with my broken heart, you are always with me."

She breathed deeply and listened to the silence. The only sound was the rustling of the leaves. Even the birds were silent in the graveyard.

Lily stood and went over to a tap at the end of the row of graves. Next to it was an empty tin can. She filled it with water and returned to the tombstone, removed the scarf from her neck, and started to clean the dusty stone set on the grave of Ron-Chaim, son of Lily and Shaul Zoref. Slowly and gently she rubbed the scarf into the indentations made by each letter, working diligently until the stone shone in its whiteness.

"There, now you're clean," she said. "Until the winds blow the dust back and make you dirty again, and then the rain will come and wash the dust away."

Lily pressed her lips against the cold stone and gave it a long kiss. After parting from her dead son, she rose and walked among the neighboring children's graves. There were Yosef and Saraleh, Moshe and Zvulun, Amihod and Shoshana, names of children who'd never had the chance to become adults and remained children, forever.

She walked the long way back to the exit. Twilight was filling the cemetery. A soft and generous light replaced the hot glare of the scorching Tel Aviv sun. And then she spied the yellow butterfly that had guided her. She smiled at it. It was only when she passed through the gate that she noticed that for the entire time she'd been at her son's grave, not a single tear had spilled from her eyes.

Eliya

"Good morning to you," Dr. Kaminsky greeted me, more cheerfully than usual.

In the week since our last session, I'd been secretly observing Lily, noting how she withdrew into herself, her silences. I'd counted the hours she was away from home, always returning late in the evening. I'd even almost managed to talk to her. My father wasn't home yet, and I found myself alone with my mother.

As usual, Lily sat by the window, staring outside.

"Why don't you ever look at the sea?" I asked her. "What are you looking for by the Yarkon River?"

"I'm not looking at the Yarkon," she answered me, without turning her head.

"So what are you looking at?"

"I'm just looking, not at anything special."

"You sit for hours and look to the east while there's a gorgeous sunset over the sea?"

"That's what I like to do," she said in a tone that signaled the conversation was over.

I stopped looking for opportunities to talk to my mother. Every time I tried, I slammed into a wall. Lily didn't want to talk to me about the weather, so what were the odds she would talk to me about herself or about our relationship?

I knew that Kaminsky would tell me again that I had to talk to my mother. I considered dozens of excuses, and in the end I decided to just tell him the truth.

"So how was the talk with your mother?" he asked in his supercilious manner, as if he already knew the answer.

"It didn't happen."

"Explain, explore, expound," he shot back, as though playing a game with me.

"My father."

"Yes?"

"My father said that this isn't a good time to ask my mother questions, because she's in a sensitive state."

"What does he mean?"

"My mother's always in a sensitive state. She wasn't even at home when I talked to my father. She's never at home. I don't have the faintest idea where she goes, and honestly I couldn't care less."

"Is it strange she isn't home?"

"No, that's the way it is. She comes home late, after my father's already made dinner."

"And what is the meal like?"

"Silent."

"Has it always been that way?"

"There are periods when she won't shut up. She complains about everything, about nonsense, speaks badly of my grandparents and of my uncle and aunt in America, about everyone."

"And why do you think your mother isn't talking now?"

"My mother's weird; you never know how she's going to react. The strangest of mothers."

"What is it about you that makes your mother angry?" The doctor leaned back in his chair as he filled his pipe. The sweet, slightly nauseating smell billowed into the room, and rather than ask him to open the window, I answered him.

"What didn't make her angry? She was angry I was dating Ari, that I married Ari, that I didn't give her grandchildren, that I look like a hippie and live like a free spirit, that Ari didn't have a regular income, and that I took money from my father. She called Ari a good-for-nothing, and she said that even if they wrote about him in the paper, it didn't make him a good husband, because how could he be a good husband if he didn't get a paycheck at the end of each month. My mother did everything to make sure I understood that I'd made a terrible bargain. In her eyes Ari was such a horrible person, and then, when her dream came true and Ari threw me out, what does my mother do? She blames me, says I must have done something wrong, or he wouldn't have left me. Ari falls in love with another woman, and she blames me."

"What did she blame you for?"

"She said that I don't know how to hold on to a man, because if I did, the Frenchwoman wouldn't have taken him. But in the same breath she said I should send flowers to the Frenchwoman, because thanks to her I got rid of the good-for-nothing."

"It seems to me," the doctor reflected, "that she cares about you a lot."

"That's what drives me crazy. After spitting fire and brimstone at me, she changes her skin and becomes soft and compassionate and deluges me with the love she was always so stingy with before."

"And the more she softened, the tougher you became."

In the hospital after I tried to slit my wrists, the worse I got, the more she was there for me. When she kissed my cheek, I turned away, but she just kissed the other cheek. For the first time I saw tears in my mother's eyes that weren't for her dead child but for me, her living child. Strange, but it was during this horrible year, when I felt I was lost in an endless tunnel, that my mother was there for me, reaching for me and pulling me out. Instead of telling the doctor all this, I stayed silent, and he, tamping down his pipe, went on.

"The two of you must talk." He was insistent. "You think you're closer to your father, but the deep connection is with your mother, and until you unravel the complications, you'll remain stuck. Until you understand the riddle of your mother's life, you won't understand the riddle of your own, so I'm asking you to find the courage to talk to her; otherwise there's no point in your coming here."

I looked over at the clock on his desk and saw that I was out of time.

I walked along the path leading to the street when suddenly I was in front of my rescuer again, the surfer from Gordon Beach.

"Third time, ice cream," he said, smiling, using the expression for when you keep bumping into someone by chance.

I smiled back, convinced it wasn't a coincidence.

"Are you following me?" I asked him.

"Maybe you're following me . . ."

"No, seriously . . ."

"Seriously. I think my appointment is right after yours. He tries to make sure his patients don't meet, but I'm a few minutes early today."

"And the last time?"

"I was a few minutes late."

"Okay, I don't get the math. When do we have ice cream?"

"You tell me."

"Who's paying?"

"I think you are."

"Okay, so I get to choose where."

"Obviously."

"Montana."

"No . . ."

"It's the closest to where I live. So I can make a quick getaway if I'm bored," I laughed.

"Okay, Montana. So in exactly one hour and five minutes."

"There's no way you can get to Montana in five minutes."

"Try me. I have a Vespa, remember?" he said, disappearing through the glass doors. Savoring the short banter we'd exchanged, I realized I'd just made a date in an hour and five minutes. What would I do till then? Go home? Change? Wash my hair? I wouldn't want him to think that I'd made a special effort for him. And why should I? He'd already seen me at one of the worst points of my life. Good Lord, he'd seen me naked, shivering, and confused. How could I have agreed to meet him? I'd forgotten how to have a casual conversation with a guy. It'd been such a long time since anyone was interested in me . . . and anyway, who said he was interested in me? Maybe he was just being nice because he'd rescued me from the sea. I decided I wouldn't go to Montana; I had no reason to meet a man I didn't even know. I would go home, go straight into my room, and lock the door. I had a goal: I had to talk to Lily, a challenge like trying to climb Everest. I wasn't about to let ice cream with some guy distract me from my purpose. I didn't have time to deal with earth-shattering questions like how I looked and what I should wear and how to hide the blush that would creep up my neck and over my face when I met him.

No, I wouldn't go home, I decided, finding some courage inside me. I would meet him, and what would be would be. I walked all the way down Gordon Street to the water and then along the beach until I reached Gordon Pool, right on the sea. On the weekends my school friends used to go there and swim in the seawater pool. I asked my father if I could go, too, but Lily interrupted and said, "You think your father robbed a bank? You go to the beach. The beach is free." So Gordon Beach had become my second home.

I climbed past the hills of gravel to Keren Kayemet Boulevard, walked by the mansion that faced the prime minister's home. I'd invented an entire life for myself in that beautiful house, light-years away from my own. I'd imagined being surrounded by friends and family against a background of happiness and joy, not the seesaw of Lily's screams and stormy silences. Now, like the former prime minister, the mansion was also gone, replaced by a four-story residential building. I crossed Ben Yehuda Street and continued along the boulevard until I reached what everyone called "Paula's store," at the corner of Graetz Street, because Paula Ben-Gurion, the prime minister's wife, had liked to shop at the modest corner store herself.

I went inside and got a roll with sliced cheese and olives, then ate it slowly on one of the benches along the boulevard. If there was one thing I'd learned from Lily, it was to never go to an important meeting on an empty stomach. My stomach rumbled with nervousness, and I couldn't eat another bite. I picked apart the soft white roll, scattering pieces for the birds, who swooped down from the treetops and made a beeline for the crumbs. At least the nerves I was experiencing had led to a good deed.

As I sat on that bench, it hit me. It was in this very area, near the grocery store, that it had all started with Ari.

I was standing by the window in my childhood bedroom, watching the raging world. Boats in the distance were being tossed on the waves. A ferocious wind had torn the asbestos roof from the divers' club and hurled it out to sea like a wild child in the throes of a tantrum flinging away a toy. There were hardly any people in the streets, and the few passersby caught in the storm tried in vain to shelter beneath store awnings.

"For thirty years," came the voice of the radio announcer, "there hasn't been a winter like this in Tel Aviv." I was fascinated by the manifestations of the weather. The flash of lightning followed closely by a thunderclap delighted me as though I were a child watching a magic show. I was suffused with joy. I adored the change of seasons, the stormy winter that arrived after a steaming, humid summer of heat waves brought to the city on the hot desert winds, and more than anything I loved the smell of the air washed clean by the rain, as though God had showered the city and granted it a new beginning.

My father was at the store, and my mother, even on a day like this, had gone off to who knew where. I luxuriated in the silence. Though in my childhood, the quietness of the empty house in my parents' absence had frightened me, as I'd grown older, I'd learned to appreciate and even to look forward to it. It was the only time when I could relax, because the constant tension Lily carried vanished with her the moment she was out the door.

An impulse sent me out into the rainy, windswept street. I chose my high-heeled boots, put on my coat, pulled a hat over my curls, grabbed an umbrella from the stand, and left the apartment. The raging wind almost blew me back. The crashing waves sounded louder than ever; the noise was deafening. I inhaled the cool, clean air and started to walk. The wind was behind me, and it pushed me up the empty street. The store doors were shut, and the salespeople sat glumly behind counters, knowing that in weather like this no one would be crazy enough to brave the elements. The cafés were empty, and the chairs usually set up on the sidewalk were stacked on the tables. The only place with side-walk seating left was the artists' café, Kassit. I sat under the awning and looked out at the rainy world. I watched a man cross the street with a dancer's bouncing step, ignoring the rain and the blaring horns of the passing cars. He sat down, without asking permission, in the chair next to mine. Marcel, the elderly waiter, came over and in his French accent asked, "What can I get you, sir?" and sir ordered a Turkish coffee in a small cup with a glass of water. He took a cigarette from the pack of Nelsons he'd put on the small round table we were sharing, lit it with a gold Ronson lighter, and sent smoke rings drifting out into the cold expanse of air. From the corner of my eye I imagined them freezing in place, but I deliberately fixed my gaze on the **BANK DISCOUNT** sign across the street. The Turkish coffee arrived with the water for the man, and although I hadn't ordered anything, I received a mug of hot chocolate. The waiter patted my head and said, "Why are you sitting outside in the rain, my lovely?" I smiled at him, and he sighed and quickly ducked back inside.

The first time I'd gone to Café Kassit, I'd been with other students from the literature department, peeking with mingled curiosity and awe at Alterman and Shlonsky, Chalfi, and Avot Yeshurun, our most admired poets, who were regulars there. Later I'd become accustomed to sitting at the café by myself, sometimes with a book of poetry and sometimes alone, like now, letting my thoughts drift.

The old French waiter had always treated me like a kind grandfather would and paid special attention to me. I didn't know what I'd done to deserve Marcel's affection, but I was delighted to adopt him. I was in my early twenties, and even though my parents' home was walking distance away, I felt alone. It was pleasant to go to Kassit every day, order a hot chocolate and a melted cheese on toast, and be served by the smiling Marcel.

The man who sat with me took slow sips of his coffee. I stole a glance at him. He had a beautiful profile, his dark, curly hair reached his shoulders, his nose was straight and suited his strong, expressive face, and a couple of days of stubble adorned his jaw. He was thin, wearing jeans tucked into cowboy boots and a black leather jacket, hiding his eyes behind dark Lennon glasses. He encircled his coffee with two fingers as if at any moment it might be snatched away. The Nelson was held between his lips at the corner of his mouth, and he sucked at it with obvious pleasure.

Although we were sitting at the same table, we didn't exchange a word. While my eyes occasionally flitted in his direction, he looked out at the street and never once looked at me.

I was hyperaware of the strange man sitting next to me. My heart pounded, and just the thought that I was attracted to him brought a blush to my cheeks. I'd never seen him before and didn't understand what about him was making me feel this way. As usual, I started to daydream. *He takes me in his arms, holds me tight, drags me to his bed, tears off my clothes, and . . .* I spilled my hot chocolate onto his jeans. Stammering apologies, I took a napkin and tried to wipe the stain off his pants, and I brushed his crotch. He looked at me in amazement, removed his glasses, and said in a quiet, steady voice, "What are you doing?"

My hand froze in the air. I stared at him wide eyed. *God,* I thought, *he has the darkest eyes I've ever seen in my life.* My breath caught in my throat. He got up, dropped a few coins on the table, and left. He had such a cute ass. I couldn't believe the thoughts I was having as I noticed how well he filled out his jeans. I watched him walk toward Keren Kayemet Boulevard, and unthinkingly, I stood, and without paying for my drink, I ran after him. The rain was still falling. I caught up with him at the corner of Gordon Street while he waited for the light to change. I stood a few steps behind him. He didn't notice me. When the light turned green, he crossed, and I was right behind him. There was a spring in his step, and he never looked around, focused his gaze straight ahead, and I followed, as if in all the world there were only us, him and me, and the rain. When he stopped at a kiosk to buy a pack of cigarettes, I pretended to examine the window of a new boutique, where music was blaring. The door was closed to keep out the storm, but the lyrics to Shocking Blue's hit single trickled into the rain, and I could hear the band belting out its song about Venus, fire, and desire. Pushing the cigarette pack into his back pocket, he continued to bounce along the street, and I smiled to myself. He veered left at Keren Kayemet Boulevard toward the sea, and I was still in pursuit. At Paula's grocery store he turned toward Ranak Street, and when he reached the steps to

Ben Yehuda Street, he made an abrupt turn and asked, "What do you want?"

I couldn't speak. I'd followed him like a cat in heat. The scent of his aftershave assailed my nostrils, and I could smell his sweat. I stared at him with longing, and all words escaped me.

He took a step toward me. *Run,* I screamed silently to myself. *Run!* But my legs remained planted on the asphalt, and he looked at me, shrugged, and went into a building. I followed him, hearing his steps, the clinking of his keys, a door opening and slamming shut. I climbed until I reached a brown door. A white slip of paper was tacked under the peephole, and it contained one word—*Ari.*

As though in a trance, I stared at the letters of his name, murmuring them to myself, "Ari," able to feel him on the other side of the door, feel his eyes through the peephole, undressing me. I placed my lips there, and at that moment the door opened, and I fell into him.

He steadied me. His grasp was strong; his hands were strong.

"Who are you? What do you want?" In his eyes I saw a mixture of curiosity and irritation and just maybe the tiniest hint of amusement at the drenched girl who'd followed him.

I didn't say anything.

"Lost your voice?"

I wanted to tell him I didn't know what I wanted or why I was following him, couldn't remember my name. But all I said was, "Ari."

He stared at me, dumbfounded. "Do we know each other? Come in," he said, closing the door behind me. A sour smell assailed my nostrils. A big, unmade bed took up most of the space, covered by a tousled blanket tangled with a sheet that had once been white and two pillows with mismatched pillowcases. There was a low table spread with a wrinkled green velvet cloth, filthy coffee mugs, and overflowing ashtrays everywhere. The shabby burgundy couch held an open copy of Hermann Hesse's *Steppenwolf.* On a desk like the one in my bedroom, attached to an overflowing bookshelf, were a disorganized pile of papers and a Hermes Baby typewriter. A bare bulb hung on a wire from the ceiling, illuminating the pitiful room.

"Sit," he told me, and I sat on the bed, as if there were no other place for me in the world. He put on a Blood, Sweat & Tears album. The song "I Love You More Than You'll Ever Know" started to play, and he sat on the burgundy couch. He placed the album cover on his knees, opened a square wooden box on the table, and pulled out a lump of hashish.

I watched him, fascinated, from my spot on his bed, watched his quick fingers expertly rolling the joint. He heated the hash with a lighter, crumbled it, mixed it with some tobacco inside one of his Nelsons, and used his long tongue to dampen the paper and his teeth to pull out the filter.

Ari lit the joint and inhaled the smoke as though taking his final breath, wrapping his lips around it and sucking. He held the joint to me, but I didn't know how to hold it. I'd never smoked one before. In the end I held it like a cigarette. I took a drag, the smoke scorched my throat, and almost choking, I started to cough. He sat beside me and took the joint from my hand. Wordlessly he motioned for me to move my head forward and suck. His nearness and the hash made me dizzy. Again and again I lowered my head to the joint between his fingers, inhaling and exhaling. We found our rhythm, taking turns to inhale, first me, then him. My head spinning, I fell back onto the bed, my feet still touching the floor. "Nothing left," he said and stubbed it out in the ashtray.

I closed my eyes. *Let him come to me*, I wished. *Let him take me*. I felt a pleasant tingling between my legs, and my nipples stiffened and poked into my shirt as though threatening to break through. My mouth was dry, and I licked my lips, slowly and sensuously like a seductive woman, not like myself. I wanted him like I had never before wanted any man. I wanted him so badly a warm wetness started to spread between my legs. My eyes still closed, I imagined him watching me, seeing what I wanted. I wanted him to touch me, to take me. My heart pounded. I had no idea who he was, but I knew that in another minute he would be inside me, between my legs, in my mouth. I felt him close to me, took a deep breath, ready for him, and then heard his voice: "Go home now."

I opened my eyes. He was sitting with his back to me at his desk, leaning over his papers.

"Go home," he repeated.

I didn't say a word.

"Are you deaf?" he asked, still not turning around. "I want to be alone."

I struggled to my feet, straightened my damp clothing, not saying that I was ready to stay there always, forever. I ignored my wet underwear, my painful nipples. With the last vestige of my self-respect, I smoothed my hair and moved toward the door. I was holding the handle, wondering if I would ever see him again, when he finally turned his dark eyes toward me. "So what's your name?"

I wanted to tell him Eliya, but instead I whispered "Lily" and closed the door behind me.

A spray of water descended on me. "Idiot!" I burst out. There wasn't a cloud in the sky, but a passing car had driven through a puddle.

The driver stuck his head out the window. "Hey, sorry, babe."

"'Babe,' your mother!" I shouted back, giving him the finger, and he stepped on the gas and was gone.

My white sleeveless top and jeans were wet, and so was the bench. I moved to another. This must be an unlucky spot for me, I thought. On the day I'd met Ari, I'd been soaked to the skin, not because of a careless driver but because of that powerful storm. *Lily,* I remembered, blushing even after all this time. What the hell had made me tell him my name was Lily? Years later Ari would say, "You've always been screwed up; otherwise why would you choose your mother's name?"

That was when he'd loved me, and I'd snuggled into him. "I wanted you to never be able to find me."

"That's why you chased me all over Tel Aviv?"

"I wanted to find you, not for you to find me," I replied in a baby voice, and he held me, grounding me in our double bed, and said, "What luck, Lily, that you found me!"

"Stop," I laughed. "It's sick. You're inside me, and you call me Lily? It's incestuous."

"Lily." He pushed deeper inside me, hard. "You brought it on yourself."

I didn't understand then how much Ari was turned on by these games of cat and mouse, how much reality bored him. I didn't know he would chase me away just because he knew I would come back, just as I didn't realize I'd walked right into one of those power games he so enjoyed that were meant to subdue me. From the moment I'd closed the door behind me, he'd known I'd be back.

When I woke the next morning still dressed in yesterday's clothes, I had a bad taste in my mouth. "The taste of a graveyard," Ari would call it a week later, when he woke in the middle of the night for another cigarette. My mascara had run, smudging underneath my eyes, and my hair was a mess.

I prayed that my father had switched on the water boiler before he'd gone to work and left some hot water and that my mother, who spent her mornings in the bedroom, staring out over the Yarkon River, hadn't come out yet. The last thing I wanted was to have her start interrogating me.

My first prayer was answered—there was hot water. I stood under the warm stream for a long time. But after only a few minutes my mother started pounding on the door. "Eliya," she shouted, "come out this instant. How much time can you spend in the shower? You could make the desert bloom with all the water you're wasting."

I ignored her. I needed a serious shower to wash away the humiliation I'd felt when Ari had kicked me out, to shed my thin skin and grow a thicker layer of protection. But my mother wouldn't let up. "Open that door or I'll break it down!" she shouted.

I turned off the water, and a terrifying silence filled the apartment. I could hear rain pouring for the second day, crashing on the treetops and the sidewalk. The broken wooden shutter on the kitchen window banged over and over. I dried myself off with a towel that had seen better days and sneaked into my room. The thought of my mother in an ill temper was too much to bear. I decided to get dressed and go out.

I put on brown corduroy pants and a black sweater and threw on the sheepskin coat I'd bought at the Jaffa flea market, and without coffee or breakfast or saying goodbye to my mother, I went out into the rain.

The cold penetrated to my bones despite the warm coat. I shoved my hands into my pockets and walked along Dizengoff Street. I saw him at Keren Kayemet Boulevard wearing jeans and a black leather coat, and before I knew it, I was following him. The rain was still falling, and my hair was plastered to my head; I'd forgotten my umbrella at Kassit the day before. Ari walked with one hand in his pocket, the other holding a cigarette, which he flicked onto the sidewalk and ground under the tip of his shoe before immediately lighting a fresh one. I followed him blindly, as though I were pulled toward him by a length of painful barbed wire, as though I had no control over my actions. Today's rain was gentler; there were more people in the streets, and some stores had their doors open. The roads were full of cars splashing water everywhere, and Ari walked lightly on the balls of his feet, as though the surrounding commotion had nothing to do with him. I tried desperately to keep up with him. When he reached Gordon Street, he didn't wait for the light to change but just kept walking, and I hurried after him. A car stopped with a screech of brakes, and I fell. The driver rushed over to me. Ari turned, and I saw the surprise in his face as he came over and asked, "Are you okay?"

I nodded.

The shocked driver said, "I don't know what happened. I had a green light, and then she was suddenly there. It's a miracle I didn't kill her."

"It's fine. She's just shaken," said Ari evenly. "Are you okay, Lily?"

Lily? I wondered, and then I remembered.

I nodded. I couldn't speak.

He supported me and helped me up.

"She's fine," he told the driver, and then he asked me, "Can you walk?"

"Yes," I whispered.

"You should take her to the hospital. Sometimes there's an internal injury, and you can't tell," said a woman who had no idea how right she was. I didn't know then how deep and internal the damage was.

Paris

The pendulum clock on the east wall of the café chimed midnight. My ashtray was filled with cigarette butts. I asked for the bill and left a generous tip, put on both the sweaters and the long wool coat, wound my scarf around my neck, put on my hat, and set out into the familiar foreign street. I was no longer the Eliya I'd been, even if I didn't know who I was now.

The Latin Quarter was deserted in the drizzle. I took a deep breath, reveling in the good smell of the rain, and suddenly I was brimful of happiness. I felt like a little girl in new rubber boots jumping in puddles. The wild wind earlier in the evening had turned my cheap umbrella inside out, but now the heavy downpour had become a soft drizzle, and I darted my tongue out to catch the drops sliding from my nose.

A stream of trumpet from a jazz club's open door shattered the night, playing an Armstrong-esque version of "La Vie en Rose." I stopped to listen.

A huge Black man stood in the entrance, rubbing his hands together for warmth.

"Would you like to come in, *mademoiselle?*" he called across the narrow street.

"*Non, merci,*" I replied with a smile and stayed where I was. He continued to call in a stream of French that I barely understood, but from his body language I guessed he was trying to persuade me to come inside. Why not, I thought. I could add it to the list of things I'd never done before, like flying to another country where no one was waiting for me, staying alone at a hotel, and now going to a jazz club in the middle of the night.

While I stood there trying to decide, the man moved aside for a couple that was ascending from the cellar club.

I recognized him immediately. It was Ari, in his worn leather coat and the gray-and-green woolen scarf I'd knitted, with his arm around a young woman who wasn't Sophie. This woman, whose body was pressed against Ari's, was taller than him, with dark hair in a short, boyish cut.

I watched Ari and the woman as they receded down the street without glancing in my direction. Was I imagining it? No, that was definitely Ari, the short torso, the head tilted to the side, the spring in his step. Yes, it was him, my once-upon-a-time love. His big hands moving in wide arcs as he talked, his windblown curls I had once adored.

Of all the clubs in Paris, why had I come to this one? And at the precise moment he was leaving? How had I seen him in Paris tonight, without planning to? As though we were in a saccharine 1950s Hollywood movie. I watched him hidden in the shadows.

And I didn't run away, nor did I run after him. And the sky didn't fall, nor did the earth crack open. I saw Ari, and I didn't feel a thing.

The man at the door again invited me in, but I went back the way I'd come, toward my hotel on Rue Jacob. The room there was more than I could afford, but I paid because of the location. I could see Ari's apartment from my hotel window. Dr. Kaminsky had instructed me to visit my past, the location of the wound. And so I proceeded, one step at a time, along my personal Via Dolorosa, stopping at every station, carrying my life's cross on my narrow shoulders.

When I woke in my hotel room, I saw it was one in the afternoon. I'd slept for twelve hours straight.

I had no time to waste. I had to complete the mission that had brought me to Paris, the toughest homework Kaminsky had given me yet. I had to confront Ari.

When Kaminsky had told me that I had to go to Paris, I'd thought he'd lost his mind. When he insisted I had to walk the same streets and sit in the café where Ari had cut me out of his life, and that under no circumstances was I to come back before I'd faced Ari, I told him to go to hell. Anything, I told him, I was willing to do anything, but I couldn't confront Ari. Because if I met Ari face-to-face, I would kill someone. Either him or myself.

"You aren't going to kill anyone," Kaminsky responded calmly, ignoring my turmoil and the fact that I was pacing in his office like a caged beast. "The only thing you're going to kill is the constant pain you feel."

"I won't be able to take it. It hurts too much."

"You're much stronger than you think you are. Go to Paris, Eliya, and come back a new woman."

So here I was, looking at my face in the magnifying mirror in the hotel bathroom as though I were being revealed to myself for the first time. I saw tiny lines around my lips and tiny, faint wrinkles etched into my forehead. They were the ravages of time, I told myself, of lost time when I hadn't seen myself, when I'd been invisible to myself, moving through the world with no substance, like wind.

As if someone had wiped the fog off some invisible glasses, I saw everything clearly and in sharp focus, most of all myself. I knew I wouldn't return to Café la Rivière, and I wouldn't waste time finding or confronting Ari.

Dr. Kaminsky had been right when he'd said I would feel like a new woman after I saw him, but it turned out I didn't need to confront him to understand why I'd almost killed myself. It wasn't Ari; it was me. Ari didn't matter. He was who he was, and he'd left my life just as he'd come into it. I didn't need to try to piece together the fragments of the life Ari had shattered. In any case, that rubble had turned to dust. My mother was right. I should thank Ari; I should send flowers to his first French lover and maybe also to his new one.

I breathed deeply. After catching a glimpse of him and not falling apart, I knew his time was past.

I felt light as a feather, as though all at once a heavy burden had been lifted from my shoulders. I pulled out my suitcase and began to pack.

I had used money my father didn't have to pay in advance for three days at the hotel, but after one day and night, I didn't need to stay in Paris one moment longer. My mission was accomplished, and I was going home. As I closed my eyes and leaned back in my seat on the plane, for the first time in a long time, I didn't feel heartsore.

But there was one thing the doctor had instructed me to do, and I hadn't had the courage to follow through. I still had to talk to Lily.

I pressed my nose to the window as the plane rose above the clouds, and I finally understood what Kaminsky had been trying to explain for so long. If I could penetrate Lily's barricade, if I could reach her, maybe I could solve the riddle of her life, and if I could solve the riddle of her life, maybe I would understand my own.

I closed my eyes and slept like a baby until the plane coasted to a stop in Tel Aviv.

Shaul

"How long is this going to go on?" Lily was furious. "Your daughter spins us like a top. Every day she wakes up with a new crazy idea, and you finance all her whims. One day she gets married, and the next she gets divorced. One day she goes to Paris; the next she goes crazy and tries to kill herself and practically kills us too. Then she goes to Kaminsky, who, if you want my opinion, is more of a thief than a psychologist. For the money he takes per hour, you can go on vacation for a week, and he fills her head with nonsense, and then she goes to Paris again and comes back again. When will it end? When? At this rate you're going to have to send me to Kaminsky as well!"

"Why are you so angry, Lily?" Shaul rose from the sofa and went over to the doorway to kiss his wife's cheek. He took her heavy bag from her hand and placed it beside her brown leather purse, helped with her coat, and hung it next to his. "You get mad at the moon and the stars, Lily. It's a waste of energy. Didn't you notice that our girl returned from Paris with a smile on her face? So maybe it was worth investing the money in Kaminsky. Remember how she came back last time? Like a ghost, half-dead. And look at her this time—the color is back in her cheeks, and today she even told me she isn't going to Kaminsky any-more, so why are you so upset?"

Lily sat down on the sofa, clearly still annoyed. She didn't ask Shaul about his day, and so she had no idea how few customers had come into the store and how deeply Shaul felt the absence of his father, who had reached the age at which he had stopped coming to work. She never asked and he never confided in her, choosing to spare her his worries about their livelihood.

"You're like a kite, Shaul, going wherever the wind takes you. It's a good thing you have me to bring you down to earth. You think you're helping her? You're not. Life is hard, and you're always trying to make things easier for her. But you won't be here forever; one day you'll be gone, and then what? What will she do when her daddy isn't there to take care of her?"

"But Lily, my dear, don't you see that Eliya's better? Why aren't you happy?"

"If you don't get happy, you don't get disappointed," she answered testily. "Enough, I have a headache from this conversation. Get me a glass of water."

Shaul went to bring the water. What else could he do? He was always so torn between the two women in his life. On one side abusive Lily, on the other angry Eliya. Eliya had returned from Paris seeking a truce, but she'd been met by an attack that had sent her flying out the front door. When Lily came home, Eliya would leave the house.

When she returned from Paris, Shaul and Lily were waiting for her at the airport. He scrutinized all the travelers, searching for the familiar, beloved face of his child. Even Lily seemed to be excited. Finally Eliya appeared, small and thin, wearing jeans and an oversize coat. "Elikush!" he shouted, waving frantically until she saw them. He examined her face apprehensively to see if anything had changed. To his surprise his daughter was grinning from ear to ear. "She's okay," he said to Lily. "The child is okay."

"Thank God," Lily murmured. "My heart almost stopped beating until she came out."

Eliya flew toward them and hugged her father as she hadn't since she was a little girl. His heart leaped with joy, and he gathered her in his arms. And now his daughter was hugging him as though she'd never grown up, and he whispered to her, "My girl, how wonderful that you've come home."

When Eliya turned to embrace her mother, Shaul saw Lily stiffen, and his anger flared, but he swallowed his fury as always and didn't say a word. He wouldn't allow anything to taint his happiest day in two years. The child had returned with a smile, and that was what mattered.

At home, Eliya told him she'd seen Ari by chance, though he hadn't noticed her, with his arm around a woman a head taller than him, and she hadn't felt a thing. She'd decided to give him a divorce, and it didn't cause her any pain. On the contrary, it had set her free.

When he returned with her glass of water, he found Lily watching television, having seemingly completely forgotten the argument they'd just had. He sat down next to her and put his arm around her shoulders.

He was exhausted after another long day at work, another day when he'd managed to sell only a very few of the pieces on display at the store. The general mood in the aftermath of the 1973 Yom Kippur War was different from the euphoria that had followed the Six-Day War in 1967. Then, the humility had been gone, and the nouveau riche had been born. Contractors had become wealthy overnight building the Bar Lev Line, the chain of fortifications along the eastern bank of the Suez Canal, when Israel had occupied the Egyptian Sinai Peninsula. A glittering society emerged, seeking the good life and striving for a local version of hedonism.

Even the small jewelry store profited from the sudden prosperity, which meant more women were buying jewelry. He and his father could barely meet the demand. And Shaul was also carried away by the possibilities of the good life. He bought his first automobile, a Simca, and he and Lily took a holiday at the Carlton Hotel in the northern coastal city of Nahariya. He was so swept away by the prosperity that, despite his father's resistance, he agreed to sell on credit. But almost overnight the euphoria was replaced by economic anxiety, and as the situation worsened, his clients' debts increased. Decent people returned the jewelry and apologized that they couldn't make their payments, but some simply vanished, leaving only their names and the amounts they owed in his neat hand in a black notebook. He had no choice. He took back the jewelry and absorbed the losses. He thought about closing. It wasn't only him; the whole country was licking its wounds. *Will the last person to leave please turn off the lights* was scrawled on the walls of the buildings. Who was buying jewelry when the situation was so dire? Again the store emptied of customers. He spent his dull days waiting to lock the doors and go home and put on his pajamas.

He was tired, troubled about work, troubled about Eliya, troubled about Lily. If he'd had the courage, he would have left them both, jumped on the next plane, and fled to his brother in America, as far away as he could get from his miserable life.

Eliya

There are days when the world is bright as crystal. When the sea is a deep blue and the sun scatters it with drops of gold. I sat on the sand on Gordon Beach and gave myself over to the sweetness of the silence, thankful for the ripples of the waves and the smell of salt and seaweed lingering in the air. After the big storm comes tranquility, and I felt as though I'd returned to a safe haven, as though I'd come home.

Even Dr. Kaminsky couldn't divert me from my decision. He berated me like an old hen when I told him I'd seen Ari at a jazz club, and not only had I not talked to him, I'd decided I didn't need to try to find him again. "You didn't follow my instructions," he reprimanded me. "You had explicit instructions. I told you to go back step by step over what almost led you to kill yourself. It's irresponsible for you to sweep it under the rug."

"I'm not sweeping anything under the rug," I answered him quietly. "There's no point in sweeping dust that disappears in the wind."

"Eliya, you're running away. Either you're a coward or you're experiencing temporary euphoria, and I really think you're making a terrible mistake."

"I threw all my fears into the Seine when I saw Ari with his latest girlfriend."

"You're talking nonsense!" Kaminsky leaped from his chair. "You haven't been miraculously cured, and you can't stop treatment before it's over. You're hurting yourself. I'm responsible for you; I can't allow this."

"You want to send me back to Paris?"

"I would send you," he answered with utmost seriousness, ignoring the sarcasm in my voice, "if it wasn't so expensive. Meanwhile, I'll decide how to continue your treatment."

I rose and told him dryly that I'd signed the divorce papers the moment I'd landed. I didn't stay long enough to see his reaction.

The sun, an enormous golden ball of fire, already slanted westward as I left Dr. Kaminsky's office. I sat on the beach and stared straight into the sun and knew, as surely as the sun sank into the sea, that I wouldn't be going back to Dr. Kaminsky. The moment I'd signed the divorce papers, it had been clear I was also divorcing the doctor and his exaggerated hold on my life. What he had to give I had already taken. I didn't need the rest. I knew exactly what I had to do. I would take my time and enjoy to the fullest the lightness and the joy I felt, which, for the first time, didn't revolve around anyone but me. I was responsible for my happiness, not Ari or anyone else. I knew I had to see all the goodness and all the beauty I'd missed during the years I'd been Ari's clinging little wife. I vowed that as often as possible I would return to the sea I loved so much, that I would always be surrounded by love. I felt like I was floating in a sea of love, as though its waves were lapping softly all around me. The sea loved me and my father loved me, and my mother, well, I'd teach my mother to love me, but first I had to teach myself to love my mother. Even if she pushed my love away, even if she turned herself into a porcupine every time I touched her. Suddenly it was clear to me. To love myself I first had to love my mother, the one and only impossible mother I had, Lily.

Eldad

For several days now he had been watching her from up in the life-guard's tower, which was shuttered for the winter. He watched as she sat down on the sand and took off her shoes. Even on the coldest days she took off her socks, too, and pushed her feet into the sand up to her ankles.

He saw her from behind, her flowing auburn hair cascading over her shoulders, always wearing the same red coat and faded jeans, sand-colored Palladium shoes, and a turquoise wool scarf wound around her neck. Her knapsack always looked stuffed and heavy, as though she was ready to jump on a train or a plane and take off at a moment's notice.

Her gaze never shifted from the sky as it filled with bewitching shades of sunset, navy, pink, and gold. And when the colors faded into darkness and the beach had emptied of people, she would pull on her socks, slip into her shoes, and rise from the sand lithe as a ballerina.

So many times he had wanted to go to her and ask why she hadn't met him at Montana that day, why she had left him there waiting for her like an idiot, holding two ice creams that melted down his wrists. He couldn't know that after the trauma she had experienced in her relationship with Ari, Eliya was terrified of embarking on a new relationship. He had wanted to surprise her and wait for her with the ice cream, thought it would be romantic. But when it had pooled in a puddle at his feet, he'd had to accept that she wasn't coming.

The disappointment caught him by surprise. For a long time his heart had been sealed off to emotions, and he couldn't remember when he had last met a woman he really liked. He didn't pursue women, didn't feel attracted to anyone, didn't go on dates. When he felt the need for sex, he would go to Sisi on Yirmiyahu Street. The place was always packed, and it was never difficult to pick up one of the girls who crowded around the bar.

Most of the time he was satisfied with a quickie in the courtyard behind the pub or in one of the boats on the banks of the nearby Yarkon River. On rare occasions he would accept an invitation from one of the girls to go to her place, but as soon as they were done, he made a fast getaway back to his room. He never shared his own bed with anyone, never met the same woman twice, and almost never remembered the faces of the women he was with.

It was different with her. When he had helped her off the surfboard on the beach, for the split second when he saw her naked, shaking with cold and dripping wet, looking at him with her piercing eyes, something flickered inside him that he'd thought had been extinguished for good. Although he quickly averted his gaze, her image stayed with him, and for the first time in a long time he felt something.

Eldad had fled from the beach that day, frightened by the reawakened vitality, and of course he had made no effort to get to know her, nor dared to imagine that he might see her again. He had accepted that he wasn't capable of opening his heart to another human being, but in the days after their unusual encounter, he couldn't get her out of his mind. He had no idea how to even begin to look for her, to learn her name or discover where she lived. How would he ever find her in the city of Tel Aviv, especially now that it was winter and few people came to the beach?

To stop thinking about her, he decided to go to Sisi. He and Ilan were childhood friends, had grown up in the same neighborhood, which sprawled from King George along HaNevi'im, Shlomo HaMelech, and

Frishman. They both went to the Dvora Kindergarten on Zamenhof Street, then to the Carmel School on HaNevi'im Street, and from there to the same high school. They hung out on the same street corners, played board games and soccer, and worshipped the Tel Aviv basketball star Ofer Eshed. They went to the same parties, dated the same girls, ate at the hamburger joint known as the California, which was owned by peace activist Abie Nathan, and spent the long Tel Aviv summers on Gordon Beach, mostly in the water on their surfboards, or sailing boats on the Yarkon River from the Pe'er Cinema to the centuries-old Sheva Tahanot flour mills and back again. They stripped and sat under the cascade of water gushing at the foot of the Reading Power Station and ate ice cream at Montana.

Young, carefree, and beautiful, they had shared an idyllic Tel Aviv childhood. Their adolescence was wild and wonderful. They were conscripted together, were sent to the Paratroopers Brigade together, and were together when they earned their wings and their maroon berets. Together they spun big dreams about what they would do once they had completed their mandatory army service. They would travel to Amsterdam, where they would buy an old Volkswagen minibus, paint it in psychedelic colors, and then set off to explore every inch of Europe. They would drive to London, continue to Scotland and maybe Ireland, cross the Channel from Dover to Calais, and end up in Paris. They stayed up nights making plans, charted their route on maps, and were as excited as small children about their journey, after which they would settle down and start to live their real lives and build their futures. Ilan was going to be an engineer like his dad, and Eldad wanted to study architecture. They would share an apartment in the Hadar neighborhood near the Technion–Israel Institute of Technology and live it up in Haifa like they had reveled in all that Tel Aviv had to offer.

And then came the war, and everything was turned upside down. Their lives changed, and their plans went up in smoke, and nothing that came afterward was like it had been before. Ilan wasn't going to become an engineer, and Eldad wouldn't study architecture. Ilan was badly wounded and lost his left eye. After almost a year in the hospital, he decided that life was too short to waste in the respectable profession his father had chosen for him, and he opened a pub on Yirmiyahu Street and named it Sisi, in memory of their commander, Yossi, whose nickname that was. He'd died in an accursed battle of that accursed war.

Although Eldad appeared unscathed on the surface, he was badly damaged. His friends had died like flies. Though not a hair on his head had been harmed, his soul was scarred, and a year later he still felt lost and had no idea what he wanted to do with his life.

When Ilan was released from the hospital with a black patch over his eye, they moved in together and shared an apartment on HaYarkon Street. Ilan's parents financed Sisi, and although they weren't thrilled at his choosing a pub over an engineering degree from the Technion, they took comfort in the fact that their son was alive and moving on with his life.

The war had changed Eldad. The young, charismatic man who had always been at the center of everything had become shy, introverted, and withdrawn. Eldad the superb athlete, who fell in love easily and was easy to fall in love with, who had the craziest ideas for the best times, whose laughter was contagious, had completely shut down. Even his sparkling blue eyes, which had always glimmered with mischief, seemed faded. Ilan hadn't heard him laugh even once since the war.

When Eldad's parents urged him to register at the Technion as he had planned to do before his army service, he told them that he wouldn't go to study in Haifa without Ilan. The thought of leaving Tel Aviv and being alone in a strange city appalled him. He preferred to remain in a safe, familiar place near his best friend. But when Ilan asked Eldad to join him at the pub as a partner, he refused. "I don't have any money, and I'm not going to take any from my parents. They're so disappointed that I'm not going to university."

"I didn't ask you for money."

"What kind of a partner would I be if I didn't invest in the business?"

"Invest by working. When we start making a profit, you can pay me back."

"Out of the question!"

"So come and work as a bartender."

"I can't imagine doing something that would keep me trapped in an enclosed space for even a few hours. I need the sea, the open air."

Ilan was worried about his friend. "At least come to the pub tonight. You've always attracted the ladies, and I need that kind of atmosphere," he said, even though he knew that these days Eldad had the opposite effect. His silent, brooding presence, his gloom, and his sadness did nothing to attract women.

Eldad couldn't pull himself out of the low place he inhabited. Despite his closeness to Ilan, he felt lonely. He spent most nights alone in their apartment, rolling joints, getting high, and listening to music, afraid to fall asleep and wake up terrified by the images from the war that pursued him in his dreams. He would wait up until four in the morning, when Ilan came back from the pub, and only then, when he heard the door click shut, would he let go and fall asleep.

He had to find a job. How much longer could he sponge off his parents? How much longer until his pride wouldn't allow him to drink on Ilan's tab at the pub? And still he couldn't bring himself to go to a single job interview. The only place he felt calm was by the sea. Ilan tried to convince him to become a lifeguard. "Just do the course," he urged him. "You're in great shape, you're a great surfer, you have twenty-twenty vision, so why not?" But Eldad knew that the vocation demanded a responsibility that was more than he was up to. The most he could manage was to sit in the empty lifeguard tower, abandoned for the season, surf once a day at Gordon Beach, and meet weekly with Dr. Kaminsky. Most of the time he felt like a dead man, living someone else's life. And then, completely unexpectedly, a ray of light illuminated his darkness in the shape of a girl he saved from drowning. Not only did she bring him out of himself when he rescued her, show him that he was still resourceful and brave when he thought he had lost those qualities, but he liked her. He liked her a lot.

"How did you let her get away?" Ilan asked when he told him. He put a hand on Eldad's tanned shoulder, glad that his friend was finally showing some interest in a woman.

"The truth is that I ran away from her," Eldad confessed, "so that, God forbid, we wouldn't get to that point where you exchange phone numbers. I took off like a scared rabbit. I barely said goodbye."

"Why did you chicken out?"

"I don't know."

"You didn't have a conversation?"

"I made a fool of myself. I thought she tried to kill herself."

"How do you know she didn't?"

"That's what she told me, but I had the feeling that she needs help, like me. I advised her to go and talk to Kaminsky. I gave her the article about him."

"And she took it?" Ilan watched his friend; with his one eye he often saw more than other people did with two.

"She did."

"And do you know if she ever went to see him?"

"How could I?"

"What's the problem? Just ask Kaminsky if a girl came to him recommended by you."

But before he could find the courage to ask Kaminsky, he bumped into Eliya.

Even then, when the opportunity fell into his hands, he made a quick getaway. The next week, he timed it so that they would bump into each other, and he even made the date to meet her at Montana.

He had a hard time concentrating during that session and kept sneaking glances at Kaminsky's clock. When the minute hand reached its appointed place, he paid in a rush and was out the door like a shot.

He jumped on his Vespa and zoomed down Ben Yehuda Street, cursing every red light that held him up. He got to Montana on time, even managed to buy her ice cream, but she never showed. The disappointment caught him unprepared. That emotion had been buried deep, and Eldad regretted that something had given it a reason to surface.

And now here she was, and for the last few days he had been watching her from the empty lifeguard booth. Observing her like a voyeur invading her privacy, not daring to approach her for fear of being rejected again. The sun set, and Eliya stood up and walked toward the lifeguard tower. But it was as if his feet were nailed to the floor. He couldn't take that simple step and go down to her. She had already walked past, and in another minute she would disappear. He was such an idiot.

Eliya

When I arrived home, I found my father despondent. He was wearing his striped pajamas under his tattered robe and pacing restlessly between the rooms.

Without greeting me, he asked, "Have you seen your mother?"

"I saw her this morning. Is something wrong?"

"She still isn't back. She never comes home this late."

"But she always comes back in the end. Enjoy the peace and quiet. How often in your life do you get the chance to be alone without Mother bothering you?"

"I don't like to be alone, and your mother doesn't bother me. She sits here beside me, and I like to sit next to her."

"Sorry, Daddy, I didn't mean to upset you, but it's very strange that neither her husband nor her daughter knows where she disappears to every afternoon."

"And what makes you think that I don't know?"

"So if you know, why are you worried?"

"Exactly. It's because maybe I know that I'm worried."

"Enough, Daddy, enough with the riddles. Either tell me where she goes or don't tell me."

"If your mother wants to, she can tell you. It's not my place to tell you."

"Once, a long time ago, you told me that she goes to Dizengoff Street and sits in cafés. But you and I both know that there's as much chance of her sitting in a café as there is that she's off visiting Grandma and Grandpa."

I don't know what suddenly made me think of Grandma and Grandpa. Once I used to visit them regularly with my father and sit on my grandmother's lap and eat cookies that she'd baked specially for me. But one day, the visits had stopped.

"Daddy, why?" I asked him. "Why did we stop visiting them?"

My father sighed. "We stopped going because I didn't want to fight huge battles with your mother. But you're a big girl—you can visit them on your own. Just make sure your mother doesn't know about it."

"Secrets again. More lies. I don't want to lie anymore for Mother," I insisted.

My heart went out to him. He looked so pathetic and lost in his pajama bottoms and his old robe. His eyes kept darting to the door, yearning for his wife to walk through it and allow his frantic heartbeat to slow. He asked me to make him a coffee with boiled milk to settle his nerves.

I brought the milk to a boil three times, just the way my father had taught me, added one spoon of instant coffee and two spoons of sugar, and stirred. But before I had poured the coffee into his favorite glass mug, I heard the door open and my father saying, "Oy, Lily, thank God, I was so worried."

"Why should you be worried? It's just a little after six."

"But it's already dark outside."

"I always come back when it's dark. Don't make a big fuss because I'm five minutes late. And why are you so pale?"

"I don't feel well. I closed the store early. Not a soul came in today in any case, and I came home. I was hoping that you would be here."

"Did you take a pill?"

"I took an aspirin. It didn't help. My throat hurts."

"All right, I'll make you a *gogl-mogl*. Just let me get out of these rags."

I walked into the room with the cup of coffee in my hand. "Here, Daddy," I said, ignoring Lily. "Here's your coffee."

"No coffee!" Lily declared. "A sick person doesn't drink coffee. I'm making him *gogl-mogl*!"

"Make him whatever you like," I replied in an icy voice, "but he wants coffee."

"He can want what he likes! Take the coffee and drink it yourself. He's going to drink *gogl-mogl*."

I took the coffee back to the kitchen and left it on the counter. My mother cured everything with *gogl-mogl*. When I was little, she'd forced me to drink that disgusting hot milk and raw egg, and it had made no difference to her that I'd always thrown up. Just as now she couldn't care less that my father wanted his favorite coffee. As always my father stared at my mother with lovestruck eyes and gave in.

Night fell, but sleep wasn't an option. The wall between my room and my parents' bedroom wasn't thick enough, and nothing in the world could induce me to listen to the noises and whispers that traveled through it. I put on my jeans and grabbed a sweater without bothering to look for my bra, took my coat, and very quietly left the house.

I decided to trace the triangle of Dizengoff, Ussishkin, and Yirmiyahu Streets. Maybe the walk would tire me out, and when I got back home, I would be able to fall asleep. The lights were already out at the basketball arena on Ussishkin Street, and couples were sitting on the banks of the Yarkon. I walked over to Yirmiyahu and the balcony of Café Baba, then crossed over to the opposite sidewalk, walking fast in hopes that none of the people crowding the balcony would notice me. Ari had loved that place, and I had sometimes joined him there, so there was a good chance that I would see some of his friends. I strode briskly toward Dizengoff. Through the door of a pub, I could hear the voice of one of my favorite singers, Grace Slick from Jefferson Airplane, inquiring whether I wanted somebody to love. I stopped for a moment to listen, and that was when I saw him. It was the surfer from the beach, my savior. He was standing in the middle of a large crowd. I hoped he wouldn't notice me. How could I possibly explain why I'd stood him up at Montana? But before I could move on, he saw me and began making his way over. I smiled in embarrassment.

"You still owe me ice cream," he said, and even in the dark I could see how blue his eyes were.

I remained rooted to the spot, smiling like an idiot, and not one of the excuses I was considering made it to my mouth.

"So . . . ," he said.

"So what?"

"So what about that ice cream?"

"I'd prefer a beer," I said with courage I hadn't known I possessed, and I tilted my head in the direction of the pub playing Jefferson Airplane.

"Let's go," he said, and we climbed up the five steps, opened the door, and walked inside. I took a step back. It had been a long time since I was in a place with so many people, and it seemed as though everyone was talking at once, everyone was smoking, and the music that I liked so much was swallowed up in the noise.

"Do you want to sit at the bar, or should we find a table?"

I hesitated for a moment, and then I said, "At the bar." There would be other people at the bar, so it wouldn't be just me and him.

We sat on the high chairs at the corner of the bar. The barman, a young, good-looking guy wearing an eye patch, smiled broadly at me. God, there were too many people wearing eye patches like Moshe Dayan after this goddamned war.

"What can I get you, beautiful?" asked the young Moshe Dayan.

"Beer." I didn't like beer, but I couldn't think of anything else. I had never much liked alcohol, maybe because Ari was so fond of it.

"Goldstar for the pretty lady," said the one-eyed barman, handing me a bottle without a glass. "*L'chaim!*"

I raised the Goldstar as though I swigged beer from a bottle every day. I didn't like it, but I took a sip anyway.

My surfer took a drink from his bottle too. He didn't say a word about our meeting that had never taken place at Montana, but I felt it hovering there between us, and I decided to broach the topic.

"I'm sorry I never made it to Montana."

"Your loss," he said. "I waited for you with the ice cream."

"I don't know what to say . . ."

"Maybe you could say why you didn't come."

"I'm sorry."

"You never thought about explaining yourself?"

"I didn't think we'd ever see each other again."

"You didn't want to meet again?"

"I wanted to, and I didn't want to . . . it's complicated."

"That's why we go to Kaminsky," he said, and he raised his bottle in the air. "*L'chaim.*"

"I don't go anymore. I had enough."

"Want to talk about it?"

"It's a long story, and we don't know each other well enough."

"So let's get to know each other." He smiled at me, but I noticed that it was with only his mouth, not his eyes.

Everyone has a story. He went to Kaminsky for a reason. To my surprise, I wanted to know what it was. He intrigued me, and I liked him. Electricity seemed to flow between us even though we really didn't know each other. We sat side by side at the bar and spoke little, every so often drinking from our bottles of beer, toasting each other, and smiling shyly.

"So what does the pretty lady do?" The one-eyed barman appeared with another beer.

"I haven't finished this one." I avoided his question.

"Don't worry about it. Have a fresh one. It's on the house."

"Why on the house?" I laughed. "It's my first time here."

"That's exactly why. We want you to come again. Not to mention that any friend of Eldad's is a friend of mine."

So his name was Eldad. It suited him.

I smiled uncomfortably, and I felt myself blushing to the roots of my hair.

"Do you know how long this guy has been looking for you? He's been through the whole city trying to find you."

"Really?" I looked over at the surfer.

He nodded. Unlike the talkative, flirtatious barman, Eldad didn't say much, but I felt that if I gave him the slightest encouragement, he would open up to me.

I finished off my first beer. My head was spinning, and I was staring openly at Eldad. I started to sip from the second bottle.

"So he just let you go?" I heard his voice over the noise of the music and the people talking.

"Who?"

"Kaminsky. He doesn't let people go that easily. He believes in lifelong treatment, like a Catholic wedding."

"What do you mean, 'let me go'?" I laughed. "He shouted at me and said that I was making a mistake. He's convinced that I'll come crawling back, but as far as I'm concerned, he's finished his job."

"Are you going to someone else?"

"No."

"So who's treating you?"

"I'm treating myself. He did his thing, and I'm grateful; then I had enough of him. And you? Are you continuing?"

"Yes," he said without elaborating. I didn't ask any more questions.

I noticed that the barman never took his eye off us. It was too much for me. After such a long period when no one had noticed me, suddenly there were two men who seemed to be interested.

I squirmed in my seat, and Eldad noticed. "Are you okay?"

"Yes, but it's making me uncomfortable that the barman is always staring."

"Oh, that?" He laughed. "Don't worry; he's not ogling you. He's looking at me."

"Sorry," I stammered. "I didn't think . . ."

"No, no." Eldad laughed tightly. "It's nothing like that. He's my friend; we share an apartment. As you've no doubt already figured out, I told him that I lost you, and he's happy that I've found you again."

"Who else did you tell? The whole city?"

"I don't know if you've noticed, but I'm not really the 'whole city' type."

I couldn't take my eyes off him. Something about him fascinated me. But the next minute I was terrified. *No,* I decided, *there is no way that I'm going to go and get involved again with someone who is going to make my life difficult.*

"Okay." I stood up. "I have to go."

"Wait," he said. "I'll walk you."

"You don't have to. I live nearby."

"I'll walk you," he insisted. I shrugged and made for the door without saying goodbye to the barman. We walked side by side in silence.

"You didn't have to leave the pub because of me," I finally said.

He looked down at the sidewalk and didn't respond.

"Do you want to maybe go to the beach?" I asked suddenly, surprising myself as the words came out of my mouth.

"Now?" he asked.

"Yes, why not."

The sea was rough, and the waves crashed loudly against the shore. We took shelter from the wind underneath the lifeguard tower.

"We've returned to the scene of the crime," I said, and he nodded.

I blushed deeply as I remembered that he'd seen me naked only a few minutes after we'd met.

"Do you come here a lot?" I asked, hoping to distract him from that memory.

"Every day, summer and winter."

"Me too, summer and winter, but I prefer winter, when the beach is empty."

"I know," he said. "I see you."

"Really?" I turned to face him. "So why did you never say hello?"

"Honestly, I was afraid of being disappointed again."

"I'm sorry," I said. "I didn't mean not to show up at Montana, but things happened in such a way that I couldn't make it."

"It doesn't matter," he said. "Maybe one day you'll tell me what happened and why."

We sat next to each other on the sand, listening to the waves, touching and not touching, our bodies leaning in hesitantly, shoulder nudging shoulder, not talking. We were sitting so close that I could hear the beating of his heart. I rested my head on his shoulder, and he put his arm around me, and we sat like that for a long time, letting our bodies do the talking.

I hadn't thought that I would ever want someone again, someone who wasn't Ari, to take me in his arms and kiss me. But when he turned and took my head in his hands and kissed me, I surrendered to it, lost myself in the old-new feeling that filled me, in the desire that I had forgotten I could feel. He was gentle, so gentle, and I took his hand and guided it over my body and sank into the pleasure that suffused me as his strong hands cupped my back and lifted me onto him. He kissed my eyes and then my neck, and his lips moved down to my breasts, and I thought that if he continued, I would pass out, but I didn't want him to stop. I wanted him to go on and on. I shuddered with the intensity of my reaction, the passion bursting from my body, and drew him deeper and deeper into me. I gave myself over to him to do with my body as he wished, and I did what I wanted to with his body, and we both gave in to the unbelievable pleasure, that pleasure that God has granted us freely as a gift, and we became one body.

When I opened my eyes, his face was right next to mine, and his eyes, glittering with tears, bored deep into mine, and I couldn't believe it. Eldad, this incredible man who had brought my body back to life, was crying. I kissed his tears, and he whispered into my hair, "Thank you."

Eliya and Eldad

In the spring of 1975, the weather was wonderful. The sea was as smooth as glass, the beach was deserted, and Eliya sat alone on the sand and watched Eldad as he balanced on his surfboard. Sometimes he came onshore, picked her up, and paddled her out onto the water on his board. Then he would stop, and they would float and bob in the gentle waves. They would sit staring into each other's eyes, and then he would hold her, and they could remain like that until the sea's movements changed and the waves grew choppier, and then he would bring them in.

They couldn't get enough of each other and spent all their free time together. Eliya became a fixture at Eldad and Ilan's apartment on HaYarkon Street. Her parents were so pleased to see her behaving normally that they left her to herself. And besides, her father was deeply troubled about their livelihood. The severe economic crisis that afflicted the country after the Yom Kippur War, the galloping inflation and the heavy taxes, kept customers away from the jewelry store. He did everything in his power so that Lily wouldn't realize just how bad the situation was. Once in a while he would bring her a piece of gold jewelry as a gift. He had spent hours fashioning a special gold bracelet for her, a chain with a heart dangling from it, and once a ring with a red stone. But to his profound disappointment, Lily never wore any of it. "Why don't you wear the heart?" he finally dared to ask her.

"Jewelry doesn't suit me," she replied. "A piece of jewelry on me is like a gold ring in the nose of a pig; it's a waste of gold, a waste of your work, a waste of money. You should take it all and sell it at the store." But he didn't sell the pieces that he'd made for her. He kept them in a red velvet box in the safe. When the time was right, he would give the jewelry to Eliya.

◆　◆　◆

Eliya was glad that her parents were preoccupied and left her to her own devices. Even Lily seemed content that sparks of life had returned to shine in her daughter's eyes and there was color in her cheeks, and she didn't ask any questions.

"It's better this way," Lily said to Shaul. "In any case, if we ask her, she won't tell us, and if she does say something, it won't be true, so as long as she isn't roaring like some lion at the zoo or hiding under her blanket, we should just leave well enough alone."

"But aren't you interested in knowing what caused her sudden mood change?" Shaul asked.

"That's how she is, one good day, one bad day. Now she's up, so let's enjoy it."

Shaul sighed, and as always he did as Lily said. Keeping the peace at home was all that mattered. And if there was a cease-fire between the two of them and if his daughter was smiling again, then fine, he wouldn't ask questions.

Eliya and Eldad

The days grew colder, and I made sure to be home every evening for supper. Only after my parents had gone into their room and I could hear my father's snores through the wall did I leave the house to meet Eldad. Mostly we stayed at his place; sometimes we went to Sisi. In time I learned to like Ilan, and I loved the friendship between them. It was a friendship between men, and I knew that I couldn't come between them, just as I knew that Ilan wouldn't come between Eldad and me. I was smart enough to accept their friendship, to grant it its place without allowing it to detract from mine.

I fell more deeply in love with Eldad with each passing day. The way I loved him was so different from the way I had loved Ari. I loved Eldad with a tenderness and compassion that arose from a growing and deepening sense of closeness and belonging. It wasn't wild lust or burning passion, nothing like the crazy, uncontrollable attraction or the total annihilation of self that I'd experienced with Ari. It was a quiet love that slowly and gently made its inroads into my heart, and I found myself watching him, thinking about him, caring for him, sensing when something weighed heavily on him or hurt him. And yet I still felt I hadn't managed to really get through to him. So I waited for the right time, knowing that it would arrive. Eldad wasn't someone just passing through my life; he was there to stay. And I waited patiently.

Weeks passed, and we met every day, but we still didn't spend the whole night together. After we made love, I would fall asleep in his arms, and he would wake me softly and tell me it was time to go home.

"I want to stay with you," I whispered to him one night, from inside the circle of his arms. "I want to sleep with you and wake up with you in the morning. I'm cold," I said, burrowing into his body. "I want to stay here, with you, in this fine place that I love so much, here in this hollow between your shoulder and your chest. This is my place."

"Go home, my love," he begged. "Go so that you don't get into trouble with your parents."

"I'm not a little girl anymore. I was married. I don't need to explain to my parents why I don't come home at night."

"If that's the case, why do you hide it from them that you're meeting me?"

"I prefer that my mother not know about us so she won't ruin everything. Ever since I slit my wrists, she guards me like a lioness."

"I would like to meet your mother," he said suddenly.

"Better if you don't." I hugged him and covered his face with kisses.

Our lives settled into a welcome routine, but we still thrilled one another. Who would have believed that I could be so lucky and that my life would change like this? Every morning we walked together to the beach. Eldad would surf, and I would sprawl on the hot sand, reveling in the rays of the sun. Then we would eat steak in pita at the Carousel sidewalk restaurant on Dizengoff or ride Eldad's Vespa to his apartment on HaYarkon, where he would cook something for us, and for the rest of the afternoon we would listen to music and make love. I felt as though Eldad were returning to me the years I had lost, the years with Ari when I had nearly extinguished myself, although now his image kept receding and was almost forgotten.

I told Eldad how I had followed Ari through the rain and walked up the stairs to his apartment when I didn't even know him, how I married him in a wedding where I felt like a stranger who didn't belong, how I had become his despised, spineless slave, and how he had broken up with me in a Paris café and then I'd lost my mind.

I told him about the period when I didn't get out of bed and how I had tried to kill myself and my mother used her fingers to stem the flow of blood and saved my life. Together we remembered that day at the beach when he'd rescued me from drowning. As I talked, he held me, kissed the tears that fell like rain, and never said a word. And afterward he put me to bed, covered me with a blanket, stroked my hair, and didn't leave my side until I fell asleep.

I awoke in the middle of the night with his strong arms holding my body. I turned to face him. His eyes were closed, and when I kissed his eyelids, he opened them and looked at me.

"Are you asleep?" I asked him.

He shook his head.

"Why not?"

"I can't fall asleep. I can't sleep at night."

"Never?"

"Almost never. Since you've been with me, I've managed to sleep for a few hours, but I never sleep through the night."

"Is that why you go to Kaminsky?"

"Because of that and other things."

"And he never gave you pills to help you sleep?"

"He did. At first I took them, but the combination of the pills and the alcohol and the hash was fatal. I became aggressive, I lost control, I didn't recognize myself, and people who knew me couldn't believe that I had turned into such a repulsive, aggressive person. My parents were at a loss. They didn't know how to approach me. They were afraid of me. Every little thing made me crazy. My father would say something that I didn't like, and I would go nuts. Once I even threw a chair at him. I became a danger to myself and those around me. My mother tried to calm me down, and when I pushed her away, she fell and nearly smashed her head. That's when I decided to throw away the pills. Like Kaminsky told you, too, it's dangerous to stop cold turkey, but I was determined to stop. I was so terrified by the fact that I hurt my mother, that I had thrown that chair at my father, that I had become a threat to everyone close to me, that I decided to stop."

"Why didn't you stop the alcohol and the drugs?"

"Because I couldn't stand the pain, and only the alcohol and the drugs managed to dull it."

"Tell me," I whispered.

He didn't say anything.

"Please tell me."

"Do you promise that you won't hate me if I do?"

"I will never hate you."

"That you won't leave me after what I tell you?"

"I will never leave you."

He looked at me as if seeing me for the first time.

"Really?"

I looked straight into his eyes, and I knew that I would never leave him even if he told me the worst thing of all.

I touched his lips with mine, and I said to them, "Tell me, please."

And he lay down beside me, and he told me.

"After two weeks at the outpost it was finally my turn to go home, but just my luck, it was Yom Kippur. What a rotten break, what a terrible waste of a weekend, no parties, no going to the beach, no cinema, no music. The bus was supposed to come to pick up the guys who were going home, but it was delayed, and we started to lose patience. And then the rumor mill got to work, and the rumor was that there was some kind of alert and no one was going anywhere. Time passed, and no one told us a thing. The next morning the rumor was proved true: all leaves were canceled.

"Before the fast everyone went to the dining hall to eat. Sisi, our company commander, came to tell us officially that we were on alert. Almost everyone was fasting. Even me. Although I had never fasted in my life, I don't know what came over me, but that year on Yom Kippur I had decided to fast. In the morning my stomach was rumbling, and I was starving. I went to shave and brush my teeth, and one of the other soldiers told me that if I brushed my teeth and shaved, it was as if I hadn't fasted, so I thought to myself, *In that case I'll go make some coffee.* But before I had managed to make the coffee, the brigade rabbi told everyone to stop fasting and eat something and that it was an order. The religious guys were still praying, wrapped in their prayer shawls, and Sisi told them to hurry up. He hadn't even finished his sentence when suddenly the shelling started, and there was this crazy noise coming from every direction. The Syrians were firing along the entire sector, the Syrian Air Force was attacking, and in minutes there was total chaos, mortars falling everywhere, precise hits on targets, utter anarchy.

"That was my baptism of fire. I didn't know what to do; all around me the guys were falling. The injured cried for help, the bombs whistled past, and I was scared to death. A few feet away from me a soldier was lying with a wound in his stomach, calling to me to come and save him, but I was paralyzed and I couldn't move. After the first barrage, which went on for about thirty minutes that felt like a lifetime, there was a lull. Two soldiers came running with a medic, and they evacuated the soldier, but it was too late, and I knew that if I had gone to find a medic when he was crying for help, maybe he wouldn't have died in their arms.

"Suddenly the shelling started again, and it was worse than before. The bombs made so much noise as they fell I thought I would lose my hearing. Planes were circling, and one of them was hit and exploded right above me in a cone of fire. I looked for a hiding place. I didn't think of returning fire; I didn't think about fighting. I just wanted to stay alive. It was impossible to raise your head—whoever did was hit, and all around me people were being picked off. APCs were damaged and stopped in their tracks; soldiers were hit and stopped in their tracks. The attack went on for five hours, five hours of nonstop shelling, and from a distance I could see the Syrian tanks advancing toward us.

"I was hysterical. I screamed like a lunatic, but no one heard me. I believed I was going to die and felt sorry for myself. So young and already dead. What would happen to my father and my mother if I died? I hadn't done anything yet; I hadn't seen the Eiffel Tower in Paris or the Colosseum in Rome, and what about my dream to travel the world and study at the Technion with Ilan and to get an apartment together? I was still just a kid; I wanted to live! I remember screaming, 'Get me out of here! Get me out of here!' But no one heard. And in the middle of all that madness, I see a convoy of APCs and truckloads of Syrian soldiers coming toward me. I'm alone. How the hell can I stop the convoy? It's all over. I'm dead. Dead! And then I hear Ilan shouting, 'Why are you standing there like a schmuck? Shoot! Shoot!' And that finally shakes me out of my paralysis, and I start shooting in every direction, out of control, not taking my finger off the trigger. The shooting is all around me, impossible to take in, and I think to myself, *This is what hell looks like.* And in front of me are Syrian soldiers trying to take over our position. Sisi, our company commander, is suddenly there in his APC, trying to stop them, but as it reaches them, he's hit at close range, and it goes up in flames. The shooting continues. Ilan shouts to me that he's going to try to rescue Sisi and another soldier who was hit, one in the head and one in the chest, and I stand there like a moron and do nothing. Ilan is hit in the face. Instead of rushing to Ilan, all I could do at that moment was scream, 'Medic, medic!' But I didn't move from my hiding place. I didn't go to Ilan, who was wounded. I was terrified. The bullets whizzed past, I heard it every time they connected, I felt like a sitting duck, and I started shooting again like a madman until I had no more ammunition. All around me hell is breaking loose, bullets are everywhere, mortars are falling, soldiers are dying, screaming in pain, and I am still shooting although my ammunition is gone. I threw myself into a trench. *It's over,* I told myself. Suddenly I heard an explosion that almost shattered my eardrum. I was thrown back, and I fell to the ground, flat on my face, surrounded by men who were wounded or dead. My body was covered in blood. I patted myself all over, and I realized that the blood wasn't mine; I wasn't wounded and certainly not dead.

"And then there was total silence, and I thought about my parents, my friends from the Scouts, the group of guys I had enlisted with, about Ilan and wondered if he was dead or alive, about our dreams that had shattered on the basalt rocks of the Golan Heights. I was so thirsty. I wanted to piss, but I was afraid to stand up, afraid to move, and I pissed in my pants. An eternity later I heard someone shout, 'Anyone alive here?'

"I crawled out. The soldiers who had come to rescue us looked at me like I was a ghost. Everyone else was dead or wounded, and I was unscathed.

"My body was intact, but my soul was bleeding. The war ended. Sisi died and left behind a pregnant wife, Ilan lost an eye, and me, I didn't lose anything, not an eye, not a hand, not a foot. I was whole! But inside I was shattered. No one else knew what was happening inside me; no one understood why instead of being overjoyed that I was alive, I walked around desolate and miserable. No one except for Ilan. He was the only one who even without words knew that I was ashamed.

Ashamed of being a coward, ashamed that I hadn't saved the wounded man who cried out for help, ashamed that I didn't try to pull Sisi out of his APC when it was hit, ashamed that I wet my pants next to the body of a soldier who died beside me, and most of all devastated that I hadn't helped him, Ilan, when he was shot in the face, and instead of rushing to his aid, I froze and then hid in a trench. He understood all of it without words; I never said a thing. When he was in the hospital, I sat at his bedside almost twenty-four hours a day. His mother called me a *zaddik*, said I was a righteous man, but I felt like a cowardly criminal, someone who had frozen, who thought only about himself and not his comrades. Someone who was seriously damaged. Ilan found Kaminsky for me. He, who had lost one of his eyes, had enough emotional strength to take care of me and to convince me to go to Kaminsky. At first I resisted. I told him that I wasn't crazy, just a coward. And he said, 'No one says you're crazy, but this doctor knows what to do with people like you. He treats shell-shocked soldiers.' I told him that I wasn't shell shocked; I was just a coward. And he said, 'Fine, you're a coward. Go to him, talk to him, and figure out why you reacted like that.' I kept on refusing until Ilan told me, 'Either you go to Kaminsky, or I am going to have you put away. They'll find the right medication to fix you up.' So I started going to Kaminsky. Twice a week I sat in his office like a zombie, refusing to cooperate. In the end he got through to me, mainly via the sea. It was his idea that we should have some of our sessions on the beach, and they were really our best ones. Suddenly I had a reason to get up in the morning. I had my surfboard, I had the sea, I had the beach, and I had Ilan, who held my hand like I was a little boy.

"And I still don't understand what happened to me. Why I froze in terror, why I didn't help my friends, why I was paralyzed, why I'm such a coward."

"You are no coward," I whispered, pressing my body into his. "You're damaged. We're both damaged, and we have to heal each other."

I held him, fitting my body to his. "I love you," I told him for the first time. "I love you as much as my life."

And he entered me, enveloped me. His hands, his tongue, and his heart were inside me, and I was in him. "My love," he whispered to me. "My love."

◆ ◆ ◆

I knew that under no circumstances should I bring Eldad home, but he kept asking. He had already introduced me to his parents, who were pleasant and polite, but still I felt that they were keeping their distance. They might have been aware of my positive influence on Eldad, but they weren't overly enthusiastic about his new girlfriend. Why should they be when he had insisted on telling them that we had met at Dr. Kaminsky's?

"You shouldn't have told them that," I complained.

"Should I have told them that I rescued you from drowning?" he laughed.

"You could have said that we met at the pub."

"I'm not so good at lying, especially not to my parents."

"It would have been a white lie."

"You're going to be the mother of my children, so it's best if they know where we met, even if it's a half lie."

"I'm going to be the mother of your children?" I looked at him in surprise. His eyes sparkled, and he was smiling.

"You haven't realized that yet?"

"So you love me."

He pulled me to him, breathed me in, and said, "More than my life."

"More than your life, huh?" I wanted more. Eldad rarely expressed his feelings in words.

"I love you."

He gave me a lingering kiss and said, "And since I am going to be the father of your children, I think the time has come for me to meet your parents."

"Why spoil such a beautiful moment?"

"Come on, Eliya, how long can you go on hiding me?"

"I'll introduce you to my father. We can go visit him at the store."

"I'm more interested in meeting your mother."

"You have no idea what kind of a minefield you're stepping into."

"Eliya, my love, you said that we have to heal one another. You are treating my wounds, you anoint them with your love, and I feel them healing thanks to you. Let me heal your wounds. You said that Kaminsky told you that until you mend the relationship with your mother, you won't be able to repair yourself. You hold the key, Eliya; you just have to open the door. Let me walk through that door with you so I can be there for you, so I can hold you when it hurts, catch you if you stumble. I'm not afraid of your mother."

"That's because you haven't met her yet," I said, smiling.

And so one evening I brought him to my parents' house. When we got there, Lily was still out, and my father, as usual, was in his pajama bottoms and his threadbare robe, sitting on the couch in the lounge drinking his coffee and reading the paper. He was so surprised to see me walk in with a young man that he spilled some of the coffee on his robe.

"Hi, Daddy," I said shyly. "This is my boyfriend, Eldad Arbel."

"Pleased to meet you," he said, rising from the sofa.

I could tell from his expression that he liked Eldad right away. Later he would tell me that what he liked the most was how Eldad and I looked at each other.

"So what do you do with yourself?" my father asked him.

"He's getting ready for university," I hastened to answer for Eldad. "He's going to study architecture at the Technion."

"Very nice. And in the meantime, what do you do for a living?"

"He's training to be a lifeguard. He's a fabulous surfer."

"A surfer," my father murmured. "That sounds good. I'm going to prepare supper before your mother gets back."

"What were those lies about studying architecture at the Technion?" Eldad turned to me when my father disappeared into the kitchen.

"They aren't lies; they're half lies, just like telling your parents that we met at Kaminsky's. And anyhow, you really are going to study at the Technion. You're going to follow through with the plans that you made before the war, to become an architect, to travel the world, to have children with me. I never lie to my father."

He laughed. "I see you've got my whole life planned out."

"Our life." I kissed him. "It's all worked out down to the last detail."

My mother walked in at that moment and couldn't believe her eyes. There was her daughter kissing a strange man in the middle of the living room.

"And hello to you too," she said harshly.

"Hello, Mother," I replied. "Meet my boyfriend, Eldad."

"I didn't know you had a boyfriend." She gave Eldad's extended hand a limp shake. "Since when do you have a boyfriend?"

"Three months now."

"You've been hiding him from us for three months?"

"Not hiding him. I thought it was too soon to bring him home."

"And what makes you think that now isn't too soon to bring him home?" She spoke to me as though Eldad weren't in the room.

"Because now it's serious, and I wanted you to meet the love of my life."

Lily looked Eldad up and down. "So now he's the love of your life. I hope you understand, young man, that every few years my daughter replaces the love of her life. She doesn't know that a woman falls in love only once in her life," she said, and she turned on her heel and left the room.

"I told you. I told you that she's evil and she would ruin everything." I sat down, drained.

"She isn't going to ruin anything," Eldad promised me. "We're going to soften her up."

Throughout the entire meal, Lily stared at Eldad without saying a word, and only when we had finished eating and he got up to help me clear the table did she ask, "So, young man, where do you work?"

"He doesn't work, okay?" I burst out. "He's unemployed. Happy?"

"Eliya, that's enough." Eldad spoke to me gently but firmly. "I'm in an in-between phase at the moment," he told Lily. "I finished my military service after the war, and it took me time to recover. Ever since I met Eliya, I've been doing much better, and now I'm planning my future. I'm thinking of studying architecture at the Technion."

"But how do you support yourself?"

"At the moment, my parents are helping me until I get back on my feet."

The meal was over, and Eldad left. I stayed home that night, and through the adjoining wall between our rooms, I could hear my parents talking. Lily made no attempt to lower her voice.

"So he's as cuckoo as she is," she said bitterly. "Came out of the war and 'it took him time to recover.' God help us, where does she find these people!"

"Stop it, Lily." I heard my father's usual imploring tone. "Why are you always looking for something negative? He's a lovely guy. Who knows what he went through during the war? Who knows what pain he's carrying? And he's planning to study at the Technion."

"And in the meantime both he and she are living off their parents. Quite the pair they are."

"It's none of our business how he lives."

"But how she lives is our business. It's time for her to get a job and stop eating up all our savings. How long do we have to carry her on our backs? And who will carry us when we get old? Certainly not her."

My father tried to steer the conversation in a different direction. "Lily, it's all going to work out. Look at Eliya. Finally we know what put the color back in her cheeks."

I heard him tell Lily that Eldad seemed like a very good person from a good home, a hero who had fought on the Golan Heights during the Yom Kippur War. I could feel how happy he was for me, how hard he was trying to counteract Lily's venom.

"So what if he fought in the war?" Lily squashed his enthusiasm. "What's the big deal? Everyone, except for that good-for-nothing who ran away, fought in the war. What's so special about that?" My father didn't respond, and she continued, "Not to mention that he has no profession, and a man who doesn't bring home a paycheck at the end of the month . . ."

"I know, I know." Uncharacteristically, my father interrupted her, saying wearily, "A man who doesn't support his family isn't a man."

Lily

On some days Lily felt mellow, at peace in the world. She listened to the silence disturbed only occasionally by the chirping of birds, was aware of the rustle of the leaves, and inhaled the wonderful sweet scent of the citrus orchards mingled with the hyssop growing wild among the orange trees.

And to think that she experienced this beauty, this smell, the smell of life itself—of all the places in the world—here in the children's section of the cemetery at Kiryat Shaul. It remained the only place where she could breathe easily, where she felt at peace. The only place in the world where she really wanted to be, and when the sky was streaked with shades of gold, she could even smell the sea.

Only here, near the grave of her baby, did she feel serene. No one disturbed her, as no one disturbed the rest of the dead children. Sometimes cries of grief broke the silence, but even they couldn't disturb her tranquility. Those cries, like the funerals, were far away from her, on paths that didn't lead to the children's section. More than once she had witnessed the funerals of dead children, seen them dig the new tiny graves, observed the tombstones, the candles in the lanterns placed there by the devastated parents, the statue of an angel set atop the resting place of a little girl. But as the years passed, the children's section filled up, and a new section was cleared. God didn't distinguish between adults and children; both continued to die. How unjust the world was, Lily thought. One person just began a life and died, and an elderly person who lacked the strength to go on with his life and longed to die continued to live. A sick person who yearned to remain alive weakened and died, and a healthy person wanted to die, slit her wrists, and lived. Lily could not understand the choices God made. Why did one receive such a short allotment of time while another was granted long life? What divine logic could explain why a woman carried a child in her womb for nine months and was overjoyed by him for a year only to have him cruelly wrenched from her?

The *bishara* had told her that God only took from those who had great emotional strength, from those who could withstand the pain. "Be comforted that God thinks you are strong," she had said. But it was no comfort at all, not then and not now. After the *bishara* died, she searched for answers from others. Went to everyone who she thought might be able to tell her why her baby had died, why God had taken him so soon. She sought out those who read tea leaves and those who read cards, went to mediums who held séances using cups and those who preferred candles. Each of them was paid with money she didn't have, and no one ever gave her an answer. And after consulting a woman who spoke with the dead, who told her, "Only people who have done something truly terrible in that world are punished terribly in this one," she finally ceased her quest.

She was exhausted from trying to understand. From the day when her baby had died, so many years ago that she had stopped counting, she had been a bereaved mother in hiding. She never dared tell anyone that every day she traveled on two buses to reach the cemetery where her baby was buried.

Shaul preferred to forget, not to talk about the baby, not to recite the mourner's Kaddish hymn, not to visit the grave, not to remember. And when she lit a candle every year on the anniversary of his death and placed it next to the photograph on the night table by her side of the bed, he never said a word.

Shaul had never come to the cemetery, and Eliya, what did she know? She had no connection to her dead brother. After the tantrum she'd thrown when she was ten, when she'd hid his photograph, she had never asked about him, not even once. She behaved like an only child, as if another child had never existed before her in her family. God had punished her twice, Lily felt, first taking her cherished baby and then giving her a child who only embittered her life, a daughter who seemed like the child of some other woman who had been planted in her womb. What had she done to deserve such punishment? She took a deep breath. Thinking about Eliya always confused her. When Eliya had refused to get out of bed for a year, when she'd tried to kill herself, when she'd wanted to be institutionalized, Lily had thought to herself, *Good Lord, this is even worse than when baby Chaim died. The baby died and that was the end of the story, but Eliya continues to wreck our lives and her own life every day that she lives.* God forgive her for the thoughts she harbored. How could a mother think such things about her daughter.

It was only when Eliya was in mortal danger that Lily finally felt close to her. When Eliya was weak and exhausted and her lifeblood nearly streamed out of her, Lily preserved that life with her very fingers, pressed down and prayed that the blood would stop flowing out of her daughter's body. That was the first time she had felt that Eliya was her child, and she would do whatever it took to save her. But the moment Eliya began to improve, they had reverted to sinking knifelike words into each other's flesh. She knew it was she who had cast the first blow, suddenly terrified by the closeness that had developed between them. By trying to push away Eliya, she could return to that safe place of anger and alienation, a place where there was no kindness or compassion. Lily knew she was not permitted to truly be close to another human being, not even her daughter, her own flesh and blood, because if she ever again felt destiny's boot smashing into her belly, she would die.

◆ ◆ ◆

Darkness was descending on the graveyard. Lily traced the inscription on the gravestone with her fingers in a farewell to her child, kissed it, and hurried toward the exit. But when she reached it, the gate was locked. "Hello, is there anyone there?" she shouted, hoping that some of the workers might still be nearby, but no one replied. Like a person possessed, she began to run along the main path, knowing that she would soon arrive at the adjacent military cemetery. It wasn't fully dark, but the shadows were lengthening, and she was alone in the graveyard. When she finally reached the gateway that connected the two cemeteries, she heaved a huge sigh of relief. There were people there. Since the Yom Kippur War numerous graves had been added to the military cemetery, which was often referred to now as the City of Youth. So many young people had died in that war, and many parents came each day to wash and adorn the gravestones and tend small gardens there. Lily observed the parents stooped over their children's graves, and suddenly she didn't feel alone in her bereavement. She walked among them and felt that they shared the same fate.

As Lily walked serenely toward the exit, she stopped to wash her hands at the tap by the gate. She turned to a woman who was standing there and asked, "What time do they close this gate?"

The woman answered, "Never. This gate is always open."

It was now mid-September. Almost a year since Eliya had met her new man. After initially ignoring Eldad, Lily had grown fond of him. It was obvious that he had a positive influence on Eliya. She had finally left home and moved in with him to the apartment he shared with his one-eyed friend on HaYarkon Street. Lily had been there only once. It was Eldad who had invited her, of course. It was actually a nice apartment, full of light. Two old armchairs and a small table were arranged on the balcony, and Eliya's boyfriend had made her a cup of sweet, strong black coffee, just the way she liked it, and behaved like some kind of English gentleman, pulling out her chair and taking her coat.

And Eliya had changed. She exuded a softness that she hadn't had before. She was thinking about completing her studies at the literature department and had started working as a waitress at the pub owned by the one-eyed man. And Eldad was teaching children how to surf at Gordon Beach, a temporary job until he became an architect. Who knew, maybe one day he would amount to something.

Eliya's troubles seemed to be over. The girl had stolen two years of Lily's life, maybe more, if you counted the years she had spent with the good-for-nothing.

What would she not give to be like Eliya, a young woman in love, to rush into adventures thoughtlessly, recklessly, with no idea how things might turn out.

She quite liked Eldad's one-eyed friend. If only she were twenty years younger, she would embark with him on the kind of fantastic adventure that filled her nights with unquenchable yearnings. And suddenly, like a frightened virgin about to enter her marriage bed, Lily was shocked by the feverish thoughts in her mind.

It's not that I don't love Shaul, she reasoned with herself. *He's a good man. He's my savior and my protector. I would be lost without him. But I must admit that he is an ordinary man, and he lacks passion.* They hadn't made love for a very long time, and even then, it was she who had moved toward him in bed, parting her legs. He was always delighted as a child, but when he was finally ready, it was over before it had begun, and he lay sprawled heavily on top of her. Two minutes later he was snoring, and she was lying there wide awake, miserable and frustrated. Then she would move her fingers down inside her own juices, still mingled with the secretions from his body, and pleasure herself until her body was transported and she had to bite her lips so she wouldn't wake him, but Shaul remained snoring on his side, oblivious that his wife had slaked her passion on her own.

Suddenly, it wasn't enough for her anymore. She wanted to feel another body against hers, someone else's skin igniting hers. She wanted to be swept away in the arms of a real man; she wanted to feel that fire that she saw in Eliya's eyes that had never burned in hers; she wanted that glow that she saw in Eldad's eyes when he looked at Eliya. She had never felt anything like the flame she saw burning between Eliya and Eldad, the secret glances they exchanged, after which they disappeared into some corner of the apartment to devour one another with their eyes, their hands, their lips. Oh hell! She was jealous of her own daughter.

Lily couldn't sleep at night. She bit down on her pillow and tossed and turned, throwing off her covers, pulling them back, getting up, lying down again. She felt as though she were losing her mind. A mother didn't envy her daughter. But hadn't it always been this way between her and Eliya? Hadn't she been jealous of Shaul's love for their daughter? Of the good-for-nothing's love for her, and now of Eldad's love? And suddenly it was so clear to her—how had she not seen it before—it was because they were so similar. Everything she disliked about Eliya was what she disliked in herself. Instead of being angry with herself, she was angry with Eliya. She had to admit that she and Eliya were incredibly similar. Even strangers could see that Eliya was a copy of Lily, the same green eyes, the same high cheekbones, and the same sensuous lips. They even had identical dimples. The only thing she didn't inherit from her mother was her golden hair.

She and Eliya were more similar than either of them would ever admit, but Eliya had received everything that Lily never had. She had loved two men to the depths of her soul and been loved by both in return, while Lily had never in her life loved with passion. Not only had her heart never been broken, but her heartbeat had never even quickened for any man. Until she met the one-eyed man. He looked at her with his single eye, and she felt that he saw her as a man saw a woman.

It caught her unprepared. She had no idea how to deal with her mortification when she realized that she was drawn to him as a moth to a flame, and she knew she must never get close. If she allowed herself to be pulled toward that fire, she would get burned, and her life would go up in flames. And yet she sought it out—and unfortunately she knew just where to find it.

She had to see him. Her body ached with desire for him, even though she knew she was heading for disaster. She could be his mother. But he was appearing in her dreams. She fantasized about the heights of passion they would reach. She wanted to pummel his strong young body, to scrape her fingernails down the rippling muscles of his back, to scratch him, to break through his shell, to expose whatever was inside him, and to crawl in there. Her fantasies filled her nights and her days, even when she visited the cemetery. *This is a sin,* she told herself. *I am defiling the sanctity of my baby's grave with my head full of thoughts of a man who isn't his father. What a terrible thing. If my son were alive, he would be the same age as the one-eyed man.*

And yet, with no regard for the consequences, she went to visit Eliya at the pub. She knew full well that no one would ever believe that she was there to see how her daughter was or because she missed her. Her lie was ridiculously transparent. And she went anyway.

Eliya didn't even have time to be surprised by her mother's appearance at the pub. She was too busy running from table to table, balancing her full tray, taking orders, and serving drinks. "Mother, what are you doing here?" she asked, but she didn't have time to wait for an answer. The music was earsplitting, but to Lily's surprise it didn't bother her; her body might be aging, but apparently her heart was still young. All of a sudden she loved the kind of loud guitar music that usually drove her crazy. The smoke stung her eyes, but instead of waving it away, she longed for a cigarette. Lily Zoref, who had never smoked in her life. So she sat down at the bar next to Eldad, who didn't say a word about her inconceivable presence there, and asked him for a cigarette. She inhaled and immediately had a coughing fit. Eldad brought her a glass of water, and the one-eyed man winked his single eye and served her a drink in a tall glass.

"What's this?" she asked him.

"Whiskey and cola."

Lily grimaced, and he laughed. "Want something stronger?"

Stronger? She didn't even drink the ritual wine for the blessing on Friday night. She sipped the whiskey, surprised at the pleasant tingling in her palate and the smoothness with which it slid down her throat. The one-eyed man moved his lips and said, "*L'chaim.*" She downed her drink and asked for another.

"Mother, are you drinking?" Suddenly Eliya was pelting her with questions. "What are you doing here? Did something happen to Daddy?"

"Why should anything happen to your father? You don't come to see us, so I came here."

"I don't come to see you?" asked Eliya as she piled her tray with bottles of beer and the glasses that the one-eyed man was handing to her. "We were over to see you yesterday. Right, Eldad?"

Eldad nodded but didn't get involved. Eliya hurried off to serve another round of drinks.

"How does she keep all the bottles from falling off?" Lily asked Eldad.

"At first they did fall off." He smiled. "But she's a fast learner, your daughter."

"That's true," the one-eyed man added. "Super talented. She must get it from her mother."

"Get it from her mother," Lily scoffed. "That one is Daddy's girl, no doubt about it."

"She may be her daddy's girl, but she's beautiful like her mother." He smiled, leaned down close to her, took her glass, and poured her another drink.

Was she imagining it, or was he flirting with her? Her head was spinning from the alcohol, but she was sure he was staring at her openly. Good Lord, what would Eldad think, she wondered. What must be going through the minds of all the young people at the bar? An old hag like her, making a fool of herself in front of Eliya's boyfriend and at the place where she worked? She was drunk, that was for sure, and she couldn't stop this crazy dance with the one-eyed man. He winked at her, and she couldn't take her eyes off him. He gave her a smile, and she returned it. He flattered her, and she giggled like a sixteen-year-old. Or was it all in her head?

What had she imagined? That she would sit at the bar and he would fall at her feet like a piece of ripe fruit? What had been going through her head when she'd taken all her clothes out of her closet and couldn't find a thing to wear and ended up in her usual rags, then put on gold earrings and a necklace of red beads, hoping they might compensate for her dismal clothes? What could she have been thinking when she'd applied red lipstick three times and each time wiped it off her cracked old lips? And then she'd lied to Shaul and told him that she had a doctor's appointment and she was already late.

"What kind of doctor's appointment at this hour?"

"It's a gynecologist," she lied. "I'm seeing him privately."

"Why do you have to see a gynecologist? Did something happen?" he asked, overwhelmed with concern.

"Why should something happen?" She lost patience. "These are just women's matters that you know nothing about," she shouted over her shoulder. She just managed to catch a glimpse of his astonished expression before she slammed the door behind her. He was already accustomed to the fact that she disappeared for hours every afternoon, but to leave the house at eight in the evening? That had never happened before.

What was she thinking? That she would sit at the bar and drink some magic potion that would shave off twenty-five years and she would suddenly be young, and then she and the one-eyed man would live happily ever after? God help her, she had completely lost her mind.

Her head was spinning, and she could feel her bowels twisting and the evening meal she had eaten with Shaul rising in her gorge. How shameful. She had to get back to Shaul, to her man who accepted her as she was with all her neuroses. She had to get back to that safe space within her own four walls. She had to . . .

"Mrs. Zoref." Eldad was holding her arm and trying to steady her. "You are totally drunk."

◆　◆　◆

Cruel blades of sunlight slashed through the window and pierced her eyes. She had forgotten to close the blinds, and the sun had woken her too early. She shielded her face with her hand and rolled onto her stomach in an attempt to escape the blinding light. Unsuccessful, she decided to get up, but her body refused. Her limbs were like lead, and a headache pounded mercilessly at her temples.

Her side of the bed was in total disarray. The sheets were crumpled and damp with sweat. Shaul's side was smooth and neat as always, the pillow, sheet, and blanket aligned and pulled tight with military precision. She placed her feet on the cold floor to stand up, but her body slumped. She stank with a sour smell of perspiration, and her breath reeked of alcohol. She found the strength to move falteringly toward the window and close the blind. She teetered toward the kitchen, filled a glass from the faucet, and rinsed her dry mouth. Crawled to the bathroom and saw her reflection in the mirror. Her hair was wild, and her face looked haggard. Her mascara had run in black rivulets down her cheeks, and vestiges of her red lipstick were stuck in the creases in her lips. She quickly washed off the makeup. God, what had gotten into her last night? Who knew what she had said and what she had done? Good Lord, how badly had she disgraced herself? Had the one-eyed man taken advantage of the fact that she was drunk and made a laughingstock of her? Or was it she who had made a fool of herself? She remembered that he had poured her whiskey, then more and more, and smiled at her with little smirks rife with innuendo, tempting her. Or was it she who had sent him little flirtatious smiles, full of promise, she who had tried to seduce him? What the hell had she been thinking? That he would rescue her from her life of crushing boredom?

She couldn't remember how she had found her way home. How she had opened the door and who had taken off her clothes, dressed her in her nightgown, and put her to bed. Had she undressed herself, or had Shaul undressed her? And how had Shaul reacted when she'd come back in a drunken stupor so late at night? So many questions and not a single answer.

Determined to clean herself up, she took a shower. She stood under the scalding water for a long time, scouring herself with a rough bath sponge until her skin was red and raw, in an effort to cleanse herself of her shame. The hot water finally ran cold, shocking her out of her torment and reviving her. On her way to the bedroom, the big clock in the kitchen told her that it was already one o'clock. She had slept away half the day, and soon Shaul would be home for his afternoon rest. The last thing she wanted was to confront him. If she didn't hurry, she would be late for her baby; she had two buses to catch and a half-hour walk. Today of all days she needed to talk to him. She needed the peace she found there; then she would know how to go on.

◆ ◆ ◆

When Lily finally arrived at Kiryat Shaul, it was already late. Short of breath, she hurried over and rested her face against the cold gravestone. "Hello, my child," she whispered. "I'm sorry I'm late. I hope I didn't worry you. Mommy's here. Everything's all right now." The stone felt pleasant against her cheek and soothed her. She kissed it and burst into tears, unable to stem the flow.

"Why are you crying?" She heard the sweet voice of her baby welling up from inside her. "Why are you crying, Mommy?"

"I'm crying for you," she told him, "and I'm crying for myself and your sister and your father. My longing for you and for what we might have had if you hadn't died hurts so badly."

"But Mommy"—she could hear the baby's voice bright and clear—"I was part of your life for only one year, and Eliya has been yours for her whole life. Why, Mommy, why don't you allow Eliya to heal your yearning?"

"I am a bad mother, my child. I have a rotten heart. All the love I had in me I gave to you, and there is no more love inside me, not for Eliya and not for your father. And now, I am no longer satisfied with the safe, quiet love of your father, and I seek an adventure that may cause great grief and sorrow. I can't control it, my child. Your mother has lost her head over a man who could be her son. My child, tell me what to do."

"Mommy," her baby whispered to her, his voice like the sound of the wind, "follow your heart. Don't listen to what other people say. Don't do only what is permitted," said the voice emanating from her heart. "Mommy, do what makes you happy."

As she did at the end of every visit, she kissed the letters of her dead baby's name on the gravestone and leaned over the small plot. His words echoed in her mind. It wasn't the first time that her dead baby had spoken to her from within her. She thought that perhaps she had what the *bishara* had, the ability to communicate with the dead. Although unlike the *bishara*, who spoke with all the dead, she could commune only with her own baby. If she could have spoken with all the dead, she would certainly have talked to the woman who'd given birth to her, who had most likely been dead for some time now, and asked her why the hell she'd abandoned her.

Lately she found herself wondering often about that woman who was her mother. She, who had sealed off her heart from any emotions related to the woman who had given birth to her, had begun to ask questions to which there weren't any answers. For who could tell her who her mother was? She sometimes wandered the streets, following strange women and searching for a face that might remind her of her own. She recalled the time she had gone into a store on Dizengoff Street because she'd seen through the window a woman who looked familiar. Her blonde hair was swept up on her head, and she had the same slim body Lily had, the same small breasts she so despised in herself. She recognized something of herself in that woman, who was engrossed in a conversation with the saleswoman and didn't notice her. Later she followed her out of the store and down the street. When the woman disappeared into a building, Lily stood outside for a long time, trying to imagine which apartment she lived in and what it looked like inside. Later she scolded herself, What the hell was she thinking? That it was her long-lost sister who would lead her to the mother she had never known?

◆ ◆ ◆

Night had fallen by the time she returned home, and the dark stairwell frightened her. She switched on the light and rushed up the sixty stairs until she reached their third-floor apartment. She waited outside until her breathing returned to normal, and only then did she open the door. Shaul, dressed as usual in his old pajama bottoms and worn robe, sat waiting for her. The table was set for supper. The plates were side by side, flanked by the knives and forks, the salt and pepper shakers between them, the salad, Halloumi, and slices of white bread placed in the little straw basket, everything ready and waiting for her as it had been every day for the last twenty-seven years. But this time, rather than comfort her, the tidily set table made her angry. What would happen if just once her dear husband would prepare chicken livers and mashed potatoes or goulash with white rice? What would happen if instead of coffee with boiled milk, they drank a glass of wine? Would the world come to an end? And what if instead of receiving her wearing those ancient pajama pants, she came home to find him dressed in a pair of pressed trousers and a white shirt? And rather than eat at home, what if he invited her to a restaurant? How many times had she walked along Yirmiyahu Street and envied the well-dressed women escorted by handsome men stepping out of gleaming cars and entering the Casbah restaurant arm in arm? Would she ever in her life sit in an elegant restaurant? When would she have the chance—just once—to have some fun?

She tugged off her coat and went into the bedroom to change into her house robe. But she remained standing in her bra and underwear. No, today she wouldn't put on that ratty old robe. She would put on the red dress she had bought yesterday on Allenby Street. It was a low-cut bloodred minidress that she knew she couldn't afford, the kind of dress she had never dared to wear before.

The dress hugged her curves, and Lily ran her hands down the sides of her body to smooth it out. She plunged her fingers into her bra to reposition her breasts, applied her new red lipstick, then touched her fingers to the tip of the smooth cylinder and dabbed two spots of color to her cheeks. When she walked into the kitchen, Shaul looked at her in shock, his eyes wide, not understanding what had happened to his wife, but he didn't say a word.

She sat opposite him, regarding him defiantly. He began to eat his egg, which had gotten cold, dunking the bread into the yellow yolk, not raising his eyes from his food. "So," she asked him in a petulant tone, "aren't you going to say anything about my new dress?"

"Wear it in good health," he mumbled.

"Don't you think it's nicer than the old rags I always wear?"

"It's nicer."

"And it doesn't bother you that I spent nearly all the money you earned this month on this dress?"

Shaul nearly choked on his egg. He had hoped that life would return to a more peaceful state now that Eliya was happy, but now Lily was giving him a hard time. He had been terrified when she'd stayed out so late the night before. He'd even taken an expensive taxi to the cemetery, only to find the gate closed and securely locked. He'd returned home and paced the apartment in a panic, fearing the worst. He had been married to the woman for so many years, and yet he still didn't understand her.

Eldad had finally brought her home after midnight. Lily could barely stand, and if Eldad hadn't been supporting her, she would have collapsed like a rag doll.

"She needs to go to bed," Eldad said. The shocked Shaul hurried to take her from Eldad, helped her into her nightgown, and put her to bed. Only after he was sure that she was asleep did he switch off the light and return to the living room, where Eldad was waiting for him.

"I'm sorry," Eldad said. "She had too much to drink."

"To drink? Where?" Shaul asked.

"At Sisi, the pub that belongs to my friend Ilan."

"What was she doing there?"

"She came to visit Eliya at work, and Ilan gave her a few drinks. He had no idea that she can't hold her liquor."

"She came to visit Eliya?"

"That's what she said."

Shaul didn't reply. Even if it was hard for him to believe that Lily had gone to see how Eliya was doing, he didn't feel that it was appropriate to tell Eldad, who wasn't yet family.

"I'll go now," said Eldad. "I'm sorry. Ilan didn't mean to get her drunk."

"Go, go," Shaul told him. "Thank you very much for bringing her home."

He didn't sleep a wink that night. He lay next to Lily, rigid with worry, and never took his eyes off her. She tossed and turned in her drunken sleep, mumbling unintelligible words. He had never seen her drunk before, certainly never been put off by the smell of her body or her breath, but now it made him feel nauseated. When he had almost dropped off, Lily woke up, agitated, ran to the bathroom, and vomited. He hurried after her, held her head, and washed her face. Then he tried to undress her and give her a clean nightgown, but she fought him off so forcefully that he gave up. He cleaned the puke from the bathroom floor. He wanted to wash off the stink of vomit and alcohol that clung to him, but there was no hot water, so he made do with washing his hands and face.

Shaul was terrified and bewildered. Lily's behavior was beyond his comprehension. How fortunate that Eliya's boyfriend had been there to bring her home, how lucky that she hadn't ended up staggering home on her own.

In the morning, he glanced over at his slumbering wife. The red lipstick had smeared over her mouth, giving her the appearance of a sad clown. He wanted to wipe it off, to smooth the creases between her eyes, but he didn't dare to touch her and quietly left the room. He dressed in the living room, folded his pajamas neatly, and placed them on the sofa. He skipped his morning coffee and left the apartment quickly.

When he came home, she wasn't there, and he assumed she had made her usual trip to the cemetery. Although it had taken quite some time for him to discover where she disappeared to every day from afternoon to evening, he had known her true destination for several years now. At first he had thought that she went to the cafés and shops along Dizengoff Street. In his lowest moments he had suspected that she was cheating on him.

"Where do you go, Lily?" he said when he finally confronted her, when he couldn't contain his anxiety and fear a moment longer. "Where do you go to every afternoon?"

"I just wander around," was all she would say.

"Where do you wander, Lily?"

"In all sorts of places."

"Lily," he pleaded, "which places?"

"What do you want from my life?" Sparks seemed to shoot from her eyes. "What do you want, to chain me up at home?"

"Heaven forbid, Lily, I would never try to stop you from going anywhere. I just want to know where you go. You're my wife, and I'm concerned about you."

"Don't worry. I always come home, don't I? So what do you have to worry about?"

"Maybe you go to Jaffa? Have you found another crazy old woman to read your coffee grounds?"

"Don't you dare call the *bishara* crazy." Now she was really angry. "The *bishara* was a good woman; she saved me so many times."

"What did she save you from, Lily?" Shaul really couldn't understand.

"From myself, from myself. She saved me from myself, may her memory be blessed."

"So is that it? Have you found a new *bishara*?"

"There isn't and never will be another *bishara*," she bemoaned. "I will never find another woman like her in Jaffa or in Tel Aviv or in the entire world. There is no place where I will find another *bishara* who will reveal my life to me, who will advise me about this terrible life I live."

Shaul ignored the latter part of Lily's short speech. "So where do you go, if not to Jaffa?"

"I go to the place that is the best place for me to be."

"Better than your home?"

"The place that is my home, where my soul is."

"What are you talking about?"

"I go to where my boy is," she said in a hoarse voice.

"Your boy?" he repeated. "You don't have a boy, Lily. You have a girl."

"I have a boy. How can you forget that I have a boy, who is also your boy."

He gazed in amazement at his tormented wife, and only then did he understand that she went to the cemetery. He took her in his arms, and she didn't resist. "Shh, shh, Lily," he whispered into her hair. "Everything's all right, my love. Go to the place where your soul is. Everything is fine, Lily. Everything is fine."

They never spoke of that conversation. Shaul calmed down—at least he knew where she disappeared to—and for a long time he accepted that there was no point fighting it or envying his dead child. Lily loved their dead child more than she loved him and more than she loved her living child, and he had learned to live with that fact.

But how would he deal with this new Lily who went out drinking and came home intoxicated? How could he cope with a woman who had suddenly started wearing low-cut red dresses and bared her arms and her legs like a streetwalker? She hadn't even worn lipstick on their wedding day, and now she was painting her lips bright red. Better to just keep quiet, he decided, to accept it and keep his mouth shut until this latest phase had run its course.

"I asked you if you mind that I spent nearly your entire paycheck on this dress."

"If you like the dress, enjoy the dress," he stammered.

"You aren't interested in why I came home drunk last night?" she challenged him. "You aren't interested in why I'm suddenly wearing a red dress? Not interested in why I put on red lipstick?"

"What do you want, Lily?"

"I want you to ask questions and not to sit here like some schlemiel in your pajamas and act as though nothing's happened."

"What's happened, Lily?"

"I'll tell you what's happened!" She raised her voice and stood up. "What's happened is I've had enough! I'm sick of coming home every day to you and your pajamas and your fried egg and your finely chopped salad. I'm sick of staring at the television and going to sleep straight after the last broadcast, and I'm sick of getting old before my time. Do you understand, Shaul? I'm bored out of my mind. I'm sick of rotting at home while other people stroll along Dizengoff, sit in Café Ravel, go to the movies, the theater, to restaurants, go on trips, while I'm stuck here with you, with your pajamas and your stupid suppers. I've had enough!" And she pounded her fists on the table, and the food and the dishes jumped and jangled.

Shaul held tightly to the table as he rose and faced Lily, and in a quiet, ice-cold voice he said, "You know where the door is, Lily. If you've had enough, walk through that door and don't come back. Go look for excitement someplace else. Drink like a drunk; dress like a whore; sit in cafés; go to restaurants; go to the theater, to Habima, the Cameri, the Ohel; go to hell—just go! Get out of this house!"

Lily's storm of emotions evaporated on the spot. She stared at Shaul in shock and disbelief. She had never seen him so decisive, had never heard him curse like that. Good Lord, he was throwing her out.

"As far as I'm concerned, you can sleep at the cemetery, next to your dead child!" he shouted and slammed his hand down on the table.

For a moment Lily faltered. Since the death of the baby, Shaul had almost never mentioned him. Now he was more fierce and determined than she had ever seen him, and he was kicking her out of the house. She pulled herself together, and without another word she turned toward the door.

"You're going to regret the day you told me to leave. You'll come begging on your knees for me to come back," she shot at him before she slammed the door.

There was only one place for her to go. She would sit at the bar and wait until the one-eyed man got off work, and then she would go home with him. He would pluck her like a ripe tomato, and she would taste his sweet body, and then, only then, would she finally be free. She stood on the sidewalk facing the pub, waiting for the line to get shorter, but it only grew longer. She realized that if she didn't get in line, she would never get in.

She was shivering. She hadn't thought to bring a sweater or a jacket and had only just remembered to grab her purse. She had her red dress and nothing else.

Suddenly she saw him.

"Eldad." She waved. He turned and his eyes widened.

"Mrs. Zoref, you're here again?"

"I want to get into the pub. Can you help me to jump the line?"

"Mrs. Zoref," he stuttered, "I don't know what to say. Does Mr. Zoref know you're here?"

"Enough with the 'Mrs. Zoref.' My name is Lily, and it is none of Mr. Zoref's business where I am. Can you get me in or not?"

"Mrs. Zoref . . ." He began again, "Lily, do you really want to get drunk again? It's not really dignified for a respectable woman like you."

"Young man, don't you worry about my dignity. Are you going to get me inside? Yes or no? Just don't stand here and preach at me. I'm old enough to be your mother."

Eldad was in a bind. He didn't want to insult Eliya's mother, but he knew that Eliya wouldn't want to see her at the pub again. She had been so upset the night before about how her mother had embarrassed her, and Ilan had only made matters worse with his imitations of the drunken Lily.

"Come on," he said, and he took her by the arm. "I'll bring you in through the kitchen."

They went around through the back courtyard. The odor of burnt oil assaulted her nostrils as they passed through the kitchen, and an unbearable racket assailed her ears in a tumult of conversation, laughter, and loud music, which blared from the speakers and set her temples pounding. Suddenly she felt suffocated.

Eldad showed her to one of the high chairs at the corner of the bar. He exchanged a look with Ilan, who winked at him. Eldad made a slashing motion across his throat, warning Ilan not to do anything stupid.

"Welcome, Queen Mother," said Ilan, smiling, ignoring Eldad.

Lily blushed. So she hadn't been imagining things after all.

"What are we drinking today, pretty lady?"

"Whatever I had yesterday."

"Coming right up," Ilan replied, and he gave her a suggestive smile.

"Are you nuts?" Eldad joined Ilan behind the bar. "You want her to get drunk again? You want Eliya to get mad at me?"

"Who's getting her drunk? A person goes to the pub, wants to relax, have a drink; who am I to refuse her?"

"Ilan, I'm not joking. I'm not bringing her home drunk again, you hear me? I don't want to upset Eliya or Eliya's father."

"Don't worry, my boy. I'll give her cola and tell her it's whiskey. She'll never know the difference."

Eliya

I thought I was seeing things. There, sitting in the crowd at the bar, was my mother, wearing a vulgar red dress.

"Mother, what kind of costume is that?"

"It's not a costume. I'm tired of wearing old rags. I felt like wearing something young. I'm not over the hill yet."

"But what are you doing here again tonight?"

"I'm not allowed to visit my daughter's place of work?"

"You've got to get her out of here," Eldad whispered to me.

I thrust my tray at him. "Take this round for me. Mother, seriously, why aren't you at home?" I lowered my voice.

"Your father threw me out."

"My father what?"

"What you heard. He told me to walk out the door and not come back."

"What are you talking about? Daddy would never throw you out of the house, even if you burned it down. Daddy can't breathe without you."

"If you don't believe me, go home and ask him."

"Mother, what did you do?"

"I didn't do anything. I just told him that I'm sick of coming home every day to his pajamas and his egg and his salad and his eight o'clock news."

"You've lost your mind."

"Why, because I want to live?"

"What does that mean, 'to live'? To sit in a pub with people who could be your children? Go to a folk-dancing class with people your own age—live."

"You go to a folk-dancing class. I'll go wherever I feel like."

"Mother, you're coming home with me right now!"

"I'm staying here. Can you give me a little more of what you just gave me?" she said to Ilan. "And put in a little whiskey this time. Don't try to trick me."

"Coming right up," Ilan laughed. "Your mother is seriously cool," he said to me. "If she was twenty years younger . . ."

I glanced at my mother and caught the expression on her face. Even in the dim light I saw her features freeze and her face redden. Only then did I realize that she was coming to the pub because of him. How mortifying! What did she think—that he liked her, that he thought she was a young woman?

At that moment she realized that Ilan was treating her like a joke, a bad joke. She gulped down her drink and rushed out of the pub.

"You bastard," I hissed at Ilan.

"I didn't say anything!"

"You dumb bastard!"

I hurried after her and barely managed to catch up with her at the corner of Dizengoff.

"Mother, wait. Mother, please wait."

"Leave me alone." She shook me off. "Just leave me alone and get back to your boyfriend and to that stupid Moshe Dayan whose mother never taught him how to behave like a gentleman."

"What did you expect, Mother? You come to the pub, drink like a fish, dress like some cheap woman—what did you expect?"

"I'm your mother. Don't you dare call me cheap."

"Look at yourself! What's with that dress?"

Lily took a few more faltering steps and collapsed onto a bench on the sidewalk, holding her head in her hands. Suddenly everything flipped. I felt like she was a little girl and I was her mother, reprimanding her. She covered her face with her hands and looked so lost. Everything was so strange—since when did we actually talk about anything real? Since when did I tell my mother what I was really thinking?

"Mother, you go home, and I'll go back to the pub. I have a shift."

"I'm not going home," she said.

"So where will you go?"

"I don't know, but I'm not going back to your father."

"Don't talk nonsense. He must be going out of his mind with worry, and I have to get back to work. Eldad is no waiter; I'm sure he's smashed half the glasses by now."

"I'm not going home. You can go wherever you like."

I was at a loss. I couldn't just leave Lily sitting like a naughty child.

"We'll go to our apartment. Sleep at our place tonight, and in the morning we'll figure it out."

"I'm not going to your apartment. I don't want to see Moshe Dayan's face in the morning."

"Don't worry; you won't see him. He sleeps at his girlfriend's. You can sleep in his room."

"I am not getting into his bed."

"Fine, so Eldad and I will sleep in his room, and you can sleep in our room. Let's go. I'm sure Ilan's going to fire me tomorrow anyway, so what difference does it make?"

As we walked toward the apartment, I stole a glance at the woman walking beside me, a woman who wasn't young but wasn't old, a woman whose face had been touched by the passing years but was still beautiful, and I asked myself, *Who the hell is this woman, and how many more*

surprises does she have in store for me? How is it that although I have known her since the day I was born, I don't know her at all?

She hugged herself, trembling in the wind that blew from the sea. Suddenly she said, "I'm sorry."

I thought I had heard wrong, but she went on, "I'm sorry you had to leave work because of me."

"No big deal, and anyway all that cigarette smoke isn't good for your skin," I said, and I smiled at her. To my surprise she smiled back.

When we got to the apartment, Lily told me that she liked it, that it smelled like the sea, and I thought, *Well, at least we have one thing in common—we both like the smell of the sea.*

"Here, take these." I tossed her a pair of pajamas. "Get out of that terrible unflattering dress."

"Why isn't it flattering? See how well it fits me."

"It may fit fine, but it doesn't work with your face. From the back you look like a young girl, but when you turn around, it's scary."

"Now you're insulting me too."

"That was a compliment. I hope I have a body like yours when I'm your age."

"You will. You'll see that you will. We have good genes in our family," she said and continued softly, as if talking to herself, "even though I don't know anything about my genes."

I pinched myself. Had the Age of the Messiah arrived? Lily and I were having an ordinary conversation. And that was when I realized that what might be a once-in-a-lifetime opportunity had fallen into my lap. I was about to have the conversation with my mother that I had always longed for.

Lily

When Lily woke up, the sun was high in the sky. She had once again
slept till midday. Her emotions were stirred by the yellow glare and the
sight of the blue sea visible through the window of Eliya and Eldad's
room. She walked over to look out at the sea. And suddenly she found
it so beautiful, so blue and so deep. No wonder Eliya loved it so much.
The promenade was crowded with people. She could hear the sound
of balls hitting paddles from the many games of *matkot* on the beach
and the familiar call of the ice cream vendors: "Ice pops, ices, chocolate
banana." The beach chairs were arranged in rows, filled with glistening men and women; children built sandcastles; bodies bobbed in the
waves, and occasionally the lifeguard's voice was heard, issuing a warning. She couldn't take her eyes off the sight. Life, people living, going to
the beach, playing games, eating ice cream, swimming, talking, laughing. It was only she who was stuck in her tiny, monotonous existence.
How had she become this gray, boring woman, bitter and angry? She
could view the sea from her windows as well, but she had never looked
out at it. When Eliya had asked her why she always looked east, she
didn't tell her that she was looking toward the place where her baby lay.

She filled her lungs with air and turned away from the window. The
red dress lay draped over the chair. Whatever had possessed her to buy
that horrible thing? How had she ventured out of the house in it, and

how could she have put it on to go to visit her child? Her baby had told her to be free, but he hadn't told her to dress like a tramp.

The door to the room where Eliya and Eldad had spent the night was closed. They were surely still asleep. How it had irritated her when Eliya slept till the afternoon; now she was guilty of the same thing. She washed her face in cold water, squeezed some toothpaste onto her finger and rubbed it over her teeth, and laughed at what she was doing. She realized that she never laughed. Why did she never laugh? Why was she always angry, resentful, irritable? She looked at her reflection in the mirror over the bathroom sink. Her skin was clear and shining, and she gazed into her own green eyes. Her hair had darkened over the years, and there was little left of the gold that had shone so brightly when she was young. She smoothed her hair with her hand. The blonde was gone, but her hair wasn't gray yet. Her lips were sometimes dry, but they were still full, just like Eliya's. Eliya resembled her so closely. How had she not seen it until now? Who would have believed that it would be Eliya who would come to her aid? If it weren't for Eliya, who knew what would have happened last night, where she would have ended up. God bless Eliya. Who would have believed it, of all the people in the world, Eliya.

It was already late, and she had to go see her child, to tell him that she had done what he'd told her to do. And it had led to the spark that might grow into a radiant light shining on her and Eliya. She had to tell him that his father had kicked her out of the house and that she felt light as a feather.

Eliya

I left my parents' house and took the number 4 bus in the direction of Mendele Street. When I crossed Ben Yehuda, I suddenly saw Lily striding along, wearing a dress that she had obviously borrowed from my closet. She suddenly looked ten years younger. Her usually stooped shoulders were straighter, her steps light and nimble. She was walking so fast I had a hard time catching up with her. My parents had both gone mad, my mother dressing up like a teenager and my father sinking into a depression that I didn't know how to deal with. The day before, when I had gone to my parents' apartment, my father looked like he had aged a dozen years overnight. "Don't worry," I said. "Mother's at my place."

"Thank God." He sat down and held his head in his hands, the mirror image of his wife on the bench on the sidewalk.

"Daddy, what's going on? Lily says you threw her out."

"Oy, sweetheart, I don't know what's with her. She isn't the woman I know. She's like someone else, with all sorts of crazy ideas in her head."

"What ideas?"

"She's sick and tired of living with me. She's bored with me. She wants to go to pubs, thinks she's a young girl. I'm worried about her. I've always accepted her antics, was prepared to take it all. But I don't know how to deal with this new phase."

"Daddy, you're the best husband a woman could ever wish for," I told him, and I stroked his cheek. "She's gone off the rails."

"And how, tell me how, my child, can I get her back on track? All my life I've kept my head down and taken whatever she dished out, but this time I couldn't do it. She hurt me; she hurt me here," he said, and he placed his hand over his heart.

"Daddy." I was frightened. "Daddy, you can't take it to heart. You have to take care of your health. Instead of being angry with her, you take it out on yourself. You didn't do anything wrong."

"But it's here, the moment I have feared more than any other. My love isn't enough for your mother anymore; she's looking for excitement. She wants to live, to go out, to take on the world."

"That's what she told you?"

"She didn't have to. I've always felt that I'm not good enough for her. From the day she allowed me to escort her from the falafel stand in the Bezalel Market to her dormitory on King George Street, I have lived in fear that she might leave me, and now it's happening."

"She said that you told her to leave."

"I told her that she knows where the door is, but as soon as she closed it behind her, I regretted it, and from the moment she left, I have been waiting for her to come back. I can't live without her, Eliya. I am nothing without your mother."

He wept for a long time, resting his head on his arm, his shoulders shaking. I didn't know how to contain his sorrow. I put my hand on his shoulder. "Enough, Daddy, enough. She'll come back. For now she's with me and Eldad, and tomorrow I'll tell her that she can't stay with us any longer. She won't have a choice, and she'll come home."

"No!" he shouted. "Don't turn her out! I don't want to think about where she might go." Through his sobs, he started to mumble, "God help us, Eliya, just not there."

"Where's 'there,' Daddy? She has no one else in the world besides us. She has no family, no friends; she has no one."

"Ach, my child, all these years I've tried to hold things together and to look after us, all so our family wouldn't fall apart. I failed, my child. I've failed."

My heart broke as I listened to him. "Daddy," I said, "when I was little and Mother would have one of her fits of anger, you would tell me that when a big wave comes, you have to keep your head down and wait until it passes."

"This wave isn't going to pass," he said in despair. "This wave is going to sweep us all away."

"I'll stay here tonight," I told him, "and tomorrow I'll bring Mother home." He nodded and went into his room.

I knew he wouldn't rest until Lily returned. I didn't manage to get any sleep in my childhood room. It didn't feel good to be back in the bed where I had spent the most difficult year of my life. I got up and walked around, biting my fingernails, until finally I was weary enough to sleep. I went back to my room and lay down. I could hear my father crying through the adjoining wall. A wave of pity washed over me, but to my surprise, for the first time in my life, I didn't only feel sorry for my father. I also felt for Lily, who had caused him so much pain, but I sensed that her actions were out of her control.

Suddenly I realized it was all up to me. I was the only one who could bring my family together. I was determined to ease my father's loneliness. I decided I would reunite my father with his family and forge a connection with them myself.

When I woke up, my father was already gone. Brokenhearted or not, he wasn't going to miss a day's work. The bed in my parents' room was made, the supper dishes were washed and stacked on the dish rack, and there was a note taped to the refrigerator:

> My sweetheart, I've gone to the store. Look after
> Mother. Love you, Daddy

I ran my finger over the note, and my eyes filled with tears. I was determined to stop his suffering. I would force Lily to come home if I had to drag her by the hair through the streets of Tel Aviv.

On my way back to the apartment, I saw Lily standing at the bus stop on the other side of Ben Yehuda. Why was she waiting for the southbound bus instead of the northbound, which would have taken her in the direction of home? I rushed across the busy street, but before I could reach her, the number 4 bus pulled up, and she hurried on. I called her name, but she didn't hear me.

Confused, I went back to Eldad. "I missed you," he said, taking me in his arms.

"What a night I had," I told him. "I don't know what to do. I can't force my mother to go back to him."

"Where is she now?"

"I just saw her at the number four bus stop. I was sure she would leave here and go home. But she got on a bus going in the opposite direction."

"Come." He took my arm gently. "Let's check out the number four bus route."

I tried to remember the southbound route—Ben Yehuda, Allenby, Magen David Square, and the last stop at the Central Bus Station. "Oh no! If she went to the Central Bus Station, she could go anywhere in the country. How will we find her? What will I tell my father?"

"You're upset," said Eldad. "You can't think straight like this. How about you wait for her at home and I catch the number four and try to follow her. We'll find her; it's not like she's a little girl who's going to get lost."

I hugged him, drawing strength from him. "I'm so lucky to have you."

We parted with a lingering kiss, but I was still restless. Suddenly I decided that the best way to clear my head would be to go for a walk by the sea.

My father had told me that the first people to settle in Tel Aviv didn't appreciate life by the sea and built their houses facing away from the water. They thought the sea was only for fishing and boating. Even Meir Dizengoff, the first mayor of the city, said the sea was only good for horses to bathe in.

I used to love to walk hand in hand with my father, just the two of us, without Lily, who wasn't allowed to know that we went to visit my grandparents. I didn't understand why I was forbidden to tell her, but I was so thrilled to have my father all to myself that I never asked. One day Lily found the bar of milk chocolate my grandmother had given me, and then our visits stopped, along with our walks along the beach. I was sad to lose those walks, when my father regaled me with stories of Tel Aviv.

My favorite stories were the ones about his childhood. Every day, when his father and his uncle were at work, his mother and his aunt would take him and his brother, Shmulik, and all the cousins to the beach. The fresh sea air was always a welcome reprieve from the Tel Aviv heat waves. He described the huge baskets his mother and his aunt would pack with thick sandwiches with leek patties and slices of tomato and pickles. He told how he'd carry a watermelon on his head all the way to the beach, where they would split it open and eat it with chunks of salty white cheese. They would stay at the beach until sundown, get home late, and collapse onto their beds, asleep before their heads reached the pillows. I envied his wonderful childhood in the bosom of his family, a childhood full of aunts and uncles and cousins, so different from my lonely one. I sometimes daydreamed that I was there, too, with all those relatives, enjoying the feasts and playing with my father and his cousins. And in those daydreams, I, too, was a happy child, an ordinary child.

My father thought that the sea was a divine gift, and he'd awoken the same love in me. How lucky I was to have grown up by the sea, and that the balcony in Eldad's apartment looked out onto the beach. I could never imagine living with my back to the sea. I continued my walk along the neglected waterfront, imagining all the cafés that had lined it before I was born, as my father had described them to me, with the waiters wearing tailcoats and bow ties circulating among the patrons and serving European treats brought with them from their home countries, like cold coffee with ice cream and whipped cream topped with a cherry. I imagined the five o'clock hour when the orchestra would start to play and the patrons would rise from their chairs and dance.

Now the only places lining the promenade were gambling joints and shady bars, a far cry from its glory days. When I reached the opera house, I planned to turn back, to go home and wait for Eldad and Lily, but something stopped me from turning around. Something propelled me southward, past the remains of the Menashiya neighborhood. My heart contracted at the sight of the demolished buildings. Islands of devastation, piles of junk and construction debris thrown out to sea. I was so lost in thought that I was surprised to see that I had reached the Shabazi neighborhood that bordered on Neve Tzedek, where my grandparents lived. How many years had it been since I was here, in this neighborhood I had loved so much as a child? Its houses looked to be on the verge of collapse. Neve Tzedek, the first Hebrew neighborhood built outside Jaffa, had once been home to writers, poets, and painters, but now this once-beautiful area was known only for poverty and crime.

A wave of nostalgia washed over me, and I shivered, realizing how much I missed my grandparents. The last time I had glimpsed them had been at my doomed wedding. I was ashamed at how numb my heart had been that day, how disrespectfully I had treated them, behaving as though they were two strangers. I suddenly decided that I wanted to try to atone for my unforgivable behavior. I would go to their house, knock on their door, and apologize.

As I got closer to their home, I hesitated. I didn't know how they would receive me. What if they didn't want to see me? And what if they wouldn't forgive me for my disgraceful behavior? Would they be able to absolve me despite the fact that I had never come to see them? How could I explain all the years when we had not been in touch?

It wasn't long before I stood before their simple house. The wooden shutters were held open by metal pieces affixed to the wall that looked like tiny people. The walls of the house were weather beaten by the wind that blew in from the sea. And yet to me it seemed that time had stood still. I climbed the single step, took a deep breath, and with a trembling hand knocked on the old door, whose brass nameplate bore my last name, Zoref, right under the peephole.

My grandmother opened the door and looked at me in surprise. At first she didn't recognize me, and then slowly it dawned on her that the young woman standing on the doorstep was her granddaughter.

"The dead are resurrected! How long has it been, *querida*, since I have seen your beautiful face! Come, come inside," urged my grandmother, her eyes shining. "To what do we owe this pleasure that finally our granddaughter has honored us with a visit?"

I walked into the house with hesitant steps. But all my worries evaporated thanks to my grandmother's reaction. The warmth in her eyes melted my heart. "*Qué sana estás*, Eliya. You should only be healthy." My grandmother peppered her words with Ladino, and the language was so pleasing to my ears. "Not a day goes by that your grandfather and I don't think about you. So many tears we have shed over your father and over you, may we be forgiven for all our sins. How are you, my *querida*, and how is your husband? Only yesterday I said to your grandfather, 'Who knows, maybe we have a great-grandchild and we don't even know.' How would we know when your father doesn't tell us anything?" My heart caught in my throat when I realized that my grandparents didn't have any idea what had happened since my pathetic wedding day.

"I'm not married anymore, Grandma," I confessed, ashamed. "I'm divorced."

My grandmother regarded me in silence. I watched her slowly taking in the meaning of my words, but she recovered quickly and said, "Don't be embarrassed, *querida*. Right away I could see that that man wasn't for you! Why would a person get married at the rabbi's office? Only if they have no money to pay for a hall, or heaven forbid they have something to hide." She rested her hands on her belly. "Oh my, what a wedding he made for you. A disgrace, not a wedding. I hope he didn't break your heart, the *bastardo*."

"He broke it, Grandma, he broke it, but I managed to heal it. I have a new boyfriend who I love very much, and I'm sure that when you meet him, you will also love him."

"*Gracias a Dios*," my grandmother sighed. "Thank God. I am so happy you came to visit us. I have used up all my tears, *querida*. How can it be that a mother doesn't see her son? That a grandmother doesn't see her granddaughter? May we be forgiven for all our sins, *mi alma*. We don't have such a big family that we can allow ourselves not to see each other."

Her speech, so rich in Ladino expressions, enchanted me as it had so many years before. I had forgotten how much I loved to listen to her talk. I had even forgotten the Ladino words of love she used to shower me with. "*Mi alma*," she would say, *my soul*.

Trying to keep my emotions in check, I said, "It's a shame, Grandma, such a shame that you stopped being in contact with us."

"We stopped? Heaven forfend! Grandpa Albert and I would give our lives to see you and your father. What do you think, that we like being alone? Two old people sitting alone on Shabbat and the holidays, like two miserable wretches with no children, no grandchildren. We sit and look at each other, and we don't utter a word, afraid that if we speak, it will hurt even more. In my family we always respected the old people. My mother, may she rest in peace, she would say, 'A home without old people is like a home without water, a home without air.' But now that's enough, *gracias a Dios*, praise God. The main thing is you're here." The words poured out as though they had been pent up for years, and now they burst forth in a torrent. She could finally relieve the burden in her heart and speak her pain aloud. Perhaps, at last, it would be relieved. "If only Albert was here as well, but he is still at the synagogue."

I was afraid that if my grandmother kept talking, a river of tears would pour from my eyes and I would never be able to stem the flow. I went to her and hugged her soft body, kissed the withered cheeks furrowed with wrinkles.

"*Basta, querida*," my grandmother scolded me gently. "Enough tears. We should be happy and thank *Señor del mundo*, who makes miracles in this world. What is happening now, Eliya, it's a miracle! It's a miracle that you came to visit your old grandmother and grandfather."

"But what happened?" I asked my grandmother. "Why did we stop coming to see you? When I was little, we would come every Shabbat." I remembered waiting impatiently all week for the visits and the bar of milk chocolate that she always gave me. I would gobble it up right away. Until that one time when I'd saved a few squares. What a scene Lily made when she found me eating it in my room. In a rage she stuck her fingers in my mouth, pulled out the chocolate, and threw it in the trash, all the while screaming at my father that not only did he take me to see his parents behind her back, but his mother was ruining my teeth. As a child I hadn't made the connection, but now I realized: that was when it had happened; that was when Lily had forbidden him from bringing me here, because after that we'd never gone back. And maybe I had always known that it wasn't that my grandparents had rejected me but that it was Lily who had driven a wedge between us. At first I used to nag my father to take me to visit them, but he never responded. To make it up to me, he took me to the zoo at Hadassah Park and once even to the amusement park on Jerusalem Boulevard in Jaffa, and then I stopped pestering him. My father always knew how to make me feel better, but I'd never realized how much heartache the situation had caused him.

"Ach . . . may we be forgiven for all our sins," my grandmother sighed, jolting me out of my reveries. "I never got along with your mother, and she never got along with me. From the day your father brought her here from wherever he found her, I didn't like her. But he insisted on her, and I had no choice, so I accepted her. And then the baby, may his memory be blessed, was born, and after he died, as strange as she was before, now she went crazy, and then you were born. What a *muñeca* you were, a doll. I fell in love with you in a minute, and I wanted to come visit you every day, but your mother wouldn't let me inside your house, wouldn't let us see our granddaughter. And your father, who has a big heart but, God forgive me, a small brain, wouldn't agree to bring you here without her permission. I begged him. I missed you; I wanted to see your sweet face. I begged so hard that he finally gave in. He would give your mother 'a few hours of peace and quiet' and bring you to us like a thief behind her back. But when she discovered that he was coming here, she told him to get out, locked the door on him, and threatened she wouldn't let him or us see you. I said to him, '*Iza querido*. Do as she says; just don't leave her alone with the child, so she doesn't, God forbid, do something.' I was afraid she wouldn't take care of you. She could barely take care of herself, that strangest of all creatures our son found in the street."

"Father met Mother at a falafel stand in the Bezalel Market."

"*Nu*, that's not in the street? One day he shows up with her, and I ask, 'Who's the family? Who are the parents? Where is she from?' And there's no answer, *nada*, nothing. And after that she doesn't come anymore. Shaul says her feelings were hurt. If you only knew what a golden boy your father was before he met her, how much respect he gave us. I was sure he would marry a good girl, one of us, not that strange creature he brought us. That's it; that's what happened. There were problems from the first minute. She cast a spell on him, your mother."

I wanted to tell my grandmother that there was nothing wrong with the fact that my father had met my mother at a falafel stand. After all, I had met Eldad on the beach. Young people meet in all sorts of places. I wanted to tell my grandmother that it was no wonder that Lily didn't want to have anything to do with her, if from the start she'd made faces and called her strange, but I bit my tongue and kept quiet. I had come to atone for all the wasted years and apologize, not to argue or, worse, to upset her and start an argument. And yet my heart ached for Lily. I imagined her not as my all-powerful mother but as an insecure young woman, homeless, with no family, who visited the home of her boyfriend, and his mother scowled, peppered her with questions, didn't even pretend that she wasn't an unwanted guest, and most of all acted like she wasn't good enough for her precious son. I felt sorry for Lily; I felt her pain. For the first time in my life, I felt empathy for my mother.

Then I almost leaped from my chair, horrified. Here I was, sitting with my grandmother when my mother had disappeared. I should have been searching for her. How had I forgotten my concern for her for even a moment? I had to get back to the apartment; maybe Eldad had already found her. I had to leave.

Completely oblivious to my change in mood, my grandmother was still fussing around me. "Sit, sit, *querida*. Why are you getting up? You have to taste your grandmother's famous *burekitas*; I'm sure you have forgotten what they taste like. Come over here and eat, *querida*. Why are you thin as a matchstick? What is this? Doesn't anyone feed you?"

"Grandmother." I tried to get a word in. "I have to go now."

"Go? You just got here! I haven't had a chance to breathe you in. You don't know how overjoyed we are to see you," she said, unaware of how agitated I was becoming. "Look, look here, at the picture on the sideboard. Who's that girl with the curls and the ribbon in her hair? Your father saw how much it hurt me that I couldn't see my grand-daughter, so he gave me that picture. In tears he gave it to me and said he was sorry. 'Soon,' he would say, 'soon Lily will calm down, and we will come to visit.' But time passed, and you never came. I would comfort your grandfather and tell him, 'Don't worry—soon Eliya will grow up and come to visit us without her father, and she won't need her mother's permission.' But you didn't come. You should only be healthy, you aren't dependent on your mother's craziness anymore, and still you didn't come. Is that a nice way to treat the only grandmother and grandfather you have in the whole world?"

My eyes filled with tears. I couldn't explain why I hadn't come to visit the one place where I had always been welcomed with open arms and a warm heart. How I had allowed myself to forgo the orange seg-ments my grandmother would peel for me on a sunny winter day and feed to me one by one, how I had been willing to give up the orange jam she would prepare from their tangy peel. I could almost taste the brown bread spread thickly with butter that they would buy on the black market and my grandmother would top with a layer of her orange jam, or the salty white cheese she would buy at Mr. Elazar's grocery store opposite the Alliance School. And the sweet watermelon, whose shiny black seeds my grandmother would remove and wash, and together we would arrange them on a towel outside in the tiny yard so they could dry, and the following week she would take them out of a glass jar where she had placed them after she'd toasted them, pulling off their hard shells with her teeth and feeding me the soft insides. I remembered how she used to take me by the hand and we would go out to the small street where the neighborhood women would gather, sometimes perched on wooden stools, and she would show me off, proudly calling me her beautiful granddaughter.

I could smell the salty scent of the sea through the open windows, and everything came rushing back to me. How I had loved to come to Shabazi Street, the fun I'd had playing hide-and-seek with the children who lived there, dodging the washing hanging on lines strung from window to window all along the narrow lane.

I looked around the living room at the heavy brown furniture, the sofa strewn with pillows, each one embroidered by my grandmother's hand. A large framed tapestry, also her work, hung on the wall. The large sideboard was crowded with framed family photographs. A photograph of me stood near the center, alongside a picture of my father as a little boy, wearing a sailor suit, standing beside his mother, who was holding my uncle as an infant in her arms, and a picture of my Uncle Shmulik as a grown man with his American family. There was no photograph of Lily. My heart contracted as I realized that I either hadn't met or didn't know most of the people in the photographs. There were pictures of adults and young people, family groupings of an entire tribe, and I longed to learn about all of them. This was my only family. True, my mother didn't have relatives or roots, but I did, and I didn't know any of them.

"Grandfather Albert and Grandmother Sarina came to Israel from Yugoslavia before I was born," my father had once told me. He'd never told me more, and I'd never asked, but now I wanted to know.

I embraced my grandmother again, feeling her soft breasts, breathing in her smell of soap and lavender. My grandmother rocked me like a baby. "*Ize mía*, my girl," she murmured into my hair. "We have missed you so much."

"I've missed you too, Grandmother Sarina," I whispered. "But they're waiting for me at home." I considered telling her what had happened to Lily, what had happened to my father and to me. In the end

I decided that I shouldn't. I turned toward the door. "I have to go now, Grandmother, but I promise to come back."

But she wouldn't let me go. "Won't you stay a little longer?"

I gave her one final hug. I felt so good, as though I had come home, as though I was exactly where I was meant to be. And for the first time in my life, I realized, *This is what family feels like.*

"Grandmother," I said in reverence and love, "I have to go. My boyfriend is waiting for me at home."

I wondered once more if I should tell her the real reason that I had to tear myself away from the fierce embrace in which we held one another, but before I could make up my mind, she burst out, "You aren't going anywhere, *querida.* Any minute now your grandfather will come back from the synagogue, and we will sit down and eat lunch. And for once it won't be just two lonely old people sitting down at the table. Your uncle in America comes to visit every few years, but your father lives on Dizengoff, and he doesn't come at all. *Haida querida*, enough saying you have to go. Come and help me set the table. Your grandfather got old, and he can't help me anymore. He spends all day at the health fund or sitting around with his friends. They sigh and gossip, a bunch of foolish old men who can sit for hours and tell stories about the old days in Monastir, which is worthless now."

"Monastir?" I had never heard the strange name before.

"Ach, *querida*, Monastir is the name of our city. We came to Israel from there. A beautiful city, Monastir, a small community, where everyone knew everyone because we all lived in the Jewish neighborhood, right next to each other. What a life we had there, and what a synagogue. It was a palace, not a synagogue. It was so beautiful, so luxurious. And the parocheth, the curtain on the Holy Ark, in your whole life you've never seen a parocheth like it. My mother told me that all the women in Monastir embroidered that parocheth with golden thread, each one in her turn, and it would go from house to house until they finished it. And when it was finished, they hung it above the Holy Ark in the

Kal di Aragon Synagogue, which was the name because our ancestors arrived there after the expulsion from Aragon in Spain. And there was a house of Torah study and a school and a cemetery they called the House of Life of the Monastir community. And what a cemetery! All the gravestones made of marble and at the head of each one a Magen David, so heaven forfend they wouldn't make a mistake and think a goy was buried there and not a Jew."

I was fascinated and wanted to hear more. Nonetheless, when she paused to take a breath, I tried again: "Grandmother, I really must go." But it was pointless.

"You aren't leaving before you kiss your Grandfather Albert's hand. It's the least he deserves from you." I gave in. I would wait until my grandfather returned. I would do as my grandmother asked and kiss his hand, and then I would say goodbye and run all the way back. I hoped that by then Lily would be home safe. Until then, I decided, I would listen to my grandmother's stories and try to fill in the gaps of all that had been kept from me over the years and strengthen the blood connection between myself and this woman, who never stopped bustling around and talking.

"So is Monastir in Yugoslavia?" I asked my grandmother. "I've never heard of a city with that name."

"Today they call it Bitola. It is a small city in Macedonia, which is in Yugoslavia. First it was the Turks who ruled there, may their name be blotted out, evil sons of evil. And today it's the Communists, may their names be blotted out, even worse than those Turks."

"So we are Yugoslavian?"

"No, *querida*, we are Monastir Jews, and that is what we will always be, and our language is Ladino, Spanish, not like the languages they speak in Yugoslavia."

It was obvious that my grandmother enjoyed showing off her knowledge of geography and that she relished the opportunity to voyage back in time to her childhood. Spellbound, I drank it all in.

"The house of May Their Memories Be Blessed, my dear parents, was on the main road in the Jewish neighborhood, a big house with a *cortijo*, a big courtyard, inside and plants flowering in pots. Next door to us was a school for teaching Torah to the little children. The house where Albert, your grandfather, lived was on the same street, above his father's store. His father was a well-known jeweler. Even the goyim, may their memories be blotted out, would come to our neighborhood to buy gold from him. Even when he was little, your grandfather would go to the store with his father and learn how to work with the gold, until he was better than his father. Their store had much success and brought to them, praise God, a good living.

"My family, may it be blessed, didn't lack for anything. My father, Shmuel Nachmias, was an apothecary. Our medicine store was right next to the Zoref family jewelry store. And not only the Jews but many non-Jews, lots of goyim, would stand in line for cures, because my father was a big expert. They all gave him respect and called him Doctor. And it's true he often gave medical advice to people after they told him what was ailing them, and he saved them a visit to the real doctor, which cost a lot of money. May his memory be blessed, my father was a *zaddik*, a righteous man. On Friday at the synagogue he would give medicine even to people who couldn't pay; because of him they also called the synagogue the apothecary. And he wasn't only a *zaddik*; he was also wise. People would come to him for his free advice. They would come hungry and leave feeling full even though they hadn't eaten a thing, because he filled them with so much wisdom.

"The Zoref and the Nachmias families were like relatives. And from the days when Grandfather Albert and I were *chiquititos*, tiny children, the families agreed that we would marry. And when the time came, we had a big wedding at the synagogue, and after the ceremony there was food fit for kings, and we ate and danced and laughed until morning. Ach, what a wedding we had. They talked about our wedding all over Monastir.

"So that's it—both your grandfather and I came from good families. Now you understand, *querida*, why it was important to me that my sons would also marry brides from good families? But what can you do? Man makes plans and God laughs. My sons, may God help me, brought me one daughter-in-law from the street and one from America. One is no good and the other is terrible."

My grandmother's last words upset me. I didn't like her referring to my mother as a woman from the street. I was relieved that I hadn't told her about Lily's disappearance, since she already had such a low opinion of her. Who knew what she would have thought if I'd told her. All I wanted was to make peace within my estranged family so that the anger would fade and the arguments be forgotten. But every time my grandmother called Lily an ugly name, it seemed to burn my skin.

"Come, Grandmother, let me help you set the table," I said, to change the subject.

"Thank you, *mi alma*. Here, put these plates on the table. These are from my wedding set. My mother gave them to me as part of my dowry. I dreamed of passing them on to my daughter. But what can you do—God gave me only sons, and I thought, *It's all right; I'll give them to Shaul's wife when he gets married*, but I didn't want to give them to your mother. She didn't respect me, and she wouldn't have respected my mother's dishes."

Such a shame, I thought, so many wasted years. These beautiful dishes could have been laid out on the table at my parents' house; we could have been eating off them at family meals with my grandparents and carrying on the traditions that had begun in faraway Monastir. I pictured my Great-Grandfather Zoref sitting at his worktable in his store in Monastir, with a monocle on his eye, the better to see as he hammered out a gold bracelet of his own design. I imagined my Great-Grandfather Nachmias in a white cloak, thick-lensed glasses on his nose, as he stood at the counter in his apothecary, in front of a glass-fronted cabinet lined with rows of small bottles containing medicines and potions that he prepared for his customers. In my mind's eye I saw the homes where my grandparents had grown up, the tapestries adorning the walls, the china cabinets where the elegant sets of dishes were displayed, the sideboards holding family photographs, the soft sofas upholstered in floral fabrics, the bookcases that accommodated the holy books, the large dining tables around which the families would gather. I imagined the paved courtyard with a well in the center and the pots overflowing with colorful plants, in a distant place, in a distant country, in a distant city whose name I had never heard before today. Entire lifetimes bound up with my own, by virtue of a lovely set of dishes whose patterned plates I now held in my hands.

We set the table together in silence. I carefully put down each fragile porcelain plate, outlined with a band of gold. *When I marry Eldad, this is the wedding present I will ask my grandmother to give me, and I will take such good care of it, and I will pass it down to my own daughter, and the set of dishes from Monastir will be the common thread that runs through our family, a constant reminder of where we came from and where we're going.* I wanted to share my thoughts with my grandmother, but I hesitated. Maybe it was too soon. I had to allow her to become accustomed to my presence. After all, I had descended upon her unexpectedly, and I sensed that the old woman was still digesting my reappearance in her life. Slowly, slowly, I decided, I would follow her rhythm.

"We should only be healthy; the days of the Messiah have arrived," my grandmother murmured. "I used to set a table for twenty people. Do you know what a family we have? Ach, you, may we be forgiven our sins, you don't know anyone. Not your Uncle Shmuel or his wife, who your mother used to call 'Her Highness,' and not your cousins. Not Isaac, your grandfather's brother, and his wife, Hannah, and their six children and their daughters- and sons-in-law and their grandchildren. We used to meet to recite the Friday-night kiddush and eat our Shabbat meal together, and on Shabbat afternoons I would make up a pot of macaroni *hamin*. My slow-cooked Shabbat stew. We would alternate hosting, one time at our house, the next time at Isaac and Hannah's, such a big family around the table. It was a comfort, for we missed the rest of our family that remained in Monastir, which was so big that on Seder night we would take down the doors that separated the rooms and push together many tables so there would be room for everyone. But ever since your father stopped coming and Shmuel left for America, I stopped inviting anyone over. I'm ashamed that our children have left us alone, and since I don't invite them, they don't invite us. You could say that your mother broke up the family." My grandmother paused to sigh and wipe her eyes.

"Tell me more about life in Monastir, Grandmother Sarina," I encouraged her, ignoring her harsh pronouncement about Lily. "I want to know everything."

"Oy, *querida*, where do I begin? I was seventeen when Shaul, my father-in-law, may he rest in peace, came to ask for me from my father, Shmuel, may the Lord avenge his blood. We were engaged right away, and then, a month later, we were married."

"So fast? You were only children!"

"We certainly were. I may have been married, but I was still tied to my mother's apron strings. I wouldn't leave her side until she said to me, 'Enough, Sarina. You are a bride; go to your husband.' Truth be told, *querida*, at first there was nothing at all between your grandfather and me. I wanted to stay with my mother and my sisters, and he wanted to stay with his brothers. His best friend was his big brother Isaac, who was a member of the Zionist youth movement called Blue White, and he came to live in Israel and worked in the citrus orchards in the city of Petah Tikva. Later he moved to Tel Aviv, and one thing led to another, and he started to manage teams of construction workers, and he started to do well for himself. He got married, he had children, and he wrote to your grandfather and begged him to come here. In his letters he wrote that Tel Aviv was a beautiful white city, and he promised that if we came, he would help us get settled. Your grandfather got excited, and he wanted to go. Me, the minute he started talking about it, I was afraid. I was afraid to leave my family, my mother and my sisters, my little brother, Eliyahu, who was the apple of my eye. I told your grandfather, 'Over my dead body we're going to Israel. I am not leaving my mother or my sisters.' I loved my life in beautiful Monastir, even though the goyim, may their names and their memories be blotted out, didn't care for us.

"So many tears I cried, *querida*, how I sobbed, but nothing helped. Even my mother told me there was nothing I could do; a wife must follow her husband. So I went. I wept and I went; did I have a choice? And the whole way on the boat I threw up all my insides. I thought I was seasick. I didn't know I had your father in my belly. How should I know? What did I know about life? I was a young girl with no mother to explain things to her, no sisters to lean on. *Wai de mei*, how I cried! I filled the sea with my tears. All the way from the port in Saloniki to Jaffa Port, I never stopped crying.

"In Jaffa, Isaac was waiting for us and drove us in his automobile to his house here on Shabazi Street. What can I tell you, *querida*—the way he described Tel Aviv to us and the way it looked was day and night, earth and sky. He said a white city, Riviera. But it was not white and no Riviera. All the way from Jaffa, sand and sea, camels and Arabs, and flies, so many flies, Lord help us. I was lucky I had the fan I brought from Monastir. If not, I would have lost my mind. But still I soon fell in love with Tel Aviv, because of the sea. Sometimes I thought the people in Tel Aviv lived on the beach and not in the houses. Every hour of the day, from morning till late at night, people were on the beach. They had winds from the desert, the khamsin, much worse than today, and me with a baby in my belly sweating like a horse and heavy as a bear, and to cool down a little from the heat, we went to the sea, and I would go into the sea, and only in the water could I breathe."

"I love the sea too," I told her. "Every day I go to the sea."

"Oy, *querida*, after you and your father stopped coming, every day your grandfather and I went to the sea, and only there were our hearts soothed. There's nothing like the sea; it heals the soul. From the moment we stepped off the boat in Jaffa, I was in love with the sea, but you can't eat by enjoying the sea. Your grandfather had to find work; soon the baby would come. He had a profession—he was a jeweler—but he had no money to open a store, and no matter how many times he went to all the jewelers on Herzl Street and Allenby Street and asked for work, he couldn't find any. Those were hard times here. People barely had money for food, so how could they buy jewelry? The other jewelers hardly had any work for themselves. So Isaac gave him a job helping him build houses in Tel Aviv. But your grandfather was a jeweler; his delicate hands weren't made for rough building work. He wasn't made to carry sand and stones on his back like a camel. And it was time already to leave Isaac and Hannah's house, where we had stayed too long. Your grandfather said we didn't want, God forbid, to argue with our family; better to leave before the quarrels started.

"Fine, but where should we go when I have a baby in my belly and your grandfather has no work? In the end, Isaac found someone from Monastir with a jewelry store who would take on your grandfather, but the store was in Jerusalem.

"I cried and cried. I didn't want to move to another city, and even if my sister-in-law and I were like a cat and mouse sometimes, I didn't want to leave my only friend in the country. Times were hard; the Arabs in Jaffa were shooting at the Jews from the Hassan Bek Mosque, and every other day you heard about someone who was murdered. And in the middle of all that we took our suitcases and we moved again, this time to Jerusalem. We arrived on the eve of Yom Kippur. We were preparing for the fast, and then the world turned upside down. The Arabs were rioting and screaming. Why? Because on that Yom Kippur eve, for the first time, the rabbis decided to set up a barrier at the Western Wall to separate the men from the women. The Arabs thought the

Jews were trying to take over the place that is holy to them. Then their mufti, the evil Nazi, may his name and memory be blotted out, Haj Amin al-Husseini, promised them that whoever killed a Jew would have a place in paradise, and they shouted, *'Udrub adbach al Yahud!'* and the bastards rushed out of Damascus Gate and killed a Jew in the Bukhari Quarter and continued to HaNevi'im Street and the Georgian neighborhood and burned down houses and a synagogue and moved on—they should all go to hell—to the Mea Shearim neighborhood of the ultra-Orthodox, and if it wasn't for a Jew named Aharon Fisher who took a pistol and shot the bastard in the head who was leading the Arab mob, God knows what a disaster there would have been. Luckily they grew afraid, and they ran away. And I thought, *Thank God, it's over.* But it wasn't over. It went on the next day, in Hebron. Arabs fell on Jews and slaughtered them like sheep. They slaughtered children in front of their mothers, slaughtered fathers and mothers in front of their children, cut off pieces of the men's bodies, raped the women, burned houses. The bastard British didn't intervene to stop the massacre. What a disaster, may God have mercy. Even in other countries they wrote about it in the paper, what happened in Hebron.

"All that fear in my heart, I was afraid it would enter the heart of the child in my belly. I was shaking with fear, and I was all alone, no mother by my side, no family, and my husband working all day in the jewelry store, from sunrise till sunset. You understand, *querida*, how miserable I was? Luckily I had good neighbors, and they helped me, and I would stay with them during the day until your father came home from the store. I was terrified that my water would break while I was home alone."

"When the time came, was Grandfather with you?" I listened in suspense to her story.

"Thank God it happened at night when we were sleeping. My water broke, and your grandfather took me to Misgav Ladach Hospital, and your father, may he be healthy, was born, and we gave him the name

Shaul after Grandfather Albert's father, and a year later Shmuel was born and received my father's name, and that was before we knew that we would never see our fathers again. And after that, no more. My womb closed. God didn't want to give me more than two children. If only I had five or six children like my neighbors, then maybe now, with Shmuel in America and your father, who prefers your mother to his own mother, I wouldn't be alone, may we atone for our sins."

I placed my hand on hers. "You won't be alone anymore, Grandmother. I promise you, I will always be here for you."

"With God's help," she whispered. "Ever since we lost our families, I'm afraid to dream. And oho, *querida*, how I used to dream! When we came to Israel, I would dream about Monastir, about my father and my mother, about my sisters and my baby brother, Eliyahu, may he rest in peace. I prayed to God to bring them to the Land of Israel or to take me back to Monastir. I would imagine that I lived next to my mother and she helped me with the children; I would imagine my sisters, who were married women now, and I wasn't at their weddings. I missed little Eliyahu, and I wasn't at his bar mitzvah. And your grandfather missed his family, and we would lie in bed at night, the two of us, and dream out loud about the day when our families would come to this country and once again we would be one big happy family and our children would have grandparents and aunts and uncles and cousins. Oh, how we missed them, how we dreamed, how we hoped! But then came the great disaster. I still can't talk about it without my voice catching in my throat. Forgive me, *querida mía*; it doesn't matter how many years have passed. I cannot take in that disaster. Who knew, dear God, who knew that such a thing could happen?"

"What disaster?" I was confused.

"The Holocaust, *querida*, the Germans, may their names and their memories be wiped off the face of the earth, and the goyim who collaborated with them and were even worse than they were."

Of all the things my grandmother had told me, this was the one that left me in shock. I hadn't had the faintest idea that my relatives had perished in the Holocaust.

"I didn't know," I whispered. "Grandmother Sarina, I never imagined . . ."

"How could you know, *querida*, if your father erased us? How could you know? Who would have told you? The entire Zoref family, except for Uncle Isaac and Grandfather Albert, and all the members of the Nachmias family except for me were burned in the gas chambers. Nothing is left of them. When the accursed Germans entered Macedonia, they gathered all the Jews in the capital city, Skopje, lined them up on the banks of the Vardar River, not far from the big bridge, and forced them all into a tobacco factory. From there they put them on trains to Treblinka. No one survived.

"I had such beautiful memories of the Vardar River. When I was a little girl, the whole family went on a trip to Skopje, and we had a picnic on the riverbank, exactly where they made the Jews line up. Ach, what a world, how beauty became horror. There was so much evil in the world in those times."

I was sitting on the edge of my chair, my eyes glistening with tears. "And how did you find out what happened? How did you find out that they perished in the Holocaust?"

"After the war we hoped and prayed that someone was still alive. Survivors began to arrive in Israel on immigrant ships, and we searched among them for people from Monastir. We did everything we could. We asked; we searched; we called the radio program everyone listened to that helped people to find their relatives; we listened to every broadcast, hoping someone was looking for us, that someone had heard the message that we were looking for them. But *nada*, not one of us had survived. There are hardly any people left in the world who speak Ladino."

"Grandmother, how did you go on living after that?"

"It took a long time until we could start to live again, *querida*, until we had to accept that Isaac and his small family were all that remained. When your mother was pregnant with May His Memory Be Blessed, we asked your father to name the baby, who we prayed would be born healthy and strong, after one of our relatives who we lost in the Holocaust, but your mother said that she and only she would decide what the name of her baby would be, and she called him Ron."

"But his name was Chaim," I protested.

"Later. Before he died, they added the name Chaim, *life*. Maybe she hoped the new name would give him life, but the name didn't help and God didn't help, and the poor baby died when he was a year old. I was so angry at your mother. May God forgive me, I hated her for not agreeing to give him the name of a relative who died in Treblinka. When the baby died, my heart broke for her. But we are believing people: 'The Lord gave and the Lord has taken away; blessed be the name of the Lord.' Your mother, she didn't forgive the Lord. All the time she cursed Him, and all the time she grieved and she cried. Even when she was pregnant with you, and even when you were born, she couldn't stop grieving. When I asked again if they would give the new baby to be born the name of my little brother, Eliyahu, she didn't care anymore, and she accepted your name without a fuss."

"I knew," I told my grandmother, "I knew that I was named after one of Father's uncles who died. I didn't know he died in the Holocaust. I didn't know he died a child."

"One year after his bar mitzvah," my grandmother whispered.

For years I had suffered with the name Eliya. No other girl was called Eliya. Children made fun of me, calling me Eliyahu the Prophet. So many times I came home in tears and asked my father to change my name to Ilana or Ofra, any normal Hebrew name like all the other girls had. But over time I learned to love my name; I enjoyed having a name that was special and liked the fact that no one else I knew had the name Eliya. I felt as though it suited me perfectly.

"You know, Grandmother, for a long time I have felt such deep pain about the Holocaust, but I never understood before now the depth of that pain. Only now do I understand how personal it is. Every time someone calls me by my name, the name of little Eliyahu echoes through time. I am named after a boy who was murdered in the Holocaust; his blood flows in my veins."

"*Dios mío*, Eliya." My grandmother kissed me. "What you are doing to me—my kerchief is soaked through with my tears. I haven't cried like this for so long. I can't remember the last time I talked about my family, and when was the last time I hugged you, *querida mía*. But enough, enough crying! *Basta!* We must be happy! Today is a day of miracles; we should open a bottle of wine like we used to do in Monastir when there was a celebration. We Jews from Monastir, we love to be happy and to drink wine. Come, *querida*, come, let's dry our tears and drink wine even before your grandfather comes home."

At that very moment my grandfather walked in. He looked exactly as I remembered him, a small man with a kind face. My grandmother bent over and slapped her thighs as she exclaimed, "Oh, welcome home. Finally you're here. Look, Albert, the dead are risen. Look what the wind has brought us."

I ran to him, and he opened his arms to me as if we had never parted. "Welcome back, welcome back," he murmured. "How your grandmother and I have missed you."

"I told her," said Sarina. "But now enough—she already said she's sorry. We have forgiven her, so let's sit down at the table."

"Said she's sorry for what?" asked my good grandfather. "It's not her fault that we haven't seen her for such a long time; it's our fault that we gave up. We should be apologizing to you, Eliya, not you to us."

"I should apologize to you, Grandfather Albert. I'm sorry that I haven't come to see you for all this time, even when I didn't need my mother's permission anymore."

"Eliya," he said in a gentle voice, "it's not only your mother who is to blame for us not seeing each other; it is us as well. Every stick has two ends."

"What nonsense you talk, Albert," my grandmother interrupted. "Your brain is getting too old. Are you saying we didn't want her to come see us? How we cried and hoped that she and her father would come."

"Fine, fine, enough, Sarina. The main thing is that she's here now. Let's sit down to eat. You must have missed your grandmother's chicken *sofrito*. Many traits your grandmother has, some good and some less good, but her best one is that she knows how to prepare *sofrito* like no other woman. Your grandmother is the queen of the kitchen."

His words softened her, although it was obvious she was angry that he had said that the blame for our long separation rested equally on them. We sat quietly and ate the *sofrito* that had pride of place in the center of the table. I had forgotten the taste of that tender chicken that melted in my mouth, the delicious flavor of the potatoes baked in its juices.

"So how is your father?" my grandfather asked suddenly, and only then did I realize that my grandmother hadn't asked about him at all.

"He's usually fine," I answered, trying to decide whether or not to tell my grandfather what was going on.

"*Nu*, praise God. The main thing is that he's usually fine."

"Yes," I said, and the words seemed to tumble out by themselves, "but now he's very worried."

"Did something happen?" my grandfather asked, looking genuinely concerned.

"My mother's going through a crisis, and he doesn't know how to deal with it."

"Again with a crisis," my grandmother exclaimed. "Her whole life, it's one crisis after another with that one."

"Quiet, Sarina," my grandfather said, raising his voice. "What is wrong with your mother?" he asked me softly.

"I don't understand, and Daddy doesn't understand," I told him, although I was still unsure whether I should reveal my family's secrets. But they were also my family. And maybe they knew something about Lily that my father and I didn't know. "She wants to leave home," I said.

"Praise God, now she decides to go, after she's already ruined the family for us." My grandmother couldn't keep quiet.

"Sarina!" My grandfather pounded on the table with his fist, and the glasses and the silverware rattled.

"What do you know about Mother?" I asked. "From the time before I was born, what do you know about her life before Father married her?"

"We don't know anything, Eliya," my grandfather replied. "Your father never talked about her with us. He knew that your grandmother was unhappy about the relationship, and so he never talked about Lily."

"I tried to find out what I could," my grandmother burst out again. "I asked where she was from, who her family was, but she didn't say a word. There was no one from her side to ask for her hand for our son as the tradition goes, no one. Afterward your father said that she has no family and no one in the whole world, only him. I asked where she grew up, and he said in an institution of the Jewish Youth Aliyah organization. So I asked how she got there, because they aren't born there. So where was she before? All we knew was that she lived in that women's dormitory on King George Street; that's all."

"You too, *querida*?" asked my grandfather, looking at me with compassion. "You also don't know anything about her?"

"I know that someone left her at a convent when she was a baby—that's what Daddy told me. The nuns raised her until she found out that she was Jewish, and then she ran away."

"*Dios santo.*" My grandmother was shocked. "She grew up with nuns in a convent? He never told us that."

"Why should he?" My grandfather regarded her harshly. "You wouldn't accept her from the women's dormitory, so what chance was there that you would agree to welcome her from a convent?" He turned to me. "And what was your life like, at home?" he asked, ignoring his wife.

"Daddy kisses the ground she walks on, and she never got along with me."

"What a surprise," my grandmother interjected again. "She never got along with anyone. Why should she get along with her own daughter, her own flesh and blood."

"*Basta*, Sarina!" my grandfather thundered. "We are finally on the train, and you keep trying to take us back to the station. It's over; what was, was. Now our granddaughter is here in our home, praise God. Now everything is fine, and it will be even better. From this moment forward, you are not to say a word about your daughter-in-law, do you hear? Not one word. You have done enough damage." My grandmother seemed to collapse in upon herself. We finished our meal in silence, and then I helped to clear the table and dry the dishes.

"It's getting late, and I really have to go," I told them. "I'm worried about my father and also my mother."

"Go, *querida*," my grandmother said. "But don't forget to come back."

"I'll be back," I promised. "But please, Grandmother, stop being angry with Mother. So many years have passed, and it's time to make peace."

"I promise, *querida*. I promise we'll start over, turn over a new leaf."

"Thank you, Grandmother. From now on we will be a family like every other. You will no longer sit alone on Shabbat and holidays."

"The Messiah has come," she repeated. "Do you believe, Albert, do you believe in miracles? Today a miracle happened. Remember this day, Albert, the day we got our granddaughter back."

I embraced my grandmother and kissed her two wrinkled cheeks, and then I went over to my grandfather and kissed his hand. He placed his other hand on my head, closed his eyes, and recited the Sheheheyanu blessing, said on special occasions: "Blessed are You, Lord our God, sovereign of all, who has kept us alive, sustained us, and brought us to this season."

◆ ◆ ◆

When I finally got to my parents' apartment, I found my father pacing like a caged lion. He was still in his work clothes. "Where were you?" he shouted as he never did. "It's not enough that your mother disappeared; you have to disappear too. What do you two want, to drive me insane?"

"Mother isn't back yet?"

"No, she isn't back, and you disappeared, too, so I left the store in the middle of the day, and I'm going crazy! I asked you to take care of her. Where were you?"

"The last time I saw her, she was getting on the number four bus that goes to the Central Bus Station."

"Good Lord, Eliya, and you didn't stop her?"

"I didn't manage to reach her before she got on the bus, and it drove away before I could get on."

"If she was headed to the bus station, she could have gone anywhere. How will we ever find her now?"

"Eldad went to look for her. You haven't heard from him?" I paused and looked my father in the eye. "Daddy, think hard. Where could she have gone?"

"There's only one place I can think of," he said, "but you don't have to go via the bus station to get there. She would have taken the bus to Tzahala and continued on foot."

"On foot to where?"

"To the cemetery at Kiryat Shaul. She goes there every day, Eliya. She's there from afternoon to evening. To visit her dead child."

"How do you know that?" I asked, horrified.

"For almost thirty years she has gone to the cemetery every day."

"And you don't go with her?"

"'The Lord gave and the Lord has taken away.' He took the baby and gave you to us, and ever since you were born, I prefer to be here with you, my living child, and not with the dead child. But to this day your mother has not stopped visiting her dead child."

"You never tried to stop her?"

"And if I'd tried, would I have succeeded? Your mother is stubborn as a mule, and once she makes up her mind, nothing will stop her."

"Daddy, this is a mental illness! He died years ago. You knew that you should send me to a psychiatrist. Why didn't you send her?"

"Shh, shh, Eliya, why are you talking about a psychiatrist? Did your mother try to kill herself? All she does is go every day to light a candle on the child's grave. There are worse things."

"Like us not being in contact with Grandfather Albert and Grandmother Sarina?"

"Why are you mentioning them all of a sudden?"

"I was there today. I visited them."

He was silent for a moment, as though struggling to absorb what I had said. When he turned to me, I could see tears in his eyes. "And how are my dear, elderly parents?"

"They miss you, Daddy. Just like Mother can't stop missing her dead child, they can't stop missing their live child, the one who lives so close. For them, it's as if he's dead."

"Oy, Eliya," he said so softly I could barely hear him, "not a day passes when I don't think of them, when I don't want to go to the old neighborhood to visit them."

"So why don't you go? Why did you stop going? Why did you stop taking me there?"

"Because your mother told me it was them or her, and I chose her."

"Grandmother Sarina said that Mother split up the family. To force you to choose between her and your parents is cruel. She not only separated you from them but also me from my grandparents. That's what Grandmother told me. But Grandfather said that it's also their fault, not only Mother's fault."

"He's right, my child. When I met Lily, she had no one in the world. I brought her home, and I hoped that we could be the family she didn't have, but from the start my mother wasn't welcoming. She interrogated her like someone from security services. Is it surprising that she didn't want to visit them? And after we were married and our first child was born, instead of bringing us closer, your mother distanced herself further. She demanded that we cut off contact with them. And I knew that if I didn't do what she wanted, I would lose her. And I didn't want that to happen, just as I don't want to lose her now. Where the hell is she? I'm going to have a stroke because of her." He wiped his face with a large handkerchief, the picture of a broken man.

"I'll find her, Daddy. I thought she would be home by now. She must be at the pub or at my place."

"The pub? What kind of a custom is that, to go to the pub? I don't understand anything anymore. Not the way she behaves, not the way she dresses, and not the places where she is suddenly spending her time. A woman who never in her life left her house alone after eight in the evening is suddenly sitting in crowded pubs? The world has gone mad, and your mother has too. I'm coming with you to look for her."

"No, Daddy." I felt so sorry for my father. His familiar world was slipping through his fingers, and he looked like a lost and bewildered little boy searching for the hand of an adult to cling to. I would give him my hand; I would get his life back for him; I would bring back my mother if I had to go looking for her all over the country.

"If Mother comes back," I told him, "I think you should be here. In the meantime, I'll go look for her. But before I go, Daddy, I want to ask you for something."

"Anything, my child," he said. "Anything."

"When Mother comes home and everything returns to normal, can we go all together to visit Grandfather and Grandmother? Can we be a family again?"

He hugged me, and our tears ran together. "I promise," he whispered. "There is nothing in the world that would make me happier."

I ran almost all the way to the bar. A song was blasting through the speakers. I glanced at the bar, but my mother wasn't there, and Eldad was nowhere in sight. Ilan was busy filling glasses and loading the waitresses' trays with bottles of beer. He handed me a bottle. After a pause, he interrupted my thoughts, asking, "Is everything okay with your mother?"

"What do you think, after she came here, sat at the bar in that red dress, and tried to pick you up as if she was some nubile twenty-year-old?"

"Come off it, Eliya. She didn't try to pick me up. She came here to have a little fun, to feel a little young. What's wrong with that? Do you really think she would try to pick up her daughter's boyfriend's best friend?"

"I don't know what to think anymore, and now she's disappeared."

"Where has she disappeared to? We're in Israel, not America. How far could she go?"

"I have no idea. The last time I saw her, she was getting on the number four bus in the direction of the Central Bus Station."

"So maybe she had some errands to run. She's probably already back home."

"She's not there. I suddenly feel like her mother instead of her daughter."

"Hi." Eldad appeared by my side and kissed me on the mouth.

"Where have you been?" I whispered in his ear, kissing him back, pushing my body into his.

"I walked the streets looking for your mother, hoping I would bump into her, but nothing. I walked the length of Dizengoff, Ben Yehuda, Ibn Gabirol. I searched the bus station. Nothing."

"We have to go to the police," I declared.

"The police? I don't think they'll pay any attention to us, Eliya. She's only been gone since noon."

"So what should we do? Sit here and drink, while my mother is missing?"

"Come," he said and took my hand. "Let's go to your father; he must be going nuts. We'll wait for Lily with him. She'll come home eventually. Where else could she go?"

On the way to my parents' place, I told him about my reunion with my grandparents. I told him everything I'd learned about my family history, and then I started to worry about Lily again.

"We'll find her, and after we do, everything will change for the better. You did something very brave today, my beautiful woman. You did a good deed as well, asking your grandparents for forgiveness and renewing the connection with them before it's too late. But now you face the toughest mission of all; now you have to talk to your mother."

"I'm worried about her, Eldad. Deep down I feel that something bad is happening to her, something that has turned her world upside down. I think . . . I know what she's looking for."

"What is she looking for, my love?"

"My mother is searching for her roots. I have to find her and go on this difficult journey with her so she won't have to travel that path alone. I want to know who the real Lily is, because the woman we know has been wearing a suit of armor woven of thorns so she won't be hurt again. There's no child in the world who could emerge unscathed after being abandoned by its mother as a newborn infant at the entrance to a convent on a freezing, snowy night."

Lily

The sight of the huge building filled her with terror. She had forgotten the tremendous height of the surrounding walls but not the gates, which were always locked. She also remembered the staircase that led to the clearing and the cypress trees that surrounded it, encircling the large, well-tended garden, in the center of which stood a grape arbor and a vegetable patch. She could picture herself as a little girl dressed in her blue convent smock, down on her dirt-stained knees as she made tiny wells in the earth with her small fingers and dropped in seeds for tomatoes and peppers. She remembered the stone-paved paths that curved into secret corners where she'd loved to sit to escape the ominous silence within the convent and the nonstop whispering of the girls—which to her ears sounded like the buzzing of a swarm of bees—who didn't dare to raise their voices for fear of the wrath of the nuns. Lily remembered the large main hall, with its painted floor and high decorated ceiling, and the painting of the baby Jesus in his mother's arms, which covered most of the central wall. So often she had stood in reverence, staring at the picture of the beloved mother and her infant son. And she remembered well how her stomach had contracted painfully, as it did again now, because her own mother had never gazed at her with that same expression of love and compassion. She remembered the sofas and chairs upholstered in red velvet upon which she had been forbidden to sit, the black grand piano that she had been forbidden to touch. Once she had lifted the cover that protected the keys and pressed down with her tiny fingers, astonished by the sounds she produced, unaware of the approach of one of the nuns, who slammed down the lid on her fingers, drawing blood. The nun ignored her blinding pain and loud wails, grabbed her by the ear, and locked her in a tiny upper chamber. Hardly any light penetrated the small high window, through which she could see a little piece of sky. She had been imprisoned in the cold, frightening room for many long hours only because she had wanted to play the piano. She could still conjure the heavy scent of incense from the church, the sour, mildewy smell of the nuns, and the musty odor of the convent's stone walls, as well as the sound of the bells calling the occupants to prayer, the wind whistling through the leaves of the trees, and the rustle of the nuns' habits as they moved like ghosts along the corridors.

As she faced the imposing building, she experienced the same paralyzing terror as she had as a child who had fled this place so many years before.

The convent was situated in a nineteenth-century building and had originally been populated by stern Catholic nuns sent to Jerusalem to spread Christianity by doing charitable work among the poor of Jerusalem. They devoted most of their time to the abandoned children who ran wild in the filthy streets, starving orphans dressed in rags, eating what they could find, banding together in rival gangs, stealing and selling whatever they could. Some sold the use of their younger siblings' bodies or their own, for a pittance, to the Turkish soldiers. The nuns gathered as many of the children as they could house and provided them with food and a roof over their heads. After the Ottoman period, during the British Mandate, they also took in children whose parents couldn't take care of them for economic or other reasons, as well as children who were handicapped in some way, blind, deaf, or ill with chronic diseases. Despite her young age, Lily had always wondered how the nuns, who were busy every minute of every hour of every day with charitable acts, could be so insensitive and coldhearted.

Now she wondered whether young girls still lived within the thick walls as she had, abandoned to the care of the nuns. She remembered the other girls who had lived with her, many of whom were orphans like herself, some from families too poor to keep them, Arab girls and Jewish girls all sleeping in the same drafty hall, where narrow iron beds lined the walls. She remembered the thin mattresses that stank of urine, filled with straw whose stalks often poked through the coarse fabric, piercing her body like needles. She remembered the creaking metal springs that supported the mattresses and often woke her when she or the other girls moved in their sleep. Her mind filled with images of the huge kitchen, where the sparse meals were prepared, and she could almost smell the gruel bubbling in the enormous pot and the soup that had the odor of dirty laundry and always made her feel nauseated. But her strongest memory was of the day when she'd made the decision to run away from the enormous stone walls that imprisoned her.

Lily recalled the small chapel that had been her refuge when she'd sought solitude away from the prying eyes of the nuns. The chapel was located deep inside the garden and was usually deserted. Except on that fateful day when Sister Rose had come in. She could still hear the gentle nun's soft voice telling her how there's no love in the world like the love of a mother, and she remembered how her small heart had beaten. And then the harsh face of Sister Katherine loomed in her memory, and she recalled being told about how she had been placed on the doorstep at the entrance to the convent on a freezing, snowy Christmas Eve, about the note attached to the blanket in which she'd been swaddled, and about the drawing of the Star of David in clear, straight lines, which had convinced the Mother Superior that Lily's mother was a Jewess. Strange how all the years of strict Christian upbringing, years of praying to the crucified Jesus and his holy mother Mary, fell away in an instant when she understood that she was born a Jew. Strange how even as a young girl, she suddenly understood why the walls of the convent seemed to be contracting. Although she had never known any life other than her years in the convent, she had always felt as though she didn't belong. From that moment her restlessness was intolerable, and she began to plan her escape. Hungry and filthy, dressed in what remained of her blue convent smock, eating leavings from the market and trash from the gutters, she wandered the streets of Jerusalem until the good women of the Memorial to Moses club rescued her and took her to the boarding school in Herzliya.

And so here she was, many years later, standing at the entrance to the place from which she had fled, the place that hid the secret to her life. For maybe, if she knew who her mother was, she would know who she was. She didn't recognize herself anymore. She reached out and grabbed hold of the pull rope and gave it a tug. The sound of the reverberating gong sent her reeling back in time. She recalled how when she had heard it echoing through the halls, she would press her nose against the windows to see who was knocking, who was approaching from the unknown world beyond the convent.

She stood as if frozen in place. After some time the gate opened to reveal an elderly nun who observed her with curiosity. "May I help you?" she inquired in English, and Lily, as though her tongue were glued to the roof of her mouth, couldn't make a sound. Again the old woman asked, "Yes, madam, what are you looking for?"

Lily couldn't take her eyes off the nun's face. Furrowed with deep creases, it looked ancient, but the large blue eyes could only belong to Sister Rose. Good Lord, she was still alive, and suddenly Lily was overcome with terror that Sister Rose would grab the hem of her dress and pull her inside and she would be locked away, imprisoned, and would never be able to get out again. Without another glance at the nun, she turned on her heel and ran as if pursued by a pack of demons. Still panting hard, she caught the first bus back to Tel Aviv from the Central Bus Station in Jerusalem.

What had she been thinking? That she would reach the convent and they would supply her with the answers to her questions? Why had she suddenly thought that they knew something about the woman who had given birth to her? And why was she thinking about that woman now, may her memory and her name be blotted out, the woman who'd condemned her to life as a waif?

The *bishara* had told her that if she married Shaul and they had a family, she would set down new roots for herself, but what kind of family had she made? A family with a dead child and an estranged child. A child she had never embraced, never held lovingly in her arms, never told that she loved her. On the contrary. All she had ever done was distance the girl from her. And only now, dear God, only now did she understand how very much she loved her. But she had no idea how to tell her.

Her heart filled at the thought of Eliya. A tremor of emotion ran through Lily as she recalled the last few days. Despite their ambiguous relationship, Eliya hadn't left her side, had invited her to sleep at her home, had even given up her own bed for her. She had not been critical of Lily's embarrassing behavior, not gotten angry at her. Would her daughter ever be able to forgive her for the way she'd treated her? And Shaul, what crime had her good man ever committed to deserve being treated so shabbily? It wasn't his fault that she was unhappy. Shaul had cut himself off from his parents to please her and walked on eggshells to avoid making her angry. Her brain feverishly processed her swirling thoughts, and her breathing was shallow.

The bus pulled into the station, and she hurried off and stopped the first taxi she saw, never mind the expense. She had to get to Kiryat Shaul. She had to get to her child. The taxi let her off at the gate to the cemetery, and she ran to Ron-Chaim's grave. It was the only one surrounded by flowering plants, which Lily nurtured assiduously, the only one with a memorial candle, which always burned inside a small box she had ordered specially. It had cost a considerable amount of money, which she had saved by putting some cash aside each week from her housekeeping money. Lily practically fell on the grave, lay across it, and kissed the letters that spelled out her dead child's name. Gradually the thoughts in her head abated and she felt calmer. Her body cooled, she breathed normally, and her heartbeat slowed to its usual rhythm. "Thank God," she murmured, her lips fluttering over the cold marble. "Thank God, my child, finally I am here with you."

She closed her eyes, and then she heard the voice of her child rising from within her. "Go home," he whispered. "Go to Shaul; go to Eliya."

"How can Shaul help me? What can Eliya do for me? All my life I have been alone."

"You chose to be alone," the child whispered. "You pushed them away."

"I didn't want to be alone. I wanted a family to take the place of the family I never had."

"And you received a family," the child continued in his hushed voice.

"You call this a family, my child? This is a broken family. God didn't protect my family."

"God gave you a family," the boy continued in his gentle voice that singed her heart. "You are the one who was supposed to protect it. God wasn't supposed to do that for you."

She listened to the voice of the child that came from within her soul, and tears flowed from her eyes. He was right. God had bestowed a gift upon her, and she hadn't even untied the ribbon. What could she do now? How could she turn back time? She had to beg forgiveness of Shaul and apologize to Eliya. She should kiss the feet of her in-laws and beg their forgiveness too. With her own hands she had destroyed the gift God gave her, the family that was granted to her. How, dear Lord, how could she repair what she had broken?

Eliya

The gray clouds were gone and the sky was clear and blue, but it was still cold. I buttoned my coat and plunged my hands into my pockets. In one of them was the note my father had given me, with the number of the burial plot. He had copied it from a piece of paper that was wedged inside his identity card. Like my mother, he also took the dead child with him everywhere he went.

I entered through the large open gate. There were no other people to be seen at the cemetery, and I was scared to death. I had never been in a graveyard before. Even when classmates of mine had died in the Yom Kippur War, I'd preferred to pay my respects at their home during the shiva period of mourning rather than attend a funeral. The dead scared me, and a cemetery without another living soul filled me with terror.

I ran along the path, taking note of the numbers of the plots and the names on the tombstones. God, God, God! What had I gotten myself into? What if I didn't find Lily? I generally preferred not to disturb God, but this time I prayed with intent and a true and honest fear that nearly paralyzed me: "God, please let me find my mother. Make this nightmare end."

And then I saw her, bent over the grave. It was undoubtedly Lily. Her thick hair blew in the wind, and her body leaned forward, her face resting on the horizontal marble slab.

I didn't know whether I should reveal my presence or remain hidden, but while I was trying to decide, the heavens opened. I was suddenly drenched to the skin.

My mother remained sprawled across the stone on top of the small grave, seemingly oblivious to the rain. Now I was sure that Lily had gone crazy. What normal person would lie across her dead child's grave in a rainstorm so many years after his death? I was suddenly sorry that I had told Eldad not to come with me. Maybe he could have picked her up in his strong arms and carried her out of this ominous place.

"Enough!" my mother screamed. She banged her head against the marble stone, once and then over and over.

"Mother, stop!" I ran out from my shelter, took Lily in my arms, and held her, and with a strength I hadn't known I possessed, I managed to lift her off the grave. "Mother, calm down," I cried, but Lily continued to cry, trying to break free of my grasp.

"I can't stand it anymore. I hate being all alone in this world!"

"You're not alone, Mother. I'm here."

"Not alone. I'm not alone." Lily repeated my words as though she was reciting a mantra. "I have the baby. I'm not alone."

"Mother, the baby is dead, but I'm here. I'm alive."

"You're alive, but I'm dead. Like the baby Ron-Chaim, I'm dead."

My heart opened to her, and I held her tight. I had never held my mother before. Her head reached to my shoulder, and I was astonished at how small she was. Like a little girl, I thought, like a frightened bird. How different she seemed now from the way I had perceived her all my life. I felt a wave of immense pity for her.

"Mother, you're bleeding," I cried. In all the excitement I hadn't noticed that a trail of blood was dripping from Lily's forehead and staining my jacket. I quickly unwound my scarf and used it to stem the flow of blood. Her lipstick was smudged, the kohl she had used to line her eyes was running down her face, and the blood that had dripped down gave her the most bizarre appearance.

And then all at once the rain stopped, the sky cleared, and the air grew fresh and clean. Lily stopped crying. An unearthly silence reigned in the children's section of the Kiryat Shaul cemetery. The only sounds were raindrops dripping from the trees and Lily blowing her nose.

"Mother, let's go," I pleaded. "The rain has stopped; let's get out of here. Father is waiting at home. He's out of his mind with worry."

Lily moved away from me without a word and walked over to the cypress trees where I had been hiding. She returned with a rag that had been inside a bucket, wrung it out, and quietly began to wipe the rain off the white marble gravestone.

I approached Lily cautiously, as she continued to clean the grave diligently, scrupulously, and I whispered, "Mother."

She turned toward me as if noticing me for the first time.

"Eliya," she asked softly, "what are you doing here?"

"I came looking for you."

"Looking for me?"

"I almost gave up. I thought I'd never find you. Father said this was the only place where you might be, by the grave of . . ." I couldn't say the name of my dead brother.

Lily finished my sentence for me. "Of the baby Ron-Chaim."

"Yes," I said softly, "his."

Lily continued to wipe away the streaks left by the rain, cleaning out and polishing every crevice that time had worked into the stone, paying special attention to the letters of his name. "Ron," she whispered. "That's what I called him when he was born. What a beautiful name Ron is, a name of joy, of happiness, the name of a child born to spread delight. One year, Eliya, for one year he made me happy, and ever since it's been years of pain that won't ease, pain that catches me here"—and she placed her hand over her heart—"and chokes me here"—and she placed her hand across her throat. "And it's so strong, this pain, and it strangles me, so that the only place where I manage to escape it is here. When I lay my face on the marble stone, I can breathe. Here I can speak the truth without worrying that my words may burn; here I pour out my heart to him, consult him, ask questions, and receive answers."

"You ask a dead baby for advice?" I found that hard to believe.

"He talks to me and I hear him."

"How does he talk to you? He died at the age of a year. He didn't know how to talk yet when he died."

"Many years have passed, Eliya. He matured, grew up, became wiser than anyone I know. He saves me."

"He almost made you crack your skull. How does he save you? If I hadn't been here to stop you, you would have cracked open your head."

Lily was quiet for a moment as she looked at me, taking me in from head to toe.

"You don't understand," she said. "It was he who sent you to save me; it's the baby Ron-Chaim who sent you so you could stop me."

"It was Father who sent me, not the baby. It's Father who's sitting at home now and going out of his mind with worry, Father who hasn't slept a wink since you disappeared. Not a baby who you won't allow to rest in peace because you don't have the courage to accept his death."

Lily placed her hand on my face and stroked my cheek.

"My child," she murmured, "my poor child."

"Mother, it's scary here. Please, I'm begging you. Soon it will be dark. Let's go."

"Come," Lily said. "Come sit here on the ground beside me. There are some things I have to tell you. After that we'll go."

"The ground is wet, Mother. Come and tell me what you have to say on the way home; there's time until we get to the bus."

"No!" Lily was adamant. "I want to tell you here. These are things I have been holding inside for many years. I want you to hear from me why I have never been a good mother to you. I want you to sit down here beside me and listen."

Lily sat on the sodden ground, ignoring the mud and the damp. I did the same. I wanted to get out of that graveyard as fast as possible.

"Come closer," Lily said. "Sit close to me."

I moved toward her until my body was touching my mother's. To my surprise Lily took hold of my hands and placed them in her lap.

She took a deep breath, looked up at the sky, and seemed to be overcome with emotion.

"From the day I emerged from the womb of the woman who left me like a dog at the entrance to the convent in Jerusalem, I have been alone. It's true that you and your father live with me in the same house, but I feel completely alone in this world. That's how it is: someone who is born without a mother to nurse her at her breasts, to hold her when she cries, to cover her when she's cold, to comfort her when she's hurting, will always feel alone, and it doesn't matter how many children I have, and it doesn't matter how much your father loves me; I'm alone.

"I don't know who the woman who gave birth to me was, but one thing I know for certain. To her I was a terrible thing; otherwise she wouldn't have thrown me away like that. She was certainly frightened and had no one in whom to confide her panic and her fear. I don't even want to think about how miserable she must have been, and what an outcast. Imagine, to be an unwed mother today is a scandal, but it was so much more so in the twenties, when I was born. What that woman must have suffered."

I was amazed at the peace that had seemingly descended on my mother, who was speaking calmly and fluently. Here I was, finally having the conversation that Dr. Kaminsky had insisted that I have with her. Here was the opportunity to tell her what was in my own heart. And I would not allow this chance to slip away. Now it was my turn to take a deep breath. I said, "And did you place your hand on your belly when I was inside you? So that I could feel you? Not for one day in my life did I feel wanted or that you ever loved me. You are exactly like your mother."

Lily was silent for a very long time. She kept her eyes on the wet ground, but she never let go of my hands. Finally she gazed straight into my waiting eyes and said in a whisper, "I was afraid to feel. I believed that if I behaved as if there was no baby in my womb, then the pregnancy would go smoothly and nothing terrible would happen to the baby and God wouldn't take him from me as well. But you kicked me from inside. It was as if you were saying, *I'm here, and you can't ignore me.* And so I prayed to God to bless you with physical and mental health. I begged God to watch over you so that, God forbid, you wouldn't die like your brother died."

"So why did I always feel as though I was some kind of punishment that God gave you? That you would have preferred that I was never born?"

Lily sighed, and I realized that I had hurt her deeply. When she tightened her hold on my hands, I saw tears in her eyes. "When you were born, I hoped that the soul of Ron-Chaim would move into you. I hoped that the darkness would lift and my black heart would be filled with light. But the soul of Ron-Chaim was not inside you. You had your own soul, and among my other sins I couldn't find room in my heart for the light that you brought into the world. I didn't see the gift that God had placed in my arms, and I chose to remain in darkness. Your luck and mine was your father. Your father loved you for me as well."

She paused, as though searching for the best words. "Guilt, my daughter, is not atoned for. You carry guilt on your back like a cross you must bear all of your life; there isn't a minute when I am not carrying it. For the wrongs I have done to you and to your father, no atonement will suffice. In order for you to be able to live your life and love the children you will have someday, in order for you to be happy and at peace, you must know that you did not come into this world forsaken and alone. You weren't born abandoned, as I was. You were born to a father who is willing to give his life for you. And I too. I know you think I don't love you, but you must know I would die so that you may live. I am not asking you to forgive me, but I am asking you to understand. I was born to a woman who didn't want me and threw me away. I felt like a small

animal that had to fight to survive. And then into that great darkness
there penetrated a ray of light. I met your father, I started a family, I had
a baby, and for the first time in my life I fell in love—I fell in love with
the baby. He was mine. He beamed his love at me in his little smiles,
in the way he latched on to my breasts and was nourished by my body.
He became me, and I became him. And then, when finally I was happy,
God came and took my child, and once again I fell into the black pit
of despair that I had known as a child. Except that this time the pit was
deeper, and the void was infinite."

"Mother," I asked gently, "when you think about the woman who
abandoned you at the convent, are you angry at her?"

"I used to be angry," she replied. "I was terribly angry. I didn't want
to know a thing about her. When I was a young girl and went to the
Arab *bishara* in Jaffa who read my coffee grounds, I told her, 'I don't
want to know about my past. If you see something, keep it to yourself.'"

"I thought the only person you consulted was your dead baby?"

"I only started talking to the baby after the *bishara* died. I believe
she directed me to talk to him. When he died, she told me to go home
and lie with your father so that the soul of the dead baby would enter
the new baby who would be born to me. But you—what can you do—
you were born an absolute original. He was mine, but from the moment
you were born, you were your father's child. No, Eliya, you weren't
him."

"And that's why you didn't love me, because the soul of your dead
baby didn't enter my body?"

"I loved you, God help me, of course I loved you, but the forces
of evil stole my heart, locked it up, and threw away the key. And it
wasn't until you almost died in my arms that I realized that for all those
years I had been afraid that if I allowed myself to become attached to
you, there would be another disaster. Do you understand, Eliya? I was
afraid to feel like a mother again; I was afraid that if I loved you like I
loved Ron-Chaim, once again God would take what was mine. I felt

cursed. I felt as though everyone I dared to love came to harm. I was afraid that you would die, like he died. When you tried to kill yourself, I knew that if I lost you, I would also lose myself. For the first time in my life, I could feel the woman who gave birth to me." She placed her hand on her heart. "Here, in my heart, I felt her. I felt as though she was inside me, sending the strength of the biblical Samson into my fingers so that I could stop the blood flowing from your veins, sending me the strength to be strong for you. Because if you had died, I would have died with you."

"Mother," I whispered, "Mother, I am so sorry for you, and I am so sorry for your mother. Do you realize now how hard it is for a mother to give up her child? Do you understand that she gave you up to save you?"

"I understood that," Lily said, "on the day when I was about to lose you."

"And when your baby died, how is it that you didn't understand then?"

"On the day when the baby died, may his memory be blessed, a storm raged just like today. The heavens cried and I cried, and there wasn't a living soul who could hear my weeping merged with the tears from the sky. I was so young and the pain was so powerful that I couldn't feel a thing other than my pain. I didn't think, not about your father, who had also lost a child, not about Grandfather Albert or Grandmother Sarina, who had lost a grandchild, and certainly not about the pain of the woman who had given birth to me. I didn't have room in my heart for anyone. You should know, Eliya, that there is no worse punishment in the world than the loss of a child. A person who loses a child must have done something truly horrible in a previous life if God gives him such a terrible punishment in this life."

"Maybe God tried to atone for His deeds when He gave me to you."

"I didn't see it as atonement. I was too busy feeling sorry for myself."

"And what about me? Why didn't you feel sorry for me? Why did you never make me feel like a child who was loved? You always preferred to go to your dead baby rather than to be with me. Instead of giving me love, you gave it to him."

"Forgive me," Lily entreated. "Forgive me, for yourself, not for me."

"Before I can forgive you, Mother, I have to release this anger inside me that threatens to poison me."

My mother trembled, holding on to my hands like a drowning woman grasps a rope.

For a minute I thought I should let it go, but I knew that I had to have my say. "You only ever had harsh words for me, Mother. No kindness, no tenderness, no affection, no comfort. Why, Mother? Did I disappoint you because I didn't turn out perfect like your dead baby? Because his soul didn't enter my body?"

"You're right, Eliya," Lily whispered. "Forgive me. From deep in my heart I ask you to forgive me."

My mother, my mother who had a heart of stone, wept bitterly, wept like a child. Lily sobbed, holding her face in her hands, still trembling, and I held her, and she cried and cried, the sound of her weeping tearing through the silent, glistening graveyard. I held her, afraid that if I released her, she would revert to the Lily I had always known, and this moment, when for the first time in my life I felt that I was my mother's daughter, would vanish as if it had never been.

And that was how, wrapped in each other's arms, our tears mingled together, united as we had never been before, my father, Shaul, and my beloved, Eldad, found us at the cemetery.

Lily took to her bed the moment she got home. For three days and nights she stayed in bed, refusing to get up, refusing to eat. Shaul looked on helplessly but had to return to work. I fluttered around, forcing her to drink milky tea, feeding it to her as though she were an infant, covering her when her blanket fell off, plumping up the pillow under her head.

How similar we are, I thought as I took care of Lily. When I couldn't deal with my broken heart, I'd also climbed into bed and refused to get up. Just as my beloved father had watched over me, it was I who now took care of my parents. Suddenly I was the responsible adult in the family.

Without a second thought I moved back into my parents' home.

Eldad would join me at night, and we snuggled together in my narrow childhood bed. How I loved him for agreeing to stay with me in my cramped room, for the way he supported me as I helped my parents through their hard time.

On the fourth day Lily sat up, weak and pale, propped against the pillows. I walked in and opened the blinds. "Look at that sea," I said. "Maybe we can walk down to Gordon Beach, breathe some air."

Lily didn't respond, but she turned toward the window, where the blue sky kissed the blue sea.

"Do you forgive me?" she asked.

"I forgave you a long time ago, Mother," I replied. "Now you have to forgive yourself."

"How, how can I forgive myself after I destroyed your father's life and yours?"

"What was, was," I told her. "You can't change the past; what's important now is that we put back together what was broken, that we be a family."

"Oh, Eliya, I can't look your father in the eye after I ran away from home like that. How can we go back to being a family after everything I did to him? And what about his parents? They will never forgive me."

"They promised me they will forgive you."

"How can you know that?"

"I went to visit Neve Tzedek and apologized for not coming sooner. Grandmother Sarina is still mad at you, I won't say she isn't, but Grandfather Albert opened his arms and his heart, and then she softened up. And Daddy, he forgives you no matter what you do. As for me, I just want us to be mother and daughter. To forget the past. But for that to happen, you have to do some work, Mother, to confront what brought you to this point." I took a breath and waited for the usual onslaught. Only this time she didn't stamp her foot or shout at me.

I went on, "Now is the time to look back over your life at the mistakes you've made. This is the chance to recover, to heal from the past."

Lily looked at me in wonder as if really considering my words.

"When did you get to be so wise?" she asked. And for the first time in a long time, I smiled. And then she asked, with a seriousness that belied her fear, "You believe that old wounds can be healed?"

"I do."

"That's love, isn't it?" she asked in a soft voice. "Your love for Eldad and his love for you transformed you into a new person, into a good, strong person."

I smiled a second time. "Yes, Mother, Eldad is the love of my life, my true love. He healed me and I healed him. But I helped myself. From the moment I decided to take myself in hand, something changed in me, and a door opened. It wouldn't have happened if I had remained locked in my anger, in my hurt, in my silly pride, and worst of all, in the feeling that I was a victim. Now, Mother, get up and take a shower. The window may be open to the sea, but this room stinks."

Two weeks later we all crowded into my father's little Simca and drove to my grandparents' house in Neve Tzedek. My father was as excited as a child, and it was clear that this reunion with his parents was the fulfillment of his greatest wish. "May God bless you, my child; you are making your old father very happy. I never dared to dream that your mother would agree to renew contact with your grandparents," he said tearfully, and he stretched his hand from the driver's seat to the back seat and grasped mine. Lily sat rigidly in the passenger seat beside my father, looking straight ahead, not saying a word. Eldad and I, squashed together in the back, held hands all the way and didn't make a sound.

When we arrived, my father fell into his parents' embrace, and all of them wept. "*Dios mío*," exclaimed my grandmother. "The Messiah has come; it's the Age of the Messiah. I thought I would die and you wouldn't recite Kaddish for me. *Gracias a Dios*, come, come in, you too, Lily, welcome," she said to her daughter-in-law, who stood, hesitant, in the doorway. "Come in, come in. Why are you standing outside? And you, Eliya, where's your hug for your grandmother? And who's this? The groom?" She pointed at Eldad. "*Precioso*, what a handsome guy, welcome, welcome." She couldn't contain her excitement or her flow of words, and I was secretly grateful to her for her nonstop chatter, which filled the room and defused the tension that you could have cut with a knife.

My grandmother trundled to and fro on her heavy old legs from the tiny kitchen to the dining table, bringing out a seemingly endless array of dishes that she had prepared in honor of our visit. Each time she brought something out, she announced its name: "*Bougatsa*, with spinach so it will be kosher—I usually make it with cheese, but soon we will be eating *sofrito*, and that has chicken in it, so this time the *bougatsa* will only have spinach, but when you come on Shabbat, we'll also have *burkits* with cheese, so here you go. Eat! Enjoy! Eat, eat, Lily; you're still as thin as a matchstick, and your daughter inherited that slimness from you. You should gain a few kilos. It's not attractive for a woman to be so thin." She couldn't resist taking a jab or two at Lily.

Lily never said a word throughout the entire meal and looked less than happy to be there. She didn't even respond to my grandmother's remarks, and I wondered if she had decided to accept them as due punishment for having kept the family apart.

Meanwhile, my grandfather beamed. Later he would tell me that when we were finally all seated around the table together and the strands were reconnected and the circle was no longer broken, it was like a flaw-lessly crafted piece of jewelry, every gemstone fitted perfectly in place.

◆ ◆ ◆

Grandfather Zoref didn't speak much that day. He sat and reflected on the events of his long years. Details from his past seemed to spring to life before his eyes so that he could describe them to me.

He and my grandmother had lived in the apartment where we were all sitting for almost their entire adult lives. Jerusalem, to which they had moved when he couldn't find work, hadn't suited them. Sarina couldn't get used to the ongoing violence between the Arabs and the Jews, and she feared for her infant son, Shaul. She was frightened whenever Albert arrived home late from work. She seemed to shrivel up in Jerusalem, and anytime they visited Tel Aviv, she blossomed like a flower. In the end the family returned to live in Tel Aviv and moved into the apartment they still lived in today.

In those days Tel Aviv was a small, pretty city, whose beaches were crowded with people and whose waterfront was filled with women in their finery. He took to wearing short pants and cotton shirts and learned to watch out for camels on the edge of the road. Alongside their neighbors, Sarina and Albert dressed little Shaul in light clothing, placed him in the white wooden baby carriage, and walked along the beach.

Albert had just enough money to purchase a tiny key-money store on King George Street. His reputation grew quickly, and he soon had a loyal clientele. Young people came from all over Tel Aviv to purchase engagement rings and wedding rings, as did the wealthy matrons of Neve Tzedek, who ordered necklaces, bracelets, and rings glittering with gems. He was doing so well that he was able to buy the small house they lived in.

Sarina was happy. She sang as she pegged her washing on the clothesline and grew friendly with her neighbors. Sometimes on Saturday they attended cultural events and listened to people like Chaim Nachman Bialik, the beloved and admired poet and symbol of the new Jewish culture. On sunny winter days they put Shaul in his baby carriage, paraded along Herzl Street, and enjoyed the wonderful café life. They were well off, their son was a source of joy, and they were expecting a second child. Sarina even stopped moaning about how she missed Monastir. They had built a joyful life in the Land of Israel, and they were happy.

News of the Holocaust in Europe trickled slowly into the Land of Israel, followed by the horrifying realization that every single member of both their families had been taken. Every day seemed to bring more terrible stories, and the full scale of the horror became clearer—the expulsions, the death camps, the massacres, the starvation, the subhuman treatment, the suffering, the gas chambers. Albert and Sarina spent their days poring over their photo albums, drinking in the pictures of their parents, brothers, and sisters, and crying. Even Albert, ever stoic, wept bitterly.

◆ ◆ ◆

In the meantime, their sons were growing up and growing into two such different boys. Shaul, the eldest, was gentle and aimed to please. For him any word uttered by his parents was like a command, while Shmuel had a fire burning inside him. By the age of fourteen he had already joined a group to liberate the homeland, to his mother's great displeasure. And then the rioting began in the Land of Israel. It started with shooting at Jews in Jaffa, and then the War of Independence broke out. The British had only just left when the Egyptian Air Force started to rain down bombs on Tel Aviv. The bombing went on from the spring of 1948 until the summer. More than 150 were killed, and Sarina begged Albert not to go to work. Shmuel had already left home. He had been fighting for his country before it was established, and once it was, he fought in the Negev in southern Israel with the Israeli Givati Brigade commando unit known as Samson's Foxes. Shaul stayed to help his father at the store.

He, too, wanted to take part in liberation of the country, but Sarina made him swear not to join up. Poor Shaul was scorned as a shirker, but his fear of his mother was greater than his apprehension about what those who hurled abuse at him might do. He was amazed at the naivete of his fellow countrymen; when the Egyptian Spitfires flew over Neve Tzedek, people climbed to the rooftops to watch the show. All who did so were either killed or injured. He rushed to the shelter with his family and remained underground until the noise stopped. They emerged to a scene of total wreckage. Eighteen people from the neighborhood had been killed, most of them children and teenagers he had known by name. Later the city posted notices warning people not to go near the beach, to prevent the foolish citizens from running out to get a look at an Egyptian plane.

When the war was finally over, a period of austerity began. The young country didn't have the resources to contend with the waves of immigrants who washed ashore, and Ben-Gurion decided that the scarce food supply should be divided equally among all citizens. Every family received a ration book with which to buy oil, sugar, and margarine. Later the same system was employed for the purchase of clothing, shoes, and housewares. Each family received half an egg per day and had to share it. Shaul barely managed to keep the store on King George Street afloat, and if Isaac hadn't helped him out when he could, they would have become destitute.

My kind grandfather told me some of these things himself, in the long conversations we had now that we were a family again, and the rest he wrote in his elegant round hand in a lined notebook that he gave to me. He made me vow not to forget our family's story so that I would learn to forgive, to repair, and to mend, just as you repair an old and valuable piece of jewelry, carefully and meticulously, one link at a time. "Because even what seems broken and lost may be a treasure that is simply in need of a loving hand," he explained earnestly.

"Promise me, Eliya, that you will tell the story to your children and make them promise to tell their children, too, so that the Zoref family will never be divided again, no matter what happens."

"I swear, Grandfather," I promised him. I hugged the notebook to my chest and lowered my head to kiss his clenched hand.

Although that first reunion with my grandparents was tense, the ice gradually thawed. The lapsed tradition of eating together for the Friday-night Shabbat meal was reinstituted. I told Eldad, "I'm realizing a dream I've had since childhood, to eat the Friday-night meal with my extended family."

Lily

They were silent all the way to Jerusalem. Lily sat with her head resting against the window of the bus, her eyes closed. Eliya sat beside her, leaning back against the seat, her eyes hidden behind dark sunglasses. Her head hurt.

It was Eliya who had persuaded Lily to travel to Jerusalem to visit the convent and confront her past. To mend what was broken, "gently, one link at a time," as Grandfather Albert Zoref had said. Lily, who seemed almost childlike lately, had reluctantly agreed. She was still frightened at the thought of what she might find out, but she knew that the time had come to go through with it.

Eliya had wondered if they should let sleeping dogs lie, but she truly believed that Lily's wounds would never heal if she didn't discover the truth. Studying her mother, Eliya noted once again how small and fragile she looked. Her fine lines seemed to have deepened recently and radiated from her huge eyes, and her thick hair was threaded with more gray. Over the past few weeks her mother had seemed to age several years. Eliya gently took her mother's hand with its bitten-down fingernails and held it in her palm. Lily's eyes fluttered open, and she regarded her daughter with a questioning glance. "It's going to be fine, Mother," Eliya whispered. "We'll face it together."

"This is it," said Lily as they stood together before the imposing stone building. Lily gave the rope three tugs, and the gate was opened by a heavyset elderly nun.

"Yes, ladies?" she said. "How can I help you?" Lily stood motionless and mute. So Eliya stepped forward.

"My mother grew up here," she replied, "and she would like to visit the place where she grew up."

The nun regarded Lily and asked, "Are you the mother?"

Lily nodded.

The old woman didn't seem to recognize Lily.

"Can we come in?" Eliya asked.

"Please, but you are only permitted to visit the garden and the church. You can't enter the classrooms or the living quarters."

"That's fine," Eliya said quickly, and she gave Lily a small push across the threshold.

"Only in the garden," the nun repeated. "And remember to close the gate behind you when you leave."

"Good Lord," Lily said when the nun had walked away. "I remember the building being much more intimidating and frightening. The staircase seemed to go on and on, but there are only ten steps here."

She began to walk along the garden paths with Eliya following behind.

Lily pointed at a small chiseled stone bench. "I would sit here when I felt suffocated inside." She led Eliya toward a small chapel situated at the back of the garden. "I would come here when I wanted to get away from the other girls, none of whom liked me, and to get away from the nuns, none of whom I liked."

They entered the chapel together—a young woman who had never before set foot in a convent and her mother, who had grown up in one. Lily's eyes darted all over the room, as if she was reacquainting herself with the icons and representations of saints hanging on the walls.

"I so loved to come here, to sit in the shadows," Lily said in a hushed voice, "to smell the incense. I drew so much strength from the Holy Mother and from Jesus."

"Did you believe in them?" asked Eliya, surprised.

"Of course," Lily replied, and her voice swelled with memories. "That's what I was taught from birth. And that faith gave me strength. I identified with the crucified Jesus." She gestured toward a statue of Jesus as a baby, lying in his mother's arms, which hung above the altar. "I felt as though every day I was crucified above the altar, as lonely as Jesus was. But despite all his suffering, at least Jesus had a mother to comfort him, and I didn't have anyone."

"If you believed so deeply in Mary and Jesus," Eliya whispered, "why did you decide to become a Jew?"

"I didn't become a Jew," Lily protested vehemently. "I was born a Jew."

"How do you know?"

"The nuns told me that the person who left me on the doorstep left a note tied to my clothes that had a drawing of a Star of David. They said they had no doubt that the woman who gave birth to me was Jewish. When I heard that, I started to shake, and I felt warmth spreading throughout my body. In that moment I felt as though I didn't belong to Mary or to Jesus or to the convent, and I ran away."

"Where is that note? Who has it?" Eliya asked, excited.

"Who knows, it was so many years ago, but when I was a child, the Mother Superior had it."

"And you didn't take it when you left?"

"Who could take anything from the Mother Superior? I was terrified of her."

"Come on." Eliya straightened her skirt, looking more determined than ever.

"Where are you going?" Lily asked. She had taken a big enough step by simply visiting the convent.

"Let's go see the Mother Superior." Eliya was adamant. "Maybe they kept the note. Maybe they have more information about your mother."

"She wasn't my mother, she just gave birth to me, and the Mother Superior probably died a long time ago. And if by any chance she's alive, she probably doesn't remember."

"We'll find out soon enough."

They left the chapel, Eliya walking briskly along the path, determined to finally discover the secret of Lily's life, while Lily trailed behind her.

"What makes you think they'll let us see the Mother Superior?"

"Do you remember where her room is?"

"How could I forget? Every time I was summoned to that room, it was to receive another punishment."

"Where's the room?"

"On the second floor, at the end of the corridor."

When they finally stood on the threshold of the gloomy entrance hall, Lily took a sharp intake of breath.

"I have to sit down for a minute," she said. "I'm about to have a heart attack."

"Mother, what's wrong?"

"I can't bear the smell. I can't breathe. My head is spinning."

"Mother, you're just emotional. You have to be strong. Take a deep breath and let's go."

"I'll wait here," Lily said. "You go up. I can't do it."

"No!" Eliya knelt before Lily, who had collapsed onto a small bench to rest. "Whatever the nuns have to say, you have to hear it with your own ears. We're doing this together. Stand up; take a breath. Don't be afraid. I'm here with you; you aren't alone."

Eliya took her mother's hand.

The corridor on the second floor was dark, and the scents of incense and mildew hung in the air.

"This is the room," Lily said.

"Are you sure?"

"As sure as I am that you are holding my hand now."

Eliya knocked on the door, which was opened immediately by a young nun.

"Yes, please?" she asked.

"We're here to see the Mother Superior," Eliya told her.

"The Mother Superior is very busy. Who are you, please?"

"My name is Eliya Zoref, and this is my mother, Lily Zoref. My mother grew up here from the day she was born, and she would like to ask the Mother Superior a few questions about her past."

"I'm very sorry," said the young nun. "You have to make an appointment."

"My mother was here before," Eliya lied, "and we aren't leaving until we see the Mother Superior."

"Please repeat your mother's name." A voice was heard from the depths of the room.

"Lily," she said. "Lily Zoref."

An elderly woman with paper-thin skin rose from her chair behind an impressive writing desk whose surface was illuminated by an art deco lamp. She approached them and motioned to the young nun to allow them to pass.

Lily faced the old woman and gazed at her.

"Sister Katherine, is it you?"

"The one and only," replied the Mother Superior. "Please come in."

She settled herself behind her desk and asked Lily and Eliya to sit in the chairs facing her. The last time Lily had seen her, Sister Katherine had been relatively young and attractive. Now her face was crisscrossed with deep lines, and brown age spots covered her hands, which bulged with blue veins. Only her voice was as decisive and resolute as Lily remembered. She recalled when Sister Katherine had told her the story of how she had found her on that freezing Christmas Eve. How she had feared and hated Sister Katherine after she'd heard that story.

"So how are you, Lily?" she asked. "It has been many years."

"Not that any of you cared." Lily donned her prickly armor in an instant.

"Of course we did. We even asked the British police to look for you, but you vanished without a trace."

Lily studied the ancient nun's wrinkled face, her body heavy with age. The years had wreaked havoc on her, but her eyes were exactly the same steely blue. It was the same voice that had paralyzed her with fear as a little girl. But she was no longer a little girl, and she wasn't afraid. Now, with her daughter beside her, she would not allow this woman to speak to her as though she were still a child.

"I can see when I look at you that many years have passed since we last met," Lily said. "You have changed a great deal."

"So have you, my child," answered the Mother Superior. "The years are etched on your face as well. But what brings you here, Lily? Did you want to show your daughter where you grew up?"

"No," Eliya answered for her mother, and her young voice rang out in stark contrast to the ancient surroundings. "I know where my mother grew up. We want to see the note left by the woman who gave birth to her."

Sister Katherine regarded the two women without saying a word.

"There was a note." Lily spoke now. "You told me that the note was sewn to my clothes when you found me at the gate to the convent."

"The note that had a Star of David on it," Eliya added.

The Mother Superior sat perfectly still and silent for a minute. Then she stood and went over to a carved wooden cupboard that stood in the corner, opened its glass doors, removed a key from one of its drawers, and said, "Follow me."

She led them down a long, dark corridor. She walked with difficulty, supporting herself with her cane. "Now please wait here," she
instructed when they reached the end of the hallway.

"My mother has waited long enough. We're going with you," Eliya
declared, increasing her pressure on Lily's hand, as her mother had fallen
mute again.

"If you insist," the nun acquiesced.

Behind a spiral staircase there was a small door. The elderly nun
inserted the key and opened it.

"This is where we keep old documents," she explained.

The room was crowded with cupboards and chests of drawers
packed with brown numbered folders. The Mother Superior opened
the door to one of the cupboards, pulled open a drawer, and removed a
black leather case from which she extracted an envelope yellowed with
age. She handed it to Lily and lowered herself into one of the chairs
that dotted the room, still leaning on her walking stick. Lily and Eliya
remained standing.

"I've been waiting forty years for you to come and pick up this
letter," she whispered. "Your mother sent it one year after she left you
with us. It's the only letter that ever came from her."

"She . . ." Lily, who couldn't bring herself to use the word *mother*,
paused, then continued, "She sent me a letter, and you never gave it
to me?"

"We decided that it would be better to give you the letter when
you turned seventeen, but you ran away before we could give it to you."

The crumbling envelope bore a stamp and a return address from a
town in England.

"Your mother left Israel after you were born." Eliya turned to Lily.

"I know," Lily replied in a low voice. "She lived beyond the sea. And
you, madam"—she suddenly addressed the Mother Superior—"would
you be so kind as to give me the note that was attached to the rags I was
wrapped in when you found me."

The nun withdrew the worn note from within the leather case. "I kept it," said Sister Katherine. "I waited for you to come and get it."

Lily held the fragile piece of paper close to her face. The letters had almost faded away, and the Star of David was faint, but she could still read the words written by the woman who had given birth to her, words of supplication to the nuns: *Rescue my baby as you rescued me.*

"Here's the drawing of the white lily." Eliya was clearly moved. "The woman is asking that they name you Lily."

"That was her wish," said the Mother Superior, "and we fulfilled it."

"Did you know her? Did you know who the woman was who left me here?" Lily turned to the old nun with suspicion.

"Not at first. Though she asked that we take care of you as we cared for her, we had no way of knowing who she was. Only when the letter arrived did we know."

"Who was she?" Eliya was too excited to keep silent.

"She was a Jewish girl who knocked on the gate of the convent. It wasn't unusual. There was a terrible plague in the city. People were dying like flies; children were orphaned, lost their homes, lived in the street, and wandered lost and hungry all over the city. They sold their bodies for a crust of bread. When we took her in, we didn't ask any questions. She lived here for a year, and then, just as you did, Lily, she ran away, and we never heard of her again. Until the letter arrived."

"Did you know her?" Eliya asked.

"It was before I took my vows, so I didn't know her, but there were nuns who had known her. Only when we received the letter did we learn that she ultimately reached England."

"Is there anyone here who still remembers her, who could tell my mother about her?"

"No, my child, unfortunately all the nuns who knew her have gone to God."

Lily had been holding the envelope in a trembling hand, and now she opened it and removed a delicate piece of writing paper. It seemed miraculous that it hadn't disintegrated and that the words written on it were still legible. She read,

Dear Sisters,

One year ago I left a baby girl in your care. It is my daughter, who was born to me in sin and who I could not raise. I left her with you so that you could raise her and care for her needs, because I cannot be and am not worthy of being a mother to her. I have parted from her forever, so as not to ever see her again, so as to forget that I have a daughter, so that she will not know that she has a mother. I left her with you, my good Sisters, because I knew that if she grew up with me, she would be a bastard child and would be denied a decent and respectable life, which is what she deserves.

May God have mercy on my sinner's soul. I have done everything I can to root her out of my heart. But the heart has its own ways, and oftentimes the heart overcomes the mind. My heart will not surrender to my common sense, and I cannot manage to forget my baby girl.

Due to the circumstances of my life I cannot take her back. I cannot provide her with a home and love as she deserves. I have no recourse but to beg of you, dear Sisters: watch over her in my stead, see that she has everything she needs, and who knows, perhaps one day she will find compassion in her heart and forgive me.

You must remember me; I am Rahel who stayed with you for a year, which saved me from a life on the streets.

I beg you to grant me one more act of benevolence and to save my daughter too.

"Almighty God." The letter shook in her still-trembling hand. "And all these years . . ." Lily tried to speak through her tears. "All these years I hated her and didn't want to hear from her."

Eliya embraced her mother as she tried to make out the words written on the back of the envelope. Finally she deciphered them and exclaimed, "Look, Mother, it's her address."

Lily traced the letters on the flap. *Rachel Townshend. Teignmouth.* "The *bishara* from Jaffa was right," she whispered. "She told me that my mother was beyond the big sea. That righteous Arab woman was always right."

From deep within her chair the Mother Superior observed Lily and her daughter and nodded. For years she had prayed to her Lord Jesus and the Holy Virgin, expressing remorse for never telling Lily about her mother. For years she had entreated the Holy Mother to work a miracle and bring Lily back to the convent so she could give her the letter from her mother, and finally her prayer had been answered.

She rose and faced Lily and Eliya and said, "I thank you for coming and allowing an old nun to redeem her pledge."

"What did you pledge?" Lily asked through her tears.

"After I found you at the convent gate, the Mother Superior entrusted you to my care. You were my baby. I took care of you, fed you, changed you, and saw to your every need. I became deeply attached to you, but the Mother Superior disapproved of the maternal feelings I developed for you. She took you from me, and all the nuns were instructed to take care of you, each one in her turn. It pained me deeply to see you becoming distant from me, and I hardened my heart.

"I am an old woman, and soon I will stand before my God and pay for my sins. One of my greatest sins is the harsh way I treated you through no fault of your own. I embittered your young life. After you disappeared, I swore that as long as I was alive, I would keep the note and letter ready for you. Today you have removed a great weight from my heart. Perhaps at least this one sin will be forgiven. I am so grateful to you for coming today with your daughter and allowing me to pay my debt to you. But there is one more thing. Please, would you be so kind as to return with me to my office."

The venerable Mother Superior opened the door to her office and asked the young nun to leave them alone. "There is one more thing that I have kept for you," she told Lily. "No one else knows of its existence, not the previous Mother Superior and not any of the nuns." She turned to the wall, took down a picture of Jesus surrounded by a halo, and revealed a hidden safe. From deep within it she extracted a brown leather pouch. Once she'd loosened its laces, she inserted her fingers and withdrew a gold chain. Hanging from it was a gold Star of David with the word *Zion* engraved in its center.

"You were wearing this necklace when I found you," she said, "so I was never in any doubt that you were born to a Jewish mother. But I didn't give the necklace to the Mother Superior. You see, Lily, I hoped that in time the drawing of the Star of David on the note would fade and the fact that you were born to a Jewish mother would be forgotten. But a gold Star of David cannot fade, and so I decided to hide it and not to reveal its existence to a soul. Forgive me, Lily, but I wanted you to grow up as a Christian girl. I wanted you to feel the love of Jesus and the Holy Mother in your heart. I beg your forgiveness and compassion for hiding from you this concrete proof of your Jewishness. Here is the necklace," she said as she handed it to Lily.

Tears sprang to Lily's eyes as she received the gold chain. "The woman who gave birth to me left me something after all," she murmured. "She left me a sign."

Lily kissed the gold star, and a tremor coursed through her body.

"She left you your identity, Mother." Eliya was crying too. "She thought that if she left you this necklace, you would have an identity."

"But Sister Katherine chose not to grant me my identity." Lily's eyes flashed as she turned to the old nun. "She chose that I should live the lie that I was a Christian girl."

"I vowed to give you the necklace with the letter and the note when the time came. I never intended to keep from you what was rightfully yours," the Mother Superior answered quietly, choosing to ignore Lily's tone. "And now, I beg of you, go, dear Lily. Take your necklace, your note, and your letter and go in peace with your daughter, and permit an old woman to have her afternoon nap. Too much excitement isn't good for me at my age."

"For years I hated the woman who gave birth to me, but I hated you more," Lily said to Sister Katherine. "I hated you for never being a mother to me in place of the mother I didn't have, for not giving me any of the affection or kindness that a mother does. But now, Sister Katherine, you have atoned for your sins. Your good deed today makes up for all your sins against me."

She approached the old woman and pressed her hand.

"Come, Eliya, let's go and find my mother."

Eliya

Eldad and Shaul were waiting for us on tenterhooks. We returned to Tel Aviv late in the day, as excited as two children, and told them about the meeting with the Mother Superior and the treasure she had bestowed upon Lily.

"We have to write to your mother," my father said in excitement. "You must let her know that her letter reached you only today."

"And if she's dead?" Lily said out loud what we were all thinking. "And what if someone from her family receives the letter instead, someone who has no idea that I exist? We can't do that."

"If I may say something"—Eldad, who hadn't uttered a word, spoke up now—"I suggest that we go to the British Embassy to find out whether a woman named Rachel Townshend appears in the British population registry and, if so, whether she is still alive. After all, it's been almost half a century."

"We'll go there first thing tomorrow morning and find out," my father said.

"I don't think I'll be able to sleep tonight," said Lily, who hadn't put down the gold necklace.

"Let me put it on for you," I said, as I fastened the slim chain around her neck. "The necklace is just the first link in the chain," I promised her. "We won't rest until we find the woman who gave it to you."

Lily stroked the Star of David and said solemnly, "This is the first time in my life that I have had a sign from the person who gave birth to me. When I was young, the other girls always had something from their homes: a picture, a keepsake, a piece of jewelry. Only I had nothing. Who would ever have believed that I would have something to connect me to my roots?"

After lodging our request with the British consul, we were asked to fill out various forms. "The response," the clerk told us, "won't arrive for at least a month." He seemed to be trying to tell us that we shouldn't get our hopes up. I was so impatient I wanted to get on a plane to England, but Eldad pointed out that it was unlikely that Rachel still lived at the address on the letter.

Meanwhile, Lily and Eldad had grown closer, and she was always delighted to see him. I had moved back to his apartment on HaYarkon Street, but we came often to visit my parents. He continued to teach children how to surf, and I took time off from my job at the pub and spent my days at the university library. As I had once devoted myself to the study of literature, now I decided to learn everything I could about the city with the strange name where, at least for a time, the woman named Rachel Townshend had lived.

One day, when I was on the bus on my way home from the university, I saw a newspaper on the seat beside me. As I scanned its pages, I came to the literary section, and Ari's face jumped out at me. His beautiful face, framed by curls that reached to his shoulders; the ever-present unfiltered cigarette hanging from the corner of his mouth; his half-smiling eyes— Ari at his best. Next to the picture was an image of the cover of his new book, which had finally been published. Curious, I read the review. I was surprised at how harsh it was. It ripped the book apart, describing it as improbable, unrealistic, and, perhaps worst of all, boring. And then there was the personal criticism of the author. The reviewer maintained that Ari had been granted an exaggerated number of opportunities to prove his literary talents and that perhaps the time had come for him to lay down his pen and choose a different vocation. To my surprise it didn't give me any pleasure. I actually felt a little sorry for him. Poor guy, I thought. After a review like that he would never show his face again in Tel Aviv. But a few sentences later I read that he had left Paris and returned to Tel Aviv, and a few days after that I happened to walk past our old apartment. Through the open balcony windows I could see right into the living room. The straw lampshade I had once balanced over the bare bulb that hung from the ceiling was still there, along with the reproduction of a painting by Ofer Lellouche that I had framed and hung on the wall, and the white curtains I had chosen were blowing in the breeze. I looked at it all and felt nothing. It was simply a place where I had once lived.

I rushed home to Eldad, and when I saw him, I held him tight and thanked him. "For what?" he asked, surprised.

"Thank you, thank you for being in my life. Thank you for the two of us being together."

Exactly thirty days after we'd gone to the British Embassy, we were summoned to return. Lily was tense and silent as we walked up HaYarkon Street. Beads of sweat broke out on her face, and she began to perspire profusely. "You're sweating like a horse," I told her.

"It's hot," she panted.

"Do you feel all right?"

"Yes, but once I could run up this street, and now I can barely walk."

"Please have a seat," the consul told us with British politeness as we filed into his office. He was leafing through several folders on his desk as though he had all the time in the world.

Lily sat down heavily while Shaul, Eldad, and I stood behind her. The tension was palpable.

The consul chose a document from one of the files, cleared his throat, and said, "Mrs. Zoref, I am pleased to be able to tell you that the woman who you say is your mother, Mrs. Rachel Townshend, is alive and well and living in the town of Teignmouth in the county of Devon, at this address," and he handed her the page.

An audible sigh of relief escaped me, and Lily burst into tears. "She's alive," she said. "The woman who gave birth to me is alive. Can you believe it, Shaul? She's alive!"

My father squeezed her shoulders, took the document, and perused it. "She's a widow."

"Does it say how old she is?" I asked.

"In November she turned sixty-six," he replied.

"She was so young when she had me, only eighteen."

Lily took the document from Shaul. She read it again and again, making no attempt to hide her joy.

"I want to go to England," she said excitedly as we left the office. "I want to see the woman who gave birth to me."

"You have a mother," I said. "Why do you keep calling her 'the woman who gave birth to me'?"

"I don't know." Lily considered my question. "I have never in my life called anyone *mother*. It doesn't feel right on my tongue."

"What will you call her? Will you call her Mrs. Townshend?"

"I will call her Mother, but on one condition."

"What condition?"

"If you call me Mother and stop calling me Lily."

When had I started to call her Lily? As far back as I can remember, she was Lily, not Mother. But now everything had changed. I took her hand and looked into her eyes and said, "I promise you, Mother."

The weeks that followed were packed with emotion and activity, as Lily bounced between euphoria and anxiety. "What if she won't meet me?" she asked again and again. "What if she denies my existence and doesn't want to know me or our family because she doesn't want to disrupt her life?"

"What's the worst thing that can happen?" I asked her. "If she doesn't agree to meet you, everything goes back to the way it was before. You didn't have a mother before, and you still won't have one. But if she does agree to see you, your life will change. You'll close the circle. You'll be able to ask her the questions that you've been asking yourself all your life."

"There's only one question I want to ask her," Lily confided to me quietly. "How can a mother live with the knowledge that she has a daughter in the world who has no idea that her mother exists?"

We decided that all four of us would go, Lily and Shaul, Eldad and I. And in the meantime travel fever reigned at my parents' home. Shaul made a big sign to hang on the door of the store to inform his customers that it would be closed because he was going on vacation. Meanwhile, Lily set to packing and unpacking her suitcase, filling it, then emptying it and repacking it.

"How will we carry the suitcase to the plane, Shaul? It weighs more than the table in the living room!"

"That's why they have trolleys," he reassured her. "Don't worry, Lily. Everything's going to be fine."

◆ ◆ ◆

When the suitcases were finally packed, the passports were enclosed in a travel wallet purchased specially for the trip, and the pound sterling notes, bought according to law at the bank, were safely inside it, the clothes to be worn for the journey had been ironed and hung up, the commotion had finally died down, and we could all take a breath, Lily said, "There's just one more thing that I have to do before we go. I have to go to Kiryat Shaul and tell my son that I found his grandmother."

My father and I exchanged a glance, neither of us daring to give voice to what we were thinking. It hadn't been that long since Lily had stopped going to the cemetery every day, and we were both terrified of the moment when she would go back to visiting her dead baby.

"Why are you both looking at me like that?" she challenged us. "What did you think? That I would stop going to visit my baby? That I would forget that he is there? I will never forget him, and I am asking the two of you never to forget him either."

My father looked at my mother and said, "I agree, Lily. If we have renewed the relationship with my parents, if we have renewed the tradition of having family meals on Shabbat and holidays, we should renew another ancient Jewish tradition of honoring the dead. We should have a memorial ceremony for him on the anniversary of his death, and we should recite the mourner's Kaddish. I will say Kaddish for him, Lily," my father promised, and he kissed her on both cheeks. "We won't forget him."

"And," I said, "you can put the picture of the baby back in the living room. I am no longer ashamed of my brother who died before I was born."

Lily

London was caught up in the pre-Christmas cheer. The city's holiday preparations left the two couples open mouthed. They gazed at the colored lights strung up everywhere and the people thronging the streets. Decorated Christmas trees stood at the entrances to stores, offices, public buildings, and houses, and a children's choir stood in Trafalgar Square, its young members' clear voices ringing out like bells as they sang Christmas carols. Lily and Eliya were charmed by the ubiquitous Santa Claus figures and the glittering lights that transformed the gray city into a breathtaking spectacle.

But despite the beauty of the city and the excitement of discovering a new and unfamiliar world, Lily was restless. She wanted to get to Teignmouth, so Eldad hurried to the train station to buy their tickets for the following day.

From the moment they stepped off the train, they fell under the spell of the charming seaside town. Its tiny houses looked as though they had been copied from a picture postcard, and the long meandering seafront wended its way along the bay.

"The streets here haven't changed since the twelfth century, when Richard the Lionheart sailed from the Dart River Port on his voyage to the Holy Land," Shaul read from the Lapid travel guide he had purchased in advance of their trip at a bookstore on Allenby Street in Tel Aviv.

The clerk at the railway station counter recommended that they stay at a bed-and-breakfast, and the four of them set off along the narrow, twisting alleyways until they reached a small white house with a barely visible sign that read **BED & BREAKFAST**. They rented two rooms that looked out onto the harbor. But before they even had a chance to unpack, Lily announced that she was ready to go.

The address was for a house on one of the streets that descended toward the port. They stood at the top of the hill and gazed down at the boats anchored in the bay, aware of the deep silence. Lily couldn't help but wonder what her life might have been like if she had grown up in this charming place facing the sea instead of the cold and gloomy convent.

They were all quiet as they searched for the address and found it on the third house in a row of identical cottages.

Despite Lily's protests, Eliya had insisted that Shaul and Eldad be present when they knocked on the door. She feared the magnitude of the occasion and the reaction of the woman, but most of all she was afraid of how Lily might react. She feared that Lily's birth mother might let her down again, and the disappointment would send Lily flying back to Kiryat Shaul cemetery, to her thunderous silences, her repressed anger. She feared that everything they had achieved over the past few months would be wiped out and that once again they would be like strangers to one another. Who knew what awaited them on the other side of that door?

But now Lily was adamant. "I'm prepared for Shaul and Eldad to walk us to the house, but I don't want them to come in."

They walked down the stone steps toward the house through a small, well-tended garden. "Ready?" Eliya asked Lily, and she raised one hand and knocked at the door, while her other hand grasped her mother's. Lily's face was flushed with emotion, her lips taut with tension.

A blonde woman in her forties opened the door and said, "Yes, how can I help you?"

Lily's heart was pounding, and the blood rushed to her head. Her inner turmoil struck her dumb. A long moment passed before Eliya recovered and replied, "We're looking for Mrs. Rachel Townshend. Does she live at this address?"

"And who, if I may ask, is looking for her?" the woman inquired.

"We're her relatives," Eliya answered. Lily was still mute.

"Relatives?" the woman repeated in surprise. "Mrs. Townshend didn't tell me that she was expecting a visit from her relatives. Well then," she said, studying the women on the doorstep with curiosity, "if you're relatives, then please come in."

A long hallway led to the living room. Lily swiveled her head, walking blindly, while Eliya tried to take in the room, which was furnished with dark, heavy pieces and lit by standing lamps with different types of lampshades. Heavy curtains whose fabric matched the upholstered sofa and chairs hung at the large windows. The curtains were open, revealing a view of the pretty garden through the sparkling frames of glass. On the eastern wall, underneath a painting of a landscape, a fire blazed in a fireplace, and the mantelpiece was covered with framed family photographs. Lily stopped beside one and stared at it. She thought she saw her own face looking out at her from the picture. It was old and faded, but the resemblance was unmistakable. The same large, round eyes, the same sculpted nose, and the same dimples that the woman in the photograph had passed on to her and that she in turn had passed on to Eliya.

They walked past a Christmas tree standing by the window, decorated with colored candles and sparkling balls, tiny flowers and hearts. The tree was exquisite, and Lily's breath caught in her throat.

A gray-haired woman sat erect in an armchair by the fireplace. Her posture was so straight that if it hadn't been for her gray hair and wrinkles, she might have been mistaken for a much younger woman.

"My dear," the blonde woman said to her, "these ladies have come to see you. They say they are your relatives."

The woman's gaze roved from Lily's face to Eliya's several times, and Eliya felt a cold wave wash over her. Yet despite her frozen expression, it was possible to discern a flicker of curiosity in the old woman's eyes.

"Please have a seat," she said. She gestured to the woman who had escorted them into the room that she could leave.

Lily and Eliya sat down awkwardly on the sofa.

"So?" asked the woman after a pause that seemed to go on forever. "Which side of the family do you come from?"

Without a word, Lily withdrew the gold chain with its Star of David from the leather pouch and held it out.

The woman took the necklace, and the color drained from her face. The hand holding the chain shook, and her posture collapsed.

"Where did you get this . . . ," she began, but then she fell silent.

"I don't want anything from you," Lily said quickly, "except to know if you are the woman who put this necklace around my neck and left me at the gate of the convent in Jerusalem."

The woman looked from the chain to Lily and back again and took a deep breath, and in a barely audible voice she said, "The woman who opened the door is the sister of my departed husband, may his soul rest in peace. Neither she nor any of my family knows the slightest thing about my past or my country of origin. Would you be so kind as to give me time to speak to them before I speak to you? I cannot surprise them as you have just surprised me."

"We came all the way from Israel to meet you," Eliya declared.

"You came from Israel without letting me know in advance. I am an elderly woman, and you have burst into my home without advance notice. I beg you to permit me to prepare my family to meet you."

"You had your whole life to prepare them," Eliya cried, her eyes flashing.

"Lower your voice, please," the woman said. "We don't want to bring my sister-in-law rushing back in here. This conversation, if it is to take place, must be conducted between myself and her. As I said, no one knows the first thing about my past."

"No one knows that you have a daughter." Eliya couldn't tolerate the older woman's arrogant tone and demeanor.

"Correct, no one knows, and if you promise me that what you know and what I know will not be revealed to my relations before I tell them myself, I will receive you here the day after Christmas, and we will speak then."

"I've waited my whole life," Lily said. "I can wait another day or two."

The woman dropped her gaze, seemingly unable to look directly at Lily.

But Lily held her ground, and in a hushed tone, she went on, "But before I go, I would like you to answer one question. Why did you give me up?"

"Come closer. Take a chair and sit here, facing me," said the woman, and Lily did as she asked. Eliya was spellbound at the sight of the two women, so similar, yet so unalike.

Looking only at Lily, she said, "Listen closely and hear me out. I promise I will tell you what I have never told another soul in my life, except for my husband, may he rest in peace, and even he knew only a small part of what I will tell you. No one from my husband's family has ever heard these things from me."

"We aren't interested in your husband's family," Eliya interrupted rudely. "Whether they hear or not, it's all the same to us. We aren't family, although unfortunately we are of the same blood. So either tell us now, or I will make such a scene that your sister-in-law will have no choice but to hear from me and not from you that she has a niece."

"Eliya, calm down," Lily said to her daughter in Hebrew. "Why are you interrupting? What the woman is saying makes sense. Her family is not to blame for what she did. There's no need to throw a bomb at them. Let's hear what she has to say. Don't interrupt her again."

"The old witch will send us away without telling us anything," Eliya retorted. "We have to force her to talk."

"The old witch understands Hebrew," said the elderly woman quietly. "No matter how hard she tried, the old witch didn't manage to forget either the language or the country where they speak it."

Lily and Eliya stared at her in astonishment. It had never occurred to them that she would speak to them in Hebrew.

She turned to Eliya and scolded her, "If you can sit quietly without butting in like a young billy goat, perhaps we can agree, like civilized people, to a meeting, so that I can explain to her"—she inclined her head toward Lily—"why I left her as a day-old infant at the entrance to the convent. Nothing changes with you people. Even now that you have your own country, you remain uncouth and impatient."

"I am not prepared to sit here and be insulted." Eliya stood up. "Certainly not by you. Come, Mother. You've seen the woman who gave birth to you; that's enough."

She turned to leave, but Lily's voice commanded her to stay.

"I didn't come all this way not to hear what she has to say," she told Eliya. "If you want to, you can go, but if you decide to stay, please sit down and please be quiet."

Eliya felt nothing but hostility toward the gray-haired woman, but she had come all the way to England for Lily. So she decided to keep her mouth shut and listen to what the old witch had to say.

"Darling, is everything all right?" The blonde woman had returned and was looking quizzically at her sister-in-law and the two women facing her.

"Everything is perfectly fine," she replied. "These nice women came to wish me a merry Christmas, and now they will be on their way." She stood up. "And so, ladies"—Rachel Townshend delivered her lines with perfect British manners—"it has been a great pleasure, but I am an old woman and I am tired. I would be delighted to receive you again in four days' time. Please come the day after Christmas for five o'clock tea. And now, my dear," she said to her sister-in-law, "would you be so kind as to see my guests to the door?" She glided regally from the room.

When they were standing on the doorstep, the blonde woman said, "I don't know who you are or where you're from, but if you are family, I am very pleased to meet you. We have never met any relations from Rachel's side," she concluded as she locked the door behind them.

The next two days seethed with unbearable tension. Lily was withdrawn and refused to discuss what she was feeling, and Shaul reverted to tiptoeing around, desperate not to upset her.

While Lily and Shaul remained in their room, which Lily refused to leave, Eliya and Eldad explored the streets of Teignmouth. They went for long walks along roads that had been paved in the Middle Ages, traversed its alleyways, and visited the many historical houses that filled the town. Arm in arm they strolled to the lovely port on the banks of the river, surrounded by wooded hills, and one afternoon they walked out to the lighthouse at the end of a narrow inlet. They wandered into the small secondhand shops that sold antique furniture and delicate porcelain cups, romantic dresses, lace tablecloths, jewelry, and sterling-silver spoons. They stopped to revive themselves in one of the many tearooms and sipped hot tea that arrived in porcelain teacups on matching saucers with two tiny biscuits.

As much as she enjoyed their romantic walks—they even made love in an abandoned fishing craft that had been damaged in a storm—Eliya didn't forget for a moment the reason why they were in this cold, foreign place. She was impatient to hear the story of the woman beyond the sea, who now had a face and a voice.

Meanwhile, Lily remained in her room, staring out the window, wondering whether she could find it in her heart to absolve the woman. Would she be able to understand her motives, whatever they had been?

There had to be a terrible reason for a mother to abandon her baby. Lily had been unable to let go of hers from the first moment she'd held him in her arms, even after he had ceased to breathe, even in his grave, so how could she forgive this woman who had abandoned her when she was still alive?

It was Christmas Eve. In their room at the bed-and-breakfast Lily heard the sounds of the Christmas Mass from the nearby church. She felt tugged toward it by enchanted tendrils. All those Christmas Eves, all those Masses she had been part of as a child at the convent, appeared before her eyes. She put on her coat, and for the first time in two days she left the room, while Shaul, without a word, hurried to follow her. The grand church stood at the top of a hill. Hundreds of people crowded around the entrance and stood on the steps. Lily stood in awe and listened, transfixed, to the divine voices of the members of the choir and the congregation, to the wonderful music emanating from the organ, and tears spilled from her eyes. How strange, she thought, to find herself in a little town in southwest England on Christmas Eve, so far from the convent in Jerusalem, surrounded by total strangers, and yet she felt an overpowering sense of belonging. These fragments of the childhood that she had been certain she had buried deep in her past were floating up inside her, and she understood for the first time that to build a new life it wasn't necessary to obliterate the old one. She understood that she could merge old and new and move on from there. Whatever happened when she met with the woman who had given birth to her, nothing she could say would destroy the life Lily had built with Shaul; nothing would rupture what she had repaired with Eliya. No matter what she said, this unfamiliar woman whose blood flowed in her veins would be no more than the closing of one circle and the opening of another.

At precisely five o'clock on the appointed day, Lily and Eliya stood outside the door of the woman's house. This time Rachel opened it herself. The sister-in-law was nowhere in sight.

She led the way to the living room.

Without any preliminaries or small talk, she addressed the matter at hand.

"Even before I saw the gold chain," she said, looking straight at Lily, "I knew who you were. When I was your age, I looked exactly like you; the necklace only confirmed what I already knew."

Lily's eyes were riveted to the woman's face, searching for similarities—the dimples that had almost disappeared into her wrinkles, the slightly upturned nose, and the small ears whose lobes were a little bit bigger than her own. And although the woman's hair was mostly gray, she could imagine it once being as thick and blonde as her own.

"I also knew that it was you, before we knocked on your door," she replied.

"You knew as well," the woman said quietly. "My prayer was answered."

"Your prayer?"

"For years I have prayed that you would come looking for me. My secret was buried inside me, and I never considered revealing it, except to you. The secret weighed on me for years, ruined my life with my poor husband, who I forced to lie to his family. I am a sick woman; my end is near. I thank you for coming to liberate me from the secret, which I feared would descend with me to the grave."

"I didn't come to liberate you," Lily said. "I came to free myself."

The logs in the fireplace were turning to embers, and the fierce cold outside began to penetrate the room.

The woman went over to the fireplace and placed more logs on the fire, stirring the flames with a poker.

Then she pointed to some wool blankets folded on the sofa and said to Lily and Eliya, "Please wrap yourselves in a blanket."

Lily did as she asked, but Eliya sat immobile. The woman dusted off her hands and went on, "My husband's relatives, may he rest in peace, believed that we met in Kenya, where we told them I had lived with my family, when he was stationed there as an officer in His Majesty's army. My husband told them that he married me in Nairobi. But I met Stewart in Jerusalem. He was an officer of the British Mandate, and I was a pitiful Jewish girl whose life he saved."

"But he didn't save my mother's life," Eliya interrupted coldly.

"My dear girl," she said, turning to Eliya for the first time that day, "I understand your anger, and I respect it, but I beg of you, be patient and allow me to tell my story. Grant me what little respect you may have for me, if only because the same blood flows in our veins."

"Eliya," Lily said to her in Hebrew, "please sit quietly and allow her to tell her story. I also have a great deal to say and am holding back."

"Where were we?" asked the woman. "If I lose my train of thought, I don't always remember where I stopped and what I wanted to say."

"You said you were a pitiful Jewish girl and that your husband saved your life."

"I was a Jewess," said the woman, almost swallowing back the word. "For many years now I have been a member of the Church of England. That is what fate determined."

This time it was Lily who couldn't help but speak. "None of your relatives know you're Jewish?"

"My husband knew, but I asked him never to disclose to a soul that I was born a Jewess in British Mandatory Palestine, especially not to his parents. This arrangement suited him, and he kept my secret. From the day we sailed from its shores, he never spoke to me of my country of origin, and I never referred to it either."

She sat back in her chair, arranged the blanket over her knees, removed her glasses, and placed them on the tea table. Then she resumed talking.

"When our ship set sail, I stood on deck and watched the shoreline recede. I had already decided that would be the last time I would see the land where I was born. I left my previous life behind and embarked on a new life."

"You also left a daughter there," Lily said softly. "You left me there."

"I did it so that you could live a life of dignity and not as the illegitimate daughter of an unmarried woman."

"I would have preferred to live as a bastard with my mother, rather than as a waif without a name."

Rachel Townshend sighed and withdrew more deeply into her chair, and it was a long time before she replied. "I know that I have sinned against you and there is no absolution for my sin, but I did not leave you at the entrance to the convent to get rid of you. I did it to save you, because who knows what might have happened to us both if you had stayed with me."

Tears welled in her eyes, but she went on in a steady and matter-of-fact voice.

"I will never forget that day. I wrapped you in several layers of clothing and a warm blanket, and I did not place you on the doorstep until I heard the jangling of the sister's keys as she approached from the other side of the gate. Only when I heard the screech of the heavy lock and the gate began to open did I put you down gently and hide. When she lifted you into her arms, I left as fast as I could."

"And you didn't look back," Lily said.

"If I had looked back, I would have taken you back, and if I had taken you, God only knows what kind of a life would have awaited you."

"Awaited me or you?" Lily challenged.

"A terrible life awaited us both. Listen closely, and you'll understand who the woman was who gave birth to you and why she didn't want you to grow up with her."

Rachel

She didn't know how long she had been lying awake, staring up into the darkness, her eyes swollen with tears, her teeth chattering in the bitter cold that even the thick stone walls couldn't keep out of the narrow chamber.

The night before, her beloved had brought her to his sister, a woman she had never met, in the room where she lived with her husband and her two children. She was terrified, trembling like a sparrow, and his sister, who pursed her lips and regarded her with an expression rife with condemnation, did nothing to relieve her fear. "Don't leave me here alone," she begged him. "Stay with me." Her beloved knelt before her and withdrew a red velvet box from the pocket of his coat. He opened it and held out a fine gold chain on which hung a gold Star of David, engraved with the word *Zion*.

"This is your engagement necklace," he said, and he kissed her eyes. "Tomorrow I will bring you a wedding ring and bring you to our wedding canopy, and we will start our lives together as husband and wife." For a moment her fear vanished and she was happy. Her face flushed and her eyes glistened with fine tears. Her engagement necklace. She wouldn't wear a white bridal gown at her wedding, but she would have a golden necklace with a Star of David. When he fastened the chain around her neck, she caressed the star with delicate fingers. She pressed herself into him and whispered, "Come back soon, my heart's love. I cannot stand to be without you any longer."

"I will return," he promised her. "After this night we will never be apart again." He kissed her eyelids once more, gently disentangled himself, and left her, embarrassed and frightened, with his scowling sister and her husband, who was even more furious than his wife. Without a word, the woman threw a pile of rags onto the floor of the tiny room and motioned for her to lie down. Then she went back to her mattress, which she shared with her husband and children.

She did her best to cover herself with the rags, but the fabric was thin and the bits of cloth did not warm her. She tried to remain calm, concentrating on the sounds of the children's breathing, but the snores of the strange man assaulted her ears and petrified her. Her heart beat wildly, though she wasn't sure whether it was from excitement about her upcoming wedding or apprehension about her future. This was not how she had dreamed of being a bride, with her mother and father conducting mourning rituals and sitting shiva for her and the groom's parents ostracizing them and vowing not to be present at their wedding.

From the day when Rochel had first glimpsed her beloved standing behind the counter of his store at Jerusalem's Mahane Yehuda Market, her life had been turned upside down. She had grown up in the ultra-Orthodox Mea Shearim neighborhood, her upbringing rigid and strict. She—who had been trained never to raise her eyes to the person who was speaking to her, to obey blindly, and not to ask questions—couldn't take her eyes off him. As though she had no virtue, she followed him heedless of consequences, pursuing him shamelessly. She felt compelled to do so, her feelings stronger than she was. That man had to belong to her, and she to him.

She had always been different. Neither her father nor her mother and certainly not her siblings could understand her. They had a hard time accepting this strange bird in their midst, who was so different from everyone else. And because they didn't understand, and because this child and her questions confused them and were inappropriate in their world, they responded in the only way they knew how—with blows. Rochel was a punching bag for her parents and siblings, eventually becoming skilled at holding herself beyond arm's reach to avoid the slaps from her father and the punches inflicted by her mother, who would screech at her in Yiddish, "You poison the very air you breathe!"

Rochel had learned to absorb the smacks and fists so that she barely felt them, but the knowledge that her parents wouldn't be standing by her side under the wedding canopy was a different kind of pain, even aside from the fact that they were performing the mourning rituals as though she were dead. Her parents could not accept that she, an Ashkenazi girl, had defied their traditions and fallen in love with a Sephardic man from the Ohel Moshe neighborhood. Their daughter had done what was strictly prohibited and brought disgrace upon the entire family. She was turned out of her father's house, and her relatives were instructed to behave as if she had died. Meanwhile, his family also objected to the match and did all they could to prevent it.

Her beloved hadn't told her which rabbi would marry them or in which synagogue, but she knew that she would never have met the quorum of ten men who would encircle them at the ceremony; she wouldn't wear a bridal gown; her mother and her sisters wouldn't escort her to immerse herself in the ritual bath before her wedding; and her father would not return home from the synagogue, singing with his son-in-law-to-be. She would marry like one of the solitary women who had lost their entire family in the great plague and were left desolate and destitute.

Her heart broke, for they were the only parents she had. She concentrated on imagining her wedding ceremony, how her beloved would slide the ring onto her finger and break the glass as he said, *If I forget thee, O Jerusalem, let my right hand forget its cunning.* Over and over she murmured the Amidah prayer, moving her body on the floor as she did in the women's section of the synagogue, repeating three times, "Holy, holy, holy," her eyes filling with tears, her heart overflowing with fear, and everything whirling together in confusion until she barely knew who or where she was, and the Holy One, blessed be He, seemed to take pity on her, and she fell into a deep slumber.

She awoke to the sounds of unintelligible shouting. When the sounds formed words, she heard, "Throw her out of the house! Get rid of the *putana* so she doesn't contaminate your home as she has defiled ours! How did you allow this rebellious female into your home? Turn her out into the street; let her go back to her father and mother's house, or let her go to hell, the whore!" The house was in an uproar.

She curled up on the floor, trying to disappear into herself. And then suddenly there was silence. She heard her beloved's family leave the house. She realized that she was there alone and didn't understand what had just happened. She wondered desperately where her beloved was and why he wasn't gathering her into his arms and telling her that everything was going to be fine.

"Get up, *putana.* Get up, you *mamzer!*" Her beloved's sister was suddenly beside her, pummeling Rochel with her fists and kicking her. "Get out of here, you piece of filth," she cursed her in Yiddish to make sure she understood every word. "Get out of here, slut."

Rochel covered her belly to try to protect herself from the kicks. Bruised and beaten, she was dragged by her hair to the door and shoved out into the street, where the neighbors awaited her, and they, too, grabbed her by the hair and beat her.

◆ ◆ ◆

She escaped the pack of wolves attempting to devour her alive and stumbled away toward the fields on the edge of the Sha'arei Hesed neighborhood. Finally it was quiet, and the only sounds were the birdcalls and the braying of a donkey from far off. She lay on the ground until she could breathe normally, inhaling the sweet smell of the rich soil.

She had no home and no family, and total strangers were beating her savagely and calling her a whore. A whore? Apart from her beloved, she had never before been alone with a man. And where was he now? Why hadn't he come for her, as he'd promised he would? She shivered in the grip of fear, unsure what to do next or where to go. She tried to stand, but the mud seemed to suck her back down toward the ground.

She thought she should go in search of her beloved. After all, he must be scouring all of Jerusalem to find her. The rabbi, the quorum of ten men in the minyan, all of them must be waiting for her; she mustn't keep an honorable rabbi waiting, and her beloved must be out of his mind with worry.

Again she tried to stand and wipe the mud off her face and her clothes, but it clung to her like a second skin. She gave up, deciding to wait here for him to find her. Her beloved would take care of her. He had sworn to her that their love would conquer all.

At that moment the heavens opened and a torrential rain poured down. She stood in the middle of the field, and streams of mud ran from her head down her back. "Merciful and compassionate God," she prayed, "slow to anger and abundant in loving kindness." She removed her dress, her shoes, her black stockings, and her undergarments and stood naked and trembling in the downpour. She prayed that the rain would wash away the mud and cleanse her so that her groom would find her as pure and unblemished as the Lord God had created her.

◆ ◆ ◆

An Arab farmer found her unconscious in the field and brought her to the police station on Jaffa Road. The English policeman rushed to cover her with a blanket and warm her frozen body, and then he made her a cup of tea. "Drink slowly," he told her in English, which she didn't understand.

"She has the eyes of a crazy person," said the Jewish policeman as Rochel looked from one man to the next in panic. Her terror clouded her mind so that when they asked her questions, she couldn't respond.

The dress that the policeman brought her from his wife's closet was several sizes too large, and the shoes were far too big. He hadn't thought to bring stockings or a coat.

She sat hunched over on the hard wooden bench, leaning against the wall, her eyes focused on an imaginary spot on the floor.

An hour passed, then another. The door didn't open, and none of the policemen approached her. She got up and began to pace the corridor, until she felt as though the room were closing in on her. Then, without realizing that she had made a decision, she burst out the door and took off running. The officer who guarded the entrance didn't manage to stop her, and in a flash she had crossed the courtyard and disappeared. He called to the other men on duty, and they rushed up Jaffa Road until they reached the Mahane Yehuda Market, but it was as if the earth had swallowed her up, and they couldn't find a trace of her. Finally they gave up and trudged back to the police station.

She ran for all she was worth, kicking off the too-large shoes and wondering at the lightness she felt and her speed. She had always been able to run like a deer, to evade her big brother, who would come at her with his belt threatening to flay her. She was lucky that the Holy One, blessed be He, had granted her swift legs. She ran without stopping until she found herself standing in front of the huge convent that her mother had threatened her with so many times, saying that if she didn't mend her ways, she would leave Rochel there, to live with the nuns behind the high walls until she died, and then she would burn in hell for all eternity.

She pounded on the iron gate, but it didn't open. And then she noticed the bellpull rope to the side and grasped it like a drowning person.

"What's all this noise?" scolded the nun who opened the gate. She fell into the nun's arms, exhausted, hungry, cold, and frightened. She needed an embrace, and it didn't matter where she found it. If her rightful mother wouldn't provide the comfort she needed, she'd get it from a maligned nun.

Asking no questions, the nun led her into an entrance hall. She looked around anxiously. The room was dark, with a high ceiling and enormous paintings along the walls depicting men and women wearing large crucifixes. In her previous world, the cross represented the essence of defilement. Maybe her mother was right and she was already inside one of the circles of hell. But she found that she didn't care. She had realized by now that she had no groom and there would be no wedding canopy, that she had no home and nothing in the world beyond the walls of the convent.

The nun, who still hadn't uttered a word, led her down a wide corridor to a room lined with buckets and sinks and indicated that she should wash herself. Then she turned and left the room.

She hitched up the large dress and lifted it over her head, then stood naked on the floor beside a bucket and a large dipping ladle. She scooped the water from the bucket and poured it over her body. It was ice cold but somehow purifying. The nun returned with a brown, long-sleeved dress, white underpants, thick wool socks, and sturdy black shoes. When she had finished dressing, the nun reappeared and beckoned her to follow. They traversed more dark corridors until they reached a large hall filled with long tables flanked by wooden benches on both sides. The nun motioned to her to sit down and then brought over a copper bowl of steaming broth. She ate the soup eagerly, grateful for the warmth that filled her stomach. When she was done, the nun had her take her empty bowl and spoon to the yard by the kitchen, wash them with soap and water, and put them away. Again she followed the silent woman in her flowing habit, this time up a flight of stairs to the top floor, where they stopped in front of a door. The nun knocked, and a voice from the other side invited them in English to come in.

She stood in amazement at the entrance to a big, well-lit room. An old nun with a hefty crucifix hanging around her neck sat at a large desk. The elderly woman looked directly into her eyes. Suddenly anxious, she looked down and moved behind the nun who had brought her here. On the wall hung a massive painting of Jesus on the cross, his face tilted downward in agony, rivulets of blood flowing from his wrists nailed to the crucifix, from his chest and his stomach, his loins covered with a piece of cloth. Her body and soul were burning; she wanted to cover her eyes, but she controlled herself and took deep breaths.

The nun addressed her in English. Even had she understood, she would certainly have remained silent. After all, what was there to say? That her mother and father had thrown her out and were mourning her as though she had died? That her fiancé's family had ostracized her? And that her beloved had abandoned her on her wedding day? She could hardly tell the nun that an Arab farmer had saved her life when he'd discovered her naked and unconscious in a field and brought her to the police station, and that she had fled like a madwoman. And maybe she was truly mad, if of all the places in Jerusalem she had chosen to seek refuge in the most impure place of all, this terrible, frightening place, which her mother had repeatedly threatened to shut her up inside of for the rest of her life.

What would the nun say if she knew that Rochel had been taught from the day she was born that Jesus Christ was abhorrent? That the many convents, monasteries, and churches scattered throughout

Jerusalem defiled the city, and it was forbidden for a Jew to set foot in any of them? And here she stood before the likeness of the abominable one in this unholy place, praying that these accursed people would save her.

When she didn't respond, the old nun addressed the girl in Hebrew. "What is your name, my child?" she asked in a gentle voice.

Still staring at the floor, she replied, "Rochel."

After she said her name, the Mother Superior ceased her questions and told the nun to take her from the room. She followed the silent woman, who took her to the living quarters, showed her to a narrow iron bed in a large sleeping chamber full of other beds, and then left.

She took off her shoes and lay down on the hard bed, covered herself with the coarse gray wool blanket, closed her eyes, and fell asleep.

A few hours later she woke up feeling stronger and waited for her eyes to adjust to the darkness. Through the large window streamed the light of a half moon shining through the clouds, illuminating tall trees whose tips seemed to brush the sky. She looked around. Women and girls were sleeping in some of the beds, and she could hear faint snores and sighs. On the wall at the head of her bed hung a crucifix. She closed her eyes, bracing for the moment when the hellfire would ignite and incinerate her. But nothing happened. There was no fire, the walls remained standing, and she was still alive. Slowly she opened her eyes again and knelt on the bed, facing the cross. She extended her hand and touched it, ran her fingers across its length and breadth, felt the smooth carved wood, then traced the body of the crucified Jesus sculpted in brass, his hands stretched to his sides, his head hanging down. For the first time since she had been banished from her father's house, she felt safe and at peace.

◆ ◆ ◆

Three months later, she had become accustomed to the thick stone walls, the long corridors, the light that filtered through the stained glass windows. She no longer feared the portraits of the Christian saints that peered at her from the huge paintings hung along the hallways, didn't wrinkle her nose at the smell of the incense in the church, and was undeterred by the icons and the candles.

She had become fond of the dim interior of the chapel, where the soft light poured through the windows of the domed ceiling. The quiet and the sense of holiness that encompassed the convent soothed her. She was less suspicious of Sister Eugenia, the young nun who was responsible for her, and she no longer looked at her feet every time the Mother Superior addressed her. To her surprise, the convent, surrounded by its high stone walls and completely cut off from the outside world, infused her with a sense of security.

The rigid daily regimen left no time for privacy or reflection. Hour followed hour, and task followed task until when she was finally alone in her bed after lights-out, she was so exhausted that she fell immediately into a deep and dreamless sleep. She built a protective wall of silence around herself, and even Sister Eugenia stopped asking her about her past.

Daily life at the convent was packed with activity. The girls rose at five, washed themselves in freezing water, made their beds with military precision, and attended morning prayers in the church. From there they went to the dining hall, where each one received a deep copper bowl of porridge and hot tea in a tin cup. When the meal was over, they washed their dishes and put them away on the shelf. The girls spent all day in class. Every class comprised about twenty girls, ranging in age from twelve to eighteen, and not one of them had blonde hair like hers.

Classes commenced with an English lesson taught by Sister Agnes, which always started with a song taught by Sister Eugenia that began, "Jesus loves me! This I know, for the Bible tells me so." At first she didn't understand the words, but she liked the tune. When the meaning of the words was clear to her, she sang them with gusto. She had no doubt that Jesus loved her, for it was thanks to him that she had been rescued.

The teachers were strict, demanding that their charges sit up straight, and if their handwriting wasn't neat, they didn't hesitate to hit the tips of the young fingers with a ruler. She, who had never learned how to write, received more than her fair share of smacks.

In Hebrew lessons with Mr. Meimran, a Spanish Jewish man who never smiled, and English lessons with Sister Agnes, she felt as though she had arrived from another planet. Like the other girls in her community, she had never been to school, never learned to read and write. Sister Agnes saw how she struggled, rested a gentle hand on her head, and whispered, "The English language isn't so hard. I'm sure you'll learn it in no time."

She felt a rush of warmth for Sister Agnes and for the English language too. Rochel, who now used the Hebrew pronunciation Rahel, wanted to learn the language of the refined and generous people she had only recently encountered. The language of the kind policeman at the Mahane Yehuda Police Station, who had covered her naked body with a blanket and made her a cup of hot tea; of the Mother Superior, who didn't ask too many questions; of Sister Eugenia, who whispered more than she spoke; and of Sister Agnes, whose hand she loved to feel on her head.

Sister Mary taught religious studies. For the first few weeks Rahel blocked her ears so she wouldn't hear the stories about the Holy Mother and her crucified son. She held her breath, reasoning that if she stopped breathing, she wouldn't be truly present when Sister Mary told stories about the Virgin Mary and her son. She hugged herself tightly so that the words of desecration couldn't penetrate her body and prayed to God to make her deaf so she wouldn't hear, to have mercy on her sinning soul and protect her from Sister Mary's words so that she wouldn't burn in eternal hellfire.

But as time passed and no disaster befell her, she was amazed to find that she was captivated by the New Testament, overcome by the story of the woman from Nazareth into whose ear an angel had whispered that she was carrying the son of God in her womb.

All the prohibitions and all the fear and loathing of Christianity and its symbols with which she had been raised evaporated as though they had never been. She found she derived a deep strength from the cross, Jesus, and the Holy Mother. Like her, Jesus had also been betrayed and persecuted. He had also been forced to flee for his life. She started going to the chapel even when prayers weren't being held, sitting in the wooden pews and gazing at Mary holding her son, taking great comfort in her presence.

After six months, she had begun to master English, and she could engage in simple conversations and read and write a little. This delighted Sister Agnes, who was fond of the strange child.

There was a blind Jewish girl at the convent named Simcha who was older than all the others and had been there the longest. One day, when Rahel was sitting alone in the wooden pew in the chapel, she heard the tapping of Simcha's cane as she felt her way along the corridor. Unaware that anyone else was there, Simcha came in and sat down. Rahel regarded the raven-haired blind girl, whose skin was white as snow.

Simcha apparently became aware that she was being observed. Frightened, she called out, "Who's there? Is someone there?"

"It's just me, Rochel," she said, reverting to the Yiddish pronunciation of her name favored in the ultra-Orthodox Ashkenazi community where she had grown up.

"Lord in heaven, you should only be well, but you scared me out of my wits." For a long time the two sat side by side without speaking. When Simcha rose to leave the chapel, Rahel also stood and took her arm to support and guide her.

From then on they met every day at the chapel and sat next to each other in silence. One day the blind girl began to speak. She said that she'd been born in the Zikhron Tuvia neighborhood, by the Mahane Yehuda Market, to a poor family. Despite their poverty it was a warm and happy home until her parents died. Then the children were left alone to take care of each other.

"I was nine or maybe ten," Simcha told her, "and I got sick. I had terrible headaches, and every day my eyesight grew worse. At first I thought I would get better. But I didn't. The year that I went blind, everybody got married, and I was left alone at home. If I hadn't been blind, they would have found a match for me, too, but who wants to marry a blind girl? After everyone got married, the owner of the house came and took it back. My siblings had no room for me in their homes, so they brought me here and left me with the nuns. I've been here now for ten years."

Simcha's story moved her, and she put her arm around the older girl's shoulders.

"Why are you here?" Simcha asked. "Who brought you to the convent?"

She didn't reply at first. She didn't want to share her story with anyone, but the secret weighed so heavily on her. She knew that Simcha would never betray her confidence, so she took a deep breath and, in a quiet, detached voice, told Simcha how her groom had abandoned her on her wedding day.

"Why didn't he come?" Simcha asked.

"If only I knew. But he disappeared as though the earth had swallowed him up, leaving me with nothing but the clothes on my back in the house of his sister, who beat me and threw me into the street."

"Why did he leave you at his sister's house? Why weren't you in your own home?"

"I have no home," she told her. "My father sat shiva for me, and my mother said I was no longer her daughter."

"And what was your fiancé's name?" Simcha asked.

"Gabriel."

"Gabriel Armoza, the son of Señor Armoza from the Mahane Yehuda Market?"

"That's him," she whispered, and she went on to describe how they had fallen in love and decided to marry, against their parents' wishes.

"*Dios mío!*" Simcha was overcome. "You are the Ashkenazi girl from Mea Shearim who caused Gabriel Armoza to lose his head!"

"That's me," she said, doing her best not to reveal her emotions.

"Aii," Simcha sighed, "how he broke your heart, your man. Do you still think about him a lot?"

"Ever since he left me, I haven't allowed myself to feel the pain."

"Feel it," said Simcha. "Cry. I cried a great deal after my brother and sisters left me here. Cry; don't be afraid. I'm here. I won't leave you."

But not a tear appeared in her eyes. She sat in silence beside her friend until Simcha implored her again, "Cry. Let the tears wash away your pain."

The tears began to rise from somewhere deep within her, but they stuck in her gullet, a wellspring that couldn't burst through the dam of her throat. Her tears, like her pain, were locked away.

"Never mind," said Simcha, and she touched the other girl's dry eyes. "It seems the time hasn't come yet for you to cry. Don't worry; you will cry."

And then they rose from the pews in the chapel and returned to the sleeping hall.

Several days later Simcha turned to Rahel in the convent garden and said, "I know why he didn't come for you."

Rahel stopped in her tracks.

"Yesterday, my sister Leah came to visit me. '*Mi hermana*,' I said to her, 'have you heard the story about Gabriel Armoza and the Ashkenazi girl?' And she said, 'Of course I know it. Everyone in Jerusalem knows it.' And then my sister told me that on that night before Gabriel was to marry you, his father, Raphael, died. My sister says he died of a broken heart because of the shame. He was ashamed, may his memory be blessed, that his son didn't respect him and decided to marry you against his will."

She tried to take in what Simcha was saying. It was the first time that anyone had told her about that night, the first time she understood the meaning of the screaming and wailing in Gabriel's sister's house on the morning when she'd been thrown into the street.

"When the old man died," Simcha continued, "Señora Armoza forced her son Gabriel to swear on his father's grave that he would never see you again. She forced him to swear that you would be dead to him. Rochel, that's why he didn't come. He promised his mother; he swore on his father's grave."

Rahel didn't say a word.

"I'm sorry," Simcha said. "I know it hurts, but better that you know the truth so you don't die not knowing why he didn't come for you."

They remained sitting in the garden, side by side, each one alone with her thoughts. When she spoke, Rahel's voice was toneless and distant. "He shouldn't have sworn to his mother. He shouldn't have given me up. He knew I had nowhere to go and that my father was mourning me as though I was dead. Gabriel is dead to me. If you are my friend, swear to me now on the Holy Mother Mary and on Jesus the Savior that you will never mention his name again."

Simcha was appalled. "God help us, to swear on Jesus and Mary? I love the peacefulness of the chapel, but Jesus and Mary are not my *Señor del mundo*. Praise God, Lord of Avraham, Yitzhak, and Ya'acov, the God of Israel is my Lord."

"Your Lord has forsaken me," Rahel said quietly. "Where was the God of the Jews when that person left me and never returned? Where was the Holy One, blessed be He, when she threw me into the street with no food, no water, no place to rest my head?"

"But Rochel, that's why we have synagogues. There are merciful Jews. Why did you not go to the synagogue? Why did you come to the convent?"

"Why didn't your sisters take you to the synagogue? Why didn't merciful Jews rescue you when they dumped you at the convent?"

"It's completely different," Simcha replied, seeking to mollify Rochel. "My poor sisters, what could they do? They each have a husband and children; where could they put me? 'The best place for you,' they said, 'is here with the nuns.' My sisters come to visit me and weep. I'm like a wound in their hearts, but what's the point of being angry? There's a reason for everything, and between us, Rochel, I wouldn't call you a spotless prayer shawl. Who ever heard of a Jewish girl leaving her father's home for a man? And especially someone from an ultra-Orthodox family like yours? You should thank the Lord that they didn't kill you. You should go home, ask your father to forgive you, beg him to take you back. Endure the agonies of your soul, fast, pray, and atone for your sins. Me, I have no choice, I have nowhere to go, but you have a home; you have a mother and father. Run away from here, Rochel. Run before you are punished by heaven for your wayward thoughts."

Without a word, Rahel stood and walked away, leaving Simcha sitting on the bench in the garden.

From that day Rahel never went near Simcha again, spurning all the blind woman's attempts to breach the wall behind which she secluded herself.

Now that she had revealed her secret, she felt that the defensive barrier she had erected had been breached. She no longer felt safe at the convent and withdrew further into herself.

A year to the day since she had rung the convent bell, she packed a small bag and left, determined never to return. She had grown strong enough to confront the world beyond the convent walls. The nuns had nurtured her self-confidence and taught her English, deportment, and good manners, and she had ceased to resist the affinity she felt for Christianity.

On the day she left, the quiet road where the convent stood was deserted. If she continued up the street, she would reach Jaffa Road and the market. If she were to walk down, she would arrive at Strauss Street, which led to Mea Shearim. Those were the two last places on earth she wanted to go. She had banished her family from her mind, but she had not managed to eradicate Gabriel from her heart. Although she had vowed not to think about the man who had ruined her life, she couldn't forget his beautiful smile, his dimples, his laughing eyes, his strong warm arms. Thoughts of him kept her up at night, and he appeared in her dreams.

She walked by Café Europa at Zion Square in the city center. It was packed with Jews, Arabs, and soldiers of the British Mandate sitting at small round tables. She watched the well-groomed women with the soldiers, sipping tea from glass cups, nibbling at cream cakes. She watched the soldiers with their perfect manners helping the women take off their coats, bowing slightly, and pulling out their chairs. She stood there with her nose almost touching the glass, until one of the waiters noticed and shooed her away.

She was certain of only one thing—she would never return to her previous life. Never again would she be Rochel of Mea Shearim, nor would she be the Rahel of the convent. No man would ever raise a hand to her again as her father and her brother had, and no man would smash her heart to pieces as Gabriel had. She had no money and no possessions, but she knew that somehow she would manage.

She spent the day roaming the city, delighted by the passersby and the shop windows. All her life she had lived within the boundaries of the narrow and crowded lanes and alleys of Mea Shearim and the Mahane Yehuda Market. But here she was, walking freely wherever she chose; even her rumbling stomach couldn't quell her sense of freedom.

Along the main street she saw automobiles, horse-drawn carriages, and a hodgepodge of people of all types. There were stylishly dressed women wearing small hats, others dressed simply and modestly and covered from head to toe, mothers pushing strollers and baby carriages, Arab men in wide salwar trousers with kaffiyehs secured to their heads with agal ropes, Arab women dressed in traditional djellabas, ultra-Orthodox Jewish men whose heads were covered by wide-brimmed hats, and British soldiers in uniform. The noisy, colorful mixture thrilled her. After a year cloistered in the convent and her previous circumscribed life in her parents' home, she felt that for the first time she could breathe.

When evening fell, the lights were switched on at Café Europa, and a band started to play. She stood transfixed at the plate glass window, enthralled by the women in their evening clothes swaying to the music in the arms of handsome men in their pressed uniforms.

"Excuse me." A hand touched her shoulder, and she jumped. "Beg pardon, young lady. I didn't mean to frighten you, just to invite you for a drink."

A British soldier stood before her, smiling beneath his small mustache. She was hungry and thirsty but mostly curious about what it would be like inside the café. Without thinking twice, she nodded her assent.

"After you," he said, as he held open the door.

She had never heard such music before, never seen men and women dancing together. At the weddings she had attended in her community, the men and women had danced separately, to klezmer music performed with trumpets and violins. The men and women who moved to the sounds looked to her like figures from a dream.

Rahel's garments were plain by comparison, her sturdy shoes clumsy and odd looking, and yet there was something about her—the way she held her body erect, with her blonde hair tied back, exposing her neck, and the way she moved—that drew people's gaze. She was aware of the men's covetous glances, but rather than feel uncomfortable, she felt the power radiating from her presence. She walked gracefully to the table the soldier led her to and waited as he pulled out her chair, then sat down as though she were routinely seated in this manner and this weren't the first time in her life that she had been inside a café and in the company of a strange man.

"What would you like to drink, miss?" he asked.

She replied with the only beverage she could think of, tea.

"Tea!" he laughed. "No, my dear, let's order you something similar but much better."

He ordered brandy, and as she sipped the drink, she enjoyed how it warmed her mouth, burned her throat, and slid straight into her rumbling stomach. Without the slightest hesitation she asked him to order her another. The brandy made her head spin, and her mouth stretched in a pretty smile. The soldier couldn't take his eyes off her.

"What's your name, miss?"

"Rahel."

"Rachel," said the soldier. "What a pretty name."

And in that instant the soldier bestowed upon her the name that would be hers for the rest of her life. Rochel had slipped from Rahel into Rachel.

She danced in his arms, at first with tentative movements, but slowly she embraced the rhythm and succumbed to the melody, allowing him, with surprising ease, to lead her in the dance steps, to spin and twirl her. She enjoyed every moment, and when they returned to their table and he ordered another brandy for her, she found the courage to tell him she was hungry. He ordered a hot sandwich with melted cheese and tomatoes, and she wolfed it down. He looked at her curiously and asked, "When did you last have something to eat?"

"Not long ago," she lied, "but I love to eat."

"You certainly can't tell. You're nothing but skin and bones."

She regarded him with her big green eyes and asked for another brandy and another sandwich.

When she had finished, the soldier wiped the crumbs from the side of her mouth with a white napkin and tried to kiss her. She pulled away, and he tried again. This time she pulled away a little less vigorously, and he was encouraged. He helped her to her feet. "And now, my dear, the time has come to continue our evening elsewhere."

He signaled to the waiter, paid the bill, took hold of her elbow, and steered her out of Café Europa.

She knew exactly what was going on. She had lost her innocence when Gabriel had abandoned her to a cruel fate and left her alone in the world. She had to survive, and as a survivor she knew exactly what was expected of her. She had two options—to flee from this man while she still could and spend the night in the street, or to go with him to his room, let him do as he pleased with her, and sleep the rest of the night in a warm bed. She chose the latter option. Her heart and her soul were out of reach of the soldier. As far as the rest of her was concerned, she would just have to manage.

The British soldier took her to a cheap hotel on one of the streets adjacent to Zion Square, paid the clerk at reception, and led her to a staircase. He could barely get himself up to the second floor, and in his drunken state he fumbled with the key. She took it from him and inserted it in the lock.

There were two single beds with a small night table jammed between them. The soldier collapsed onto one of the beds and pulled her toward him, but she resisted, her body rigid. She clenched her teeth, closed her eyes, and prayed, *Almighty God, king of the universe, I beg You, in Your mercy, prevent me from feeling. Make this thing that the soldier wants to do be over quickly. Forgive me, master of the universe. Absolve me of my sins. Have mercy on me.* The soldier, blind to what was transpiring within her, babbled in a drunken voice, "Come, my dear little one, my sweet girl. Come to Daddy. Be nice to Daddy."

His sweaty hands on her arms were like slimy iron grips. She tried to evade him, but he tightened his grasp and pulled her body onto his. She forced herself to lie down beside him on the narrow bed.

"Not like that, my little sweet one. Come lie on top of me. Help Daddy to take off your most unnecessary dress."

He tried and failed to take off her clothes. "Help your daddy; that's a good girl," he continued in his drunken stupor, while she, for whom the effects of the alcohol had vanished, moved to the edge of the bed, endeavoring to get as far away from him as she could. He pulled her back roughly and pinned her down. He lifted her arms, and she grabbed hold of the metal headboard. She held on so tightly that she felt as though her blood had stopped circulating. Finally he managed to push her dress above her head. She lay as if nailed to the bed, her hands still grasping the metal frame, the garment covering her face, shaking and scared to death. Her thin legs and her breasts were exposed, and all that was covering her were her oversize convent underpants. The drunken soldier burst out laughing. Leering at her, he said, "Let's get those ridiculous underthings off you, my beauty, and see what they're hiding down there."

She squeezed her legs together, and he flailed at her underwear.

"Help your daddy, darling. Daddy really wants to see what's hiding in your funny pants." He began to make babyish noises as he climbed on top of her. But the moment his weight pressed down heavily atop her, she felt as though a sheet of steel had been inserted between them. He might succeed in penetrating her body, but he would never touch her soul.

The soldier was too drunk to take off his trousers, and he ground himself against her, fully clothed. She lay perfectly still, and after three attempts he groaned, slumped over her, and fell asleep.

His breath stank of alcohol. Trapped underneath him, she used every bit of strength she could muster to push him off. He was as heavy as a tree trunk, but she managed to wiggle out from underneath him, to pull down her dress, and to slip into the other bed. She covered herself completely, closed her eyes, and descended into a deep sleep.

In the morning, when she woke up, the British soldier's bed was empty. She sat up and checked that her body was intact, that she was still wearing her underwear and her dress. Everything was in place. She wondered where the soldier had gone, although she didn't really care. Memories of the previous evening came flooding back. A tremor rippled through her body. God, who had abandoned her, had twice answered her prayers. The soldier hadn't managed to get what he wanted, but what would happen next time? Would her luck hold? And even if it did, how long would it be before she met the soldier who would have his way with her, and then what would become of her? She took a deep breath, trying to recover the good feeling she had felt when she'd awoken.

I have to stop being afraid, she told herself. *I slept the sleep of the just in a bed, inside a room, and not out in the street.* Jerusalem was full of terrifying homeless people who wandered the city at night seeking easy prey. Better that she should choose her own opponent rather than be cornered by him. She had to protect herself and not rely on anyone. From this day forth she and she alone would be responsible for her welfare and manage her own life. She would be the predator, not the prey.

There was a jug of water on the windowsill, and she sipped from it and then splashed some of the water onto her face and neck. She opened the window, closed her eyes, and allowed her upturned face to be caressed by the rays of the sun, which was already blazing down from the sky.

Sharp raps on the door interrupted her reverie. "Hello, hello! Open up!"

She went to open the door and found a hotel employee standing there.

"You have to leave now," he told her. "The soldier only paid for a night, not the whole day."

"I'm leaving," she told him.

"If you aren't down in five minutes, I'll be up here again," he threatened.

After he left, she straightened her clothing and examined herself in the broken mirror. She had to get rid of the convent dress. She had to get hold of some money and buy herself one of those delicate, fashionable dresses that the attractive women at Café Europa had been wearing.

Just before she walked out, her eyes swept over the dilapidated cubicle one last time. She felt sure that this wasn't the last time she would spend the night in some musty room in a cheap hotel. Then out of the corner of her eye she spotted some money that had been wedged between the wall and the night table between the two beds. As she retrieved the bill, a wide smile lit up her face. It was a ten-pound note.

Who would have believed that God, whichever God it was, would grant her request so swiftly. She understood that the soldier had left her money in return for services rendered. It was good that he was kind enough to pay her for the night, even though he'd never received what he was after. She knew that the money would buy her food and clothing, and she rushed to leave the hotel, ignoring the clerk, who hissed, "British whore."

◆ ◆ ◆

Rochel, now Rachel, sat at the bar at London Bridge, the club next to the Edison Cinema. She sipped a glass of sherry and moved her body to the music. The place was almost empty at this early evening hour. The British soldiers and officers would only start to arrive after sundown. She freshened up her lipstick, using a pocket mirror she took out of her purse. Her blonde hair had been cut and styled à la Gloria Swanson, her green eyes were heavily made up, and she wore a slim dress that accentuated her slender body. The Jews, she had learned, liked more ample women, while the British were partial to a body like hers, which reminded them of the women at home.

She lit a cigarette and swung her foot, shod in a high-heeled sandal. The club where she worked was just a few minutes' walk from her parents' home in Mea Shearim, but she felt that she was in a different galaxy.

Her world had changed drastically since she'd left the convent and made the decision to live her own life, regardless of the cost. With the money the soldier had left her, she had paid for a modest meal and a pretty dress. She had spent most of the money on the dress, which she'd known would bring her as much food as she desired. She scrutinized all the dress shops on Jaffa Road until she saw a flowered dress with buttons in front that exposed the décolletage. She went into the store, tried it on, and walked out wearing it, discarding the convent dress in the changing room. That same evening she returned to Café Europa. The soldier from the previous night wasn't there, but there were other soldiers, and after less than a minute one of them invited her for a drink and bought her dinner. She danced in his arms and later accompanied him to a hotel.

This man took her to the Zilberstein Hotel, removed her dress clumsily, and was shocked when she told him she was a virgin, but true gentleman that he was, he treated her gently, and she hardly felt any pain. The sheet of steel protected her again, and she lay still beneath his weight until he, too, fell into a drunken slumber. Then she pushed him off and washed the lower part of her body in the tiny sink in the corner of the room. She didn't feel contaminated or dirty; she was just tired and wanted to sleep. The moment she finished washing herself, she put on her underwear, crawled under the blanket on the second bed, and fell asleep.

◆ ◆ ◆

The officer woke her in the morning with a kiss and gave her a twenty-pound note.

"I hope I didn't hurt you too much, my dear," he said to her. "Truly, it never occurred to me that it was your first time."

After that it wasn't so hard. And then she had regulars, soldiers who waited for her at Café Europa to take her to a hotel.

In time Rachel met other girls who waited for the soldiers at Café Europa. One of them was Eva, who had come to the Land of Israel from Hungary. Full-figured Eva persuaded her to move from Café Europa to London Bridge.

"At London Bridge," she told her, "the owner won't make a face every time you walk out with an Englishman."

Rachel and Eva liked each other instantly. Neither of them had a family. When Eva suggested that they rent a place together, Rachel jumped at the idea.

They rented a small room in Nahalat Shiv'a, but the neighbors, who were none too pleased when the two young, good-looking Jewish women moved in, made their lives miserable. One evening when they came home, they found the words *British Whorehouse* scrawled on their door. A week later a dead cat was waiting on their doorstep, and when they went to buy food at the local grocery store, the owner chased them away, shouting, "I don't sell to the whores of the British soldiers."

Not long afterward a man knocked at their door and presented himself as an investigator for the Committee to Defend the Honor of the Daughters of Israel.

"The neighbors are complaining that you're running a brothel in your home." They vociferously denied the charge, and they were telling the truth. No man had ever entered their room. But the investigator wrote out a detailed report claiming that the two women were prostitutes and that soldiers came to their room every night, particularly on Saturday nights and Sundays, when they were off duty.

The saga of abuse intensified, and animal droppings and human excrement appeared on their doorstep, and then someone cut off their electricity. One day they found the hat of an Australian soldier decorated with a used condom. The neighborhood children took to chasing them and calling them names. The neighbors complained to the police night and day, claiming that drunken soldiers crowded round the entrance to the building and disturbed the peace. Although all the accusations were false, the police duly sent officers to their room each time, responding assiduously to every complaint.

One morning they were awakened by loud pounding on their door. Two thugs stood outside, one of whom grabbed Rachel roughly while his counterpart leaped at her with a razor and shaved off a swath of her hair.

"What are you doing, *meshugener!*" Eva screeched, trying to push the burly man away.

"Just you wait, *kurveh* of the British! You're next!" he yelled. Eva kicked him and scratched his face. He cried out in pain and released Rachel, and they both ran off.

Eva rushed to turn the key in the lock as the men returned to scream through the door, "*Kurvehs*, whores for the British! Next time we won't just shave you—we'll kill you!"

Rachel looked in the mirror. There was a long ugly bald patch where her scalp shone through. This was the modus operandi of the violent Bnei Pinchas organization, which favored marking the heads of its victims, who were any women they suspected of spending time with the British soldiers.

"*Adesh jermkam*, my sweet one," Eva cried. "What have those bastards done to you? They have ruined your beautiful hair."

"Don't cry!" Rachel commanded her. "Not one tear. My hair will grow back, so let's just forget what happened here. We will not let those bastards have their way!"

The following day, the Committee to Defend the Honor of the Daughters of Israel pasted posters on the walls of the buildings listing the names of women who consorted with British soldiers. Rachel's and Eva's names were at the top of the list.

Since the committee didn't know Rachel's family name, they listed her as Rachel Cohen. Eva Weiss was distraught to see her full name on the list. "How do they know my name?" she asked, wild eyed with fear.

The lists were the main topic of conversation at London Bridge. All the Jewish girls were frightened. Some feared for their lives, and others were terrified that their families would find out how they spent their time.

"Those criminals even list the names of decent girls," Rachel said when she arrived at the club, a scarf covering her head. "Nice girls whose only sin is that they went on a respectable date with one of the soldiers, or even those who, horror of horrors, are married to them."

"What difference does it make?" said Morris, the owner of London Bridge. "Whoever goes around with the British is a whore in the end, and if she marries one of them, then she's both a traitor and a whore." Rachel was appalled at the double standard.

From the day they moved in together, Rachel and Eva had an unwritten agreement that they would meet at home at the end of each evening.

If one of them didn't arrive, the other knew that she should start worrying. The system had worked well, and neither of them had had any reason to worry.

Until one evening when Eva didn't come home.

Rachel waited up for hours, and when Eva still hadn't returned, she decided that if her friend hadn't come back by morning, she would go to the police. When she woke up, Eva was nowhere in sight. So she went straight to the police station, which was housed in one of the buildings in the Russian Compound. The duty policeman told her that she had to wait until Eva had been missing for at least twenty-four hours, and only then would they start to investigate. With a heavy heart she walked to work at London Bridge. Weeks before, Morris had made her an offer she couldn't refuse. "All you have to do," he told her, "is sit at the bar and persuade the idiot soldiers to order drinks. You get a percentage of every drink they buy. That has to be better than going to bed with the bastards."

So now Rachel was a hostess. She sat at the bar, heavily made up, wearing revealing dresses, and chatted with the British soldiers and their officers. They drank alcohol and she drank tea. She earned considerably less than she had before, and she had to make a significant effort to be pleasant, but she preferred being bored to death to lying underneath them in bed.

"What's with the long face?" asked Morris, and Rachel told him that Eva hadn't come home the night before.

"So she probably found some chump and stayed overnight with him at the hotel. Don't you worry; she knows how to take care of herself."

"We have an agreement that we always come home to sleep," Rachel told him.

"Agreement, shagreement. She probably had too much to drink and passed out. She'll be back before you know it," he scoffed.

Before he had finished his sentence, Eva waltzed in, completely sober and radiant. "My *maminka*," she said to Rachel, "how are you, my dear?"

"Where were you?" Rachel demanded. "I almost died of worry."

"Oy, don't ask," Eva said, smiling from ear to ear. "I went to a hotel with this soldier, and I slept so well I didn't wake up until this morning."

"But we have an agreement," Rachel protested.

"True, my dear, but this soldier, he's sooo good, like sugar."

"You know, I went to the police," Rachel reprimanded her. "I thought something happened to you."

"*Oy va'avoy, adesh aniyukum*, why did you do that? No, my *maminka*, there's no need for the police. Eva made love with the English soldier all night long. I think, *maminka*, that Eva has found her very own English soldier."

A month later, the soldier was stationed in Tel Aviv, and he took Eva with him. Rachel remained alone in the small room in Nahalat Shiv'a, and they never saw each other again.

Rachel continued to drink with the soldiers at London Bridge. She knew that it wouldn't be long before she found her own British soldier, the man who would pluck her from London Bridge so she could embark on a new life.

Although Morris earned his living from his club, which catered almost exclusively to the British, like the other Jews in the Land of Israel, he hated the enforcers of the Mandate. But he had a family to feed, and they were his best clients. No Jew could drink like the British, and no Jew would spend as much money on hard liquor.

Morris liked to have his cake and eat it, too, and didn't let his emotions get in the way of his business dealings, but when it came to Rachel, the boundaries sometimes blurred. He liked her, and he couldn't understand why she preferred the British to the Jews. She was undoubtedly the most beautiful woman who had ever been employed at London Bridge. Most of the girls who worked for him were new immigrants, while she—he was sure of it—was local, although she never divulged where she'd been born or any details about her family. Jerusalem was a small city, and he could have done some digging, but he knew better than to look into her background, for he might lose her if he did anything to annoy her. She had made that abundantly clear on more than one occasion.

Sometimes he observed her as she sat at the bar, giggling with the soldiers, permitting them to caress her and kiss her. He noticed that she repulsed any attempt to kiss her on the mouth; although she smiled and laughed, her eyes remained cold, and though she appeared to be listening closely to the men, she was only feigning interest in them. But it was none of his business. If his customers were happy, he was happy, so long as the alcohol flowed like water and the register filled up with cash. Rachel was definitely his best girl. The British vied for her attention, and the barstool next to hers was never empty. They were ready to pay any price for her to spend the night with them—as much as what she earned in a month—but she never wavered.

Her new livelihood suited her. No more dank hotel rooms, no more disgusting encounters, no more selling her body. She would never return to that way of life. She was secretly grateful to Morris for showing her a way out of that dark world.

Rachel sipped slowly at the tea she swirled in her whiskey glass; the soldiers believed that she was as drunk as they were. She extracted a cigarette from a small purse that was a gift from one of her admirers. Morris lit it for her. The first clients would start to arrive soon, but they had a few minutes to themselves.

"Did you see this in the paper?" he asked her. "In one week, in the holy city of Jerusalem, ten Jewish girls married British men."

"*Nu*, so what?" she replied apathetically, exhaling a long stream of smoke.

"So what?" he repeated. "I'll tell you 'so what.' Only a week ago I heard about a Jewish girl from the Bukhari Quarter who married an Englishman, and then she died of some disease, and the *Chevra Kadisha* Burial Society refused to bury her. They say she's a Christian. And it made no difference that her father brought the city dignitaries to prove she's Jewish, that her mother cried and begged; they buried the poor woman in the Christian cemetery in Bethlehem."

"That's because the Burial Society has no respect for the dead," Rachel replied.

"You're talking garbage." Morris was incensed. "What, you think that girls who marry British men have any honor? You know how many girls have already followed the goyim? They should all go to hell."

"And what's wrong with the gentiles?" Rachel retorted. "Have you seen these British men? They treat a girl much better than any Jewish man I've ever met."

"Enough already, don't make me mad," the indignant Morris told her. "Just don't you go after some British guy like your friend. God only knows where that soldier took her."

"He took her to Tel Aviv," she said, blowing her cigarette smoke directly into Morris's face, "and he gave her a new life, better than the one she had working for you at London Bridge."

"How do you know? Maybe he threw her out there and left her in some dump."

"Don't you worry, Morris. Even if he did leave her in some dump, any dump is better than your dump."

"Good Lord, what a mouth you've grown. You were so quiet and polite when you first got here. Just be careful that you don't go running off with some British dog."

"And if I do?"

"*Tfoo*," he spat. "The Jewish Agency is to blame for everything."

"The Jewish Agency?" Rachel laughed bitterly. "You're to blame! You pay Jewish girls to sit here and make nice with the British so that they'll spend all their pounds at your club, and if you could take money from the girls who go to bed with them, you would do that, too, so stop talking garbage yourself."

"Keep your trap shut, and don't mouth off about things you don't understand," Morris ranted. "When the British came to Palestine and got rid of the Turks, there was such joy here, to the point that the Jewish Agency chose five thousand good Jewish girls to escort the soldiers to special clubs that the Agency set up just for them. Anything to make life pleasant for the British bastards and to make them love the Land of Israel, may they be wiped off the face of the earth! Who cares if they love Israel, those dogs! What didn't they give them? Young girls who spoke English, a good meal, a library, dances, tours of the land, even Hebrew lessons. What were they thinking at the Jewish Agency? That if they put young girls and young men together, the girls wouldn't end up with them?"

"Of course they would," Rachel agreed, amused. "Why shouldn't they be with them? They speak nicely, buy presents, bring flowers."

"Fine, fine, enough talking. You see those two customers coming in? Better you should stop talking nonsense and start getting them to buy drinks, the dirty dogs."

The club was even busier than usual, and the two customers turned out to be exceptionally serious drinkers, especially the one whose uniform attested that he was a corporal and who wouldn't leave Rachel alone for a minute, braying drunkenly, his hands wandering audaciously even beyond the boundaries of what passed for good taste at London Bridge.

Morris ignored the corporal's crude behavior. What did he care. The drunker they were, the more they drank; the whiskey flowed like water and the cash register chimed.

He was unmoved even by Rachel's furious expression, until she finally hissed at him, while bestowing a large fake smile on the British soldier who wouldn't take his hands off her, "If you don't get rid of this British jerk whose filthy hands are all over me, I am going to throw my drink in his face."

"Go ahead, throw the drink in his face, and I'll throw you out of here," Morris threatened her. "That's your job; you're supposed to be nice to him so that he keeps drinking. He's no worse than the others. What, you're a rabbi's wife now?"

Rachel gritted her teeth and plastered a smile on her face. The corporal kept ordering drinks, and the more he drank, the more audaciously he behaved. He took hold of Rachel and tried to kiss her neck, and when she pushed him away, he tried to grab her breast. She jumped off her stool, and just as she had warned, she doused him with the liquid in the glass she was holding.

"Hey, hey, hey!" laughed the drunken corporal. "You want to play, sweetheart, let's play." He threw his drink at her.

"Stop it!" Morris came out from behind the bar and positioned himself between them. "What are you trying to do?" he shouted at Rachel. "You want to start a fight and bring the British police in here?"

He apologized to the corporal and ordered Rachel to go around the bar to wash her face.

"I'm very sorry, mister sir," he stammered in broken English. "That girl, she drink too much, and you lose your drink because of her. I give you new drink, on the house." He refilled the corporal's glass.

Rachel strode behind the bar to the filthy sink full of dirty dishes. She washed her hands and face, sighed, and prepared to go back to her stool. She wasn't about to allow this small, unfortunate incident to ruin her job. She would apologize to the corporal; if she had to, she would even apologize to Morris the hypocrite, who cared more about money than about taking care of the girls who worked for him. She had to hold on to the job until, like Eva, she found her British soldier, who would transport her from Morris's stinking club to a new life.

Rachel dried her hands on the grimy towel hanging by the sink and returned to her stool. Morris was back behind the bar, wiping glasses. The noisy, crowded club had emptied out. The other girls who worked there were staring into space with nothing to do. Only a small group of three British officers remained. The corporal who had pestered her was also gone.

"He left?" she asked Morris.

"He left, and you'd better leave too. You brought me bad luck. Look what happened here since you threw your drink at that poor corporal."

"Poor corporal? He grabbed my breast, and you didn't do anything."

"Big deal, as if no one has ever done that before. Don't forget who you were and what you were doing before you came here."

"Go to hell," Rachel fumed and walked angrily out of the club.

What a jerk, she thought. *"Poor corporal." How dare he? He can go to hell.*

An icy Jerusalem wind blew in her face. She thrust her hands deep into the pockets of her coat, tightened the scarf wound round her neck, pulled down her hat, and strode in the direction of Strauss Street. The narrow alley connecting the Edison Cinema to London Bridge was dark and deserted. She hastened her steps. It looked as though the great, gloomy clouds that covered the sky were about to burst. Suddenly an arm snaked out and pulled her into the entrance to one of the buildings. She struggled, but the man only tightened his grip. She screamed and hit him with her fists, but he was stronger than she was. One leather-gloved hand covered her mouth, while the other dragged her deeper into the darkness. Her hat fell off, and he pulled her roughly by the hair. She bared her teeth and tried to bite the hand that covered her mouth, but he responded by pressing down so hard she almost choked. She kicked him, twisting her body, attempting to squirm away, but his hands were like a vise. He groaned in pain when her heel pierced his leg, and when his hand slipped from her mouth, she screamed, "Help!"

He hurriedly replaced his hand over her mouth and snarled at her in English, "Shut your trap, you goddamned whore!" Her stockings ripped. She pressed her legs together as tightly as she could as he tried to pry them apart. She yelled at the top of her lungs, but no one came. Covering her mouth again with one hand, he pushed her against the wall and tried to penetrate her. She felt as though she was about to die, but she was no match for him as he pushed himself into her body. Her breath caught as though a blade had been plunged into her, and she prayed that someone would come to her aid. She tried to push away the drunken soldier, but he only thrust her more roughly into the wall, and the sharp stones tore at the skin of her back.

"Get off me, get off me, you son of a bitch," she cursed him, but he ignored her cries. She didn't know which hurt more, his assault on her body or the pain of her humiliation. She felt her strength ebbing away but continued to try to disentangle herself from him. When she thought she couldn't bear it an instant longer, a scream rose from the depths of her being. A bolt of lightning illuminated the face of the filthy man desecrating her body. It was the corporal who had been all over her at the club. And when he was finished, he shoved her onto the wet sidewalk, zipped up his pants, turned his back on her, and disappeared into the dark alley.

The rain was now pelting down. Demeaned and aching, Rachel lay on the sidewalk in a puddle of rainwater. She had no idea how long she stayed there, her tears falling with the rain, her mouth a grimace of pain, her muscles screaming, waves of nausea and revulsion rising and intensifying until she vomited.

She struggled to her feet and looked for one of her shoes. When she couldn't find it, she took off the other shoe and continued in her bare feet, shaking and soaked to the bone. She limped home, making slow progress as she pushed herself against the walls of the buildings, trying to hold together her torn skirt and her ripped blouse, clutching her coat to her body.

She unlocked the door and made straight for the kitchen sink, where she scrubbed herself so hard with a loofah that she almost tore off her skin. She returned again and again to the place between her legs. She wept and trembled, unable to make the shaking stop.

Wet and still trembling, she stumbled over to the only chair in the room and covered her painfully throbbing body with a blanket. Curled up like a fetus, she sat immobile in the armchair until dawn broke. At first light she took a deep breath and vowed that she would never divulge what had happened to a soul, including herself. She would erase this horror as though it had never taken place. She would go back to work at London Bridge and learn to keep her mouth shut. She would do whatever it took to survive at London Bridge until she found the soldier who would give her a new life.

"You look like death warmed over," Morris greeted her that day. "Go wash your face and put some rouge on your cheeks so you don't scare away the accursed British."

She walked meekly to the sink behind the bar. One look in the mirror made it clear that even if she used all the makeup in the world, she wouldn't be able to disguise her pallor.

She tried to steady herself as she added a little color to her cheeks. She felt a terrible wave of weakness wash over her, but she tossed her head defiantly and held herself erect as she assumed her usual stool at the bar.

Morris's jokes didn't make her laugh, nor did the nonstop prattling of the godforsaken soldiers.

She barely managed to hold herself together until the end of her shift, but luckily for her it was a crowded night and Morris was too busy to notice that she barely engaged with the soldiers.

The waves of nausea assaulted her in the early morning. Ever since that night she had barely been able to eat, and she assumed that that was the problem. She tried to force down some food, but she couldn't do it. *This will pass,* she told herself. *It has to pass.* The fact that the corporal never reappeared at London Bridge made things easier for her. For the first few days she found herself glancing repeatedly at the entrance, terrified that he might walk in. But the bastard had vanished, as if he knew that he shouldn't return to the scene of his crime.

Not only did the nausea not pass, but it grew worse, and soon she was vomiting. She spent hours hanging over the toilet bowl, puking until she was exhausted. She was certain that she had some deadly disease and was going to die. And no one would even come looking for her.

◆ ◆ ◆

The new girl Morris had recently employed was standing in the doorway when she came out of the washroom. She took one look at Rachel, who was pale as a sheet, and asked her, "So how many months has it been since you've received the gift?"

"Gift?" Rachel stared at her, confused.

"*Nu.*" The girl had already lost her patience. "How long since you've seen your blood?"

Good God, thought Rachel, *how could I have missed that?*

"How long?" insisted the other girl.

"I don't remember . . . a while."

"Great," the girl exhaled. "Congratulations, you're expecting."

"Expecting?"

"Figure out how many months you've been like this."

She calculated how much time had passed since the British bastard had raped her and responded very quietly, "Three months."

The thought raced through her mind like lightning. Good Lord, the bastard had gotten her pregnant. What would she do now? She couldn't continue her work at the bar if she was pregnant. Morris would throw her out in a heartbeat. Where would she go? How would she eat? How would she pay her rent, and what would she do with the baby?

And once again, she felt her protective armor melting away. She was well and truly lost.

The new girl regarded her with eyes full of sympathy.

"Does your baby have a father?"

Rachel didn't answer.

"I understand," said the girl, as though she really did, and she turned to walk away.

"Wait . . ." Rachel stopped her.

"Yes?"

"Please don't tell anyone I'm pregnant. I need to keep working for as long as I can."

"Don't worry," said the new girl. "Your secret is safe with me."

◆ ◆ ◆

"Well, well." Morris smacked his lips. "So you've finally started to eat. Finally there's some meat on you, something to grab."

To Morris's delight her breasts swelled and almost burst out of her dresses, but she knew that he would soon discover her secret.

The new girl kept her promise and never breathed a word, so Rachel felt that she could trust her. Her name was Yvonne, and she didn't talk much about herself, except to say that she was new to the country and was renting a room from a family in the Bukhari Quarter.

"Why don't I move in with you?" she suggested to Rachel one day. "The family I'm renting from isn't too happy to have me, and soon you're going to need some support. I'm sure you could use help with the rent." Rachel agreed it would be a good idea, and Yvonne moved in.

Rachel quit work once she began to show in earnest, and when her time came, Yvonne took her to the Italian Hospital on HaNevi'im Street, where she gave birth to her daughter on a cold and stormy winter's night.

It was a hard labor. When they placed her daughter on her breast, she looked down at her, and an excruciating pain split her body. The profound heartache she felt hurt more than the pain of labor.

◆ ◆ ◆

On Christmas Eve, 1927, Rachel and her daughter were released from the hospital. She wrapped the baby in a blanket and unclasped the gold chain with the Star of David that she had never removed since her beloved had given it to her, then placed it on the sleeping infant. She prepared a note for the nuns: *Good Sisters,* she wrote, *please rescue my baby as you rescued me. I cannot save her.* At the top of the note she sketched a Star of David, and at the bottom a drawing of a white lily, her favorite flower. She swaddled the baby tightly and set off for the convent.

It was a long way from the hospital to the convent. Rachel clasped the baby to her chest and prayed that she wouldn't wake up. The snow was falling heavily, and it was difficult for her to clear a path with her footsteps. She was still weak from childbirth, but some force gave her the strength to keep moving. It wasn't the baby's fault that she'd been born in sin; it wasn't the baby's fault that her mother couldn't raise her. When she finally reached the convent gate, the baby burst out crying in heartrending sobs. Rachel didn't think twice. She took shelter in a narrow stone niche near the gate and put the baby to her breast. As she looked down at her, she felt that the infant was drawing in her life force, but she hastened to banish all thoughts from her mind and all emotion from her heart. She must not allow herself to become attached to the baby; she wouldn't look at her; she mustn't remember her face. If she wanted to go on living, she had to forget this baby, who had been born of her body in such blinding pain. She mustn't look at her peach-colored skin or her half-closed, long-lashed eyes. She could not let herself remember the golden tuft of hair or the dimples in her cheeks, identical to her own. She must not remember the baby, because if she did, she wouldn't be able to move on with her life.

When she had nursed her fill, the baby instantly fell asleep. One last time Rachel wrapped up the tiny body. Then she moved to the bell rope and tugged it once, twice, three times, four times. After the fourth pull, when she heard the sound of footsteps and the jangling of keys, she placed the baby at the entrance by the great iron gate and hid behind the fence. The gate opened. Only after she had seen the stern-faced nun lift the baby from the snow-covered step, adjust her against her breast, and lock the gate behind her, only then did she start to breathe again.

She made her way back to her room, and without getting undressed, she climbed into bed, covered her head with the blanket, and cried herself to sleep.

The British officer who sat next to Rachel at the bar was a perfect gentleman. He lit her cigarette and invited her to have a drink with him.

"Pleased to meet you." He extended his hand. "Major Stewart Townshend."

"I'm Rachel," she replied, and she noticed the kindness in his eyes.

"And does Rachel have a last name?"

"I don't; would you mind loaning me yours?"

"With great pleasure," he laughed.

"If so"—and she was smiling too—"Rachel Townshend, pleased to make your acquaintance."

That evening she devoted most of her attention to him, until Morris whispered in her ear that there were other soldiers at the bar as well.

"What do you care, as long as he's drinking and paying," she retorted irritably.

"He can't drink up the whole bar," he hissed at her. "Take care of the others too."

She explained to the major that she was working and she had to be nice to the other soldiers as well.

He nodded in understanding and vacated the stool next to hers.

"Just don't forget about me," he said, winking.

She drank and laughed with the soldiers, every so often glancing over at the end of the bar where Stewart Townshend sat alone, never taking his eyes off her, oblivious to the other girls trying to flirt with him, drinking by himself.

By the time she finished her shift, the bar had emptied of customers. Major Townshend was nowhere in sight. Never mind, she thought. If not him, another one would come tomorrow. She received her take for the night from Morris and left the club.

"Would you be so kind as to allow me to escort you home?" he asked, appearing suddenly behind her.

Rachel jumped out of her skin. The British officer had been waiting for her outside the entrance to the club, and now he extended his arm.

"No, thank you," she said. "I prefer to walk alone."

"I promise you that my intention is solely to walk you home and nothing more."

"I'm sure that's true, but it's a matter of principle for me. No customer walks me home, none of my neighbors know where I work, and I'd like to keep it that way. I don't want any trouble."

She hurried away in the direction of the new room she had recently rented, at the end of Princess Mary Street.

Despite her clear reply, the officer followed her, but he couldn't keep up. She broke into a run and vanished from his sight. From then on, he came to London Bridge every evening, but he sat at the end of the bar and never disturbed her. However, each night, when her shift was over, he was waiting for her outside. With infinite patience, despite her constant refusals, every night he offered to walk her home.

And then one night she gave in. From then on he walked with her after her shift, but only as far as the corner of Princess Mary Street, when she would say good night and continue alone.

As time passed, she softened toward him, and they became closer. Soon he was spending the night in her room several times a week. She no longer worried about her neighbors. He promised to protect her, and she felt safe with him. He was a senior officer with the British Mandate police, and as long as she was with him, no one could hurt her.

One morning, after they had spent the night together, he didn't rise early and hurry off to police headquarters as was his habit.

"Today," he said, smiling, "I have a surprise for you."

"I don't like surprises."

"I think you'll like this surprise. When was the last time that you were outside Jerusalem?"

She hesitated before replying, "I have never, in my entire life, been outside Jerusalem."

"Well then, my darling, today will be your first time, for today we are going to Tel Aviv."

Tel Aviv! She was instantly excited. The soldiers at London Bridge had often told her about the white city surrounded by sand near the sea, the lighthearted city overflowing with cafés and nightclubs, restaurants and parties. But she mustn't jump for joy. Instead, she had to convince him that it was difficult for her to go away with him and that it would endanger her livelihood. Just as she hoped, he took her in his arms and said, "My beautiful love, you won't have reason to work for that bastard much longer. Starting today, I will take care of you. Pack a few dresses; we aren't returning to Jerusalem today."

The journey took longer than expected, but she was enjoying the drive so much that she lost track of the time. Stewart was focused on the poorly paved road that connected Jerusalem and Tel Aviv, which twisted and turned among the green fields and the rolling hills. Every so often a car full of passengers drove by, but most of the cars on the road were British military vehicles. At the checkpoint on the outskirts of Bab al-Wad, the soldiers saluted Major Townshend and waved them through.

Rachel felt uplifted. The green fields and flocks of sheep on the slopes of the Arab village of Bayt Mahsir looked to her like a scene from the cinema. When they finally arrived in Tel Aviv, she gasped. She was spellbound by the blue sea and couldn't drag her eyes away. She gazed into the distance, hoping that the day was not far off when she would sail into that horizon, far, far away from the shores of the Land of Israel, British Mandatory Palestine.

Stewart drove the jeep along the beach until they reached the Tavor Hotel. She couldn't get enough of the ultramarine sea, the golden stretch of beach, the tiny white houses, so different from the gloomy stone structures in Jerusalem. A lovely building sat on an inlet.

"That's the casino," Stewart told her. "We'll go dancing there this evening."

The people in Tel Aviv looked different from those in Jerusalem. The women wore wide-brimmed hats and held white parasols to protect their skin from the sun, and the men were dressed in light-colored suits and had straw boaters on their heads. Families walked along the seaside, where mothers pushed baby carriages, and she turned her face away, for the sight of the babies pierced her heart.

The beach was crowded. Half-naked women dressed in what looked to her like undergarments and men wearing tight clothes in which what was normally hidden in their pants was outlined prominently lounged on beach chairs that were arranged in rows along the water. Others played ball games, and still others bobbed in the waves.

In their hotel room, Rachel put on a flowered dress that left her arms and legs bare, pinned up her blonde hair, dabbed some perfume on her wrists, behind her ears, and near her throat, and regarded her reflection with satisfaction. Stewart came up behind her, placed a long string of pearls around her neck, and kissed the spot under her upswept hair. She turned to him and smiled. She was almost happy.

They walked along the promenade. A beautiful young woman and a British officer in uniform. Here as well there were many who glared at them with hostility. She tightened her grip on Stewart's arm, and they continued their walk. She could not accustom herself to the hateful stares, but she had learned to ignore the harsh words that were launched at her. She inhaled deeply, breathing in the scent of the sea, held herself erect, and walked at her officer's side with her head held high.

When they passed Café San Remo, she saw him. He was sitting at a café table, and the moment their eyes locked was sufficient for her to discern the shock in his. Gabriel. Her knees buckled, and she leaned against Stewart for support. He continued to walk and talk, oblivious to the torrent of feeling swirling inside her.

"Let's go back to the hotel," she said, feeling that if she remained there, she would die.

"My poor darling, aren't you feeling well?" he said, suddenly realizing that she hadn't heard a word he'd been saying.

"No, I suddenly feel weak."

They went back to the hotel, but she felt as though she could hardly breathe. *God,* she thought to herself, *why did I have to see him?*

She went into the bathroom and studied her reflection in the mirror. The shock and fear on her face were plain to see. Then she pulled herself together, washed off all her makeup, and reapplied it carefully. She looked herself in the eye and vowed, *I will not allow that bastard to destroy my life a second time. I will walk out of this room with a huge smile, and I will make love to Stewart like I have never made love before. I will not allow Gabriel to ruin what I have worked so hard to build. He will not rob me of my ticket out of here.*

However pretty it was, Tel Aviv was not the goal. She wanted to leave this suffocating land, to put as much distance as possible between herself and the accursed place where Gabriel lived, and to never return. She fluffed her hair, stretched languorously, opened the door, and went, smiling and sensuous, into the arms of her lover, who was waiting for her on the bed.

◆ ◆ ◆

That evening they went to Café Pilz. Rachel wore her best dress and highlighted her cheekbones with extra blush. The waiter escorted them to a table on the balcony. A cool breeze blew in from the sea, the tables were covered with starched white cloths, the high-quality porcelain dishes gleamed, the menu was varied, and the service was sublime.

An orchestra played, and couples gravitated to the dance floor. Stewart asked her to dance, and she pressed herself against him, resting her head on his shoulder.

"My darling," he whispered into her hair, "are you enjoying yourself?"

"I'm in seventh heaven."

"This is just the beginning, my love. We are going to have such wonderful times, you and I. I promise you that every opportunity I have, we will come to Tel Aviv."

She pressed her lips to his for a long and tender kiss that lasted until the end of the song.

One day, she thought, *we will be far away from Tel Aviv and this awful land.*

When they returned to Jerusalem, she informed Morris that she was leaving. He tried to convince her to stay. "Your Englishman will go home and leave you here like a dog," he warned her. "Don't trust the British bastards; he's only using you while he's here. When he goes back to England, what will you do?"

"I'll go with him."

"Fat chance of that," he snorted. "Maybe when hell freezes over, he'll take you. You think he would marry a girl like you? He'll marry a fine girl. You don't know these sons of dogs like I do. For years I've watched them here, turning good Jewish Palestinian girls like you into whores. And then they go back home and leave the girls here to cry. What a pity that you live in a dreamworld. The Messiah will come on his donkey before that man takes you home with him to England."

"When Stewart leaves this country, I'm leaving with him, whether you like it or not," she said, and she exited the London Bridge, determined never to return.

A short time later, Major Townshend was transferred to a position at the British detention camp in Cyprus near Famagusta. Standing next to him on the deck of the ship that set sail from Haifa Port was his new wife, Rachel Townshend.

From the moment she stepped onboard the ship, Rachel didn't look back. She knew that she would never return. She was leaving behind a family that mourned her for dead despite knowing that she was still alive, a man who had broken her trust and her heart, a baby who was the result of a rape, a year at a convent, and a questionable past. Her protective armor traveled with her and would shield her heart and soul for many more years, ensuring that nothing hurt her and nothing touched her.

◆ ◆ ◆

On that night, belowdecks, as she lay in her husband's arms after tender lovemaking, she made him swear that he would never mention where they had met, not to her and not to anyone else.

"I want us to start over," she told him. "Promise me that you will never tell a soul that I am a Jewess from the Land of Israel."

He promised her, and in fact he was pleased, because he, too, wished to forget the circumstances in which they had met and the way she had earned her living at that time.

Rachel closed her eyes, filled with relief at the thought that she had finally left her homeland behind, a country that held only bad memories.

What she didn't know then was that part of it would remain with her for every single day of her new life, and that was the thought of the fate of the baby she had left at the iron gate of the convent on a freezing-cold Christmas Eve in Jerusalem.

Lily

The heavens were shot through with beams of a soft grayish light by the time Rachel finished her story. She leaned back in her chair, exhausted, her eyes closed, her mouth a round O. The wrinkles around her lips had smoothed out, and a pink blush colored her sunken cheeks, making her look like a much younger woman. Her breathing had slowed with the incredible relief of laying down the burden of a lifetime.

Lily sat motionless on the sofa, her eyes also closed, but tightly, as if in prayer. Eliya placed a tender hand on her mother's, aware that her mother's heart was racing.

"Let's go!" Lily opened her eyes at once and commanded Eliya. "We're leaving."

Eliya jumped to her feet.

"So that's it then?" Rachel Townshend asked Lily. "You came all the way from Israel to meet me, and now that I've told you my story, you don't have anything to say?"

Lily ignored her and left the house without a word.

Only when they had climbed to the top of the stairs and reached the crest of the hill that looked out to the sea did Lily stretch out her arms and allow a word to burst forth in a tremendous shout: "Why?"

Rachel Townshend, standing at the doorway to her home, heard that cry.

"Why, God, why?" Lily screamed again, and then she collapsed in Eliya's arms.

"How could she leave me like that, just to go back to being a whore for the British? How did she change her spots and become a lady, while I was living like a waif, a motherless child, a child without a home . . ."

"I didn't leave you to be a whore for the British." Rachel suddenly appeared beside them. Eliya was stunned that an elderly woman who walked with a cane had managed to get up the steps so quickly. "You can hate me—I deserve it—but I do not regret leaving you at the convent. You grew up to be a decent woman; you have a good family, a daughter who loves you. If you had stayed with me, you, too, would have become a whore for the British. What chance would you have had with me for a mother? In Jerusalem in those days they would have shaved your head and excommunicated you. They would have persecuted you and abused you, a bastard child, the daughter of a whore for the British. What kind of life would you have had if I hadn't left you there?"

Lily regarded her with eyes filled with pain. "But why didn't you try to find out what happened to me? Why did you only write one letter to me and then never write again?"

"I never stopped writing to you. I wrote to you every day," she replied, and she motioned to them to follow her as she walked carefully back down the stairs to her house. Lily and Eliya regarded each other, both wary of consenting, but in the end they followed. She walked through the front door, but instead of returning to the living room, she led them to the back of the house and opened a door. It was her bedroom, where the windows were hung with heavy curtains, made from the same fabric as the cover for the four-poster bed that stood in the center of the room. Rachel lit the chandelier and crossed over to a dresser covered with family photographs. In the center was a photograph in a silver frame portraying a handsome man with a mustache, dressed in the uniform of a British officer. It was flanked by more pictures of the man and Rachel at different stages of their lives and photographs of smiling children in the arms of young couples. Eliya couldn't stop staring at the pictures. All her life she had fantasized about having a big family with aunts and uncles and cousins, and here she was standing before a whole slew of relatives—and her heart was empty. All she felt was a burning anger that seeped into her stomach and then spread through her chest.

Rachel opened a drawer in the dresser and withdrew a thick leather-bound notebook. "Here," she said to Lily. "Here is what I wrote to you every day of my life. I wrote to you in secret so that my husband wouldn't read it, so he wouldn't know. Here, take it. Written here are my longings for you. In here I wrote about my life without you, about my regrets, and in here are buried my sorrow and my tears."

Lily took the book from her hands and leafed through the closely written pages.

"You wrote to yourself," Lily said as she perused the leather-bound book. "Not to me. To yourself, you wrote to ease your conscience. If you had written me a letter, even once a year, there wouldn't have been so many wasted years of pain and loneliness. I don't need your secret diary. A pile of yellowing pages cannot atone for a lifetime of bitterness. Come, Eliya; let's go. Everything that had to be said has been said. There's nothing more for us to do here."

"You don't want to read what I wrote to you?" asked Rachel in anguish.

"No! I have received answers to the questions that plagued me. I have seen the hard-hearted woman who dumped me with the nuns."

Rachel stood facing Lily, blocking her path to the door.

"Maybe you're wrong," she said to her. "Maybe you haven't received all the answers. Maybe the answers are here, in this book that you don't want to read."

Lily appraised the bedroom, and her eyes alighted on the family photos. "And what about your children?" She was practically screaming. "Did you tell them that their father met you in a vile bar in Jerusalem?

Did you tell them that you aren't a princess their father brought home from Kenya as you led them to believe?"

Rachel took a deep, shaky breath. A frightening silence filled the room, and she turned away from Lily and Eliya to face the window that looked out over the rose garden. Finally she turned back, and in a quiet, expressionless voice she said, "There was no one to tell. I don't have children."

Lily and Eliya looked at each other in surprise. Rachel sat down heavily in an armchair, and it was clear that standing had tired her. She placed a hand on each knee and continued, "After I gave birth to you, my womb sealed off, and I never got pregnant again. My husband, Stewart, couldn't understand why two healthy young people couldn't manage to have a child together, but I knew why. It was my punishment. God punished me for abandoning a day-old baby at a convent in Jerusalem. I had failed the test that God set for me, and in His eyes I wasn't worthy of being a mother.

"For many years I despaired over my inability to give birth to a child who could grow up in a decent home with a father and a mother, a child I could shower with the care and love that I couldn't give you. In time I learned to live with the punishment that God chose for me, but I was in torment over the thing that I never revealed to a soul in all my life—I have a daughter in the world, and I don't know whether she is dead or alive. I have a daughter in the world, and she doesn't know of my existence and my suffering and my yearnings and, mostly, about my regret.

"My life with Stewart was a good life; he took care of my every need, and I took care of him. We learned to live with the fact that we would never have children and ignored the pity doled out by our relatives and acquaintances who viewed us as a pathetic, childless couple. We appreciated each other and enjoyed one another's company. We were surrounded by Stewart's kind relations. His father and mother accepted me with open arms and didn't ask any questions, as did his brother and sister-in-law and their children and their extended family, who have lived here for generations. Stewart, may he rest in peace, died ten years ago, and ever since I have been alone in this house on the cliff overlooking the sea. Divina, my sister-in-law, who is also widowed, comes to visit me twice a week and helps me out if necessary. Her children and grandchildren visit me every Christmas and Easter, and the pictures on my dresser are of them, but the rest of the time I am alone, a woman tormented by the knowledge that she has a daughter in the world but no idea what became of her."

Lily didn't speak, and Rachel went on, "You think you have received all the answers, Lily, but you are mistaken; you have received only a small portion of them. If you read my diary, you will hear my longings for you, my concern, my prayers, and what I beseeched God every day: 'Please, in Your great mercy, watch over my daughter, bless her with a good and happy life, and grant her physical and emotional health.' I prayed only for you. I never dared to pray for myself; I never dared to ask God for what I wanted more than anything else—to meet you before I died. I never thought I would meet you in this world."

"You wouldn't have met in the next world either," said Eliya in a hard voice. "My mother would be in heaven, and you would be in hell."

"Why didn't you look for me?" Lily asked, ignoring Eliya. "Israel is a small country. How is it possible that you didn't get on a boat and come looking for me?"

"And what would I have told my husband? Once we realized that we could never have children, we learned to accept our fate. But the slightest breeze could have capsized our lives, demolished what we had built. If you have been cast out in the street once, the fear of being homeless never leaves you; it is always right here inside." Rachel placed her hand on her heart. "It is always here, waiting to ambush you."

"You don't have to tell me about that fear," Lily shot back. "Thanks to you, it lies in wait for me as well. But why didn't you tell your husband that you had a daughter? If he loved you as you say he did, he would have done everything in his power to help you find me."

"From the moment we reached England, my husband never once mentioned my previous life, not to me or to anyone. He forgot how we met, and he came to believe the story that he had fabricated. If I had told him that a British soldier had raped me and left me pregnant with a child who I abandoned at a convent, he would have collapsed. He knew enough ugly details about my past, and I chose to spare him more pain and kept quiet, but you have to know all the details, because it is the story of your life. You were born to a pathetic mother who had no choice but to sell her body to survive. You were born to a young woman who was preyed upon by a drunken Englishman on a night when even God cried over what he did to her. My husband transformed me into a decent woman, gave me a family, rescued me from hell, and brought me to safety. It wasn't my choice," Rachel went on, "that things happened that way. Destiny determined that you be born to a woman who had sinned and chose my husband to save me and heal me. It's not your fault, but it's not his fault, either, and so I chose not to break his world asunder, and I kept your existence a secret. It took tremendous courage and great love for him to marry a woman like me and bring her back in deception and lies to his parents' home in England. It required determination and a very strong character to keep the secret for so many years and never once to slip up and say anything to suggest that I wasn't the Christian girl they believed me to be. I could not bear to cause him any more suffering."

Lily stared at Rachel, speechless. Eliya waited for another of her mother's outbursts of fury or pain, but it didn't come. Rachel continued.

"I don't dare to ask you to forgive me. I just ask God to grant me a last act of grace and allow you to understand the circumstances that caused me to behave as I did. My daughter, I pray to God that I have not contributed to your burden of suffering by telling you my story and that you won't feel any more pain than you already do."

It was the first time that Rachel had addressed Lily as her daughter, and the younger woman felt her heart expand. Despite the resentment she felt toward Rachel, she admitted to herself that it was a wonderful feeling to be addressed as "my daughter," something exceptional to feel that she was someone's daughter.

Silence descended on the room as the three women tried unsuccessfully to make sense of their thoughts, if not their feelings.

Lily was the first to break the silence. "I don't know what to say. My English may not be good enough to understand what is written in your diary, but whatever is written there cannot compensate for the price I paid for the new life that you chose for yourself. You sailed off to England and lived happily in peace and prosperity, and I lived a terrible life in which I didn't know a moment's peace. Even when I married, even when my children were born, I never stopped thinking about the woman who didn't want me. Even when my husband was holding me in his arms, even when I held my children, I felt abandoned, miserable, alone. I always felt that I lacked something that would make me whole. I was on the verge of madness, and if it wasn't for Shaul, my wonderful husband, who refused to give up on me even when I embittered his life and made it insufferable, I would have ended up in the street, just as you left me.

"Come, Eliya," she said, and she left the diary lying on the dresser. "I don't need a diary to tell me about the woman who gave birth to me. I have already heard more than I wanted to."

Shaul and Eldad, tense and silent, waited for them at the top of the hill, looking alternately at the house and out at the boats and the waves. The minutes dragged and the weather turned colder, with strong winds blowing in from the sea as the sky filled with black clouds. Shaul's limbs felt stiff, but worse for him than the bitter cold, which even his heavy wool coat and ridiculous woolen hat couldn't keep out, were the thoughts about what Lily might be going through as she finally confronted her past. He was tired, his legs ached from standing for so long, and he could barely feel his toes, squashed together in his too-tight boots. He paced along the hilltop, withdrawn, his eyes repeatedly pulled to the staircase that descended to Rachel Townshend's house.

Eldad, who wasn't a heavy smoker, found himself chain-smoking. He, too, worried about Lily, as well as Eliya, who was escorting her mother on this difficult journey so soon after the two of them had finally opened their hearts to one another. It was admirable, he thought, that after years of distance and anger, Eliya was now at her mother's side at the center of her conflict with the woman who had cast her away. He knew that Eliya would be strong for her mother, but he wondered what it would cost her.

"What are you thinking about?" Shaul asked. "You seem so far away."

"I'm thinking about our two women, who are as strong as steel," said Eldad, and he offered him a cigarette, which Shaul waved away.

Shaul reflected for a time before answering, "You know, Eldad, even steel has a breaking point. If what this woman, Rachel Townshend, is telling Lily and Eliya now burns like fire, then even our steely women may crack."

Not for the first time Eldad was aware of how much he loved and admired the quiet and humble Shaul Zoref, who always seemed to bow to his wife's whims and idiosyncrasies. His voice was soft as butter, and he seemed to be pleading whenever he spoke to her, appearing at first glance to be nothing but a doormat she stepped on time and again, but he was in fact a strong man. It was his resilience that held together the shaky foundations of the strange family that Eldad was now bound to through his great love for Eliya. Without Shaul the family would have shattered. Shaul Zoref was a gentle man with an iron will.

Turning to Shaul, he said in a soft voice, "I know that you want to wait for Lily here, but let's go back to the room and wait for them there, as it seems to be taking longer than we expected."

"I'm not budging from here until I see Lily walk out that door and come up those stairs," was Shaul's decisive response.

"It's starting to rain," Eldad pointed out. "What's the point of getting soaked? And I'm feeling pretty tired."

"If you're tired, go back to the bed-and-breakfast, but I'm not leaving. Who knows what she's going through?" Shaul sighed. "No, Eldad, I can't leave. I have to be here for her when she comes out."

So they remained standing, exposed on the hilltop, the wind whipping their faces. Then without warning the rain started to pour down. The wind picked up and almost knocked them off their feet, and there was nowhere for them to shelter.

"Let's go back, Shaul. There's no point standing here and getting totally soaked. Let's wait for them in a warm and cozy room. They will both need a hot cup of tea when they get back."

For the thousandth time Shaul glanced at his watch. Two hours had passed since Eliya and Lily had walked through Rachel Townshend's front door, and the rain showed no sign of abating.

He could continue to bite his nails inside the bed-and-breakfast. Sopping wet and cold, his toes pinched and painful, he realized that Eldad was right. Better to return to their rooms, order a pot of tea, and wait inside. When the loves of his life returned, they would need a lot of warmth and love.

"I don't want to stay in this awful place for another minute. Let's pack. I want to leave today."

Shaul couldn't soothe Lily, who couldn't stop crying. "I never should have come to England, Shaul. I never should have met that woman; I didn't need to hear about the man who planted me inside her. It would have been better for me to go on living with the black pit that I have lived with all my life. I knew, Shaul, I always knew that I shouldn't ask questions. When the *bishara* tried to tell me things about my past, I stopped her; I told her that I didn't want to hear anything. Deep down I knew that the woman who gave birth to me was no saint, but to find out that she was a whore for the British? In my worst nightmares I never imagined such a thing."

"Calm down, Lily," Shaul pleaded. "This is not good for your health. Remember, when the incident occurred, she was working as a hostess at a bar. She was no longer"—he paused—"doing the work she had done before."

"What difference does it make, Shaul? Why do I need to find out that I was born in the garbage?" Lily stared at him with pain-filled eyes.

"My Lily, don't forget that she was born in an ultra-Orthodox Jewish home, where God resided within the walls. It was her cruel fate that she was taken from there. She was a good girl who was led astray, and the goodness in her she bequeathed to you. The woman who gave birth to you did nothing out of malice but only because she had no choice. She has already received her punishment, not from you but from above. Maybe it's true that because of what she did, God sealed her womb and prevented her from becoming a mother a second time. Who knows better than you, Lily, that there is no heavier punishment than to live in the world without the privilege of being a mother."

Lily listened to Shaul, and she understood the wisdom in his kind words. She relaxed and sank into his arms. She breathed deeply, occasionally shuddering with a dry sob. He stroked her hair and whispered in her ear, "You can't change the past. My love. Come, I'll give you a sleeping pill to help you rest. When you wake up, we'll go home. In a day or two we'll be back in Tel Aviv."

With infinite gentleness he removed her shoes, lifted off her dress, and dressed her in her nightgown. He touched her as though she were a fragile baby whose bones might break if he handled her too roughly. He covered her with the thick blanket and switched off the bedside lamp.

Shaul sat in an armchair and watched over his wife. Her features, which had been so contorted after her meeting with Rachel Townshend, were finally peaceful. She slept with her lips slightly parted, her thick hair falling on her face. He carefully brushed the hair away and kissed her softly on the cheek. *Rest,* he thought. *Tomorrow we will try to repair what broke within you today, but for now, rest.*

Eliya

My heart was overflowing. "What my mother told you and my father," I told Eldad when we were alone in our room, "is only the smallest part of the story. At first I didn't believe her, Madam Rachel Townshend with her perfect English accent. I mean, how is it possible that this woman who behaves like the queen of England was a hostess in a bar for the British in Jerusalem? How could it be that this Englishwoman with her impeccable manners was a whore for the British? I couldn't believe that this Christian woman who decorates her Christmas tree so beautifully was a kosher Jew who grew up among the ultra-Orthodox Jews in Jerusalem's Mea Shearim neighborhood." Still worked up, I added, "This strange woman is my *grandmother*."

Eldad held me. "We are all actors in God's theater, my beauty. He directs our lives and moves us around like pieces on a chessboard."

"It's all my fault. If only I hadn't forced her to come to England," I said ruefully.

"You're wrong," said Eldad. "She needed you to walk beside her on this journey to visit her past. Better to live with the truth, however difficult it may be, than to live a lie. My love, you're the one who said that to me, don't you remember? It was you who forced me to confront what happened to me during the war and to say aloud the words that almost destroyed me from the inside. Following your advice is what finally released me and allowed me to open myself to the world. You'll see: Lily will live a better life, even knowing the truth of her past."

All the drama began to take its toll. I was exhausted, and my thoughts were spinning. "Let's put this awful day behind us," I said to Eldad. "Tomorrow we'll pack and get out of here. We came to do good, and we did bad."

"No," Eldad insisted, "we didn't do anything wrong, and I don't think we should leave before your mother forgives her mother."

"Forgives her? How can she forgive her? If she had been a decent person, she would have kept her and raised her and given her a new life, just like she did for herself. But she didn't do any such thing. And no matter what she says now to justify herself, it will never give us cause to forgive her."

Eldad looked at me and stroked my cheek.

"Let's just go to sleep," I finally said. "We're both tired. In the morning we'll get up to a new day, and we'll be wiser."

"And maybe also a little more forgiving." He smiled as we snuggled into each other.

◆　◆　◆

The suitcases were packed. I sat with Shaul and Lily in their room, and we waited for Eldad to come back with our train tickets to London.

Lily was very quiet, lost in thought in the armchair by the window, staring vacantly outside. I sat next to her on the edge of the windowsill, enjoying the view of the sea. If it hadn't been for all the emotional turmoil, I would have liked to stay on for a few more days to enjoy this lovely, tranquil place that was so different from Tel Aviv.

But I was frightened about what the future might hold, what might happen to Lily if she reverted to the aggressive, withdrawn woman she had been not so long before, who found comfort only at the cemetery, with her dead baby. I was afraid that all the profound changes of the past few months—the wonderful closeness we felt for each other, the relationship we had built so carefully with my grandparents—would be undone. One look at my father's gray face told me that he shared my anxiety.

Lily

"At the convent they taught us that forgiveness among people is the condition for divine forgiveness." Lily's voice broke the silence in the room. "It's been years since I thought of anything they taught us there. But ever since we met that woman who gave birth to me, I keep hearing the things that the nuns said, like, 'First there is forgiveness, and only after people forgive one another does God forgive.' But what can I do if I can't forgive? What can I do when I haven't believed in God for such a long time?" Both Shaul and Lily looked over at her, trying to catch her eye, but she kept her gaze fixed on some distant spot near the ceiling.

They all turned at the sound of a light knocking at the door.

Eliya walked over and pulled it open. To her surprise, it was Rachel Townshend who greeted her. Bewildered, she automatically moved aside as the elderly woman made her regal way into the room, supported by her walking stick. Lily couldn't conceal her astonishment.

"What are you doing here?" she asked. "How did you find us?"

"I live in a small town, and it's not every day that tourists arrive here from Israel," she replied. "Aren't you going to introduce me?" She turned toward Shaul.

"This is my husband, Shaul," Lily said. "Shaul, this is Rachel Townshend, the woman who gave birth to me."

"Pleased to meet you." Shaul hesitantly took her wrinkled hand, clearly uncertain what to say. He took in the beautiful old woman who Lily so closely resembled.

"And so," Rachel said, "I see that your suitcases are already packed and you are about to depart."

"Yes," Lily replied, "my future son-in-law went to the train station to get our tickets."

"Fine." Rachel paused for a long moment before she spoke. "I see that you want to escape this place as fast as you can, but before you return to your country and your life, I would like to speak to you alone, just the two of us."

"I think we have said everything that we have to say."

"My daughter," said the woman, and again Lily felt her heart skip a beat at the sound of that word. "I am ill, my heart is damaged, and the doctors don't give me many more years to live. You have already come all this way. Won't you hear me out one last time?"

"I will listen," Lily agreed, "but I want my daughter and my husband to hear you too."

"As you wish."

Lily vacated the armchair and invited Rachel to take her place, while she sat facing her on a straight-backed chair. Eliya and Shaul stood by the window behind Lily's chair. From where they were standing, they could see Rachel's face but not Lily's.

"Lily . . . ," said Rachel Townshend in a faraway voice, "I gave you a name when you were born. I called you Lily for my favorite flower, the flower I had dreamed of threading through my hair on what was meant to be my wedding day. At the bottom of the note I drew a white lily, and beside it I wrote its name, *lily*. I hoped that the nuns would give you the name that I had chosen, and which to my joy suits you so perfectly.

"Lily," she said softly, as though caressing the letters of the pretty name with her voice. "Ever since I arrived here on the ship, every Friday my husband did as I asked and brought me a bouquet of white lilies from the flower shop, and I would arrange them in a vase and look at the beautiful flowers and think of you. I would imagine you as a one-year-old, then at two, at three, as a child, a young girl, a young woman, and I would wonder what your life was like. And I cried. How I cried, and my husband didn't understand why the flowers made me cry, and no matter how often he asked, I wouldn't tell him, and finally he stopped asking, despairing of ever receiving an answer. My mother-in-law thought I was breaking down under the burden of the sorrow of being barren. Time did not heal the wound that has festered in my heart from the moment I left you at the entrance to the convent on that terrible night.

"You said, Lily, that I sacrificed your life on the altar of my new life. You believe that I was happy at the expense of your misery, but believe me, my daughter, not a day has passed that I didn't think of you. There was not a single moment of joy in which my heart didn't ache, and I couldn't share my longings for you with anyone, not even my husband."

And then came the voice of Eliya, who once again couldn't keep silent. "How is it that he could endure the knowledge that you were a whore?"

"Eliya," whispered Lily, "please, this is between me and her. Allow me to fight this battle on my own."

"I understand why your daughter is angry," Rachel said evenly. "She has every right to feel that way, as do you. My husband could live with my past, but he would not have been able to live with that story."

"And do you think"—Lily's voice was barely audible—"that I can live with that story? That I can live with the knowledge that I was the result of the rape of my mother, who was a whore?"

"May God help us," whispered Rachel Townshend, "but that is the truth, for my sins."

Lily's voice broke. "I don't know if I can live with that truth. I don't know if I can forgive you."

"Lily." Rachel gazed steadily into Lily's green eyes. "You are not to blame that I blindly followed a young man who destroyed my life, left me cut off from my family and alone in a cruel world. You are not to blame that I had no choice but to work in the oldest profession of all in order to survive, you are not to blame that a drunken English bastard raped me, and you are not to blame that I left you with the nuns. None of it is your fault, Lily."

Rachel paused and took hold of Lily's hand, looked more deeply into her daughter's eyes, and continued, "Those are the whims of fate, my daughter, which trifled with me and with you and kept us apart all our lives. Those caprices have made us who we are today."

Mother and daughter were silent for a time, and then Lily said, "Here, take it," and she unfastened the gold chain around her neck. "It's yours."

Rachel Townshend ignored the outstretched hand.

The air in the room seemed to thicken, the only sounds those of the breathing of four people, frozen in their places. Despite the stormy weather, Eliya opened the window, and an icy breeze blew in, rippling through the tension. The mournful blaring of a ship's horn could be heard, and two birds flew close to the open window.

Finally, Rachel Townshend spoke again. "My daughter," she said, and her voice seemed to float in the charged air of the room, "a person's life is composed of three days—yesterday, today, and tomorrow. That is the basis of our lives on earth. We cannot change yesterday, and so all that remains is to live today and pray for tomorrow. I will not take back the necklace, my daughter; it has been yours since the day you were born. When I wrapped it around your tiny form, I wanted whoever found you to know that you had an identity. That you were a Jewess, just as the woman who gave birth to you was a Jewess."

It was a few moments before Lily was able to respond, and her voice was soft and choked with tears. "I don't want the necklace. I don't want it to remind me that I was born to you. From the day I was born,

I have felt as though I have been paying for a sin I didn't commit, for something in my past, and I had no idea what it was. Now I understand: I have been paying for the sin of my mother who gave birth to me, for your sin. I paid with great pain; I paid with the life of my child; I paid by embittering the life of my husband, by nearly destroying my daughter's life. Were it not for her nobility of spirit and generosity of heart, I would have missed out on the chance to experience the love of a mother for her daughter, the love of a daughter for her mother, just as you and I missed out. I almost passed on your fate and mine to me and my daughter. This is the price I paid for being born to a woman who abandoned me to my fate, and for that there is no forgiveness."

Shaul, who had yet to say a word, moved to stand in front of Lily. He held her face tenderly in his two hands, kissed her eyelids, and whispered in her ear, "Forgive, Lily. Forgive, my beloved wife. Don't forgive for her sake but for yours. 'As it is forbidden for a person to be cruel and refuse to be appeased, and when the person who wronged him asks for forgiveness, he should forgive him with a whole heart and a willing spirit, even if he aggravated and wronged him severely.' Think about our life, my darling Lily, the home we have built, our daughter, who is now with you every step of the way. The two of you only came together after Eliya found the strength in her heart to forgive you. Only when she forgave you did her heart open to you, and only after you were forgiven did your heart open to her. Forgive her so that we may return home to Tel Aviv and go on with our lives."

Lily's eyes filled with tears, and she collapsed into Shaul's arms, her body swaying to the rhythm of her sobs while he held her. She knew that those arms would always embrace her, hold her up, and never let her fall.

Eliya

I was overcome as I watched my mother and father in each other's arms, listened to my father's wise words, understood what my mother was feeling. And then I looked over at the woman who was my grandmother. She, too, was observing in wonder the moving expression of love embodied in my parents' embrace. How was it possible, I thought, that for nearly half a century this woman had borne the dark secret of her past alone? How was it possible that she had never slipped up, never said a word that might give it away? How was it possible that in all the years she had been living in England, she had never encountered a single person from her past until we'd arrived?

All at once, with no inkling or intention that it would happen, my heart filled with compassion for the strange woman who was my grandmother. For the first time since I'd met her, the alienation gave way to closeness. I studied Rachel Townshend leaning on her cane, and she was no longer the evil woman who had abandoned Lily but my grandmother, whose terrible life story and cruel fate had led her to behave as destiny had determined she would. I thought about the wrenching decision she had made to abandon my mother, believing that by doing so she was saving her from a life of poverty, shame, and contempt. And for a fleeting moment I felt for her.

It was amazing, I thought, how we were connected to one another by invisible filaments of blood and destiny, how my grandmother's fate had influenced that of my mother, and how my mother's destiny had influenced mine. How could a woman I didn't know be rooted so deeply inside me? Although we had never chosen it, our lives were entwined. We shared the same destiny, which bound us together whether we liked it or not.

The words flew out of my mouth seemingly of their own accord. "Forgive, Mother," I pleaded. "Forgive so that this pain will come to an end, so that you can start to breathe again."

"Only someone who knows how to forgive knows how to love," Eldad said. Our agitation had been so great that no one had noticed that Eldad had been standing in the doorway for some time.

"All of us," he went on, speaking softly, "have already proved that we know how to forgive and how to love."

Suddenly my mother turned to me, and we held one another, sobbing, our tears mingling together.

When our tears were spent and we were sitting quietly in the aftermath of the storm of our emotions, Rachel Townshend spoke again, but in the cadences of Rachel, the young and innocent girl from Mea Shearim in Jerusalem. "Today," she said, "Almighty God has corrected the injustices that He has laid in my path so plentifully all through my life. Today He who sits on high absolves me of my sins, having brought you, my daughter, and you, my granddaughter, to my door. He who sits above us has finally decided that the time has come to cease these measures of suffering—my suffering for the sin I committed against you, your suffering for a sin you didn't commit, and Eliya's suffering, which flows in the blood that binds her to us."

I felt as though I was hearing ancient words. I tried to hold on to them, to repeat them to myself silently, to sear them in my memory.

"I did not have the privilege of raising you, my daughter. I didn't watch your transformation from girl to woman, I did not escort you to your bridal canopy, I wasn't at your side when you gave birth to your daughter, but even if you never want to see me again, no one can separate you from me. Until the day I die, I will remember this day. Thank you, my daughter, from the bottom of my heart, for traveling all this way to find me. I thank you, my daughter, for granting me the privilege of meeting you and your family.

"I don't dare ask that we meet again, but before we go our separate ways, grant me a last gesture of kindness and keep the necklace."

The necklace was still in Lily's hand, but instead of putting it on, Lily turned to me and fastened it around my neck.

In surprise I looked down at the Star of David between my fingers and slowly traced each of the letters in its center that spelled the word *Zion*, brought the shining shape to my mouth, and kissed it. I looked over at my mother and my grandmother, scarcely believing the miracle that I was witnessing. The sound of the ships' horns was audible in the distance, and a soft, cleansing breeze brushed into the room through the open window now that the storm clouds had been swept away.

And then Lily spoke in a voice imbued with tenderness. "This"— she pointed at the necklace hanging around my neck—"is a gold chain of generations. You, my mother who gave birth to me, gave it to me when I was born, and now I give it to you, my daughter, and when the time comes, you, Eliya, will hang it around the neck of your daughter, and she in turn will pass it on to her daughter. And in that way the gold necklace that I received from my mother at the gate to the convent in Jerusalem will be passed on from generation to generation in our family, like a connecting thread, for we are all joined to each other with strands of blood and tears."

My mother kissed me. And then she turned to the armchair, knelt before Rochel from Mea Shearim in Jerusalem, and kissed her frail hand. She looked into her eyes, which glittered through a film of tears, and for the first time uttered the word that she had longed to say her whole life: "Mother."

About the Author

Photo © 2022 Maya Baumel

Sarit Yishai-Levi is a renowned Israeli journalist and author. In 2016 she published her first book, *The Beauty Queen of Jerusalem*. It immediately became a bestseller and garnered critical acclaim. The book sold more than three hundred thousand copies in Israel, was translated into ten languages, and was adapted into a TV series that won the Israeli Television Academy award for best drama series. It also won the Publishers Association's Gold, Platinum, and Diamond prizes; the Steimatzky Prize for bestselling book of the year in Israel; and the WIZO France Prize for best book translated into French.

Yishai-Levi's second book, *The Woman Beyond the Sea*, was published in 2019. It won the Publishers Association's Gold and Platinum prizes and was adapted for television by Netflix.

Yishai-Levi was born in Jerusalem to a Sephardic family that has lived in the city for eight generations. She's been living with her family in Tel Aviv since 1970.

About the Translator

Photo © 2020 Avi Hoffmann

Gilah Kahn-Hoffmann moved from Montreal to Jerusalem after studying theater, literature, and communications at McGill University. Starting out as a freelance journalist, translator, writer, and editor, she became a feature writer at the *Jerusalem Post* and, subsequently, editor of the paper's youth magazines. Later, during a stint as a writer at the Israel Center for the Treatment of Psychotrauma, she discovered how fulfilling it is to work for the benefit of others and moved to NGO work in East Jerusalem and the developing world. In recent years, she's come full circle to her first loves and spends her best hours immersed in literary translation.